REQUITAL

A Novel

Trevor Summons

Authors Choice Press
New York Lincoln Shanghai

REQUITAL

Authors Choice Press
an imprint of iUniverse, Inc.

iUniverse books may be ordered through booksellers or by contacting:

iUniverse
2021 Pine Lake Road, Suite 100
Lincoln, NE 68512
www.iuniverse.com
1-800-Authors (1-800-288-4677)

Originally published by Minerva Press London

ISBN-13: 978-0-595-41721-6
ISBN-10: 0-595-41721-3

Printed in the United States of America

To Mr And Mrs Charles Bader, for their help and continuous enthusiasm

Prologue

There was a slight hissing on the secure line that crossed the English Channel from GCHQ (Government Communications Headquarters), located in Andover, Hampshire. Control sat deep within the shabby building that housed all the communications that Her Majesty's Secret Service needed to carry out most of its covert activities. Control tapped his foot impatiently as the number began to ring. On hearing the voice, he immediately used the name that she had not heard for two years.

'Maggy, it's me.'

'Yes,' came the accented reply. 'I'd hoped that you had gone away.'

'You still owe me one last time, Maggy.'

The accented voice agreed that, yes, that had been the bargain.

'I know that it always comes hard after so long, but getting you away from that mob you were tied in with took a lot of effort out of me, I can tell you.'

Maggy recognized the personalization of the remark, as if Control had had no help whatsoever to carry out the operation that had given her her freedom. But the freedom was obviously not complete – yet. She tried to keep the anxiety out of her voice.

'What do you need?'

The voice that replied was tired, experienced, and very direct.

'We have been watching our friends to the west rather carefully. There seems to be a change in their direction. It's worrying us. Frankly, we need to harness the more violent element before too much damage is done. At the same time, we think that there's a chance that one of their higher-ups might be coming unglued. We've had our eyes on him for some time.'

'Just your usual watchers, I suppose.'

'Something like that. It's amazing what these computer models can run out these days.'

'So what are my orders, then?'

'We think that they'll send out the word for some help. The usual channel, small ad in the papers. We'll let you know when it appears. Then you run with it. Do what you can to steer it through. We're looking to score some points on this one, if it happens. There's a package with profiles on its way to you. Good luck.'

'Thanks a lot. But this is the last time, correct?'

'This will be the last time, Maggy, I promise.'

The hissing line went dead.

Chapter One

Belfast, 1992

The stained walls of the deserted garage reflected the grim, thudding sounds of the beating. The victim sagged against the restraints as the two IRA 'soldiers' weighed into his broken frame. The man's face was a bruised and cut mess. His arms, exposed from his soiled singlet, were blue with cold and no longer made any attempt to defend. It was the standard treatment for a confirmed runaway, and Mitch O'Doule stood in the shadows watching the treatment as he had done so many times before. In about another ten minutes, after the man had been beaten to a pulp, he would be shot through both kneecaps and left alone to crawl out into the rain.

Mitch had been the judge and jury on this whole sorry business, from the moment they had found Mickey Behan gone from his job at the bakery. It took a week of inquiries and then they caught him up at his cousin's farm, close to the border. The stupid idiot had dropped four pistols into the hands of his sister's boyfriend, who was a Protestant insider and then just plain run for it. What had it been worth to him? Two or three hundred pounds at the most, and now he would walk like a cripple for the rest of his life.

Still, he would have a life. That was something, Mitch supposed, as he turned away from the scene and went out into the wet evening. What he himself was considering would result in similar treatment, but extended, then a week of agony and starvation, and finally, execution. The IRA dramatically expanded its harshness as the rank of the traitor increased. A year ago, a sergeant had been caught passing information directly to the English authorities. He had been beaten, shot through the legs and then, two days later, set in front of a firing squad and executed. His body was hurled from a speeding car right at the gates of a British command post.

Mitchell O'Doule was a full colonel, one of the inner group, and a thirty-year veteran. His treachery would be the worst crime ever conducted by such a person. If he was caught, then his death would be the sort that could be told to successive generations, in the hope it would never ever happen again. As he turned his back against the damp wind and flicked his cigarette lighter, he heard the sharp crack of the .22 round being fired into first one kneecap, and then, *crack*, into the other. He shuddered. He drew deeply on the cigarette, and then forced himself into the gray interior to witness the end of the punishment.

'You'll remember this for the rest of your life, Mickey,' he heard himself saying. 'You'll walk stiff-legged to show what you did to the cause, and they'll always know you're a traitor.'

In the gloom, he could hardly make out the wretched man's face as the bundle huddled, whimpering and sobbing, in a corner. It was just as well, as Mitch was sick to his stomach, and nodding brusquely at the two others, he slammed out into the deserted street to make his plans, and to shake off this last sickening experience. As he walked away, he remembered how he had come to his momentous decision. From that moment, such scenes as he'd just witnessed revolted him and preyed on his mind. He could hardly believe that he'd been in the forefront of it all for thirty years. How could he have stuck it?

But two months earlier, just before his forty-fifth birthday, Mitchell O'Doule realized he'd had enough. He had been aware of a changing situation at the top for quite a long time. But a request from a cell operating close to the border received such enthusiastic approval from the War Council he knew the time had come for him to pass on the responsibilities to other hands.

The fact was he was tired of the fight. Tired of the ceaseless hiding and running. And, especially, tired of the never-ending violence.

After five minutes' walk from the disused garage he went into the saloon bar of The Rover. He ordered a pint of bitter and took it to a corner seat and slumped down. He didn't give the impression of being a professional terrorist and on every 'most wanted' list of the British authorities. Such a dangerous man would surely look the part, but to a casual eye he fitted in with the bland, well-used surroundings of the pub.

He was a tall wiry man with quick nervous movements. He had a full head of very dark brown hair that regularly flopped over eyes of the clearest pale blue. Sunk deep in his narrow pale face, they constantly moved around, giving the impression of someone who was never totally at ease with his surroundings.

The landlord came across the stained carpet to empty the ashtray at Mitch's elbow. He lifted the heavy china bowl and shook it into the bin he carried with him. Then, with a deft flick, he wiped a paintbrush around to remove the last particles of Mitch's Player's Medium cigarette.

'You waiting for anybody, Mr Mitchell?' Those in the know only referred to him by the one name, like a lord or a film star.

'No, Stan,' he replied, 'just taking a quiet drink for myself. Makes a nice change to be on one's own, I can tell you.'

The landlord shambled back to his side of the bar.

Mitch once again sank back into his thoughts, remembering how he had begun his turnaround. He could hardly believe what the fools wanted. It was completely against the policy they'd been using for the last twenty years.

At first, he'd become angry. Then, he decided to try to bend his attitude to the decision. But this forced him to recognize he was facing a crossroads. One way led along the traditional path that all his years of training had incubated, and the other was where his heart and mind were pulling him. By the end of the meeting, he knew his time had come, and he was no longer in touch with the way the game was now to be played.

He had seen it coming, of course. The Pan Am bombing over Lockerbie in Scotland should have alerted him to the sort of publicity that was bound to appeal to the younger element. Before that, the bomb in the German discotheque that killed scores of young American servicemen had shown the world the effects of full-scale attacks on personnel, rather than property.

But the War Council's policy had always been for attacks on the infrastructure and not the population. It made the most economic sense. The faithful donors that provided the Noraid funds out of North America had a great aversion to killing innocent people, whereas they were only too happy to cough up substantial sums to blow buildings to smithereens. His colleagues on the council knew almost to the penny the cost of even one innocent life in the collecting boxes that were still the financial lifeline of the fight for freedom. Such a complete change meant his collectors in the Boston and Chicago areas would complain bitterly as they, in turn, were questioned about the horrors these planned explosions would wreak on the awaiting British public.

Deep in thought, he left his seat and went out to the cold toilet, built onto the side of the pub. Standing facing the white-tiled wall, he once again allowed his mind to return to his present difficulties. Damned fools will get us all hunted down and killed, he thought. Looking round he saw the evidence of the changing times even here in the outside loo of a grotty pub. No more the sharp witticisms of bygone days written on the walls. Today it was all so-called gang markings, gothic letters that were meaningless to those outside the group. After pulling up the zipper of his corduroy trousers, he took a few moments to study the alien messages. Nothing amusing about it at all, he thought, and shaking his head, he returned to the warmth of the saloon bar.

Sitting once again with his back to the corner, he noticed the glass had been refilled during his brief absence. He acknowledged this with a silent toast to his companion, then pulled out a folded newspaper and commenced to read, thereby cutting off any further discussion that the landlord might feel obliged to offer. He tried to read the stories that the editors believed to be of importance to the world at large that day. But Mitch failed to appreciate their significance, and his eyes glazed over as he continued to ponder his present situation.

His father had begged him not to become involved with the Army all those thirty years ago when he was a bright-eyed fifteen year old. He was destined to follow in the family tradition of working at the shipyard, like father and grandfather before him. He was destined to pass from his youth all the way to his retirement and collect his gold watch and pension at the age of sixty-five. Had it not been for the 'incident', he was as certain to travel that road as a train is to follow its steel track.

Then one night, just before he turned fifteen, he and his friend, Billy McPherson, were coming home from a youth hall in the Crumlin Road, when they were ambushed by a gang of boys from the Protestant side of the city.

Mitch found out later that Billy had shown signs of interest in a sister of one of the group, and more dangerously, she had shown equal signs of interest in him.

Silently, and with the awful dedicated malice that can only come from the true zealot, the boys beat Billy senseless, while Mitch was held helpless in the shadows. When it was over, Mitch knew Billy was badly hurt, and his opinion was confirmed by the ambulance team who took his friend away to die later in the hospital.

Shocked, with a feeling of guilt at his impotence, together with an anger at the injustice of it all, Mitch wandered around in a daze for more than a week. Eventually, Father Mayhew took pity on the boy and recommended a spell away at a camp he knew on the shores of Lough Neagh.

Into the second week, Mitch was beginning to forget the scene that had been his constant companion for most of his waking moments. It was then that he was approached by one of the 'gatherers'.

He was, after all, a prime candidate, young, in shock and grieving. To listen to the soft words of recruitment was an easy task. To accept the reason and logic of a people persecuted for their life and their religion was the stuff that made for fanatics. And, over the next decade, that was what Mitch became – not immediately, as he sat each day of the remaining vacation taking his instruction, but more when he was left alone to brood on his accepted lot of being excluded from all decision making, in the six counties north of the Irish Free State of Eire.

Gradually, he pieced together how he and his people had been stripped of their rightful lands by the invading English; how that accursed race had filled his homeland with rival Protestants that took away all the Catholic rights, making them poor and dependent on the handouts of the arrogant rulers. He came to believe the only way was to fight for true independence from English rule, and become at one with the island as a whole. Brendan Murphy, the gatherer, did his job well and planted his deep seeds of hatred in the fertile mind of Mitchell O'Doule before releasing him back to an unsuspecting family, initially unaware of his traumatic conversion.

Formed out of the remnants of those older men, who had followed on from Michael Collins at the Battle of the Dublin Post Office in the twenties, the group reasoned that the only way to continue was to recruit the young. Without this new blood, the old fire of revolution would die out and there would be no end to the tyrannical rule from across the sea.

As Mitch leaned against the corner, staring sightlessly at the newspaper before him, his memory traveled back to those first exciting involvements, where he would be on watch while his colleagues struck a blow for the Irish people. He smiled as he remembered the pathetic efforts to blow up police boxes and railway lines with ineffective explosives, often produced out of twelve-bore shotgun cartridges. Several of the men had injured themselves in the process of building bombs from the dangerous substances, and yet there was an excitement they all shared.

When his father suspected Mitch's involvement, the young man at first denied it, but then he allowed his pride to come through and he told his father that he was not going to spend his life working for the bloody English. He was going to put an end to it and not buckle under like the rest of the men in the O'Doule family. His father, a lined and stooping man, lashed out at him for the first time that Mitch could recall. Then, with tears filling his anxious eyes, he went from the room, offering fruitless words of caution.

It all seemed so long ago. Time seemed to fly when you looked at it a certain way, and yet it could hang so slowly when you wanted things to happen quickly. Like the first time he had actually been on a job.

As always, it seemed it had been raining all day as the three of them started out across the fields. There was Jimmy O'Rourke, Buster Lynch and himself. Jimmy was the leader, a man of twenty-four, eaten up with anger at the way life was. He had lived with a drunken father and a slut of a mother in a filthy house down by the docks. You could tell from his face that he hated the world, and particularly the people in it.

Buster was only a few months older than Mitch, but he had an air of confidence about him that made him seem a lot older. He was the one who carried the bag full of explosives they were due to plant.

The target was a small farmhouse being used by some Royal Ulster Constabulary sympathizers – the sort of scum that mixed with the Catholics and then reported back to the RUC any unusual goings-on.

This was in the days before the great flare-up in 1969, with the marches and the rise of the movement. Bernadette Devlin and her cronies didn't know what they were starting then. A decade before, things were much quieter. It was much more underground, easier, in a way, to strike that blow for freedom. One didn't have to compete with all the others in the world. But, of course, the Establishment, who owned the media, would not print any old story about an explosion. It had to be newsworthy. And it had to take its place after the other news, like cricket scores, balance of payment reports and political speeches.

It took the words of a young long-haired girl with academic aspirations to light the bonfire of fanaticism that would boil the blood of an oppressed people. Then the money began to pour in and the people began to march and hope and fight and die for the cause.

Mitch reached for his pint and drained it with a grimace. In spite of his Puritan views of drinking, there seemed some occasions when there was nothing else one could do. He pulled himself up and took the few steps over to the bar. Stan could see from his face that this was not a good time to start up another one of those empty conversations at which so many of his trade are gifted. He filled the glass and accepted the gilt round coins that Mitch pushed across to him.

Sitting down once more, Mitch lit another Player's and wiped away the tear that formed in his eye with the ascending fumes. He could almost feel the excitement again as he ran across the field with Buster and Jimmy.

That night was very dark, and the rain hung in the air as if suspended. They were worried the fuses would be damp and they would fail in their mission. A dog barked and they froze, standing like thin hunched statues. Obviously, the animal was concerned about something else, and it fell silent once more. They hurried to the corner of the house. Their information was that it was in the living room where the men from the RUC would gather for their evenings, enjoying the camaraderie and the sport of hunting down their own kind.

The three would-be terrorists squatted down and took out the bomb. It was made from an old McVitie and Price biscuit tin. It looked very fragile, and Buster handled it carefully. On top was an Ingersol alarm clock, a red and a white wire attached with sticky tape to both sides. Round the hammer between the bells on the top of the clock were two pieces of rubber, to stop any possible contact as they carried the device around with them.

Sitting in his quiet corner, Mitch shivered as he remembered the coldness of the night and heard again the young voice of Jimmy handing out his instructions. 'Mitch, you get over to that corner there and keep a close watch out.' Jimmy had a rasping tone that even in a whisper came across as threatening.

As Mitch stood straining his eyes and ears, he could hear the scrape of the trowel against the earth, as the two others scooped out a hollow at the house's corner to lay the bomb in. They had planned to direct the explosive force towards the building by pushing earth around the outside.

The dog started up again as the three of them moved away from the house.

The clock was fully wound and due to ring its bell in ten minutes – more than enough time for the young recruits to reach a safe distance but be close enough to see the results of their work.

They made themselves walk away from the scene. 'Jesus Christ Almighty.' Jimmy had hit a stone with his foot and fallen over, knocking the wind out of himself. Buster jumped about six inches in the air and Mitch had to halt his escape long enough to drag Jimmy up and cool Buster's nerves down. Eventually, in a hollow of damp grass, they lay panting and staring towards the house, trying not to shiver and betray their fear to each other.

The bang was the most exciting thing that Mitch had ever heard in his life. The hair stood up on the back of his neck and gave him goose bumps all over his arms and legs. For a moment there was a split second of silence, following a flash of orange and yellow, then the noise reached them. It was enormous, and with it came the satisfying secondary sounds of breaking glass and squealing metal.

The latter noise was the gutter above the corner, as the explosion wrenched it away from the wall. Unfortunately, due to their haste and lack of skill, this was really the only damage to report. Not nearly enough earth had been piled around the bomb, and the force of the explosion had merely blown outwards away from the house.

With a smile, Mitch remembered the saying about one of his older male relatives made by the man's wife, 'All talk and no do.' Just like his bomb, 'All noise and no destruction.' Still, it had got him into the ranks and got him started. A few more such bangs and he was being noticed by the higher-ups. He was quiet, reliable and respectful. He was also bright and learned quickly, a decided advantage when surrounded by people who mostly came from the lowest orders of society. Their only aspirations were to do as much damage as the home-made bombs were capable of, and then go out and get as plastered as possible, before falling into oblivion.

Jimmy O'Rourke died after picking on a British soldier who, unfortunately for Jimmy, was not in the same alcoholic condition. Buster Lynch fell off a roof in the dark, trying to win a bet that he could cross over in a practice escape from the forces of law. He broke both legs and was no use to anyone afterwards. Mitch had heard that he had taken over a pub somewhere in the South long ago.

Mitch stubbed out the end of his cigarette and drained his glass. He realized that he was well over his normal limit, but then today was kind of a celebration, almost a new beginning. He toyed with the idea of switching to a Bushmills, but decided to stay on the bitter. That way he would not suffer too much the next morning. The evening was drawing in and Stan was going round pulling curtains and stoking up the fire. Mitch settled back into his corner, and turned his face away from the entrance when two young people came into the bar.

They were very young, probably no more than nineteen, full of uncertainty and awkwardness. The girl sat demurely at the other end of the room away from Mitch, and kept her eyes lovingly on her boyfriend, as he attempted to ferry the drinks across the carpet. His nervous progress created even more stains, as in the fashion of the day, the glasses were filled to the brim.

Mitch could not help thinking about himself at that same age. Not for him the carefree evenings of a date, with the possibility of a kiss and a cuddle after the pictures. He was more involved with planning and implementing raids and robberies, beatings and frighteners.

He still felt bad at some of the things he had been willing to do. Sometimes he could see the faces of his victims and hear their screams for mercy, as he and his fellows laid into them with belts and sticks. He had even shot three or four traitors himself, before he earned the rank to command others to do it for him.

It was not that he now regretted his actions. It was more a sorrow he felt for the whole state of the difficulties that his country was in and a feeling of depression that, after thirty years of struggle, he had made no difference to the situation. If anything, things were worse than when he started.

Now the vote had been made to carry the war into the lives of innocent citizens, rather than just wrecking their property. The cell from Derry had asked for, and were going to receive, the infamous Mephisto bomb, something that, if properly placed, could kill hundreds of people. Up till now, the rule was to keep to buildings. 'Don't endanger human lives; it's bad for the fund raising.' But now the youthful element was restless for more results. They were not prepared to wait for things to turn. Who could blame them? The IRA had been waiting for results for generations. The bombings had not worked, so perhaps this was the way.

A giggle of youthful laughter disturbed Mitch's thoughts. He had a passing feeling of remorse that he was presently engaged on such profound business when he should by rights be enjoying himself in more relaxed company.

As soon as he had heard the way the meeting was going, he decided he would have to play along. The mood of the committee was too aggressive to allow any real dissent. He could see the power was passing to the young ones, and he quietly demurred.

They voted unanimously to move the fight to the public, to have one huge assault on as many areas as possible, to make as much noise and create as much damage as the infamous Mephistos could create. To hell with Noraid and their diminishing funds and to the devil with Sinn Fein and their interminable political solutions that never worked. They would turn to others for help to escalate the fight. After all, some little time ago, the Libyans had offered to send a shipment of arms over and some advisors, too. The Red Army Faction and the remnants of the Baader-Meinhof Gang were also looking to produce more effect internationally.

This was why Mitch had to get out. He could not go on. After thirty years in the front line and very little to show for it, he wanted out. He wanted some of the things that other people took for granted: a family, a home, children, routine, all the things he had lived without, while he struggled towards what? He looked over at Stan, who was smiling at the two young lovers.

All he could say for himself was he had achieved a certain notoriety that would not have happened if he had gone into the shipyard. He had money, but nothing to spend it on. He had no friends outside the cause, and those inside had little to offer him in terms of real companionship.

The bar was filling up now. More young people were flooding into the smoke-filled room. Laughter and music were impinging on his troubled thoughts. His mouth felt gravelly and his head felt light. He could see from the lack of sheen on the coats that the rain had stopped. It was time to walk his thoughts through, something he tended to do when he really needed to think. He returned his empty glass to the now bustling Stan, pulled his tweed cap on his head and pushed through the frosted-glass door out into the night, his mind full now of only one thought – escape.

Chapter Two

Ballyhean, September 1786

Paddy O'Doule came through the door of his cottage. He was in a bad mood, which was not a normal condition for him. He was well over six foot tall and, in the undernourished times at the end of the eighteenth century, that was quite a feat. But Patrick Michael O'Doule, or Paddy, as everybody called him, was born big and had stayed that way for all his twenty-six years.

He was the epitome of the gentle giant and, normally, nothing upset his calm disposition. This was quite an achievement, for in those far-off days, life tended to be one disaster and complication after another. But today's difficulty was even too much for Paddy. His brother, Sean, had decided to divide the farm. This made his pale blue eyes blaze under his thick thatch of dark brown hair, cut into a bulky fringe.

Two years earlier when their father had died, Sean and Paddy together had made the sensible decision to keep complete the land that they leased and not to turn it into two small plots and run the risk of losing the advantage of the discounts the local tradesmen allowed on property over a certain acreage. Now Sean's shrewish wife, Bonnie, had nagged him into parting from their plan and going it alone. She had some fancy scheme to grow flowers for the English gentry. That would give her more money than the traditional potato crop, grown with some rye in the fallow seasons. Paddy thought they were both crazy, but he didn't know what to do.

Potatoes had been the staple crop in Ireland now for over one hundred years. They were rarely a problem. Of course, the diet was boring and there was never enough meat to go around. The English took most of that to feed their troops in whatever skirmish they were engaged upon around the world. But with the damp climate and hard work, a man could make a living and have enough left over for a few small luxuries, maybe a visit to the fair, or a few ribbons for Katherine's hair, bought off a traveling peddler.

Paddy threw himself into his wooden armchair. Like him, it was big, but it comfortably supported his two hundred and twenty pounds, and had the familiar scuffs of many years of use. The peat of the fire hissed and popped, as he kicked at it with his boot. Hearing him clumping about, his pretty wife, Katherine, came out of the kitchen, which was built onto the side of the house. She stood quietly in the doorway with a wisp of red hair falling down from the bun she wore at the back of her head. Like her husband, she was a quiet person with a gentle outlook on life. She could see from the way Paddy was hunched in his chair that things were not well.

'So what's brought you home early in such a mood?' she asked.

In reply, Paddy just kicked more life into the fire and sank even lower into his seat with a sigh.

'Now it's not like you to go sulking on me. Do you want me to bring you in some tea to warm you up?'

Without waiting for a reply, she turned back into her steam-filled little annex, and poured some boiling water onto the leaves. They had been used before, but with care, one could get a good three brews out of each ration. As a farmer's daughter, she knew the ways of thrift, which was just as well. With the vagaries of the seasons, one could never foretell when times would become very hard indeed. Removing the metal strainer from the thick china mug, she poured a little milk in, together with a spoonful of honey. It was the way Paddy liked it. Then, she brought the mug into him and sat down at his feet, beside the fire.

He may be in a foul mood, she thought, but at least it's early enough for a quiet moment before the bairns come charging in.

Becky, Michael, William and David were four unruly children who ranged in ages from eight to three. Thank God, since little David was born, she had seemed to stop having any more. As she sat still beside Paddy, she thought with a grim smile of the old saying that babies were God's punishment for making love. Well, she had been fortunate in her punishment. The four of them were a delight to her and Paddy.

'So, do you want to tell me about it, then?'

Paddy had already taken a good swig out of his mug, and she could tell from his posture that he was beginning to settle down.

'It's that damned Bonnie,' he said. 'She's convinced Sean to split the farm. You know how dangerous that is. Higher prices for seeds and supplies, and all the problems of boundaries, of course. Then what about the three pigs we have, and the horse? Then there's all the implements. What about those?'

In her special way, Katherine sat silently, realizing the questions he was asking required no real answer. Pretty soon he would begin to rationalize the whole situation, and that would be the moment to offer her advice. They stared into the smoking fire and Paddy sipped his tea. The difficulties ahead were obvious to Katherine. Apart from the ones he had been mentioning, there were others less obvious.

'Damn that Bonnie,' he mumbled under his breath.

'She's always getting stupid ideas. Wanting to climb up her social ladder. At what cost?'

'I feel sorry for poor Sean,' Katherine replied. 'He's such a nice man, and now we'll be daggers drawn with each other.'

'Now there'll only be the one family to plead with the agent about overdue rents. Two husbands united together with wives and children always mean more muscle at the difficult times. Now what'll we do?'

Katherine stood up and put her arms around the now silent Paddy, and whispered words of comfort. He responded with an embrace of his own, and they began to talk about what they were facing in the future together. Since they were fourteen, they had been able to work out the many problems that came their way. Once they married when Paddy was sixteen and Katherine a month or two under that age, they had been fortunate to move into the family house with their own curtained-off room. That was a rare luxury in those crowded times.

Within a year, Paddy's mother died after a lifetime of drudgery and illness; then, after another two years, the old man passed away. Now the house was all theirs, and the additional space was usually filled up with children playing. Altogether it was a good life that Katherine and Paddy had carved out for themselves in the green land of Ballyhean.

To placate his anger, Katherine ran through the benefits she saw for them. He in return agreed that, compared to many, they were fortunate. Then they began to tackle the new problems of dividing the farm for Bonnie's foolish flower scheme. It did not take long.

The day was growing dark as the door burst open and Becky, the eldest child, came scampering into the room, followed closely by the other three. They jumped onto their father's lap, and using him as a stepladder, they flung their arms around their mother's neck. Eight little feet stamping around on him took Paddy's mind off the immediate problems, and he entered into the game of rolling around with his children.

After the family had eaten and the four little ones had gone through the nightly ritual of kneeling by the bed to say their prayers, Paddy and Katherine returned to the table next to the kitchen. This had always been their spot in the house, since their life together began. In the beginning, they would sit quietly, waiting for the two older people to nod in front of the fire, so they could draw the thin curtain across the room and attend to the appetites of the newly married.

There was nothing either of them could do to change the situation now developing. Like most of their neighbors, they had both come from large families and had relied on the old saying that blood was thicker than water. In the O'Doules' case, this meant the two brothers would continue to benefit from a large farm and from the help that two families working in unison would derive. That was now a thing of the past, and there was no good complaining about it. Best to just do what one had to, and let the good Lord provide. In the meantime, there was the matter of informing the authorities. And this meant the recorder, as well as the agent.

Both of these officials resided in the nearby city of Belfast, and so it was agreed, before the candle was snuffed out, that Paddy would make the day's journey there, while Katherine would attend to the new boundary. This would be a line of chalk, until a privet hedge could be encouraged to grow, thereby separating the land for ever.

They both agreed the implements would be divided and the pigs fed equally until the time came for the slaughter; then they would share the meat accordingly. As for the horse, they would have to take its labor in turn, until they could find a permanent solution.

No doubt the two brothers would stay on good terms, but with the inevitable division of interests, both families would drift apart. The most important thing was for their own family to pull together, and become as efficient as possible in the months ahead.

Paddy slipped his heavy boots off and unbuttoned his thick woolen trousers. They both knelt together beside the pile of bales that made up their bed, and silently invoked the help of the Lord above to see them through this present crisis. Afterwards, had any of the four children been awake to hear, the only sound that was audible was Katherine's whispered plea, 'Do be careful, Paddy darlin'. I think I'm safe but we don't want another little mouth to feed at the moment.'

The next day saw the start of three days' planning for Paddy's trip to Belfast. He had only been there twice in his life before, once to report his mother's death and then again to repeat the exercise for his deceased father. He had never visited the agent before. Normally, rent was paid at the door of the tiny cottage when the agent's man arrived at the start of every month.

A crop of new potatoes had been freshly dug out of the dark rich soil, and it was agreed Paddy should take a few bundles along to the central market. The prices there were known to be the best in the land, so he hoped to make the trip turn a small profit.

With the money from the potatoes, there were some things that Katherine wanted: a length of cloth for the confirmation outfits of the four children, and a pot of dark blue dye. With one older girl, and three younger boys, she would be able to change the color of the clothing to give the appearance of different clothes for each ceremony, remaking the girl's dress into smart tunics for the boys. In the country, everybody knew what poor folk did to get by, but that didn't matter; appearances were judged to be very important, particularly for any religious ceremony.

The smallest boy's feet were woefully large and the family was without a proper pair of boots for him. William, two years older, had tiny feet so there were no hand-me-downs available. The poor little mite was having to run around with his feet tied up in rags and rope. Some kids were like that all the time; some even had none at all. But Katherine had her standards, so new boots for David were to be purchased.

If the potatoes fetched a good price, then there were also a few items for the kitchen that Katherine had her eye on.

'Those rascal tinkers only bring the thinnest pots. No good for a slow-cooking stew,' she would constantly say. 'Paddy, if you could see yourself clear to buy me a good iron pot, one with an extra-thick bottom, you'd be amazed at the difference you'd taste.'

Three days later, as planned, they filled the little trap with the sacks of potatoes, some blankets and a food supply. Then he was ready to mount up and be off. There were mixed emotions at his leaving. Belfast seemed the other side of the world, but his journey was necessary, and there would undoubtedly be treats for all when he returned. With a final assurance to Katherine that he would be home as soon as he could, he clicked the horse into action and the small trap moved smartly down the winding lane.

Paddy began to sing as soon as he was out of sight of his home. He liked to sing quietly when he was working on the land, and today he was doing it because he felt alone. There was a feeling that something was wrong. He couldn't put his finger on it, but he felt ill at ease. He was not a superstitious man, but he felt as if he was not quite in control of things.

This was not an altogether unusual experience for him. There were many things that were a mystery to him in life. He did not fully understand how the seasons changed for instance, nor did he understand how things grew, or why the rain fell down so regularly. All three things were of great importance to him, and yet he could not work out why they occurred. When he came upon this type of problem, he would choose one of the old ballads and sing. He had a fine baritone, and when there was music in the village church, which was only about four times a year, the priest would always ask for his attendance in the chancel. Beyond those occasions, however, his songs were nearly always inaudible.

As the distance lengthened from his little village, he settled down and began to come out of his strange mood. It was silly to be worried, after all. He was a big man whom few would tackle, and he would be coming back along the same track the day after next. In three days, he reasoned, he would be back home with his beloved Katherine and the little ones. When all was said and done what more could a man want from life?

On the outskirts of the city, he decided he would pull the trap over to the side of the road and spend the night beneath its shelter. He slipped a nosebag over the horse's head and, after taking out his supper of cold potato and sweet bread, he pulled a tarpaulin across the damp ground. Then he wrapped a blanket tightly around himself, and tried to fall asleep.

Unfortunately, Paddy had long ago lost the ability to drop off in an instant, as he had done in childhood. His mind played on his new problems with the farm, and as soon as he started to fall asleep, the noises in the night jolted him awake. On top of that, the horse would constantly move around in its shafts. Most upsetting of all, however, was the same feeling of disquiet that had remained with him since he left his home.

As the dawn dragged its light across the sky, Paddy felt he had hardly closed his eyes, and he felt stiff and sore.

Nonetheless, he took a swig from his bottle of cold tea, to start the day off, and munched on another cold potato. The weather was chilly but clear. He was grateful for it being the month of April. Such a night would have been difficult a month or two previously. Having finally got his eyes open, he removed the nosebag from the horse, pulled himself up into the trap, gave a flick of the reins, and the journey began again.

The city was busy. It was always busy. Probably it was busy at midnight, Paddy thought. When did these people ever get to bed? He felt strange and out of place as the horse jogged along. He even tried a couple of songs out loud to help him on his way, but when he received some strange looks from people, his voice faltered and grew silent.

It took him much longer than expected to find the recorder's office, but, eventually, he made his way to the dockside area where that dignitary earned his living, writing down all the facts to do with the running of His Majesty's province of Ulster. There was a lot of lining up, then scratching of pens on papers, accompanied by bored looks from the smug clerks, as Paddy stumbled his way through the procedures necessary to confirm the arrangements that he and his brother, Sean, had agreed upon, albeit reluctantly on his part. The whole business must have taken nearly three hours.

Looking back on it, two of the three hours were probably the reason for the extraordinary change of fortune that Paddy was to experience. Had the recording only taken one hour, he would most certainly have gone straight round to the agent on the other side of town, purchased his items and been on the way back home before nightfall. As it was, Paddy came out of the recorder's office, frustrated with the city, feeling lost and homesick and with a terrible thirst.

Katherine had few complaints about her adoring

husband but, if pressed, she would say the one thing that scared her most about him was his inheritance of the famous O'Doule's thirst. His father had had it, as had a couple of uncles. It almost had a life of its own. And it could strike when least expected. Among the women of the family, it was generally joked about, because, with the amount of work needed to run a farm and the lack of a decent pub anywhere near, there was little chance for the thirst to surface. Anyway, Paddy was far too happy in his life with his family to fall victim to the horrors of the bottle that haunted many less fortunate.

Unfortunately, far from home and in the unfamiliar surroundings of the city of Belfast, the thirst hit Paddy just as he left the dockside recorder's office. As he hurried down the moss-covered steps, he saw the swinging sign of The Rover Inn right opposite. He decided he would call in for a pint to settle him down for the rest of the day. The Rover was a small establishment. There was only one bar, and as Paddy pushed his way inside, he could tell it was a jolly place. There was quite a throng of people enjoying themselves during the lunchtime break.

The smell of stew and hot bread, joined with the strong odor of navy tobacco and beer and the general atmosphere, instantly gave Paddy an appetite to go with his thirst. He only had a little money, and he knew he must not stay long with the horse and trap tied up outside. However, he was determined to wet his whistle, and at the same time, eat a bowl of stew, if he could afford it.

Surreptitiously, he pulled out his money and counted out his total wealth. It came to just over two shillings. It was plenty for his needs and he approached the bar confidently. Unfortunately, he was using rural pricing in an urban setting, and he was horrified his bill for the two items reduced his cash by one third. This figure sank even lower after he decided he simply had to have one last pint before leaving for the agent's office.

On his way back to a table near the door, with his pint in hand, he stumbled. Due to the packed number of patrons, he spilled some of the beer on quite a few around him. He was most apologetic, and tried to wipe off the results, but only succeeded in spilling more. A small red-faced man took the emptying pint out of his hand, and suggested that maybe the best thing that Paddy could do was to buy a half for all those who had been splashed. Paddy, anxious to make amends, agreed, but was amazed at the number of people whom he seemed to have inconvenienced. Judging by the throng at the bar ordering on his account, he must have been very careless indeed and have affected nearly the whole room. He stood resignedly at the end of the queue, and after topping up his own pot, was faced by the appalling revelation that the bill came to seven shillings and sixpence.

As the revelers cleared away, Paddy was left standing there with his mouth open and a blush of extreme embarrassment on his face.

'I – I'm – er – sorry,' he stammered. 'I – er – didn't – er – realize it would be – er – so much.'

The landlord, who up to then had seemed a particularly jolly fellow, lost all sense of humor, and stood before Paddy with his hand held out.

Paddy's face grew redder. In a sudden fit of inspiration, he stammered, 'I've – er – got some lovely spuds outside in my trap. They're fresh from the country. Er – would you take some as payment?'

It took a while for the landlord to respond, but slowly he relaxed his daunting expression and agreed to follow Paddy outside to inspect the quality of the potatoes. Fortunately, they were indeed very fresh and also very good. A couple were cut open with a knife and the insides inspected for any trace of mold or disease. The flesh was firm and white and the new skins came away from them with only a little rubbing.

'I'll give you ten shillings a bag,' the landlord offered, and Paddy countered with his price of fifteen, a huge amount for such ordinary stock. After going backwards and forwards several times, the price of eleven shillings and sixpence was agreed upon, and the sack was hefted inside.

Now, if Paddy had collected his change and left, he would have been fine. Unfortunately, the landlord, believing he had received the best of the deal, insisted on buying Paddy a final drink. This pushed him over the edge and unleashed the thirst that Katherine was so afraid of. Paddy spent the rest of that day working solidly through his stock of potatoes and making many new friends. He was amazed at how popular a stranger from the country could be.

It was quite dark when his money finally ran out. He didn't care. He had enjoyed a marvelous day, and he was feeling fine. He had been made very welcome in this city, and he now intended to spend another night under his trap before completing his business the next day. After gathering up his scarf, hat and coat, he began to take his leave of all the friends that he had made.

He had been unaware of the discussion that had been taking place at the end of the bar. In his state of *bonhomie*, he would not have recognized the significance of the two men talking to the landlord and occasionally glancing in his direction. Both were wearing long cloaks, which covered their frames from shoulder to mid-calf. An observant person would have recognized that from under the cloaks, hem protruded bell-bottomed trousers. Any further clarification would have been easy once the observer spotted the tarred pigtail that each man wore above his cloak. As Paddy staggered out of The Rover into the cool night air, both men broke off the conversation and followed him.

Chapter Three

Belfast, 1992

Two hundred-odd years later, Mitch O'Doule pondered his future in that self same spot, unaware of the fate that had befallen his great-great-great-grandfather just outside The Rover. He would have been very surprised to know that this had been the scene of radical changes of direction for both of them. Mitch's had been a voluntary slow evolvement, coming as it did with the realization that his organization was about to embark on a path contrary to all its previous directions.

As he left the pub and turned up the rain-slicked street, breathing in the damp air, his mind was far removed from any thoughts of his ancestor. In fact, at this time, he did not even know of the man whose life would so affect his own. Mitch was getting his new thoughts in order. He would be leaving everything behind, and he'd better think hard how he could do so without a trace.

The immediate area of The Rover would not have been recognizable to the earlier Paddy O'Doule as his descendant headed away into the night. The pub had been all but destroyed twice in the intervening years. The first time it was from a stack of bombs landing courtesy of Adolf Hitler in 1943, but the second time it was more self-inflicted. After the first rush of enthusiasm for civil disturbance in 1969 the two sides decided to carry the fight into each other's territories. This meant deliberate attacks on pubs since they were the focal point for meetings – both political and social – and also the hang-outs of the prime movers of both sects.

Although not of particularly sound construction, The Rover had remarkably retained enough of its fabric for the license to remain intact until repairs could be effected on both occasions. Today, it was on a neutral street corner and served all persuasions, although Stan, the current landlord, managed to imply loyalty to both groups. This was a remarkable feat shared only with priests and newspaper vendors.

It was quiet in the street, as the majority of residents had become inured over the past twenty-odd years of strife, and confined themselves either to their houses or their moving cars during the hours of darkness. Mitch trudged on with his shoulders hunched and his eyes flicking occasionally from side to side. Over the long years, he had kept safe by being totally aware of what was going on around him, and although his automatic pilot was fully on as usual, his primary thoughts were concerned with survival in the longer term.

Mitch's problem was how to disappear. He, of all people, knew there was never any voluntary retirement from the IRA. There were only three ways out. You could leave in a coffin as a result of some heroic action or treachery. If you were found guilty of some lesser crime, you might stagger away limping, with no kneecaps. If you were too old or too useless to carry on, the powers that be might let you fade away through benign neglect. As a full colonel and active member of the war council, it was going to be difficult for him to pretend uselessness or premature senility. As for the other alternatives, Mitch, although far from squeamish, felt he needed neither the pine box nor the tubular steel walker. He had to find another way.

A car swished by, its tires sucking at the now drying

pavement, its lights spotlighting the drabness of an area that had been at war for over twenty years. As he turned farther away from the docks, Mitch passed a street of shops. Their windows were now boarded over and covered with the same graffiti that had been present on the walls of The Rover's outside toilet. Mitch smiled at the memory of the old saying, 'It's an ill wind that blows no good.' It was the glaziers who initially benefited when the outburst of urban violence first erupted. These traditional businesses soon adapted to the opportunities of short-wave radios and walkie-talkies in order to be first on the scene after a bomb blast. Sometimes they were putting in new glass even as the police arrived. Eventually, shopkeepers found that the population cared little if the windows were covered with glass or plywood, and soon they opted for the more permanent solution.

He had been there throughout all the excitement of those early days, learning about new ways to frighten the bloody British and blow up their spy networks. It was just like a real adult-sized game of cowboys and Indians, or cops and robbers. The 'Army' created a camaraderie that few of them had ever experienced before. They shared a bond and an ambition. Also, they shared money – lots of it. In fact, a fortune had passed through Mitch's hands. Unfortunately, little of it had stuck to his fingers. He had managed to salt a little of it away in an account in Jersey. It produced a small amount of interest every year, but it was hardly sufficient to allow him to retire. Finance was just another area of difficulty he had to overcome.

Mitch had by now reached an area he regularly used to lose any tail that might have been put onto him. It was a long street of terraced houses. Five of the occupants had volunteered the use of their premises for any of the senior rank to use for such a purpose.

The street was open-ended and, like many in Belfast,

backed up to an exact duplicate. Each hall had a rear door, which opened onto a small yard. It was possible to jump over the dividing walls and exit through another house on the same side, as all the back doors were left open. Alternatively, one could go over into the yards of the houses at the rear and do the same thing on that side. The security was also such that there was always a lookout on either street to ensure complete safety. Years before, the British army had become aware of this method of 'bombers' going to ground, and stopped the local population leaving their doors unbolted. This prevented escaping men from running into any house in the area and lying low. The locals responded by installing identical locks and keys, which allowed the same complete access for the escapees.

Mitch looked briefly up the street and saw a man standing just outside the circle of a street light. There was an almost imperceptible movement of the man's head, enough to indicate that all was clear. He entered a house a quarter of the way down the street and made his way through the cramped hallway. He worked his way around a motorcycle, which was dripping oil into an assortment of pans underneath it. Its smells combined with the evidence of what had undoubtedly been fish and cabbage for that night's meal.

He had no idea who the owners or tenants were. They were obviously upstairs in bed, and probably would not even hear his intrusion. He picked his way carefully to the back and opened the glass door. Outside was a low wall leading to the inevitable outside lavatory. Mitch could not help wondering if it was the Irish lot in life to have to spend all their lavatorial time in draughty, damp and cold facilities. Maybe it's some sort of divine retribution, he thought, as he vaulted over two different walls.

His exit into the other street was a mirror image of his entrance, minus the motorbike and the smells. As he left and checked the lookout on the other side, he became aware that this sort of thing was starting to get him down. It really was time to get out. He walked round the corner, opened the door of his own parked car, and climbed inside.

The drive to his home in Ballyhean took him longer than normal. He was well over the limit with the amount of beer he had consumed, and he had no wish to be picked up by the police for such stupidity. The time alone in the small Ford Fiesta was ideal to put his mind to his present problem. He had to find a way to escape from all that he knew and to disappear, without ever being discovered.

Like most of the senior officers in the IRA, he enjoyed quite a degree of freedom. Appearances could be changed fairly effectively, particularly in a climate that required a lot of outerwear and even umbrellas. The addition of a smoking pipe or a fat cigar altered the shape of the mouth. False mustaches and beards were often worn when in areas of high population. Various hats kept the face in shadow and many of the men who were on the wanted lists of police forces on both sides of the Ulster border had become adept at changing their shapes with padding and their height with high-lift shoes.

Nonetheless, although he would have looked extremely ordinary to all these but the most discerning, Mitch kept a constant lookout as he drove along the deserted roads of the province, his mind desperately searching for a solution.

Exactly what turned his thoughts back to the O'Doule family at that moment, he never would recall. Perhaps it was the sight of the fields in the mottled moonlight that jogged his mind back to the horrors of Ireland's history. It was not unusual, of course, for those in the forefront of the movement to constantly dredge up all the injustices of the past. Perhaps remembering the dreadful potato famine in the mid-nineteenth century – considered to be the worst neglect of all – he naturally thought of his own forebears.

He recalled those who had been taken, those who had escaped, and more significantly, those who had lived and escaped before the blight struck.

Several of the O'Doule family had managed to get to America and start a new life. Little contact had been preserved over the years, and Mitch automatically rejected any thought of escape to that country. He would be too well known and the hunters would soon find him through the networks that handled the finances. They combed each area and knew too many sympathizers.

How many O'Doules had suffered and died in the famine which swept across the land in black waves of hunger and disease, he would never know. Undoubtedly, most of his relatives had suffered from various degrees of privation. They came from farming stock, he knew, and with that a thought flashed into his mind: Australia.

He couldn't remember which relative it was, but one of them had sailed on one of the first ships to settle in Australia. Mitch didn't even know what had happened to him but the word Australia hit him like a thunderbolt and a big grin spread across his thin lips. It was far enough away for sure – there was nowhere farther. It also had few sympathizers for the cause, and with his accent, he would meld with the natives as so many before him had done.

Now all he had to do was to plan how to make his way there. He had about fifty thousand pounds in Jersey, but that would hardly allow him enough security to ward off the rigorous inquiries that would undoubtedly be made. He would need nearer to ten times that figure to quietly sink into anonymity and safety.

As he continued his quiet journey, he began to form the beginnings of a plan that could solve many of the difficulties. It would need a lot of nerve, a hell of a good piece of acting, and some luck. But it could be done.

He had known for some time that the goal of unification

had long since passed. Its achievement, in fact, would mean the end of a life high on the hog for many of its so-called proponents. Once Ireland was one, how would these men justify their existence? The answer was to keep the conflict bubbling along and keep taking funds from gullible romantics.

Sinn Féin, the political wing, which meant the boys in suits who had no stomach for the blood and guts of the fight, were meeting secretly with representatives of the British Government. The war council sneered at the futile attempt at efforts to reach an accord with people who were known to be among the most devious on earth. And, anyway, what was the point of talking to the Brits when Ian Paisley and his Protestant gang would never agree to reunification, as long as one drew breath. The fact that the man had the audacity to call himself 'the Reverend', made every self-respecting Catholic shake his head in wonder at such an affront to decency.

As he drove the remaining few miles to his small flat above a converted barn on the outskirts of town, the feelings he had been having for many years fell completely into place. It was all so obvious and it made him feel sad and sickened with himself. He had played along willingly, but at the cost of losing all meaning in his life. He was like a child who had been chasing a soap bubble. Now the bubble had burst.

He parked the Ford in its customary place, facing outwards between two trees. It allowed little of itself to be seen from the dark lane and offered a fast getaway if needed. He stood for a moment, breathing in the air and allowing his thoughts to accept the inevitable; then he went inside. After putting on the electric kettle, Mitch took out the old atlas on top of his bookshelf. It was hardly used. After all, when one's boundaries were mostly within a few hours' drive, one didn't need to know too much about faraway places.

He flipped open the pages until he reached the large Mercator projection. It showed the earth chopped up like a segmented orange. It particularly showed how far away Australia was, when compared to the distances of his own beloved country. As the thought came over him, he felt a sinking in his stomach. This meant he would have to say goodbye for ever.

The kettle began to steam and fill the small cooking area with its moist heat. Mitch cursed it, and walked over to the hot water, pouring it into some instant coffee. As he looked around at the flat, he realized that it did not show much for his life. This was not surprising for one who traveled from place to place nearly every three months. There had been no time to collect things, no time to acquire personal possessions, and no time to forge deep relationships. Perhaps in a new life there would be the opportunity to change all that. His mood of depression swung to one of elation. Maybe there would be time to put down some roots.

He carried his mug back to the table and stared at the map. Yes, it certainly was a long way away. But, today, one could get anywhere in a few hours. His problem was to arrive with enough independence, and without detection.

The ashtray was almost full to overflowing and the light was beginning to stream through the small windows, when Mitchell O'Doule at last went to bed. He had a contented smile as he turned away from the dawn and went to sleep.

At around twelve o'clock the next day, he left the flat, looking more individual than he had in a long time, with a smart tweed jacket and check shirt and yellow tie. Perhaps, having wrestled with his thoughts for nearly twenty-four hours, he instinctively felt the need to brighten his appearance in keeping with his new direction.

He drove about five miles to the farm, which had been the central command's meeting point for the last two months. Parking in the open barn used for that purpose, he strode purposefully through the back door and went into a windowless room.

His arrival had been flashed to those already at the farm as he had made his way along the route from his flat. The IRA were nothing if not technically *au fait* with all the latest modular phones and ultra-high-frequency radios.

Sitting at the ops-planning table were two colonels, Mike Ryan and Taffy O'Brian. Taffy had received his nickname through once getting drunk at a rugby match and yelling for the wrong side. He was five years younger than Mitch and, despite being among the most ruthless of the high command, had an uncharacteristically impish sense of humor. He looked like a jovial clown with a pink face and thinning hair, but he was personally responsible for the deaths of over fifty people.

Mike Ryan was younger still. He was only thirty-one and no one could be in any doubt about his effectiveness as a cold-blooded killer. He had an almost saturnine look about him with a sallow complexion and a nose like a beak. His unblinking eyes looked out from deep sockets, and one could almost feel the tension in the air when he was around. It was significant that when the vote had been cast earlier in the week, he was automatically in favor of escalation of the war into the realm of the public. Mitch was against it. Taffy hesitated at first, but then sided with Mike. The other three who made up the full committee went along with the escalation scheme as well. This meant that Mitch had been completely outnumbered, and that was a dangerous position to be in.

As he took his place at the table and stared at the maps with their highlighted markings and coded dots and crosses, Mike Ryan slid his eyes over and sneered, 'So, how's the people's defender today?'

The remark was in poor taste, and if delivered to anyone

in a junior position, would have carried a serious level of danger. But within the high command, Mike's tone was well known and generally forgiven. Taffy had once said that if they calmed him down with them, he might go all the way and be a softy with the enemy.

'Bloody tired, if you must know, Mike.'

'Christ, you haven't been up all night screwing some bird, have you? Thought you were past all that.'

Mitch let that one go as well. He didn't need to reply, as everybody knew that Mike's taste in women was for the most unpleasant of whores, whom he mistreated abominably.

'No such luck, I'm afraid. I got pissed down at the docks last night and hangovers just seem to be getting worse these days.'

Taffy reached behind him and rang a buzzer.

'I'll get you a "livener" and an Alka-Seltzer, if you like.'

'The Alka-Seltzer would be great but I'll pass on the "livener", thanks all the same, Taff. We old folks have to take it a bit easy, you know.'

The door opened and Matt, one of the younger staff, came in to take the order for pills, coffee and a Bushmills for Taffy. There was a silence that followed when all that could be heard was Mike lighting one of his foul-smelling cheroots. Once it was lit and his head was wreathed in a pall of noxious smoke, he mumbled to Taffy to tell Mitch what they had been discussing. Puffing on his cheroot, he leaned back in the chair, which let out a metallic squeal. Mitch was reminded that Mike always seemed to have one annoying habit or another working all the time. How he had put up with him for the last few years, he couldn't imagine.

Taffy went over to a bookcase on the side of the room and pulled out an AA (Automobile Association) map of the British Isles. On it were a number of circles – some ten or twelve. Mitch saw at once that they were centered on the major cities in England and Wales.

'So, you've decided to give the Scots a break, have you?'

'We reckon with the Scottish National element making itself felt over there, it's only going to be a few years before they break away. There's no point in pissing 'em off at this stage, is there?' Taffy replied.

Mitch was finding it hard to work up any enthusiasm for this conversation, but he knew he had to play the actor's role, or be doomed. He leaned forward and read down the map.

'Newcastle, Blackpool, Leeds, Manchester, Birmingham, Norwich, Reading, Cardiff, Bristol, London, Southampton and Bournemouth. What the bloody hell are you doing with Bournemouth? It's full of old ladies.'

Mike Ryan blew out a fog of smoke and drawled, 'Yea, Mitch, and every one of 'em votes. The ones that survive will be on to their MPs by the next post. It was Taffy's idea. I think we should go along with it.'

Taffy took a sip of Bushmills and pointed to all the targets.

'We plan to hit every city over a one-week period. As far as London is concerned, we'll blow Oxford Street, Bond Street, the City and Victoria station one morning at about nine – get all the workers just arriving. Then we'll hit the suburbs one hour later. Watford, Staines, Croydon, Stratford. Then we hit the other cities a couple of days later when everybody is starting to relax. This time we go for the hotels. They're all in the centers of town and they're full of executives on business. People with positions, people who will be missed. By the end of the week, Mitch, they'll be going crazy with panic.'

Mitch had to agree it would cause terror and total confusion. It would also cause an outcry around the world and a complete halt to funds out of America. Those folks would never stand for it. A point that he had labored to argue at the vote, obviously to no avail. The committee was determined to carry out its plan. He could see it in their faces.

'So, we better start thinking about how to organize this little jamboree, gentlemen.'

Mitch looked at his two colleagues carefully. There was a moment's awkward silence and then, from behind his smoke screen, Mike sneered, 'I thought the senior colonel was against our plans. What brings on this change of heart, may I ask?'

Mitch regretted the lack of a drink. It would have given him a prop at this difficult transition.

'This has always been a democratic movement, Mike. You all know my reasons for initially being against the plan. But as the majority are in favor of it, at least we should see that it goes off to maximum advantage.'

'There you are, Mike,' Taffy interjected. 'I told you he was a company man. He and I have been through a lot, you know. We were knocking off the bloody Brits when you were still in school.'

The last remark, Mitch could have done without. Mike was a difficult and suspicious person. He did not need him to be any more aggravated than was his natural state.

'Okay, let's cool it down,' he quickly interjected. 'What we've all agreed to do is mount a major campaign that will cause us to be elevated in the eyes of the other freedom fighters around the world. This is just as well. We don't have the muscle power to perform this size of campaign without their help.'

Mitch began his speech with severe misgivings. The shields had fallen off his eyes in the last couple of days, and he could not help feeling that his voice sounded false. Strangely, though, with his position in the movement and the way his former colleagues looked at him, it became very easy to slip once again into the role of leader. After all, it was one that he had enjoyed for more than ten years.

'You all know we don't have the materials to make the kind of noise that's needed. Has anybody thought about how we are going to lay our hands on these Mephistos, anyway?'

There was a mumbled noise from Mike, in the act of stubbing out his cheroot to the sound of another squeal from his chair. Taffy sipped his Bushmills and stared at the wall opposite. Mitch looked harshly at them both. When you boiled it all down, they were pretty pathetic.

'Well, for a start we better make contact with some other groups. Does anyone remember the signal for assistance?'

'Something to do with putting an ad in the *Irish Times*, wasn't it?' Taffy volunteered.

Brilliant, thought Mitch. These guys are going to be down the drain in a big way when I'm not here to think for them.

'So we put an ad in the *Irish Times*. What sort of ad then, Mike? How about "IRA needs foreign help to blow up British cities"? Then we could give the address here,' he added with sarcasm.

'Okay, Mitch, you've made your point. Let's just get on with what we have to do, shall we? You set up the funds and we'll set up the bombs. We can't all be wonderful at everything.'

Mitch felt a lift just above his belt buckle. Maybe this was going to be easier than he thought. Still there was a way to go yet, and he didn't want to overplay his hand.

'Okay, Mike, I'll get the Mephistos, and you two set up the targets. Are you both quite happy with that?'

Both antagonists nodded their agreement. After all, they much preferred being involved with the blood and gore – provided it wasn't theirs, of course.

In truth, the end of the deal that focused on manpower

was not such a big problem at the moment. Britain was a very easy target in general, provided you left out museums, airports, and anywhere royalty went. Huge buildings had open doors to anyone wearing a suit and looking reasonably respectable. The days had long since passed when the IRA would send unshaven drunks in ill-fitting clothes into areas of high risk. The game had become more sophisticated than that. Today's terrorist knew how to melt into the background, leave his briefcase in a vulnerable spot, and vanish without a trace.

Also, since 1989, the number of willing volunteers for such activities had increased dramatically. Ironically, this increase was the result of activity by the British Secret Service. It had exerted pressure on its allies on both sides of the vanishing Iron Curtain to assist in the clearing up of the IRA cells that were operating all over Europe.

IRA activity had previously been under the control of the police Special Branch, supposedly working hand in hand with the Secret Service. In reality, before the change in direction, there was the usual interdepartmental wrangling and refusal to pass over important intelligence.

Within Ireland, the Brits had good contacts and knowledge. Once cells had been established outside the United Kingdom and Ireland, however, they were virtually undetected, provided they kept clear of local infringements. With the new intelligence, though, the nets had tightened around the men hiding in Europe. Initially, no one could understand what had happened, but in the middle of the night, doors came crashing down and sleepy, hung-over, Irish rebels were hauled off to cold foreign jails, and left to languish.

It was the biggest sweep any of them could remember. At least fifty active 'soldiers' were arrested and found themselves in the hands of the Brits, who imprisoned them under various obscure acts. It was all done with a minimum of fuss and virtually no publicity. Those who had been warned in time made their escapes and more than seventy were now holed up in remote locations all over Western Europe, waiting for the midnight call.

Mitch knew, as the months passed, these formerly lone operators were coming under the discipline of their units; they would easily be available for the sort of onslaught the central committee was now planning. Also, several of the more fanatical operators feared the highly secret talks that were taking place with the British Government. They wanted some action before the politicos arranged a cease fire.

Had he been as genuine as he hoped his two companions thought him, he would undoubtedly be looking at the more difficult side of the operation. Mephistos were the most effective anti-personnel devices known. They would fit into an average suitcase and could be detonated remotely, long after the carrier had made his escape. The countries that had them – mostly the USA, Germany, England and Russia, fiercely guarded them – but there had been talk of some finding their way into Iran, and long-time opponent, Iraq.

Mitch probed the workings of Mike's mind concerning the way he intended to set up the network of 'carriers'. As he suspected, the job would be performed by 'respectable' soldiers who were only too pleased for some action and, of course, a big bonus.

Taffy volunteered to work with Mike's side of things but said he would be available if Mitch needed him for any special duties.

'It only remains for me to call up our friends across the waters, and see who wants to help. The last contact that we had was down in Barcelona, if I remember right. But let's see who we get.'

Mitch walked around the two of them and pushed the

bell. Returning to his seat, he wrote swiftly on a ruled piece of paper. *Urgently Seeking Reliable Foreign Antiques. Please Contact As Soon As Possible To Arrange For Viewing.* Mitch looked up at the young man in the doorway.

'What's the PO box we're using at the moment, Matt?'

'I think it's 4936 in the Republic and in the North –'

'That's okay, Matt, I only need the one down there.'

He added the number to the message and handed it over.

'Now, Matt, see that this gets into the small ads as soon as possible at the *Irish Times*, in Dublin, and make sure it goes through our most secure channel.'

'While you're resting yourself, Matt,' Taffy interjected, 'bring me another Bushmills. Anybody else want anything?'

Mitch and Mike asked for coffee, and Matt disappeared with his orders and the message.

'Well, gentlemen, we'll have to wait and see what comes out of the woodwork. But until whatever it is surfaces, it promises to be a quiet week.'

Chapter Four

Belfast, 1786

Paddy never knew what hit him. He had barely put his hand up to remove the nosebag from his horse, when the billy club caught him on the side of the head and he went down in a heap. He became aware of being carried in some sort of sheet, before he passed out again. Eventually, he came around in a dark damp room to the sound of groaning and other human noises. He felt terrible. His head hurt really badly and his mouth tasted like a sewer.

'Bejesus,' he moaned, 'where the bloody hell am I?'

He rolled over onto his side in an attempt to get up and found someone else trying to do the same thing. They both fell back immediately, once they felt the other in their way.

'Who the 'ell are you?' a disembodied voice cursed at him.

'I'm Paddy O'Doule from Ballyhean on my way to the agent's office.'

'Well, you're not on your way there any more, Paddy O'Doule. You've been pressed.'

'I feel flattened, I can tell you. Where the hell am I?'

'Can't tell you that, mate, 'cos I don't know misself yet. Don't you know what "being pressed" means?'

The voice had a harsh ring to it although it seemed friendly enough. The accent was strange, certainly not from around those parts. Paddy tried to get up again but couldn't make it. Something about his head and the complete darkness stopped him from getting further than his knees, before he sank back onto the floor.

'Don't keep buggering around, you'll fall over all of us here, great clumsy mick.'

'I'm not Mick, I'm Paddy –'

'O'Doule, yes, I got that message already. Look let's start again, shall we? I'm Chipper Johnson from the great city of London, came to Belfast on a merchantman bound for 'merica, fell out with the chief mate – bastard called White. So they gimme me papers here and tells me to piss off. "Good riddance," says I, and I settle down to a few of them special ales you micks like. Come out the bleedin' pub, and wallop. Never knew what hit me but I knows who did. The bloody press-gang and no mistake.'

'What do you mean "the press-gang"?'

Paddy was mystified. Chipper's accent was very hard to understand, as Paddy had never met a real foreigner before.

'Gawd help us, you straight out of the bogs or something, mate? Everybody knows about the press-gangs. How the 'ell do you think His Majesty keeps his ships afloat? You don't think that anyone would volunteer, do you? Blimey, you're a bloody caution.'

This statement caused Chipper to start laughing. At the same moment the room gave a lurch. Paddy stared around wildly into the darkness, and grabbed hold of what turned out to be Chipper's leg.

'Hold on a mo, mate. Careful where you're grabbing. Christ, you ain't one of them, are you?'

This was all very confusing to Paddy, and he was about to ask Chipper for another explanation, when a door in the roof opened and a hose was pushed through. A shouted command from somewhere outside was given and a thick jet of water came sluicing through the confined space.

In the light, Paddy could see that there were about fifteen men in various states of discomfort before the jet hit him full in the chest. Fortunately, it passed quickly over him and he could see his voluble companion dripping wet beside him. Chipper was small. He probably looked even smaller at that moment, like a drowned rat. Paddy laughed at the sight before the jet hit him again. Now it was Chipper's turn to laugh. Then the hose was turned off and the trapdoor closed.

'Bleedin 'ell. You're a bloody big'un, Paddy, and no mistake. We'll have to watch out for you. The big ones always get it tough. How come they got you in the first place?'

'I don't remember. That's the truth. I was having a few in The Rover, I think it was called. I came outside and that's all I can remember.'

'Same old story, mate. Can't go into a decent boozer anymore these days, but there's some navy bleeder with a cosh waiting for you. It's bloody Nelson, you know. He's going through us like a dose of salts. There won't be any of us left at this rate. Christ, I've only just got out. Got onto the *Magpie* to earn a bit on its way to 'merica and here we go again. Still, you wait till I get's me chance. They'll let me go once they know I've been in before. No chance for you, I'm afraid. You're prime meat for the fleet. Eh, that's good, innit? Must be a poet and don't know it.' He chuckled at the dreadful pun.

Once again, the trapdoor opened and this time, a ladder was lowered to the floor. A rich English voice called, 'All right, you men. Come up one at a time. No more than one on the ladder, or my men will be forced to assume that it's mutiny. That means you'll be shot.'

The wet prisoners gradually rose to their feet and, mumbling, shuffled over to the foot of the ladder. One or two were decidedly unsteady and had problems making it to the top. In spite of the man's warning, they had to be pushed up by the others. Paddy followed Chipper up the steep steps and stumbled out onto the curved deck above. As soon as he stood up, he opened his mouth and was about to say something, when he was hit from behind and fell down again.

'That'll be enough out of you for a start,' a voice shouted at him.

He was about to leap at the man when the small Londoner pulled him back.

'Don't hit 'im again, Mister. He's a bit daft and can't help hisself.'

Grabbing Paddy's arm, he helped him to his feet and pulled him over to the line of men standing in their individual puddles, staring wildly at their strange surroundings. They were on the deck of a three-masted ship, moored to a bleak dock. Away towards the stern, Paddy could see the main part of the town, but here, there was nothing but an empty dock that had seen better days. The ship itself was quite small and was covered with lines of rope, and canvas tightly rolled around the masts.

He and his colleagues were pushed, complaining, into two short bedraggled lines. The wind was blowing from the open sea, and it made them feel cold and miserable. Around them in a tight circle stood two dozen sailors, all holding pistols and clubs, one in each hand. Obviously, there was no way to fight one's way out of here.

Above them on a raised deck, a small boy marched proudly into view. Hanging down in front of him was a red, white and blue drum that gleamed in the early morning light. Shifting the instrument, he began a fusillade of strokes that attracted everyone's attention. As the crescendo stopped, an officer marched up, and reading from a roll of parchment, he informed the gathered throng that they were now officially part of His Majesty's royal navy, unless they had some reason for not volunteering.

Chipper nudged Paddy and stuck his hand up.

'Scuse me, Sir. I've served five years before the mast with Admiral Randolf Jones. I don't think I need to do it again.'

The officer, who was on the point of departing the scene, looked down at the scrawny little man beneath him and then to the rough team of seamen behind the new recruits.

'Belcher,' he shouted.

The man who had hit Paddy stepped forward and landed a swipe on the side of the Londoner's head. Chipper saw it coming and rode the punch.

'Does that mean request denied, sir?' he called up at the departing officer. This time he didn't see the punch coming and it threw him to the floor. Strong arms gripped Paddy as he made to interfere in the scene.

'Don't even think about it, feller,' Belcher's voice warned.

The officer turned away from the scene, preceded by the drummer boy, and the new recruits were left to the mercy of the professionals.

Belcher walked slowly round the group and then kicked over a wooden box on which to stand. Mounted on his dais, he seemed a formidable man. He was well over six foot with a face lined and etched by years of weather battering. His hair was greased and waved into a short pigtail. This ended in a stump of tar and an oily black ribbon. Around his stout waist he wore a tight sash into which was fixed a cutlass of considerable age. The blade had been sharpened and honed until it had almost lost its original curve. Nonetheless, it gleamed in the morning light and gave its owner a piratical look, which was heightened by a black patch over his left eye.

Belcher turned his malevolent single gaze across the assembled group of fifteen beneath him; they all watched his performance with some alarm.

'Right, you bunch of filthy micks, my name is Belcher – Bosun Belcher to you scum. I'm here to turn you useless pieces of pig shit into proud sailors. God help me, the task gets more and more difficult,' he mumbled to himself.

'Scuse me, Bosun Belcher,' Chipper piped up. 'I'm not a bloody mick, I'm English and proud of it.'

Paddy knew that this was not a wise comment at this stage, and Belcher obviously concurred with this view as he promptly jumped down off his box and came charging over to the talkative Londoner. Pulling a length of twisted rope from behind his belted sash, he hit Chipper round the head and shoulders several times.

'That's enough out of you, you bloody little cockney swipe,' he roared at the cowering man at his feet. 'Any more and you'll kiss the gunner's daughter. And that's no idle threat.'

There was no more comment out of Chipper, so Belcher returned to his elevated position and continued with his diatribe.

'From now on, you have only three masters you ever have to worry about, God, His Majesty and me, in that order. Now, for your information, God doesn't give a shit for any of you and His Majesty ain't here, so you better just concentrate on me. Now, I'm not a hard man. Many of your new shipmates around you will tell you that. In fact, most of them will tell you that I'm a good person, even a caring person.'

At this remark, there was a quiet groan from the others assembled around. Belcher fixed the group with a humorless stare.

'What your new shipmates will tell you is that, unlike God, or His Majesty, for that matter, I don't bloody well forgive sins. I only punish them. There's no confessional on my ship, so the best way for you to survive your time with me is not to commit any sins at all. Rule number one is DO

IT NOW.' His voice shouted the words out across the deck and rang in all their ears. 'That's right. Never think. Just do it now.'

There was a stunned silence to accompany Belcher's first rule. He seemed pleased with the effect and continued, 'Rule number two is DO IT QUICKLY.'

Once again the stentorian voice boomed the three words out across the ship. There was a light echo back from the shabby buildings of the dock.

'Your shipmates will tell you about a number of other necessary regulations that go to the running of a man-of-war. But always remember the most important two. Now, as to your exact situation. You are aboard His Majesty's ship *Distinction*. Here you will learn to fight the French under the protection of his Lordship, the Admiral Lord Nelson. If you do your jobs, two things will probably happen. One, you may survive, and two, you may be allowed back to your flea-infested homes, and your pox-infected families, God help them. The period of time that you have volunteered your exclusive services to the royal navy is three years. Chief Gunner Sande will show you what you will need to know to become part of the ship. You will call him Chief. That's all. Stand easy. Oh yes, I nearly forgot.' Belcher turned back from his planned retreat and stared at them all one more time, saying, 'If any of you should think about leaving us prematurely, one of three things will happen to you. You will either be hanged, flogged, or, if I'm in a bad mood, keelhauled. Carry on, Chief.'

With that, Belcher walked off his podium and a new man took his place.

Paddy had noticed that Chipper had become more rigid with the last few words of Belcher's speech. At the mention of the term keelhauled, the little man had positively shaken. To Paddy, it was all completely unintelligible. He was having difficulty understanding what on earth was going on. The accents were hard to follow; also, to a young man from the countryside with little contact outside the village, such threatening talk was totally beyond his life's experience.

Chief Gunner Sande was a different type of character altogether. He looked like a man who had rarely missed a lunch in his lifetime. He was sweaty, oily, dirty and initially looked like a lot of fun. He was also treacherous, if you were on the wrong side of him, was immensely strong, and had a tendency to homosexuality, as Paddy was to find out later.

'Right then, you men,' spoke up the chief in a strangely soft voice that caused those whom he was addressing to strain forward to hear what he was saying. 'The first thing to remember is that my name is S-A-N-D-E, pronounced Sand, and not S-A-N-D-Y. I get very upset when people call me Sandy, don't I, Mr Abbot?'

A thin stooping man, with a large mustache and a squint in his left eye, solemnly nodded.

The chief continued, 'You are all now in the service of His Majesty, aboard one of the finest ships in the royal navy. You are here to kill Frenchmen and make their wives into widows. In fact, this ship is better known as the "French Widow" for the service that she has so far performed. I am proud to claim much of the responsibility for this fine reputation. Now, how many of you fresh young Irish farmboys are married?'

Paddy noticed that about ten of the group including himself raised their hands. Chipper beside him was the first to stick his hand in the air.

'Well, if you want to ever see those rosy cheeks of your young darlings again, you'd better listen to me. My job is to keep you safe as a fighting unit. You are no good to His Majesty, Lord Nelson, or anyone else, dead.'

The chief's voice had begun to rise in volume. The soft,

slightly lisping tone was all but gone as he warmed to his subject.

'Now, firstly, let's get you into pairs. For those of you out of the bogs, that means in twos.'

There was a scurrying about at that, as fifteen undisciplined men tried to pair off with a neighbor. The chief jumped down and grabbed arms and shoved bodies until he was happy with the pairs around him. The one man who was left over, called Reilly, was given over to the thin man, Abbot. Reilly was a fresh-faced youth of about seventeen. He had not raised his hand at the question of marriage but had stood sobbing quietly throughout the proceedings. Paddy felt very sorry for the boy, and hoped that he might be helped by the obviously more experienced Abbot.

The pairs of people had been matched by Chief Sande according to size. As he bustled about, he explained that it helped to have gun crews about the same size, as it made the team equally balanced. Paddy's partner was a surly, dark-complexioned man who said his name was Welch. He looked tough, and Paddy noticed that the regular sailors left him well alone. He wore a gold ring in his ear and seemed perfectly at home in his new surroundings.

Just when everybody was settled, there was a rumpus at the edge of the group. Paddy hardly needed to turn his head to realize that it was Chipper up to his tricks again. He was in the grip of one of the sturdy sailors and was pulling this way and that, obviously trying to release himself. The chief tried to shout at the struggling pair but Chipper would not quieten down.

'You bastards, let me go. I'm telling you, he's not normal, and without me he'll put us all in danger. I'm not going down on this floating piece of shit without a fight.'

With one last tug, he wrenched his arm free and pushed himself between Paddy and his skulking companion, Welch.

The chief, in the meantime, bustled over to the red-faced Chipper and began to shake him violently by the shoulders until his teeth rattled. All softness had gone from the voice now. Only the hard accents of veteran seamen came through as they shouted at each other.

'I – I'm sorry, Ch – Chi – Chief, b – b – but the mick's n – n – not quite right in the 'ead. 'E needs me to 'elp 'im out, like. W – w – we'll work as a team if you'll let us.'

Chipper had developed a most amazing ability to look whipped into total submission under these circumstances. As a result, the one doing the whipping usually left off before too much damage was done.

Paddy stood looking in amazement at the scene unfolding before him. Had he known it, he would probably have been ashamed at the talk that was going on about him. With his big unruly mop of dark brown hair, he gave the impression that he was dumb. The chief had stopped shaking long enough for Chipper to repeat his demand, that only he could work with the big mick, as he called him.

'Right, that's enough,' Chief Sande bawled. 'Get over there, Welch, and let these two idiots work together if they must.'

Chipper grinned up at Paddy and punched him on the arm. Paddy felt as lost as ever. The pain from his hangover was not helping either. Since he had come on deck to face God knows what, he had been in a sort of dream. He had never been more than ten miles from his village and his home in his entire life, apart from the two other occasions that he had been to Belfast. And they were quick turn-around, daytime adventures, with only a stop on the way.

He had led a blameless simple country life. True, it had been hard at times but it was a life that completely lacked fear. As a child, of course, he had been scared of childlike things, like the dark, the stories of witches and the leprechauns, and when he was very small, the local bully.

But this was different. He was out of his element, out of his area and out of his mind with the fear of it all. He did not enjoy the feelings of complete submission to these bullying men, with their cocksure ways and their arrogant swaggers.

Chipper seemed to take it all as a sort of cruel joke. He had been through it all before, he said. The other men around him were either weeping, like young Reilly, were stoically staring at their new masters, like the tough-faced Welch, or, like Paddy, were standing in a sort of trance.

The chief's benign side returned and standing once more on his makeshift podium, he beamed around at them, showing several gaps in his loose mouth.

'So, now that we've got you all sorted into nice little pairs, let me tell you how we are going to progress from here. First, each pair will have a senior man assigned to them. Then you will learn with him, and with my help, what it means to serve aboard "The Widow". You'll be glad to know that the captain has provided lavish lodgings for you all.'

At this, the veterans let out a rumbling grog-laden chuckle, which the chief seemed to enjoy.

'So, we'll send you below to enjoy your fine quarters, while we get this vessel on the high seas where she belongs.'

The sailors herded the men to a hatch, and down some steep steps into a large murky room that stank of stale sweat and tobacco. As they tumbled into the new space, they all let out various oaths and cries of relief that they were still alive and away from the threats above deck. Paddy and Chipper made their way over to the center of the room to select the quarters for their enforced stay. As he negotiated his path along the sloping deck, Paddy kept banging into the swinging hammocks that hung suspended from the roof. Once at their destination, Chipper held one of the hammocks to allow Paddy to hoist himself aloft, then, with a practiced swing, he climbed up into the next and said, 'Well, I suppose this is the time that I have to really explain what it means to be a "volunteer" in His Majesty's royal bleedin' navy.'

Chapter Five

Ballyhean, 1992

Mitch realized that the time for playing games was over. At least he could no longer afford any games within his own mind. This was a very dangerous business. Somehow, he had to maintain the hard, criminal mindset that had kept him at the top of the cause for over ten years, while at the same time he had to remove himself intellectually and emotionally. The stakes were high: his very life.

Over the next few days, Mitch kept away from his colleagues on the war council. This was not difficult, for, at heart, the leaders were mostly quite lazy. They would often joke that, outside of terrorism, they would all find it hard to earn a living actually doing work. He spent much of his time after the meeting had ended lying around his flat over the barn. His mind was in a whirl. He made endless kettles of boiling water for tea, and spent many hours poring over his atlas.

On the third day, he woke early and had the urge once more to pull out the atlas. As he sat hunched and unshaven, looking at the great land mass of Australia, he glanced to the east and noticed, nestling in the Pacific Ocean, the small island of Norfolk. At the time it meant very little to him, but as his eyes roamed around the page, his attention kept coming back to the tiny speck. Something about the name gnawed away at his subconscious. He decided to think about its source while shaving, and went into the cramped bathroom and ran the tap. He stood staring at his tired face in the steaming mirror while the water ran from cold to hot.

As happened so often in his life, the solution to the problem occurred to him as half the graying whiskers were being scraped away. He had heard the name 'Norfolk Island' from his great-aunt, Mildred. She would tell him stories about life years ago, and Norfolk Island was always used by her to describe a place of horror. In her words, it was the home of 'incarnate evil'. It also had something to do with the relative who had been to Australia. Apart from that, he could remember very little about the stories, and not that much about Great-Aunt Mildred. She was probably dead by now, anyway.

On the other hand, he knew his Aunt Kathlene was still living in the North, about two hours' drive away. As he wiped the traces of lather off his face, he decided to pay her a visit. Wearing a greenish sweater and a gray trilby hat well down over his eyes, Mitch drove the Fiesta deep into the countryside. His aunt was a widow who lived in a small terraced house on the outskirts of St Mary's. This was an obscure village with little to commend it except a few factories turning out electronics, courtesy of generous grants from the British Government.

He had known his Aunt Kathlene all his early life, but it was the old lady, her mother, whom Mitch used to enjoy visiting. He loved to hear her ranting and raving about the Brits, while her quiet daughter moved in and out of the tiny rooms, dusting and cooking. Kathlene, or Aunty Kate, as he called her, had married unhappily. Before the errant soldier had departed, he had left her with two babies and pains in the stomach about which the other women in the family would shake their heads knowingly. The venereal infection proved easier to treat than her feelings of rejection.

The two babies had grown into strong boys and both

had gone to find jobs in America. As Mitch was several years older, he had lost contact with them both, but he sent Christmas greetings to Aunty Kate each year. Fortunately, this branch of the family had no relationship with the IRA or any of its political associations. The boys were long gone, heaven knows where, and his aunt had spent most of her life dealing with microscopic welds on printed circuit boards.

Mitch tried the radio as he drove along the quiet country roads, but the programs that he could tune into were either political interviews or strident pop music The first made him feel impotent and the second ancient. He impatiently stabbed the off button and gripped the wheel harder.

At least the day was good and bright. As he continued on his journey, Mitch looked around at the lush green countryside with its neat and trimmed fields. This was a tortured land that he had tried to free from oppression. Its history was one of violence and it seemed that it was as far from a solution as when he had joined the movement. And yet, something had changed. The leaders had lost their souls. No longer was the ideal one of independence and unification with the rest of Ireland. Today, it had become one that was obscured by power and money.

Maybe that had always been the case, although somehow Mitch did not believe so. When he became a member of that inner clan of organizers, there was a 'mission' in everything they did. Men met and discussed how Ireland would become one, how it would be finally free and happy, and how it would enjoy the richness of its heritage and its natural farmlands, without paying huge fees to its absentee landlords. Of course, much was myth that fed upon itself and produced justification for lives spent only in the pursuit of violence. The result was inevitable, and produced the likes of Mike Ryan and Taffy O'Brian. These two pathological thugs didn't even bother to indulge in patriotic speeches, these days.

Some of the others who had sat on the war council were more mature – more Mitch's age and older. The talk ranged over the great days of the 'Troubles' and the famines that swept over the land. They talked about de Valera, Collins, and the characters who had made up Ireland's past. But the new men coming up through the ranks into controlling positions had few memories of the old days, and even less interest. To them, the path was the future, not the past. And that meant money, and they didn't care where it came from. The standing council of five now contained four of this element.

When he reached St Mary's, he had no trouble locating the familiar row of houses. He cruised slowly down the street looking for the end terraced house. During the hasty phone call after breakfast, Aunty Kate had said that she would be very happy to see him any day, and that she normally was home about three thirty in the afternoon. Mitch said he would try and get down there in a day or two and promptly left that lunchtime. Once security is in your blood, he thought, it's almost impossible to remove. He hoped that Aunty would not be too upset at his early arrival.

Parking the small Ford along the road, he walked the last few yards and rang the bell fastened to the glass door. He watched the progress of the occupant walking towards him.

'Well, Mitchell, I thought you said in a few days. Still, as you're here, you'd better come on in. It's good to see you. What's it been? Three, four years? You're getting older, you know. Well, so am I, for all that. Not so quick on the old pins these days, I'm afraid.'

Mitch thought that Aunty was a bit more talkative than he remembered, but then she was on her own these days and probably needed to make up some time when she had a visitor.

She was also not as tall as he remembered, and her red

hair was almost white now. Her blue eyes were hidden behind National Health glasses, and she peered around intently as she flicked a duster about the already immaculate furniture before Mitch sat down. She bustled into the small kitchen and produced some strong tea and a plate of ginger snaps. It was good to see that some things never changed.

One's own maturity was an exception, of course. When Mitch was a little boy, he never liked the taste of ginger combined with tea. Somehow it brought out the heat of the biscuit. Nowadays, he didn't mind a bit. In fact, he gobbled down a couple of the thick pastries while his aunt surveyed him from over the rim of her blue Wedgwood cup and saucer.

'So, rumor has it that you're one of the high-ups in the revolution these days.'

She may always have been quiet, but when she had things on her mind, Aunty spoke up. Things did not change with her either, it seemed. In answer, Mitch smiled and lifted his cup in tandem with the woman sitting opposite in her well-worn armchair with the lace anti-macassars. The two of them sat for a while, enjoying the warmth and comfort around them.

'Well, I guess one's not supposed to talk about such things, and no doubt you think you know what you're doing. I'll not pry into your business. Still, I can't believe it's just chance that's brought you all the way out here, to see a lonely old woman. So, Mitchell, what can I do for you?'

'It's sort of a family matter, Aunty Kate. Something I've been trying to remember Aunt Mildred telling me years ago. I wondered if you might remember the tale.'

'Give me your cup, Mitchell, and I'll fetch you a refill. Some more ginger snaps?'

She hurried out to the kitchen, as Mitch settled back

comfortably in his chair. It was very quiet sitting here in the well-used parlor. Mitch thought of how many hours Aunty Kate must have spent whiling away her life here, free from all danger and tension, apart from the normal things that people worried about. The thought gave him that same empty feeling inside him again.

'You look awfully down sitting there, Mitchell. Is there anything wrong?'

'No, Aunty Kate. I was just thinking about how my mam used to bring me over here when I was small. It was always a happy time for me. Life was pretty simple, as I remember.'

'Well, maybe for you, Mitchell, but then you were only a very little boy. For us it was adult problems, as usual. Mother was quite a tartar, you know. But then you only saw her as an old lady full of stories. Still, I'm glad you have happy memories of coming here. It was a long time ago, you know.'

Mitch was surprised at the directness with which she spoke. Perhaps Aunty Kate needed a one-on-one situation to make her voice heard. Putting down his cup on the little carved table at his elbow, Mitch pulled out his packet of Players and handed one over to his aunt. She accepted it together with the flaming match, and they both sat back, regarding each other. He watched her closely, checking her reaction to his prepared opening. It was important that he did not leave any trail that could be linked to his intended departure.

'An old friend of mine is selling up and leaving Ireland.'

'Like a lot of people,' Aunt Kate interrupted. 'Ever since the Common Market, it's been the same.'

'Well, this friend was asking me what I knew about where he was going. He's decided to try his luck in Australia. I remembered that we had a branch of the family over there and, in particular, I can recall Aunty Mildred telling a tale about someone going to Norfolk Island. Unfortunately, I couldn't remember anything else. I wondered if she had told you about it?'

'Told me about it, Mitchell? Mother never stopped going on about it. I know you don't want to talk about your involvement in "The Cause", I think you call it, but I've often thought that it was in many ways due to that silly old woman's tales. I'm sorry to talk about her that way, but you know she caused me a lot of grief, particularly at the end of her life. She never showed any concern for my situation, bringing up two boys without a husband. It was me who had to work at the factory every day. She just used to sit in that same chair that you're sitting in right now and demand to be looked after. And, underneath, there was so much bitterness. Somehow it didn't seem natural. The extent of the bitterness, I mean.

'Her husband, my father, died in the last war, fighting in France. It was nobody's fault. He got drunk and fell out of a moving train. He had only just returned from leave; I was born nine months later. I never knew him. She blamed it all on the English. She blamed everything on the English. How they had taken her man, raped the countryside, stolen all Ireland's wealth and killed the good people. How she blamed them for my father's volunteering for the war I never could work out, but then I suppose hatred twists people's minds.

'The link with Australia is through her great-great-grandfather, I think – I can never remember how many generations back. He was known as Paddy and he ended up down under. I don't know all the aspects of the story, I don't think she did either. It was all sort of mixed up in her mind. She used to have a couple of bottles of Guinness, and then off she would go. All about how the English had captured her poor grandfather and sent him off to the colonies to slave for them, and how he had wreaked his vengeance. I'm sure that most of it was fantasy, but she used to hold her audience riveted and, obviously, that included you.'

Mitch stubbed out his cigarette in the brass bowl that his aunt slid over to him. Waving away the last clouds of smoke, he leaned forward.

'What was it she used to say about this place, Norfolk Island, then?'

'Apparently, that was where he turned against the English. The story goes that he was in the royal navy and served with some distinction. Something went wrong along the way and he never returned to his family. He was sent out to Australia for some crime, and spent nearly all the rest of his life there. He had been a countryman, so they say. A simple good soul, but he became twisted and sought revenge. That's about all I remember about it. Oh yes, the reference to Norfolk Island is that Mother always referred to it as the place of incarnate evil. Those were her exact words.'

'Yes, it's funny, but I remember those words, too. She must have meant them, to have lasted all the way down through time. When was it all, Aunty? How many years ago?'

'About the time of the famines here, Mitchell. Mid-nineteenth century, I think, or shortly before. Mother said that there were some letters that had told the story. I don't know where they were kept or what was in them. But she said that it told the whole story and she would never forget it. So, there you have it. It's not much, I'm afraid, but it fueled a lot of hatred in the family and I'm sorry to see that it might have corrupted you into the bargain. My belief is that what's done is done, and it doesn't help to go prying into the past to keep hatred alive. Let's face it, if you go far enough back, every family would have some complaint about some group of people, wouldn't they?'

Mitchell finished his tea, with no comment on his aunt's pragmatic view of the world.

'Do you know where the letters may be found, Aunty Kate?' he asked quietly.

'No, sorry, Mitchell, I wouldn't know where to begin. I never saw them. Mother only talked about them. They were not from Paddy, anyway. Apparently, he couldn't write. Something else that she blamed the English for. Said that they deliberately held our people back. The letters all came from someone else. Let me think a moment.'

She stared into the empty grate and rubbed her head with wrinkled fingers, bent over with the work of a lifetime.

'Yes, they were written by someone called Chipper. He had sent these letters over to Paddy's wife in the hope that she would not worry. He must have been a devoted friend to do it, Mother always said. Paddy's wife and three of the children had died in one of the first famines. Mother said that the English had taken away most of her land. There was a boy who survived, and he sought out what happened to his father. They say that he became a rebel.'

'I thought you said that Paddy had disappeared to Australia around the turn of the nineteenth century. The potato famines didn't come until what? 1845 or 1846?'

'You should have studied a bit more history at school, Mitchell. We had famines many times before the great ones in the years you mention. Mostly from over farming and bad seeding of the tubers. Famines used to come along quite regularly together with the accompanying side benefits of dysentery and cholera. Life was pretty tough for everyone in those days. Even the English, although your Great-Aunt Mildred would have none of it.'

Mitch stayed a little while longer, and took an obligatory stroll around the tiny handkerchief-sized garden, admiring the neat rows of flowers and vegetables. Then, awkwardly kissing his father's sister, he waved goodbye and returned to his car. As he was about to get in he heard a soft step coming after him. It was his aunt.

'Mitchell, as you're so interested in this Paddy and his life, there is an old box of Mother's that's up in the attic. I started to go through it soon after she died but, frankly, it was all just so much junk that I left it and never thought about it again. If I have another go at it, something may turn up. Can I send you anything that I find?'

'That's all right, Aunty Kate. Let me give you a call in a few days. I tend to move around a bit.'

'Yes, of course, Mitchell, I forgot. It was lovely to see you. Take care of yourself.'

Turning, she walked quickly back to her house. Mitchell watched her go, admiring the still stiff back and brisk walk; then he turned and got into his car.

The drive back to Ballyhean was uneventful, and Mitch's mind was firmly on thoughts of the mysterious Paddy O'Doule. He had enjoyed seeing his Aunty Kate again and regretted that it would not be long before all contact with her would be broken. Thinking further about his family, he realized that he had virtually no relationship with any of the far-flung O'Doules. Both his parents were dead, and his only sister had cut off all ties with him when he became involved with the IRA. It had been over twenty years since he had even spoken to her. He understood that she was still married to a car mechanic and had three children. He reflected that although many people viewed his life as glamorous, he had paid dearly for the notoriety and the excitement. After all, he had no one who cared what happened to him. That did not say much for forty-five years on the earth.

The small light was flashing on the answerphone as he walked back through his front door. As he rewound the tape, the high-pitched chatter gave out a brief message. He was once again invited to a 'Game of squash tomorrow morning, early. Bring your rule book.' The code meant: war council meeting tomorrow at nine. The reference to the rule book was to let him know that the advert had been responded to. He would now be on a course that would lead to his freedom.

At the agreed time the next morning, he sat with Mike and Taffy at the table. Today, they were joined by two of the younger officers. Brian Flynn was a silent moody individual, and his colleague was a tearaway who was destined for either a lunatic asylum or a prison, depending upon whether it was the authorities or the medical profession that got their hands on him first. His name was Conny Fitzherbert. He was about twenty-four, with a permanent grin that belied his violent nature. He worked with a group of similar assassins who specialized in 'eliminating' members of the opposition. This meant ambushing anybody who appeared 'intolerant' of the cause, and murdering them – all Protestants.

Even during his early violent days, Mitch had been wary of this type of element in the IRA. The cause naturally attracted men with a streak of violence in them and it suited the upper echelon to have a few loonies around to do their dirty work. Their life expectancy was usually pretty short, as they were often mowed down, or captured and jailed.

Conny Fitzherbert had lasted longer than most. Furthermore, he was ambitious, which meant that he was a danger to the council. In the old days, the seniors would have kept him out in the field to expose him to as much danger as possible. If he came through, he would be tempered down enough to move through the ranks. But the old ways were changing. Now Conny and his like could sit here and make policy decisions. Mitch nodded to him as he sat down. The permanent grin turned towards him with no noticeable difference in intensity.

Taffy O'Brian slid a cardboard file toward Mitch. It contained the page in the *Irish Times*, with a circle around the advert asking for information on foreign antiques. Clipped to the page was the reply. It was written on cheap writing paper with an unmatched envelope. The postmark was Bournemouth, Dorset, and the message read, 'Please call for catalogue of antiques.' There was added a telephone number.

'Short and sweet, eh, boys?' Mitch said and looked around the table. 'I guess I'd better make the call.'

He reached for the bell and summoned Matt into the room.

'Bring me in a secure phone, Matt. Also, let's have another cup of coffee.'

'Better make it a Bushmills for me,' Taffy spoke up.

Mitch inwardly thought that Taff seemed to be hitting the hard stuff a bit earlier these days.

Mike Ryan lit one of his cheroots and handed one over to Conny. They both exhaled plumes of foul-smelling tobacco smoke as Matt returned, pulling a cable and telephone, which he put on the table at Mitch's elbow.

The phone rang across the Irish Sea deep in the South of England. It was picked up very quickly. 'Yes.' The voice was female. Mitch tried to remove as much of his Ulster accent as possible.

'Thank you for the reply to our advert. When could we meet?'

'When you arrive here, please call this number, (202) 744320 and ask for extension 64. It will be answered on Thursday afternoons at five.'

There was a soft click and the phone went dead.

'As brief as the letter, I'm afraid. Still, whoever is behind the voice, knows what to do. Thursday is the day. I'll go next week and report back.'

There was some general talk around the table. Conny

attempted to play some macho politics with Mike Ryan, and Taffy sipped his Bushmills. The other newcomer, Brian Flynn, sat silently looking at the map of Ulster on the wall. As always, it was impossible to tell what he was thinking. Mitch withdrew without a backward glance.

Chapter Six

HMS *Distinction*, 1786

From the moment that they both swung up into their hammocks, Paddy O'Doule realized that he was going to be permanently indebted to Chipper Johnson. The little man seemed to know everything about the royal navy and how it operated.

'The thing that pisses me off the most, Paddy, is that the bleeders caught me again. I just can't understand it. Once bitten, twice shy, they say, but it obviously don't work for the likes of me.'

They reclined on the hammocks which moved gently through the thick moist air. Paddy felt extremely tired but his headache was starting to go. His first questions to Chipper were about the validity of the situation that they found themselves in. Even after the cockney's reply, he still couldn't believe that the British navy had the authority to kidnap men, and keep them prisoners on board ship, with no reparations to the families. There was not even any system for contacting wives and children.

Chipper managed to persuade him that 'pressing' did, in fact, happen on a regular basis, and bad though the method was, he had better get used to the idea as there was no escape. Furthermore, if he put his back into it, the life was not too bad. You were fed and sometimes clothed. Also, there were prizes of booty every time one's ship captured another. Some of Chipper's shipmates had salted away quite a fortune over the years.

'Threatening you with the lash and the noose is only good for new recruits. After you've been in awhile, you could jump ship any time. No, mate, there's money in His Majesty's fleet. That's what keeps most of 'em 'ere.'

Paddy regarded his new-found friend with half-lowered eyelids.

'I noticed that it was not the lash or the noose that upset you, Chipper. It was keelholing, I think he called it.'

Chipper turned to him with a whitening face. 'It's keel-HAULING, you stupid Mick, and pray God you never experience it or even see it. I came close to it only once in my life. I watched them kill the poor bleeder and then throw 'im to the sharks. I'll never forget it. Sometimes I even dream about it.'

Paddy was aware that, as Chipper talked, a faraway look came into his eyes. His frame seemed to grow smaller as he stared at the swinging hammocks all around them.

'But. Chipper, what is it that makes you so scared?'

Paddy's face grew hard as his friend explained the brutal roping of the victim's hands and feet, the lowering over the side at the bow and the two teams of men pulling the lashing, tormented body under the keel to the stern. Chipper's description formed vivid pictures in Paddy's mind of the scraping of the flesh as the man was torn against the sharp barnacles, fighting for oxygen, until he was pulled limp and bleeding out of the sea.

'The poor sod came out alive, but that bastard, White, ordered him down again and he never made it. Poor Charley, he was the best mate a man ever 'ad. Share his life with you, he would. And when he come up again dead, they cut him free and tossed 'im over the side. We was in shark-infested waters. His own blood must 'ave attracted 'em, for by the time poor Charley's body come up, you could see 'em circling round the ship. 'E was gone in a minute. I swore, if ever I had a chance to get me 'ands on White, I'd gut 'im.'

'What made them do such a terrible thing, Chipper?' Paddy asked.

'Well, we were in trouble, Paddy, and no mistake. It wasn't mutiny but we refused to eat the food. It was rotten, you see, and it was makin' us sick as dogs. White put a big bowl of the stinkin' meat in front of Charley and me, and made us eat it. I threw up on the deck and Charley asked if it was all right if he ate my share. White said okay as long as it was fast – everything's got to be fast in the royal navy, as you'll find out. Anyway, Charley now had this big bowl of rotten meat in front of 'im, with White standin' over 'im with a big grin on 'is ugly face. Charley dipped 'is 'ead in the bowl, then lifted it up quick as a flash and threw it over White. That would 'ave been bad enough, but Charley 'it the bleeder right in the face and down 'e goes. The orderlies were over Charley like flies on shit, and we both end up in the brig. I was lucky to get away with it, but poor Charley bought it all for me, Gawd rest 'is soul.'

Chipper lay still and stared silently at the deck above him. Paddy must have dropped off because there was a movement sometime later and he awoke to see the hammocks swinging in unison. The pattern of lights were changing through the thick portholes. Chipper and some of the others were clustered round the small grubby windows. They were leaving the harbor. Paddy pivoted out of his bed and clambered his way to see. The ship was distancing itself from the bleak dock. As he watched helplessly, the coast of Ireland appeared on either side of the harbor and there was a tilt of the keel, as the wind took the sails. Paddy felt a sickening nausea sweep over him. He was being taken from his country, his wife and children, his home.

Chipper came and took him to a corner of the large cabin. Making him squat down, he said, 'Now, look here,

Paddy, there's two ways you can do this. The tough way or the easy. In fact there's only the easy. If you're stupid enough to choose the tough way, the charming gentlemen above will break you. There's no escape, particularly with you being a big feller. They always set on the big ones; seem to represent some sort of threat. Now listen to me and remember what I tell you. You're daft, you see.'

Paddy stared at the Londoner and began to get up. Chipper laid a restraining hand on him.

'Now don't get upset. I know that you're okay, it's just a front for Belcher and Sande. If they think you're a gentle giant who's not very smart, they'll leave you be. If they think you're bright, they'll pick on you and you'll be dead meat. Stick with me, Paddy. I'll set you straight.'

Sitting hunched at the edge of the rolling cabin, Paddy received the first of many lessons about the modern navy. Chipper explained the workings of the crew, the non-commissioned officers like Belcher and Sande, the gun teams, and the boys working the powder lines and the rigging. He stressed how you needed to get as much food as possible into you whenever you could, and obey the two by now famous rules: do it now, and do it quickly.

'Actually, Paddy, if you think about it, the rules make sense. When you're under fire, the officers have to move quickly and they need you to act like quicksilver. Delay means death on board a fighting ship. I've seen men crushed by their own guns and die screaming over the sound of the explosions, with no one to care for them. Men have been blinded, maimed and crippled for life because they hesitated, or didn't understand an order. I'll keep an eye out for you now, but when the guns start firing, it's every man for 'imself.'

Their conversation was disturbed as the trapdoor of the cabin was thrown open. 'Grub up!' was shouted at them and the men moved to the door.

'Well, this is it,' Chipper said quietly, as he pulled himself to his feet. 'Now we'll see what sort of a ship this is. Good grub means a good ship. It's always the same. Some captains know this. Other captains steal the provisioning money and share it with the victualin' agents.'

As they came up into the bright daylight, there was a scuffle ahead. The sad young recruit, Reilly, on seeing the open sea, ran for the rail and threw himself over.

'Oh Christ, 'ere we go. Why we always 'ave to 'ave one bloody fool, I don't know. Always the same. Some silly sod 'as to 'ave a go. No bloody chance I can tell you. Don't even bother to watch. They'll pick 'im up and 'e'll be flogged, poor bleeder.'

Shaking his small head, he grabbed Paddy's arm and moved him aft to where there was a smell of cooking. Chief Sande stood at the door.

''Scuse me, Chief, but I seen it all before. D'ya mind if me and Paddy here gets some vittles. We'll be back to see the punishment. I suppose it'll be immediate?'

The chief looked wearily out to sea, where Reilly was splashing about. The poor fool was even swimming in the wrong direction, away from the land.

'Christ, they're stupid,' was all he said, and moved to one side.

There was a long table bolted to the floor of the mess, with room for about fifteen men on either side on benches that were also bolted to the deck. Paddy judged that the ship could serve meals to the entire crew in two and a half sessions. As if in reply to his thoughts, Chipper volunteered that the seating was for exactly two shifts; the watchmen would come in later. All the officers would take their food in the wardroom above, and the captain might have his in his stateroom.

'Hey up, Cookie,' Chipper shouted to the fat sweating man moving stolidly around the pots on his iron stove. 'Me name's Chipper Johnson, and this here's Paddy O'Doule. He's a bit slow, but otherwise he's okay'.

In reply, the cook pulled out two tin plates and slopped some brown mixture on each. To follow, he laid on a doorstep wedge of bread and nodded to the rough counter where a big urn of tea was steaming.

'What's your name then, mate?' Chipper inquired, refusing to take the man's silence as a put-off.

'Winston,' was the terse reply.

'Christ, not the famous Winston that sailed with Admiral Randy Jones, are you?'

'The same,' answered Winston, with a sly smile of pleasure that his reputation had carried over to the shores of Ireland.

'Well, here's a piece of luck,' Chipper continued. 'I was just telling Paddy that the acid test of a ship was the grub, and here we are getting the famous Winston's best vittles. It's a pleasure to make your acquaintance.'

Winston turned round, picked up another ladleful of what now appeared, on closer inspection, to be beef stew, and plopped it on the plates.

'Much obliged, I'm sure, Sir,' said Chipper, and made to move away.

'How come there's only the two of you down here?' Winston asked. 'The big feller looks like he could handle some work, but I reckon we'll need more than him to put the French to flight.'

Pleased with his joke, he stood back and put his thick hands on his even thicker hips, or what would have passed for them, if his fat had not covered them completely.

'We managed to get in while they picked up a jumpship. Straight over the side 'e went. What makes 'em do it, Winston? I can never see the sense of it. But like they say, there's always one.'

Winston shook his large head sadly and went back to his

steamy duties. Chipper took his brimming plate and sat on one side of the table, indicating that Paddy should sit across from him. They had positioned themselves as far away from the cook as possible, which was just as well because the first words out of Chipper's mouth were, 'The bloke's a right bastard. But we've done all right, we won't starve. He'll see us okay. But Jesus, don't get on the wrong side of him. He'll stint you out of proper rations. The stories I heard about 'im on the Admiral's ship were terrible.'

Chipper was spooning down the stew with the bread and belching as he went along. It was very hot but he didn't seem to care. It was hard for Paddy to understand every word with Chipper's mouth full, so he strained to hear.

'Admiral Randy Jones was one of the best, but he had two vices. Drink and crumpet.'

'Crumpet?' Paddy repeated through a mouthful of bread, which was surprisingly good.

'Yea, crumpet, birds, 'ows yer father, the German. You're not following me are you?'

'Sorry, Chipper, don't understand a word.'

'My mistake. Ladies, I'm talkin' about. The Admiral's real name was Randolf but everybody called 'im Randy. Christ, he'd fuck a snake if you'd 'old its 'ead.'

Paddy spluttered out some stew, and had to wipe his mouth on the back of his hand. To regain his breath, he got up from the table and collected two mugs of tea. Winston pushed a bowl of honey towards him with something approaching a smile. As he sat down again, Chipper leaned closer and continued in a quiet conspiratorial tone.

'Winston got transferred off the admiral's ship. 'E got caught shafting one of the admiral's bits of spare. Unfortunately, he was caught red-handed before the admiral had got to 'er.

'The ship was in port, and she'd come on board and wandered into the galley. Winston, over there, gave her a glass or two of grog, and when she was all giggly, he shut the hatch, and gave 'er a length. The admiral was upstairs getting all 'ot and bothered waiting for this bird, so 'e decided to take a walk roun' 'is boat. Apparently, 'e heared a bit of a shamozzle coming from the galley, and wandered in. There was old Cookie Winston givin' it a right proper seeing to. Blimey, 'e'd got 'er over the table and was doin' it doggy-fashion.

'The admiral, bein' a bit of a sport, started to move out, but the bird chose that moment to turn around and seein' it was 'im said, "Allo, Randy. Do you want to get on now? I think 'e's almost finished, and 'e's warmed it up a treat for ya."

'The admiral muttered something about it being the custom for the officers to lead the men into battle, and he was not going to change a fine tradition and start followin' 'em. Then he stormed out. Winston got transferred off the ship the next day. He was pretty pissed off about it 'cos 'e 'ad all the perks, and like 'e said, 'e didn't know it was the bloody boss's crumpet.'

Paddy laughed a bit too loud at the events as portrayed by Chipper and received a suspicious look from the main participant of the story. Both men stared down guiltily at the cooling food in silence. As they were finishing, there was an increase in the noise on deck above them.

Chipper, wiping his hand across his mouth, said, 'Well, we'd better get on top and see the whipping, I suppose. Now, Paddy, don't get this wrong in your mind. Young Reilly's going to lose some of the skin off his back. But it'll learn 'im a lesson, and the rest of the recruits, too. Don't let it get to you.'

So saying, they went on deck where the luckless young jumpship was being pulled over the side into the scuppers. He was cold, wet and looking half scared to death. Unceremoniously, he was tied to an upright deck hatch and an officer, who had not appeared till now, came out onto the forecastle. He was still chewing on a mouthful of food and was buttoning up his coat.

Chipper leaned towards Paddy and said out of the side of his mouth, 'That'll be the captain. I don't recognize 'im. But it looks like our friend, Belcher, is set for some enjoyable work, don't it?'

The bosun had removed his shirt, revealing a thick muscular body covered with black and blue tattoos. Snakes, anchors, dragons and ropes coiled their way around his limbs.

'Have a look at his back, Paddy,' said Chipper, as the burly chief turned round to face the captain.

On his back, stretching from shoulder to shoulder, and from the nape of his neck to the top of his thick leather belt, was a huge crucifix.

Paddy gaped at the sight as Chipper explained, 'The cross is supposed to stop 'im gettin' the same treatment he's about to lay out to poor old Reilly.'

At that moment the small drummer boy appeared again on deck and at a sign from the captain, he produced a drum roll.

'My name is Captain Merryview. And today I can tell you that my view is not at all merry.'

There was an embarrassed muttering from the old hands and a muted silence from the new recruits.

'You met Lieutenant Steven Jenkins when you first came on board. Now it is my pleasure to welcome you to His Majesty's ship *Distinction*, or, as you have no doubt heard her called, "The Widow".'

Captain Merryview's voice was strong yet rather laconic. His tones drifted down to the assembled hands, and left no doubt in anyone's mind that this was an officer who understood his position, and also that of the men before him.

'Unfortunately, one of you decided unwisely to cut short his time with us. The punishment for this crime is within the province of the authority vested in me. On this ship that means twenty lashes. You will all witness the punishment. Chief Belcher, commence.'

The drummer boy began a roll of his drum, and after spitting on his thick hands, Belcher picked up the handle of the lash. Attached to the two-foot-long wooden rod were nine thongs of knotted leather. As Reilly's shirt was pulled from his body to reveal a quivering white expanse of adolescent flesh, Belcher landed the first blow across his naked shoulders. There was a split-second pause as the drummer stopped. Then an animal-like scream escaped from Reilly's clenched teeth, releasing the wooden dowel that had been pushed between them. Paddy involuntarily made a move towards the boy, but Chipper was ready with a restraining hand on his arm.

'Not a movement, Paddy, I warn you. Not a sound either.'

The drummer began another roll and Reilly's back cringed away from his tormentor, Belcher. Inevitably the lash rained down again and Reilly let out another fiendish scream. Ten times the sequence was repeated and Reilly was reduced to a sagging semi-conscious wreck with his back a criss-cross of lines covered with blood. The captain had remained stiffly aloof throughout the proceedings, gazing out across the men under his command. He gave the impression of someone not entirely happy with the responsibility that he was having to exert.

'Enough, Chief,' he shouted down to the sweating man below. 'Belay there, drummer boy. Hold still, you men. Keep a lock on your mouth, Reilly.'

All three recipients of his commands obeyed instantly.

'Now, the rule says twenty lashes. But Reilly there is not going to be fit to serve Admiral Nelson if he receives his full ration. So, Chief, I'll stop the punishment. Let it be a lesson for all of you that desertion is a crime that is considered among the worst of all. Cut him down. Men dismissed.'

A bucket of sea water was thrown over Reilly's heaving back and the ratings were treated once more to that awful scream as the bosun walked off. As they were reassembled by the chief gunner, Chipper said out of the corner of his mouth, 'Well, I'll go to the foot of our stairs. A bloody merciful captain. It must be the first time in naval 'istory.'

The men were allowed to go below for their food, but as soon as this was accomplished, Chief Sande ordered a huge iron cannon to be wheeled on deck in front of the newly assembled men. Three sweating bulky men positioned the ordnance so that it was facing the group who had been placed in a semi circle to view it.

Chipper and the shifty Welch were the only men not intimidated by the muzzle of the gun that pointed into their midst. The others looked somewhat afraid, which was hardly surprising, considering the things to which they had been subjected in the last twenty-four hours.

Using the same soft voice, the chief put three separate gun crews through their paces in front of the gathering. He was able to demonstrate the workings of the gun and the procedures necessary to load, aim and fire it. Then, after positioning its barrel out to sea, he showed them all how it performed. The noise was not as deafening as everyone expected, but it was explained that the reason was because they were out on deck and not below. Down there, where the guns were fired, the noise would often be sufficient to cause a man to lose his hearing for several hours, or sometimes days.

The experienced gun crews made it all look very easy, but when it came to the turn of the new men, there were a number of hilarious mistakes. In one case the gun came loose from its lashings and started to roll across the deck, clearing all in its way. It would have crashed through the planking around the side were it not for one of the hands wedging a log beneath its wheels.

When it was Paddy and Chipper's turn, the exercise went fairly smoothly, mostly because Chipper knew what he was doing and he used Paddy to do the manual labor.

During this time, The Widow sailed steadily on. The oak beams that made up its construction occasionally creaked, and the sails suspended above on the blackened spars would crack from time to time as the wind shifted slightly. The regular seamen balanced their weight on the balls of their feet and swayed with the rhythm of the ship. They paid no heed to the chattering of the many lines that stretched above them.

When the gun exercise ended, the sun was low on the horizon. After being dismissed by the chief, the men turned and went below to their sparse quarters. As Paddy bent his head to return below deck, he was filled by an awful emptiness brought on with the realization of the loss of his wife and family. He moved slowly to his hammock, where he turned away and closed his eyes in sadness and misery, as Katherine's face floated in his memory.

There was no escape. He knew that. Chipper might help him and even rescue him from the horrors of this alien world with its harsh discipline, but the fact was it was not his world. They were not his people, and this was not his life. His existence had been rooted in the land, the animals and the farming life that had been his and his ancestors' for hundreds of years.

Talk of Lord Nelson, the royal navy and the ship on which they all floated – HMS *Distinction*, or 'The Widow', as the men liked to call it – was as foreign as if the whole package had dropped from another world. England controlled Ireland. England owned Ireland, and to some extent, protected it, but to the average Irishman, England was a million miles away from the fields and the damp sky of the ancient land of Erin. Paddy drifted off to sleep in an atmosphere of helplessness and despair. A prisoner of circumstance, he was adrift on a tide of regimentation.

Chapter Seven

Portsmouth, England, June 1992

With a squeal of brakes, the blue electric train with the yellow stripe pulled into Portsmouth station. Mitchell O'Doule jumped down onto the gray platform, pulling his canvas bag after him. He walked out of the station grounds into the bustling afternoon traffic, and headed up the road towards the car-hire business where his car was reserved. His papers consisted of an English driving license, a VISA card, an American Express card, and a UK passport, all in the name of Brian Kenneth Walker. Only the passport carried any photographic identification, so he was unrecognizable to all within the boundaries of the British Isles.

He had left Belfast by the boat across to Liverpool two days earlier. It was a route that he knew well. It was one where he could keep out of sight and remain one of the mixed crowd of holidaymakers and general travelers who flowed across the Irish Sea every two hours. Even had he been spotted by any watchers, his arrival in the depressed port of Liverpool would have led them a merry dance.

His unseen contacts had arranged a number of crossing routes with some decoys, leaving several addresses to create confusion. Once he had arrived, he was put on the back of a noisy Norton motorcycle and carried out into the suburbs. Here, he was given several tickets to allow him to cross over to Manchester and thence onto London. There, he stayed overnight in a safe house and made his phone call from a safe phone. The answer was once again immediate, and the same female voice gave him his instructions in a matter-of-fact way.

'Meet me at the cocktail bar of the Avonhead Hotel outside Christchurch tomorrow night at eight.'

He asked how he would recognize the contact and was told stiffly not to be concerned about it.

His last remaining ticket was for the 11.15 slow train from Waterloo in London to Portsmouth. It would arrive at 2.10, and he could collect a car from South Coast Rentals, three streets along from the station.

Waterloo Station had lost its rush-hour bustle, he saw, as he emerged from the Underground. There were the customary number of vagrants sleeping on the mahogany benches that were placed around this monument to Victorian steam engineering. There was a calm about the place as Mitch browsed at a cluttered bookstall, then selected his train, compartment and, finally, a seat.

He had to admit that even though his mind kept returning to his former existence, he felt completely different. From that late afternoon back in The Rover, when he had reached his decision to escape the IRA, his life had taken on a new meaning.

He had, for instance, started looking at women. This was an area where he had been underextended for virtually all his adult life. With always a new sortie or scheme to take part in, there was never any room for the time necessary to court a woman, or consider anything beyond the most basic relationship. He and his former brothers in the 'Army' would hire camp followers, or straight 'Prossies', as they called them, for weekends of drinking and fornication. However, it was always known that come Sunday night or Monday morning, the cars would return to take the women away.

In his youth, it had been great fun to see who could 'handle' the most at a sitting, but in the last few years, such behavior had left Mitch feeling cold and empty. The sport was no longer there, and he found the professional enthusiasm and false cries of ecstasy rather degrading.

Since he had landed in England, he realized that he was enjoying the sight of women going about their business. There were mothers leaning over prams, young office girls clipping along in toned-down business suits, even girls working on building sites. Perhaps it was the brief spell of bright sunny weather that was being enjoyed by all, but he was very aware that the women all seemed to look happy and be having lots of fun. Perhaps it was just his new feeling of release that was infecting his usual dour nature.

He was reminded of this unaccustomed attraction for women as he took his seat opposite a young lady in her late twenties. She was reading a copy of *Cosmopolitan* and sat leaning against the corner of the compartment. She had a somewhat severe hairstyle but it only accentuated the softness of her face lighted by the strong sunlight through the window. As Mitch sat across from her, she looked up and returned his quick smile with one of equal brevity. Mitch opened his *Daily Telegraph* at the back, to attempt the crossword. It was going to be one of the easier ones. It allowed fifteen letters along all four sides. There were none of the black squares to interrupt the compiler's skill at finding phrases to prod the solver's memory.

As he began to fathom the labyrinth, he glanced down and his eyes rested on the young woman's legs daintily crossed. They were shapely legs and his glance involuntarily rose up their length. He was somewhat amused and then fascinated by the two little bumps that appeared through the soft lap of her skirt. She was obviously wearing stockings with a garter belt, rather than pantyhose. Mitch had always liked that look.

He flicked his glance back to the crossword as he saw her eyes stare over at him. At the same time, she uncrossed her legs and tucked her feet under the British Rail seat. The train pulled smoothly out of the cover of the station.

Mitch's first impression of the ease of the crossword was wrong, or more likely, he was not in the mood to tackle it. He lowered the paper and gazed out at the passing scenery. It was depressing. Little terraced houses were crammed up against the railway track. Limp lines of washing stirred in the afternoon light and grubby children played in tiny backyards.

Graffiti was everywhere, proclaiming the territorial rights of ever changing groups of wandering youths. It was the same common sight in every area, even, he remembered, on the outside toilet of The Rover back in Belfast. Without any thought or concern for the nearby residents, it was scrawled in ever more arcane swirls, until it had ceased to be recognizable by any but the author.

The twisted writing brought Mitch's mind back to the sheaf of letters that he had looked at on the morning before his departure. He had rung his Aunty Kate a day earlier. Really, it had been on a whim; he suspected that it would be the last contact he would have with her before his disappearance. Her voice had come over the line strong and full of enthusiasm.

'Oh, Mitchell, I'm so glad you called. I found something about your great-great-grandfather. It was in the loft among Mother's things, as I suspected. When will you be over this way?'

Mitch said that he would come over the next morning early, for breakfast. His arrival at the door of the terraced house was greeted by the wafting smoky smell of frying bacon. He was ushered into the scene of the cooking activity and sat down at the well-scrubbed table.

Aunty Kate looked as pleased and smug as if she were

Sherlock Holmes about to divulge the elementary facts to Doctor Watson. She sat on the edge of her seat while Mitch consumed four rashers of thick bacon and two fried eggs. Mopping up the residue with a slab of home-made soda bread, he cocked his eye at his aunt and said to her, 'Okay, Aunty Kate, what's the great discovery? Although I'll be the first to admit that the journey was worth it just for the breakfast alone.'

She reached up to the mantelpiece over the kitchen range and brought down a small bundle of yellowing letters.

'It's a wonder that these have stood the test of time. I guess we can thank the wonderful damp Irish climate for that. Almost two hundred years old these are, Mitchell. Mother never once showed them to me. I don't quite understand that. Maybe she wanted to stop the poison from spreading any further. Although, God knows, she spread it enough with all her wild talk. Here, have another cup of tea and read through them. It won't take long.'

Mitch took the small bundle and spread the letters out on his knee. There were six in all, each on one side of a page, with a spidery almost illegible writing wandering across the surface. It took him a moment to figure out the style, particularly the peculiar S's that more resembled F's.

The signature was from someone called Chipper and, in every case, the letters were addressed to Mrs Katherine O'Doule, Ballyhean. The place names at the top read, Bucklers, Falmouth, Lanzarote, Rio de Janeiro, Cape Town and the last one from Australia. In every case, the tale was much the same. Paddy was well, Paddy loved her, Paddy missed the kids and Paddy would be home soon.

It was in the letter from Falmouth that the tone took on a slightly ominous note. Through the usual phrases, came a message that all was not well for Paddy and his amanuensis. They were in a spot of bother, to quote the literary

Chipper. They weren't sure how things would turn out. The letter from Lanzarote was the shortest of the six. It merely assured Kathlene that everything was well with her husband and that he would be in touch soon.

The tone from Rio was brighter, and full of hope for the future, except that there was talk of a delay in Paddy's return – it would be in seven years. Mitch had a passing thought that the royal navy certainly required more than its pound of flesh from its servants.

His first cursory look had not been sufficiently detailed. Mitch had completely missed the fact that the final communication was different than the others. The writing had a similar look, but it was smaller. The letter was also two-sided. On the back, the signature showed that the writer was not the usual Chipper, but Paddy himself. What had caused him to break with the tradition was that Chipper 'was no longer with me'.

The words, stretching across the yellowed page, told of a harshness that had caused the writer to swear vengeance – vengeance on those who had caused him to first be parted from his true love, and then subjected him to terror after terror.

> *The evil of Norfolk has finally made me realize that they will pay. I tell you before God, their time will come for causing such misery*

There was a simplicity in the words, but for all that there was a terrible directness that made Mitch shiver in the warm kitchen of his aunt's small house.

Standing across from him, she noticed his movement and said, 'There is the reference to Norfolk that you were interested in, Mitchell. I can't tell you what happened, but I do have some information for you about Paddy. If you want to know, of course.'

Mitchell looked up from the letters spread in front of him, then gathered them up, saying that he would like to know whatever his aunt could tell him.

'All I can remember is that Paddy never settled back home. His wife had died while still quite young, I think. The letters were kept by the last remaining son – the one that I told you became a rebel. He lived not far from here. He was a silent moody man who lived alone. Paddy did come back from Australia, and there was talk that he stayed somewhere in England. He did not live long, but before he died, there was a tale that involved the violent death of an English farmer. The rumors were that Paddy had killed him with his own hands.'

'How did you find that out, Aunty?' Mitchell asked, retying the bundle of letters. 'I thought that you knew nothing about him.'

'Well, it was the sight of that bundle you're holding. Mother never told me all that she knew, at least in one go, that is. But I think over the years she let me know everything that she had heard, and let it out in little pieces. It just took a bit of thought and I could put it all together. It was the core of her hatred for the English. I think that Paddy's story was the very beginning for our family, but that's just my idea. You can keep the letters if you like, Mitchell. They're no good to me. I think they are a reminder of things that are best forgotten.'

'No, Aunty, I'd prefer to leave them here. You see I have to go on a trip soon, and I haven't got anywhere to keep them while I'm gone.'

'Are you going anywhere nice, Mitchell? A long way south of here for instance?' A smile played at the corners of her mouth.

'Look, Aunty, let's not fence around. You know that I have been involved in some pretty dangerous stuff all these years. Well, I don't want you to be implicated at all. You don't belong in my world, and you should just forget everything that has happened over the last few days. I'm okay, but it's best that you forget about me for a bit. I may have to be gone for quite a spell, and you don't know anything. Is that okay?'

'All right, Mitchell, I don't approve of most of the things that you and your wild friends do, but you're family, and that means I'll respect your wishes. No one will learn anything about you from me. After all, I'm just an old retired factory worker. What could I tell anybody? Nonetheless, I hope that, if there is change in your life, it will involve you getting together with a nice young wife and raising some children. Our branch of the family could do with some heirs.'

Mitchell sat for a moment finishing his tea, then he handed the letters over to his aunt and gave her a quick kiss on her lined cheek.

'Keep up the good work, Aunty, and thanks for the breakfast. I'll see you soon.'

Those probably had been the last words that he would ever speak to his kind aunty, Mitch thought, as he continued to stare out of the window of the rocking train.

The pretty girl left the compartment at the third stop – Woking. She gathered up her purse and a small suitcase from the overhead rack, and stepped down onto the platform with not even a smile to Mitch, who watched her leaving with a small feeling of regret. She had been one of those thousands of people whom one meets in life, never more to return. He continued for a moment to enjoy the lingering thought about the stockings and garter belt.

The rest of the journey through the Hampshire countryside to Portsmouth remained uneventful. The weather was mild and the sky had stayed clear all the way through to his destination. As Mitch strolled along the busy Portsmouth street towards South Coast Rentals, however, there was an ominous look to the clouds as they built up in the west.

The pinched-faced girl at the car rental company stopped filing her chipped nails and offered him an upgrade to an automatic Audi. He decided to accept the increase in luxury, and paid his deposit with his new American Express card. Reading the directions to the M27 motorway, he left the converted mobile home and walked over to the dark blue vehicle. There was a pristine new smell to the inside, and Mitch noticed that there were only two hundred miles on the clock.

The M27 was one of the country's newer motorways, and it ran parallel to the old A27. Mitch had been along both roads in his past and vaguely remembered some of the place names that he passed. The clouds continued to build in the direction he was heading, and he tried out the windscreen wipers to make sure that they worked if he was caught by a sudden downpour.

The brick monolith of Portsdown castle stared ominously down on the fast-moving traffic as Mitch headed towards the west at a crisp eighty miles per hour. As he had plenty of time before his evening meeting, he decided to take a small diversion and drive through the great port town of Southampton.

He had visited the city first when he was a small boy. One of his uncles was going over to America, and a number of his relatives had been invited along to see the great man off. This was in the days when Southampton was known as the busiest passenger port in the world. This reputation was brought on in part by the city's unique situation of having two tides each day. Mitch remembered that this was because the water not only moves straight up the Solent, but also because it goes the long way round the Isle of Wight.

As a small boy he had been excited by the number of

funnels and masts belonging to all the ships that were anchored there. As he drove across the Itchen bridge, however, he was disappointed to see that there were now only the stunted shapes of container ships, and their uniform boxlike cargoes. The whole place seemed much smaller today, and he weaved around in the local traffic, looking for signs of recognition that never came.

The Roman wall was everywhere, but both within it and without, Southampton had undergone the usual faceless urban renewal that was so much a part of life everywhere else. Somehow the modern style aged worse than the styles of other eras, thought Mitch, as he made his way along the docks towards the edge of the city. The Regency, Georgian, Victorian and Edwardian structures grew old gracefully, but the stuff that had been erected since the Germans had dealt their massive blows just looked tawdry.

'So much for progress,' he mumbled to himself as he took the A35, towards the New Forest.

As he passed over the bridge into the small satellite town of Totton, the first splashes of rain fell. At the same time, he spotted a signpost to Beaulieu and Bucklers Hard. With the recognition of Bucklers, his mind jumped to the clear image of the spidery handwriting of the letters sent by the mysterious Chipper to his great-great-grandmother, Katherine.

Checking the pale digital figures on the Audi's clock, he decided that he would make the time to visit the place. The roads were slick with water when he reached the small parking lot that served the entire community of Bucklers Hard. Now a tourist resort next to the stately home of Lord Montagu of Beaulieu, it had once been an important shipbuilding center for the royal navy, stretching back to the time of Henry VIII.

Mitchell poked his umbrella out into the rain and followed it, slamming the car door shut behind him. As he ran across the car park to the ticket booth, he grimaced with the thought that, even though he had lived all his life in one of the most rain-sodden countries in the world, he still hated the bloody stuff.

There were very few people intent on enjoying the delights of the museum this late in the day, so Mitch had the place to himself. He wandered around looking at the story of the shipbuilding that had gone on during the time of Admiral Lord Nelson. He read how the forest had been almost depleted of trees to fill the needs of an island race, intent on preserving its identity against waves of invaders. Since the Norman Conquest, many would-be invaders had attempted to gain a foothold in the country, but largely through the efforts of the royal navy, all had been repulsed. Even the latest, in the form of Hitler, had failed.

Having had his fill of the evidence of Britain's glorious past, Mitchell left the museum. With his head stooped against the driving rain, he made his way to the tiny village of Bucklers Hard itself. In spite of the weather, he could see that it was a delightful place. One small wide street of terraced houses looked out onto a grass cover. The original surface of many a village before the onset of tarmacadam, the grass had been kept that way for the curious eyes of the tourists. A couple of donkeys munched on the rich grass while standing in the lee of the buildings, out of the rain.

Mitch found the pub at the bottom of the street, next to The Master Builder's House. This was the original home of the architect of the ships that would win at the Battles of the Nile and Trafalgar. Inside the bar, there was evidence of the twentieth century in the form of plastic and Formica, and also the usual slick advertising. Taking a pint over to a side table, Mitch cast his mind back to how it must have seemed those two hundred years ago. What his ancient relative might have been doing here, he had no idea. He knew that Paddy O'Doule was in the navy, and he was pretty certain that he was not there voluntarily. The term 'pressing' was known to Mitchell, and he was certain that that was the reason Paddy O'Doule had served the crown.

In spite of his new attitudes, Mitch had no love for the English. Sitting here in the heart of the small town that had created the fleet to help build up England's power, he felt the old stirrings return, strengthened by the thought that one of his own family had been an unwilling part of that power.

Poor old Paddy, Mitch thought, as he stared at the rain streaking down the windows and over the protruding bottle bottoms that had no doubt been added for authenticity. I wonder if you ever had a pint here, and how did you feel about it all those hundreds of years ago?

Mitch had become somewhat used to his feelings of confusion. Some mornings, he would awake automatically, thinking in the role of a colonel of the IRA. This could last for several seconds before he would come back to the status quo. Then he would react in three different ways: extreme happiness at the thought that he was out of it all with a new life to look forward to, ambivalence regarding whatever might happen to him, or sorrow at the loss of a way of life that had been at his very soul since he was a teenager. With thoughts of the unknown Paddy swirling in his head, and with the depressing downpour, his present mood had swung firmly to the sorrow. He had to force himself to smile at the barmaid as he ordered another pint.

Most of the other occupants of the bar seemed similarly depressed. But pulling himself together, Mitch decided that their reasons were almost certainly less profound than his. He had done a complete one hundred and eighty degree turn in his existence, and he was about to turn traitor into the bargain. With the resulting furor and search for revenge that would take place, he was entitled to feel a bit thrown. As he trod this mental path for the umpteenth time, he allowed himself a smile, which was taken as a signal by the plump barmaid who had been watching him slyly. However, Mitch raised his glass to her, drained it and, buttoning up his mac, left the hostelry to face the elements once more.

Turning his collar up against the rain, he wandered around the little village. The donkeys had gone somewhere and the grass-covered street was deserted, apart from the occasional resident darting from one house to another, engaged upon some domestic errand.

He walked slowly down to the river which bent elegantly off into the distance of the Solent. The fiberglass cabin cruisers and yachts clinging to their taut mooring ropes were a far cry from the vessels that must have been launched here for Nelson's captains. These simple, plastic, waterproof pleasure units that would rarely leave the confines of their immediate areas were so different from the wooden, top-heavy men-of-war that creaked their way down slipways to face the fury of both enemy and ocean.

He stood for a while enjoying the solitude of the scene, then, checking his watch, he decided to continue on his way. As he climbed back to the car park, his final thoughts were that Paddy must have seen a very different sight here at Bucklers Hard.

Mitch turned the Audi out of the car park and headed back once more towards the west. The light was beginning to fade, but the rain at least was easing up. He would have time to check into the Water Lodge, take a bath, and make his eight o'clock appointment with the contact in plenty of time.

Chapter Eight

HMS *Distinction*, 1786

For the next three days, as Paddy's ship sailed slowly south, he and his new-found shipmates practiced gun drill after gun drill. Their every waking hour was devoted to priming, loading, aiming and firing the iron weapons that were strung along two separate gun-decks under the main upper deck.

They were called out of their hammocks by bosun's whistle, sent to Winston's mess room by whistle and dismissed by whistle. Within two days, Paddy understood all the various sounds piped up by Bosun Belcher from the little silver instrument held in his fist. Even the slightly different tones conjured up by Belcher's deputy would send Paddy scurrying to the next post.

He behaved like an automaton which was exactly what was intended by the officers of the royal navy. He and his fourteen fellow pressees had to become a part of a fierce fighting team before they faced the enemy. Following the flogging of Reilly, the new recruits were wary of those in authority on the ship, which was the intent of the punishment in the first place.

Paddy had no difficulty in playing along with Chipper Johnson's suggestion that he act 'daft'. He felt completely disoriented, and, under the circumstances, looking foolish came quite naturally. He was not so out of touch, however, that he did not see the looks he received from the more experienced ratings. It was as if they were expecting trouble from him, purely on account of his size.

The whole point of the recruitment exercise was to intimidate any likely rebellious soul into submission. This submission would then gradually be elevated as each man began to look upon the ship and his mates as a world unto itself. It was to be a world that could support and sustain a man in the ruthless search for enemy treasure. The true goal of each man aboard was to leave the navy rich from plunder.

Until that moment of acceptance, the royal navy's first disciplinarians – the non-commissioned officers – knew that activity was the best deterrent for a rebellious spirit.

Paddy responded to all of Chipper's advice in the firing of their gun. After a day, they were the best team among the newcomers, and Chief Sande turned his harsh and sarcastic eye away from them to seek easier targets, still struggling with the awkward commands and materials.

All the time that they pushed and pulled, and rammed and plunged, Paddy had this ball of unhappiness in the pit of his stomach. It only surfaced when he lay swinging gently in his hammock at the end of each exhausting day. Then, Katherine's face would float out of the gloom at him, and he would once again feel that inner sense of emptiness at the loss of his wife, his family and his home on the farm. By the sound of the others in the gloom, he was not the only one beset by such memories, as some of the men openly sobbed before sleep took hold of them.

On the morning of the fourth day, Paddy was awakened with the others by a shouting from the entrance to their quarters, 'This little lot belongs to you men, so sort out who's is what. Don't get any ideas about wrongful use. Captain Merryview's got some strong opinions on that score.'

So saying, the deckhand opened a sack and several

knives, belts and other personal belongings fell in a heap under the hammocks.

'Christ, a bloody week early,' Chipper spoke up. He swung onto the floor and scrabbled about through the possessions until he found a thick belt with curious markings all over it. 'Thought I'd 'ave to wait a bit longer afore I met you agin, Madonna, me little beauty,' he said softly to himself.

The other men joined him around the pile of items and each took the things that had been confiscated when they first came on board.

The small cockney talked animatedly to them all, 'Now listen 'ere shipmates, we've got ourselves a good 'ome aboard the Widder. What the man says, goes. Don't go usin' these 'ere stickers on anyone aboard, otherwise we're all for it.'

Paddy found the rough-handled knife that had been his since childhood and stuck it in the thick leather belt that was also within the pile. Chipper came over and took it in his hands, turning it over and over.

'We'll 'ave to work on this a bit for you, Paddy. This may be okay for a country boy, but you're in the bleedin' navy now, you know. We don't 'ave sloppy workmanship in His Majesty's bleedin' navy.'

So saying, he reached round the back of his belt buckle and withdrew a thin blade and handed it over to the Irishman to see. It was a beautiful thing with an ivory handle that fitted neatly in the palm of the big Irishman's hand. All over the ivory was a delicate design showing a ship harpooning a whale. The details were so fine the drawing seemed to come alive in Paddy's hand as he turned it over.

'Where did you get it, Chipper? It's beautiful. I've never seen anything like it in my life.'

'That's becos you're just a stupid great mick from the

bogs. If you'd been anywhere, I mean anywhere at all, you'd 'ave seen it many times. It's carved ivory from the narwhal. It's called scrimshaw. I done it meself. Took a bleedin' long time an' all, I can tell yer. Remember I told yer about Charley, the bloke what got keel 'auled. Well, he 'ad spent a lot of time on whalers in the Arctic. He learned me 'ow to do it. And the design on the belt too. 'E said that was from the Eskimos. Now see the size of it, Paddy. About an inch thick an' about seven inches long. Long enough to slip into a man's ribs.' He smiled in a crooked way.

Paddy turned it over again in his hands and watched the filtered light gleam across the length of the steel. It reminded him of the instruments he had seen veterinarians use on their infrequent and expensive visits to the farm.

'It slips in the back of the buckle 'ere. 'Ave a look, mate.'

And so saying he took the knife back and slipped the sharp end into a slot in his belt and in a second it had disappeared, the handle cleverly hidden behind the rustic decorations on the leather.

'She's always there when you need 'er see?'

Chipper further explained that if you wore another prominent knife and it was removed, a search would reveal nothing else. In foreign lands, a weapon was very necessary. Paddy said he didn't think he liked the idea, but Chipper insisted that it had saved his life a couple of times. The same design had done the same thing several times for the now long since dead Charley.

'Seamen are always fair game ashore, me old mate. They get a few under the belt; then on the way back to the ship, bingo, they're in trouble. Thieves'll rob yer blind, but with Madonna 'ere, they're in for a surprise. Yer lie there quiet like, then you reach in an' out she pops. You 'ave a dagger that'll slip into anyone's chest and the party's over.'

Paddy stared at Chipper in wonder. Right before him he was hearing plans for cold-blooded murder, the most terrible of crimes against God. His mouth hung open as Chipper rambled on about the merits of the slim-bladed knife, so blasphemously named Madonna.

Chipper could see that his new friend was having a difficult time with his explanations, so he leaned over, tapping the hidden weapon. In low tones he said to him, 'Look, Paddy, you've got to get it through yer thick head that this is a different world yer in. There's no more Katherine and the kids. There's no more brother Sean and his wife. There's no more farm, or even Ireland. Out 'ere, on the sea, a man 'as to look after 'isself. I'll teach you all I can, but in the end, it's up to you. No one else will look out for you. Not the bosun, Captain Merryview or God 'isself. They told you that the first morning, and they told you right. Trust me, Paddy, believe 'em.'

The little cockney's tone was such and his expression so sincere that Paddy patted the small man on the shoulder and nodded his head. Then he went up on deck to think on what he had learned. It did not take him long to realize he needed to take his friend's advice. This was a different life, and if he was to come through it, he should be prepared to adopt new rules. Two days later, he had the opportunity to witness, at first hand, the difference in a sailor's life to that of a simple farmer.

For some time, HMS *Distinction* had been cruising ahead of the wind, keeping some verdant countryside on her port beam. As the ship's bells tolled midday, they came about and headed in a northerly direction. There was still land on their port bow, which the older hands called the Isle of Wight, but ahead they could see that there was a larger landfall. There was great excitement as the crew recognized they were on their way to Pompey – the sailors' term for Portsmouth. Several bell-bottomed members began a jig after the day's rum ration.

Paddy had at first been hesitant at the serving of the

daily tot. He was well aware that it was the demon drink that had landed him in these present circumstances. However, it was generally considered to be a compulsory medicine, and he not only complied, he looked forward to the thick strong potion, compliments of 'is Majesty. He was also fortunate the measure did not unleash the O'Doule thirst, with its inherent dangers.

The destination of Pompey put a lot of pep into the dancers' steps, which were accompanied by a fife and a penny whistle. Over on the rail, Chipper beckoned to Paddy to join him.

'You can see they're getting all fired up, can't you?'

Paddy agreed there seemed to be an atmosphere he had not felt in his limited experience so far. Chipper went on to explain that, once they were in port, there would be shore leave for everyone, that is, with the exception of the new pressed men.

'We're not to be trusted yet. Too new and not members of the club. Still, leave it to me, an' we'll be set up a treat. Just wait an' see.'

With a crafty wink, he went below, and Paddy was left to see the end of the dancing before Chief Sande used his rope end on a few backsides, to get them all back to the unending drills.

Later that day, the ship berthed and lay alongside the dock of Portsmouth. As Chipper predicted, all the men were allowed ashore, except the new recruits and a guard to keep an eye on them. In compensation for their incarceration, the pressees were allowed the run of the ship except the officers' quarters; they also had a large additional ration of rum.

Each day, at midday, a wooden barrel was wheeled onto the upper deck. The bung was removed and Winston, the chef, would march up to the barrel and insert a brass and copper pump through the hole. He would operate this pump to give each man his ration in a small tin mug and, at the end of the ceremony, he would remove the pump and march away, with the words, 'Rum ration complete, Sir.'

Chipper had alerted Paddy to what happened immediately prior to the removal of the pump. Not in every case, but at least twice a week, the cook would pull out the handle of the pump, and then take out the measure.

'That means 'e's got a whole pumpful over 'is arm, yer see. If the handle is pushed in, it's empty. But extended it's full. Then 'e goes down below and squirts it all out into a case 'e's got there, and we'll get it when the time's right.'

This right time came immediately after the shore party left. Winston came up on deck with his pump and his own barrel. He also had a small slate and wrote down everybody's name before he started to pour out the potent brew. It didn't take long. Within twenty minutes the whole crowd of seamen, jailors and jailed alike, were roaring drunk. An attempt was made to start up the old jig again, but the sense of balance needed for it was missing under the influence of the grog. The men then tried to wander around looking for mischief, but only collapsed into little heaps on the gently sloping deck and fell into a drunken sleep where they were.

Paddy and his friend, Chipper, had made it back to their hammocks, clutching each other and giggling like a couple of schoolgirls. Here they were at least comfortable for the couple of hours the navy rum took to wear off. They would have been asleep much longer but the noise that started up above them on the wooden deck shook them awake, with dry mouths and stiff limbs. Both of them clutched at the pain in their foreheads as they stared about. Paddy was completely lost, but as always, Chipper understood the relevance of the din and swung himself down on unsteady legs saying, 'Come on, Paddy, I bet that's Winston on his way back for the main course.'

The tall Irishman groped his way towards the daylight at

the top of the hatch after his friend, the noise increasing with his every step. The drunken men who had not enjoyed the depth of their hammocks had been awake long enough to have started all over again. The rum barrel was unsupervised, and one or two ratings were slumped over its remaining contents. The others were strung out along the side of the ship, leaning over and shouting themselves hoarse.

Paddy and Chipper pushed their way through the throng and were greeted by the sight of Winston, the cook, shepherding a crowd of women up the gangplank. There must have been about twenty various females, all made up in the bright colors of their trade. Even to a country boy from the backwoods of an Irish farm, the type of trade was obvious.

Chipper had no difficulty recognizing the situation either, and gave Paddy an enormous dig in the ribs.

'Christ, Paddy, look at the tits on that big redhead. I wonder 'ow much old Winston wants for that 'un.'

The woman he was pointing to had very little clothing over her top half and was spilling out of her bodice as she made her way aloft. The sight was like the two mainsails of the ship in a full wind. Her hair was a bright orange-red and shook out from her head in ripples of dyed excitement. But she was not the only one who looked attractive to the wild men cheering and jostling at the top of the gangplanks that supported their progress.

Winston's choice was catholic, to say the least. The women were of all types. As they drew closer, unfortunately, the images of sensuousness became mixed with tawdriness. Many had most of their teeth missing and the feminine complexions were overpainted with an excess of powder and rouge that gave all their faces a uniform clownlike quality. What good points each of them had were generally highlighted by bright colors or a lack of clothing.

Legs were prominently displayed along with bosoms. Hair was brightly colored or wrapped in scarves. But if Winston's selection had come from the ugliest portions of hell itself, the men would still have goaded themselves on into a fit of raunchiness that sent itself out into waves of sound to the visitors.

Winston worked his way to the front of the women, then held his hand up to halt their progress. Rapping on the side of the ship, he called for silence.

'These lovely ladies have agreed to come along and spend some time with you gentlemen.'

The waiting men set up a great cheer at the news. Winston continued with the tone of a stern vicar giving news to his eager parishioners.

'Now, there should be a lovely lady for each of you but, if any of you are not satisfied or can't do his duty, please see me afterwards, and I'll take his name. Otherwise, he'll pay the usual fee.'

The term 'fee' registered with Paddy, but at that moment the women made a move to come aboard and the men grabbed them in a tremendous rush and he was almost pushed to the floor.

Chipper had made a beeline for the big redhead and was pulling one of her arms with one of the guards pulling on the other. The woman must have said something to the little cockney as he released her hand, which she used to hit the other man in the face. Then she put both arms around Chipper and pulled them both out of the struggling melee.

Paddy was gradually moved towards the back of the mass as men and women both were fighting to pair off. He had never experienced anything like it outside of a bar-room brawl, and once again his overall innocence found him wanting in this rough life afloat.

Couples were now kissing and feeling each other in a wild drunken abandon almost beyond belief. The effects of the rum were still working on most of the men and they staggered about, wildly clinging onto their partners. Unseen in the general throng, a fiddler and a boy drummer had come aboard and under Winston's direction were playing some spirited shanties.

Those couples who were not intent on tearing the clothes off each other's backs immediately started to dance in an attempt at some social grace, however limited. Paddy could see Chipper wrapped in the plump arms of the redhead as she rotated round the deck to the music. As the fiddle's sound reached the ears of all those still on deck, it was the women who took each man to the small area where the dancing took place, and made them calm down and settle into a less heated situation.

A tall dark woman with a short skirt and large brass bangles in her ears grabbed Paddy's hand and before he knew it she was guiding him in a brisk waltz, much to his surprise.

The group of dancers staggered around, with the men taking every opportunity to feel the soft and unfamiliar curves of the women, who made little effort to discourage them from their goal. Breasts were flaunted and legs were entwined around waists as the music twisted and turned. Lips were pressed hard against other lips and there was an energy and excitement that reached across the normally regimented and frigid decks of HMS *Distinction*.

The tall girl with the brass earrings had an accent that Paddy found difficult to follow. She said she came from Spain and her name was Esmeralda. Other than that, her conversation was mostly a series of four-letter words which she no doubt thought would be attractive to men.

Chipper had been whisked off below decks with the large redhead, and in small groups the dancing broke up, with more and more following his example. Even the fiddler and boy drummer had succeeded in making liaisons and had disappeared, seeking more private quarters away from the late afternoon sun. Eventually, it was only Paddy and Esmeralda who stood looking out across the empty deck at the bustling port below.

Paddy knew what was expected of him and what was going on in every portion of the ship. However, he was simply too new in this brutal world and too unfamiliar with promiscuity. Having never experienced any other woman but Katherine, he was completely stumped about what to do next. Esmeralda seemed similarly lost. This was the first sailor who had not hurriedly taken her. Normally, there was never any interest in conversation or other social formalities, and there was never any need for assistance from her. In her short career of some six months in the business, she had learned to neutralize her feelings of disgust during the buffeting and panting that she was subjected to by concentrating her thoughts on the empty hills of her home outside Madrid.

There, in her sun-washed village, she had been rejected by the church as a nun, and her alternatives were to work in the hot and dangerous kitchens of the local bakery, or run away. She chose the latter, and it was in the port of Bilbao she had fallen for the proposal of a drunken Portuguese captain with flashing black eyes. He used her lustily for the rough journey over to Portsmouth, and then unceremoniously dumped her once his ship was refitted. She was quick to learn the basic needs of men and had, with her lean sultry good looks, attracted a number of repeat customers who paid the going rate and treated her with enthusiastic respect. Nonetheless, she kept a slim stiletto in the confines of her boot, in the event things ever turned nasty.

Feeling lost and rather ashamed of his lack of appetite, and lacking a common tongue, Paddy smiled guiltily at his foreign companion. There was a stern-faced guard at the top of the gangplank, and Paddy was escorting Esmeralda past his steady gaze, when Winston appeared on deck.

'Christ, Paddy,' he shouted across to the tall Irishman, 'what the fuck are you doing? You're not letting 'er leave without a proper seeing to, are you?'

Paddy looked around and saw the cook striding across the deck towards them. His bloated face had a concerned and drooping look.

'You better let me take 'er below or my reputation will be shot. You come along, too.'

Taking the slim Spanish woman by the hand, Winston gently but firmly guided her down the companionway towards the mess room that he considered his own personal domain. Paddy clattered along behind them, and not for the first time since his experience in the royal navy, his mouth hung open like a trap. There, around the cramped quarters, in the area where normally a dozen or so male seamen shared their meals, were five women, all naked. They sat boldly on the floor with their arms resting languidly on their raised knees. Two of them were smoking small pipes, the aromas from which were adding to the musty animal smells in the small room. They looked up with bored expressions as Winston brought his latest conquest through the door.

'I thought I'd done for the day,' Winston said to nobody in particular, 'but I guess one more won't do any harm.'

So saying, he kissed Esmeralda firmly on the lips, and then reached down to the hem of her split skirt, grasped it and drew it up in one movement over her head. She stood there dumbly, her mind already beginning to focus on the sun-baked hills near Navacerrada. Winston, whose trousers were exhibiting a large bulge, lifted her up with only her calf-length boots on, and put her on the mess room table. Obligingly she lay back and bent her knees up. Paddy's jaw was still in the down position and continued to remain so as

Winston let his breeches fall to the floor, and entered the willing woman.

The other prostitutes on the floor paid little heed to the bucking, swaying Winston as he went about his task. Only Paddy seemed to have a fascination for the scene being enacted in front of him. No one seemed to be at all embarrassed by the activity, least of all Winston whose eyes were closed and who was beginning to pant and sweat over the still form of Esmeralda. She, in her turn, lay back on her elbows with a quiet smile on her face, and her eyes almost shut. The weight of Winston seemed to have no effect on her, and as his rhythm increased, she merely lay flat on her back and began to pick her nose.

Paddy found to his disgust he was beginning to become aroused. This fact was noticed by one of the sitting women as well, and she made a move to reach up and fondle him. Paddy looked aghast at this and turned away from the scene to return to the fresh air on deck. As he reached the top step into the sunlight, he heard Winston let out a gasp, which was followed by a small round of applause from the earlier recipients of his favors.

If Paddy thought he was to receive some relief from the bacchanalia that had been present in the mess room, he was very much mistaken. As he wandered around the ship trying to shake the image of Esmeralda's spread body from his mind, he was confronted by scenes of lasciviousness at every turn. Members of the ship's crew, who had been pressed with him, were now being joined by the older hands and the women that they, too, had brought back on board. Bodies lay interlocked, either asleep or moving frantically, in every nook and cranny throughout HMS *Distinction*. To Paddy it was disturbing but at the same time exciting, as he had never seen humans together like this before.

He went up on the Fo'c'sle, where there seemed to be

no one about apart from one of the guards who had released himself from his earlier occupation with a cross-eyed black woman. The man's name was Silver, and he wore a large silver earring in recognition of this.

Paddy said to him, 'I've lived on a farm all my life, and I've seen animals perform all the acts that I thought possible, but this has been something I could never even imagine.'

Silver replied with a sly smile, 'Never underestimate the appetite of the royal navy's finest. The enemy does every day, and they regret it. But if you think you've seen everything, just come with me a moment.'

He looked around the Fo'c'sle and over onto the main deck, before he gestured to Paddy to follow him towards the bosun's quarters. Putting his finger to his lips, he beckoned Paddy down the short dark passageway to a doorway at the end. Silver, the guard, opened it without a sound. He allowed the door to open only a couple of inches and pointed inside. Paddy craned his neck to see. Lying on a flat bed was Chief Gunner Sande, completely naked, with a similarly unclad drummer boy on each side of him. There was a smile on his sleeping face and a trace of rouge on his bloated cheeks. The two boys, one the permanent drummer boy and the other who had come aboard with the fiddler, were stirring gently beside the bulk of the sweating chief. There was a smell of depravity in the tiny cabin as well as the sickly smell of rum, which came from an overturned bottle on the bed. Silver closed the door silently, and both he and Paddy crept away.

'With Winston it's crumpet, but with old Sande it's bum. Each to his own, I say, but why mess about with kids when there're plenty of birds in port? Can't understand it at all. Still, they do say as it's legal three days out from port, but tied up alongside – why bother?'

As they came out on deck again, Paddy could see

Winston's group of women, including the now dressed Esmeralda, making their way towards the gangplank. Esmeralda happened to look up as she put her foot on the step that would take her back on firm land once again. Seeing Paddy standing there with Silver, she waved and blew him a big kiss. Paddy actually reddened at the sight, and Silver dug him in the ribs with a snigger.

Gradually all the 'visitors' left the ship, and the routine of preparing for the next stage of the voyage was put into effect. Paddy returned to his hammock and opened a porthole to allow some fresh air in to replace the acrid smells of spent passion. Chipper was asleep in his hammock with a contented smile on his face. Paddy thought he looked a lot younger than his reported thirty years.

The next morning there was a rigorous roll-call. Bosun Belcher showed some delight that there was only one absentee, and Chipper whispered to Paddy there'd be another flogging when the shore patrols made their inevitable arrest. With a stiff wind blowing, they raised sails and drifted out into the calm waters of the Solent. The crew members were alive with stories of their conquests, both afloat and ashore. Like those who told about their occasional fishing expeditions, they elaborated greatly on the frequency and quality of the relationships that they had enjoyed.

With the exception of Paddy, nearly everyone seemed to have exhausted his sexual reserves, and the satyr, Winston, had managed one over his normal quota. He had also increased his earnings for the services provided for the company stranded on board. Paddy tried to keep a brave face on it. He certainly was not happy, having spent a restless night in his hammock with alternative visions of Katherine and Esmeralda, alive in their respective nakedness. His accompanying arousal branded him as just as bad as the rest of the men – with the exception of Chief Sande's particular peccadillo.

No formal announcement was made, but all aboard soon knew that their next stop was to be the busy ship-building port of Bucklers, with its dock, known as the Hard, lined with new vessels for the expanding royal navy. Its location lay west and north of Portsmouth, which meant that 'The French Widow' – as she was now known to all aboard – had to resort to the time-honored method of towing to gain direct access against the prevailing wind.

Paddy was selected for a place in the small boat that had the job of pulling the ship along. He found, as his companion, Welch, the tough-looking sailor with whom he had originally been paired that first morning aboard.

Welch was a surly and difficult man, but he had some five years' experience in the service, and had volunteered again. The previous day, he had, like most others, become royally drunk, but had selected the prettiest of all the women that Winston had brought on board. As they strained over their long oars, Welch explained that Doris was his regular and he had been going with her for nearly two years.

Portsmouth was his home town, and Doris came from the next street over from his home. She was a prostitute, which he didn't like, but there was no alternative for a girl who could neither read nor write, and for whom hard work was anathema. She had poor health and giving sex for money was not hard for her. Like Esmeralda, she closed her eyes and tried to forget it. As for the protection that was needed by all in that trade, she had Welch's brother, Jim, to look out for her. Welch had stayed on board because it was more a home than the cramped quarters he would have to share with his mother, sister and brother. And besides that, it was quite normal for wives to come on board or even live there during times of long harbor duty.

Paddy found the discourse of interest as he bent his back over his oars. Welch was, like Chipper, a mine of information about navy life and the men who shared their floating home. He also told Paddy the reasons for their visit up the Beaulieu river.

Captain Merryview had been in charge of a vessel called *Venture* last year. He and his crew had been caught sailing outside Dieppe by a squadron of French cutters. They were faster than the *Venture*, and also knew the coast and where to hide on that north coast of France. *Venture* made good account of herself, but during a period of grappling with the enemy, she caught fire. Captain Merryview, with great leadership and skill, fought off the French sailors and captured the ship to which *Venture* was tied. He escaped through the fog with another French prize in tow. It turned out this ship, *The Grenoble*, was brand new and was destined for Bonaparte's personal use.

In recognition of his great escape and the capture of such a prize, Merryview was allowed his pick of the new fleet being built in the New Forest. Completion was some months off, but they had permission to view progress of the shipbuilding before putting to sea.

The information kept Paddy interested as they made their slow way along the green coast of Hampshire. They kept close inshore with the small boat leading the now sailless *Distinction*. The woods of England had a foreign look to Paddy's eyes, but nonetheless, it was a very beautiful place, and he heard only the lapping sound of the water moving past the hull and the creaking of the oars in their rowlocks.

Pipes of tobacco had come out on the deck, and Paddy could see Chipper leaning out of the gun's porthole where they practiced every day. In all, it was a peaceful scene as the bosun in the lead boat worked the tiller to take them across the breadth of Southampton Water to enter the river where many of Nelson's ships would first feel the shimmering water under their keels.

Chapter Nine

Mudeford, July 1992

The Water Lodge was one of those buildings in England that could have been designed as a nursing home, a large house or a school. The fact that it was now a hotel in its eightieth year was pure coincidence. As Mitch signed the register for the receptionist, who looked far too young to be regularly employed, he recognized the type of establishment that he was entering. He declined assistance with his bag from a bellboy whose pasty face and rounded shoulders were somehow at odds with the crispness of his uniform and his offer of physical help.

He pulled his black bag, together with a small trail of gravel that he seemed to have collected from the outside, into the dark recesses of the establishment. As he made his way to his room on the ground floor, Mitch could imagine the clientele that normally walked the short hallways. This was retirement haven, or commercial travelers' refuge, an escape for regulars who sought anonymity from the demands of the local buyers, or refuge from widowhood and loneliness. Where did operations find these types of places? he asked himself. There was a faint smell of disinfectant like the waiting room in a doctor's office, as Mitch pushed the heavy brass Yale key into the lock.

He almost played a game of shutting his eyes on entering the room, as he felt he was sure to know exactly what it would be like. However, he could not be sure where that annoying piece of furniture for supporting suitcases would be, so he decided against this. The suitcase support happened to be tucked out of the way, but everything else was crammed into a tiny room decorated in pastel green with plasticized mahogany everywhere. There was a minimal bathroom with rubber hoses to convert the bath's taps into a shower mechanism. In all, it was not the sort of room that one wanted to spend much time in. But that was probably why the management still supported a resident's lounge with a large television set.

Mitch had caught sight of this facility as he made his way to his room, and also seen the several old ladies grouped around the screen as it blared out its evening news. Mitch had no desire to enjoy such a life for at least another forty years. 'God, what a future. Perhaps a Mephisto in there would put them out of their misery. Maybe I'm not doing them any favors at all,' he had smiled, grimly, as he passed.

He ran hot water into the bath, and decided to wear his lightweight suit for the evening's meeting. It was a dark brown wool suit that he had hardly worn. He felt it made him look distinguished, and he rather liked the color. He hung the suit over the bath to let the steam rise and take out the creases. Then he put on the small TV to listen to the news while he soaked away the damp and stress of the journey.

Gaddafi was ranting and raving again, and Saddam Hussein was playing tricks with United Nations inspection teams. Some unknown had won the UK snooker championship, and the stock market was up. The weather would continue unsettled for the rest of the week, and there was a storm expected near Iceland.

Mitch lowered himself into the hot water and realized that nothing much changed in the world; it was the same old formula day after day. Well, he was going to try to do something to throw the norm off course even if for once it would result in no headlines.

He lay dozing until the water cooled, then reluctantly got up and dried himself. He put on his suit, and chose a dark green tie – perhaps through some unconscious form of patriotism, he thought. Then, at seven thirty, he left the hotel and crunched across the pristine gravel to the parked Audi.

He had half an hour to go before his rendezvous, and so, having once found the Avonhead Hotel, he impulsively turned towards the signpost directing visitors to the quay. The light was fading fast as he drove over the narrow road that led to the water's edge. A few late trippers were walking back to their cars, trailing bags, towels and tired limp children. No doubt the people had spent the day using the small beach huts that were lined along the far-off shore.

Mitch circled the emptying car park. He ignored the printed demands to park and pay that stood beside the mechanical sentinel which served the double duty of accepting fees and producing sticky tickets that had to be displayed inside car windows. As he left the Audi, Mitch could not help thinking that his privilege of avoiding such small inconveniences in the same fashion as diplomats and royalty would disappear once he had established his normal life, wherever in the world that he might end up. There would be no more 'organization' to clear up after him.

He leaned over the rail above the outlet from Christchurch harbor and watched the sinking sun. The evening light was muted as the cloud cover dispersed the last rays of daylight.

Mitch had never been here before, but in common with his other exploits in strange places, he had read all he could in various guidebooks. These he had picked up and browsed through at the railway stations where his journey had taken him. There had been a large selection at

Waterloo, and one showing the harbor and environs of Chichester had told Mitch that the Mudeford Run acted as the only access for the water in the harbor. This evening, the run was in full flood as the tide attempted its escape from the English coastline. Two small boats were trying to gain entrance to the harbor and their outboard engines, at maximum revs, disturbed the tranquillity of the scene as their mechanical progress strained against the flow of nature.

Several mobile homes were away to Mitch's left, and their occupants could be seen through the windows of their temporary homes, preparing and consuming evening meals as the flickering lights of television sets washed across their flimsy ceilings. It was a quiet time at the end of a vacation day with little to worry the people, apart from the usual vagaries of tomorrow's weather. Mitch once again felt a stranger to such normal family emotions, and as he stood silently in the gloom, with the sound of the racing outboards competing with the rushing water, he found himself looking forward to the opportunity of enjoying such innocence, away from his normal condition of ceaseless, impotent struggle.

His thoughts were broken by the sound of people coming out of The Ferry Inn, located at the end of the car park. He had a few moments left and so decided on a small drink to settle him down, before he met his mysterious contact.

The pub was standing starkly among a number of benches, and as far as he could see, genuine lobster pots. This place really does still have some local fishing, he thought, as he entered the inn.

As if to confirm his view, there were two obvious fishermen sitting on the long bench inside the door, as he made his way to the bar. They wore stained and shabby jeans, thick woolen sweaters and high rubber boots turned over at the knees. Both were of that uncertain age that many harsh professions give to their practitioners, and they could have been anywhere between twenty and fifty. They both drew heavily on hand-rolled cigarettes and looked sadly at the invasion of their local pub by brightly clad tourists and even worse, in Mitch's case, people in suits.

Mitch ordered a Bushmills. It had to be poured into a measure at the back of the bar, as the Irish brand lacked the popularity here across the water that would have allowed it premier placing among the mounted bottles with their own glass dispensers hanging beneath. He poured a dribble of water into the whiskey, and leaned on the bar after having positioned a cloth to protect the elbow of his brown suit against the spillage from earlier customers. A jukebox was playing one of the Everly Brothers' early hits in the background. Mitch watched the two fishermen out of the corner of his eye and sipped his drink.

The pub was an anachronism. It was neither a working establishment nor a tourist trap, and yet it was both. Neither side seemed to have yielded to the other. There were bits of both dotted about all over the place, and both aspects studiously ignored each other. Wildly patterned carpet competed alongside worn timbered boards. Even the bar help came from both sides of the equation.

There was a young girl pulling pints, dressed in a miniskirt and a knitted top stretched over her breasts which were too large for the bra that was trying to encase them. She had an illegal cigarette burning in an ashtray on the bar, and she served everybody as if she were late for a date and needed to leave the establishment.

The other help was a thin youth with acne, wearing faded bell-bottomed jeans and a T-shirt proclaiming the success of an American baseball team. He looked as if he had been captured during the Nineteen-seventies and retained his youth through some sort of hippy potion, an image that was enhanced by his long hair and coarse silver jewelry. The only common bond between the two was that they both shared the same cigarette that was pointed away from them both in an effort to appear that it belonged to neither.

Mitch regretfully drained his Bushmills. The two fishermen continued to talk in low unhurried voices, swathed in the pungent fumes of their roll-ups. Mitch went out into the night.

The Avonhead Hotel was a grander establishment than his own, which was a mile or so further inland. It stood overlooking the harbor and quay. As Mitch made his way through the cocktail lounge, looking for his contact, he could see the sodium lamps flickering on, away over near The Ferry Inn, with its mixture of mainly working-class clientele.

Inside the Avonhead, the customers were of a very different type; mostly respectable middle-class, middle-aged people, sipping small gin-and-tonics, and whisky-and-sodas. In the clean air there was a faint sound of Mantovani that took up the slack in the hushed conversations that were taking place in every corner.

No one looked at him and no one seemed an obvious contact, so he stood at the bar, waiting for service. Eventually, this was offered by the tall distinguished man who was acting as barman. He would have looked more at home sitting behind the manager's desk at a bank, Mitch thought, as he repeated his earlier order of a Bushmills. This was served with some flourish, and a bottle of Malvern water was placed conveniently within his reach.

Mitch noticed a tall well-built woman sitting at the end of the bar in animated conversation with an elderly woman. They looked related and, as their tones filtered over to him, Mitch thought that he detected a slight accent. He paid little heed to them and sat down facing the door. He noticed the time was more than ten minutes past the hour, when the younger of the two women picked up her drink and came over to him. She sat down in an armchair next to him and said, 'I'm sorry to keep you waiting Mr O'Doule, or may I call you Mitch?' Not waiting for a reply, she carried on, 'My aunt is rather demanding and I hate to cut her off. But she's on her way home now.'

She definitely had an accent but Mitch could not quite make it out. He watched her silently, waiting for something on which to base a comment. His first impressions were correct. She was very tall, almost six foot, with short blonde hair. She had large spectacles which heightened her gray eyes. She must have been about thirty, and she was dressed in a striking yellow suit, with a plunging neckline. In her elegantly long fingers, she held a tall glass of sparkling white wine. She looked very relaxed.

'My name is Margitte. I'm Dutch.'

She offered her hand which was firm, warm and dry.

'Well, you obviously know who I am. What have you to tell me?'

Mitch could be very direct at times, particularly when he was a little outside his comfort zone. And sitting in a strange bar, with a strange woman in the heart of his former enemy's stronghold, about to discuss a completely false plan, was totally beyond his experience and his comfort.

'All I can tell you right now, Mitch, is that I am absolutely starving. Could you eat dinner?'

As she said this, her face lit up, and Mitch could see that she was a most attractive woman. He had not eaten anything since a stale sandwich at Waterloo, and the effects of two Bushmills were making his stomach rumble.

'Okay,' he answered. 'Here, or do you want to go outside somewhere?'

She stood up and said that the restaurant here was fine. As she walked towards the dining room in front of him,

Mitch was aware that her legs were very long and very shapely.

They were seated, by a tuxedo-clad head waiter, in a bay window, overlooking the gardens. A series of floodlights showed carefully tended lawns and flower beds. In the distance he could see one or two braver souls jumping into the swimming pool, which he knew was bound to be unheated and, as a consequence, freezing.

The menu offered both a set meal and an à la carte selection. It was moderately priced and there was a filet of beef Wellington he fancied. Margitte ordered a Dover sole and a salad, and accepted his suggestion of a rosé wine.

As they waited for their meal to arrive, Mitch realized that for all the world they must have looked like a typical well-dressed couple, enjoying a vacation or a long weekend, rather than two people plotting the destruction of what could well be several thousand innocent citizens.

Mitch offered his packet of Players which she declined with a shake of her blonde head.

'To get back to business, I think it's more a question of what you are to tell me,' she said. 'After all, it was you who raised the request.'

Mitch sat quietly, looking through the tobacco smoke at her. He felt somewhat alarmed to find this new woman so attractive. She was not the sort of zealot he expected to have to deal with.

'We're looking for some sort of help, and it was offered at a recent meeting sometime back. Do you know what I'm talking about?'

The waiter produced their salads and made a great show of wielding a large pepper mill over the plates. Margitte left her fork alone, and leaned towards him.

'I'm sort of a broker, Mitch. I put interested parties together. I am rarely concerned about causes or personalities or the rights and wrongs of each transaction. I just find people who need to talk.'

Mitch ate his salad, and looked through her glasses into her gray eyes. He could see that she was a strong woman, probably very perceptive, and he had to be sure that he remained on track with his business for the Irish movement. The waiter hurried up again with the oval shape of a bottle of Mateus Rosé. He went through the needless pantomime of showing the bottle, pulling the cork and presenting both it and the contents for Mitch's approval. He seemed disappointed that his customer declined to sniff either the cork or the wine, and particularly when Mitch gestured to have the glasses poured almost to the rim.

'I can never fully understand the reasons why we have to go through all that with a wine that is probably made in millions of gallons, and up to a moment ago has been better treated than the folks that made it,' he said, as he raised his glass to her.

She smiled and said softly, 'Up the rebels!' and drank a good swallow. 'So what do you want?'

'You do know who I am, Margitte?'

Her name sounded exotic as he said it.

'Look, you're Mitchell O'Doule, colonel in the IRA, member of the war council and on the wanted list of both Special Branch, the RUC, and the Garda. If I wanted to expose you I could have done it from the outset. All I am interested in is making a match with you and whomever you want. That way I get paid, you get what you want, and we all end up happy. Except the people who I guess you have as targets. Does that help? By the way, you can call me Maggy if you like. Most people over here find it easier.'

'Actually, I think I prefer Margitte. It has a sort of mysterious sound.'

'Then you'll like my full name. That's even odder to British ears. Oh, forgive me, you probably hate to be thought of as British, don't you?'

'Don't worry about it. Technically I am, being an Ulster man. But don't tell the others on the council.'

'Your secret is safe with me,' she smiled. 'Well, let me tell you about me, as I do know rather a lot about you. My full name is Margitte Matilde Van Ednas Ledenfeld.'

The words sounded very strange to Mitch with the guttural pronunciation that was her native tongue.

'I am part Jewish, part German, part Spanish and I think there's some English in there somewhere, God help me. I'm thirty, divorced from an absolute bastard for seven years, and I live alone in Amsterdam with a cat. I am a court reporter by profession, I speak four languages, sleep alone, and need money to keep up my expensive tastes, which are art and fast cars. I have no police record and, although I am on the fringe of some revolutionary groups, I'm not known to any government agency. In fact, I don't do anything illegal. I just put deals together. Does that help?'

The waiter made another trip to the table and fussed about rearranging plates and removing the bones from Margitte's sole before serving it. Alone once again, Mitch leaned forward and in soft tones he outlined his group's needs.

'One hundred Mephistos, fully charged. Delivered, if possible, within the UK mainland, somewhere not too inaccessible. Do you know anybody that can help?'

Margitte's head was bent over her plate. Mitch could not help looking down the gully between her breasts. She was very sun-tanned and he could not detect any change in her coloring or any bra beneath the yellow costume. Was this possible evidence of nude sunbathing? He found the thought very erotic.

Margitte continued eating as if in thought, and then said, 'One hundred Mephistos are enough to blow up Buckingham Palace and half of London. You're not contemplating that, are you?'

'Well, what if we are?' Mitch answered slyly.

'Yes, you're right. It's none of my business, but the people I know would like to have some idea where their efforts would be going. Can you give me a clue?'

It was Mitch's turn to become engrossed in his meal, and he bit into a large piece of the pastry-enclosed filet steak, giving himself time to prepare his reply.

'If you know anything about our campaign, you will know that over the past ten years or so, we have targeted the odd person of influence, like Mountbatten and even Maggie Thatcher herself, down in Brighton. Mostly, though, our efforts have been in keeping the focus of our attacks on the British infrastructure. Is the sole okay?'

'Yes, it's great. Please go on.'

'Well, we think it's time for a change of direction. Let's face it, we haven't made much progress in ridding ourselves of the English. They're still in control of the six counties, and their troops still keep us under the boot of capitalism.'

'You've made some great bangs, though, Mitch, haven't you? The last one was that car bomb in the City. The biggest explosion since World War Two, the papers said.'

'That's true, but what good did it really do? Even though we tried not to, we killed a couple of people, and that upset our funds out of the States.'

'So, what do you want now? Different sources of financial supply? Is that why you put the advert in the *Irish Times*?'

'Not exactly. We have decided to step up the war to the people rather than just the buildings. Unfortunately, that will cause a severe drop-off in the money coming from the Yanks. They're a squeamish lot, and don't like the pictures on CNN from the scenes. You know the sort – ambulances rushing about, wounded people being interviewed, crying children. All that good news stuff. We need the explosives, and then we need further backing. So what can you do?'

Margitte waved to the hovering waiter and gestured for her plate to be removed. She also accepted another glass of the Mateus, then placed her long fingertips together under her chin and leaned once more towards Mitch. He tried to concentrate on her face, and not on her cleavage. He put up a game try but he failed, dismally. He knew she knew. But he didn't seem to care somehow.

'Mitch, I have a lot of contacts. Arabs, Palestinians, Lebanese, also some of the crazier anarchists. Many of them would like to put a severe dent into the English establishment. Providing the explosives should be no problem, but it seems to me that you would have to explode them before there was any talk of outside financing for your cause.'

There was a pause while they both scanned the trolley of desserts that had been wheeled up to them. Mitch, who had a sweet tooth, waved the temptation away when Margitte shook her head at the waiter.

The restaurant was almost empty now, and the staff were engaged in that unsettling routine of preparing the dining room with the china and silverware needed for breakfast. This was supposed to be done with as little interference to the remaining diners as possible. However, they were young and anxious to escape the enforced control of their daily surroundings, and there were more than a few crashes and bangs of cups onto saucers.

Now that the subject of money had arisen, the need for more caution had arrived, so Mitch suggested they find a quiet corner of the lounge to take their coffee. The head waiter was more than happy to oblige, and on their way out, Mitch could feel the mood of the scurrying staff elevate considerably. Sitting down on some overstuffed chairs, Mitch's view of the cleavage was fortunately obscured.

'So how do we make it all happen then?' he asked directly.

'It's no different from most other transactions where

one needs favors and finance,' she replied. 'First, you have to part with money, then you get help. After that you have to perform, then you get more help. Finally you get money. I assume that you are not penniless?'

Mitch assured her that as one of the longest established and most successful freedom fighters in the world, they had plenty of money.

Margitte sipped her coffee and said quietly, 'That is just as well. The people that I know do not come cheap to start with. We are talking about a high-quality, top-class operation and, like most bankers, they really only want to lend an umbrella out when the sun is shining. You will have to buy the Mephistos to begin with. They are very expensive. Also, there are a number of people in the chain; they don't come cheap either.'

'Do you know exactly how large an area these bombs can destroy?'

'I've heard that ten linked together will penetrate the average drywalls of a square block in area. That's across and up and down, if the explosion is set high enough.'

'We probably need a hundred to do the job properly. We plan to hit a number of major cities.'

'You don't plan to put any here, do you?'

'There's been talk…'

'I see.'

The numbers of dead from such a blitz would be catastrophic, not to mention the maiming and wounding, Mitch realized, as he thought these facts through, that all along he was always considering the war as a battle with soldiers, and informants, combatants who knew the risks. The sort of terrorism that was now being considered by his former colleagues was murder, nothing short of bloody murder. He looked up to see Margitte watching him, almost covertly, from behind the rim of her cup. Her glasses magnified her eyes, and Mitch felt as if she could see completely through him. He felt himself color and raised his own cup to cover his blush.

'Such a large shipment would come quite expensive. It would almost certainly cost upwards of seven hundred and fifty thousand pounds sterling or one million American dollars. Could you raise that amount?'

Mitch had thought about half that amount, but that was before he was told about the range of the bombs. There was certainly enough in various deposit accounts in Europe. It would take a couple of weeks to get it all together. He felt his palms sweating as he began to calculate the quantity of money and the size of his intended crime. There would be no forgiveness for such theft. He would be hunted everywhere. He came to the end of his accounting. He knew roughly what the banks held, and if the full amount was taken out, the IRA funds would be virtually depleted. Mike Ryan, Taffy and crew would be very very angry.

Looking into Margitte's magnifying lenses, he said, 'It'll be tight but I think we could come up with that sort of money in a few weeks.'

They both sat back against their respective chairs, and Mitch lit another Players.

'You should really give that up,' Margitte said. 'It killed a couple of my relatives, and my aunt – the one I was having a drink with when you arrived – has serious emphysema.'

'I know I should, but it would take a complete change in my life. I don't know when that will be.' Mitch thought, God, if this all falls down I must get myself a job as an actor. I seem to be able to switch from role to role. Dangerous stuff.

'Is your aunt English then?' Mitch asked out of interest.

'Yes. She was born here before the war and came back for schooling and stayed. She was married to a clergyman and settled down here on the south coast.'

'I was wondering why you were here. Just visiting, are you?'

'Actually, I'm on holiday. Quite legitimately. I'm very fond of this part of the world. It's right in the middle of what the Brits call the sunshine triangle. It gets more sun than anywhere else on the island. Sunshine is very important to both the Brits and the Dutch. Holland gets the weather after they're finished with it here, you know. I've been coming here for years. Here and Devon and Cornwall. It's all so compact and quaint. For a city girl like me, it's wonderful to roam around and see some hills and variations in scenery. I suppose, if you go through with your plans, I'll stop coming. I'm sorry I had to find out. It would be kind of hard to spend time in a place that one had helped devastate. I shall miss the old place.'

'Well, it was you who asked, remember.'

Mitch tried to make his voice harsh. After all he was the customer, and he didn't need a guilt trip laid on him.

'Have you a number I can call you on? Just to let you know the money is okay.'

Margitte pulled up her leather purse and fished around in it for some moments. Mitch could see that there was a huge pile of materials crammed inside. She took out a small notebook and glanced up at him. He was not fast enough to take his amused eyes away from the purse's opening.

'Don't judge me by the state of my handbag. I'm really very organized, you know. Here are three numbers that should reach me. I'm leaving tomorrow afternoon and should be at the first number by Saturday night. I'll be there for two days.'

She scribbled down the information and tore out a page, and in so doing, she ripped the sheet in a diagonal.

'Sorry about that but hold on a moment,' and diving into her purse once again, she produced a small roll of Scotch tape and peeled off a strip. As they both bent over the task of trying to mend the paper, Mitch was aware of her flowery perfume, and the fact that, although they were perhaps more than necessarily close for such an operation, she did not seem to find the proximity uncomfortable.

Settling back once again in the small lounge with only the ticking of a tall grandfather clock in the corner, Mitch caught the eye of a passing waiter, no doubt intent on going home, and called him over.

'How about one for the road?' he suggested to Margitte.

'I'd like a small Hine if they have one,' she replied.

'Make it two,' Mitch said to the waiter, who wearily nodded and withdrew.

The two cognacs arrived quickly, as if their delivery might bring to an end the hotel's need to continue its service for the day. Mitch and Margitte sat quietly, enjoying the feeling that their business, for the time being at least, seemed completed. As far as Mitch was concerned, he also relished the prospect of another chance to spend time with the attractive Dutch woman with the dark tan and the elegant figure.

'I don't think we need to cover any other points at this moment, do you?' Margitte said, putting down her empty snifter on the mahogany and brass table.

Mitch said that as far as he was concerned, they seemed to have done all that was expected of them by their various masters.

'That only applies to you, Mr Colonel of the IRA,' Margitte said in a low whisper. 'I have no masters, I am only accountable to myself. Remember, I neither support your cause nor denounce it.'

'I know, I know, you're just an in-betweener. I'll try and remember for the future.'

Standing up, Mitch could see again that Margitte was almost as tall as he was. They walked out to the front door, and it seemed the most natural thing in the world for him to lean forward and kiss her lightly on the cheek. It was truly a most innocent parting, but for Mitch it broke a sort of physical barrier, and her perfume lingered on his mouth as he climbed once again into the rented Audi. Pulling out of the driveway, he caught sight of her standing motionless in the doorway. She waved her hand quickly and went back inside the hotel.

Chapter Ten

Bucklers Hard, 1786

Although pulling HMS *Distinction* across the Solent had been hard work, Paddy found the exercise rewarding. The steady rhythm of the oars dipping into the water took his mind off the constant worry about his situation. He was alarmed that Katherine's face was receding in his mind, and that he was adapting too easily to the harsh life aboard one of His Majesty's fighting ships.

Back home, his life had been very routine, even dull. Every day was dictated by the weather or the seasons or a crop or a saint. Here, life was dictated by the bosuns who took their orders from the officers. In both lives, he was not completely in charge; it was something that had never bothered him before, but it was starting to bother him now.

He missed the children terribly, and he missed the small comforts of his home. But as he was becoming aware of the size of the outside world, he was beginning to experience the first glimmerings of a feeling that he would like to have a say in how he lived in it.

He thought about the farm as he pulled on the rough oar. He remembered the long back-breaking hours, planting seeds and pulling up tubers from a wet earth that didn't want to release them. He was as much a slave to the process of producing a living there as he was a slave to Bosun Belcher and Gunner Sande. Something inside him started to form. Surely, it didn't have to always be like this?

Was there never to be the freedom that other men enjoyed? As he thought about these things, something began to emerge for the first time in the placid Irishman. It was resentment. He was shaken out of his private world by a shout from behind him.

'Take a look at that, Paddy, my boy.'

It was Chipper, calling from the most forward gun-port of the towed *Distinction*, and pointing ahead of the rowboat. Paddy looked around behind him, and saw in the distance a forest of bristling masts and rigging. Half a mile or so ahead, scores of ships were in various stages of work, both in the water and along the banks. Some seemed to be only skeletons that looked like fish discarded after a meal. Others were tied to the shore, where painters slapped pitch and varnish on their completed sides. Late in the afternoon though it was, Paddy could hear the sounds of repeated hammering and the soft cutting noise of saws biting into the wood that was slowly being formed into boats of war.

Some two hundred yards from a ship that was in a very advanced state of readiness, the order was given to 'Up oars'. Then both fore and aft anchors were lowered over *Distinction*'s sides to bring the man-powered trip to a halt. The rowboat fell back, and Paddy and his colleagues were helped back on board.

'Extra rum for the ship's engine,' shouted Bosun Belcher, and Winston came up from his steamy quarters with the pump and the barrel. All the rowers were lined up and rewarded with an extra tot. Paddy noticed that Winston's pump was returned below decks in the full position. In spite of himself, he was beginning to understand how the navy worked. Chipper and he leaned over the side, staring at the slow-moving river beneath them and at the work that was going on ahead.

'This is where Capt'n Merryview's boat is being built. I don't know which one it is, but they say it's the best that

Buckler's master builder has ever designed.'

Chipper explained how the shipbuilding process worked: how the weatherproofed logs were formed and then laid along the keels, and how the ship then grew upward with its ribs and coverings slowly added by all the various craftsmen. He could point out the carpenters in their leather aprons, and the blacksmiths, toiling over their forges that would hiss and send out showers of sparks. Paddy breathed in the aroma of split pine, oak sawdust, pitch, tar and the woodsmoke that settled over them in soft layers from the nearby forest.

'This is where we'll beat the French,' Chipper said, as he gazed up stream at the activity. 'You see, Paddy, we let the navy run down once before, one hundred years or so ago. Now that we've built it up again, we'll never be beaten on our own home shores. Maybe that's why you lot have had such a hard time with us. Somehow, we just don't feel safe with you on the left of us, and the French on the right. I suppose you'll never understand, but we feel trapped if Ireland is run by people who are more faithful to Rome than to London. Still, here I am sounding like a bloody politician, and all you want is some fun. Well, let's see what we can do about it.'

At that moment, there was a sound of a whistle being blown; it was echoed by several others, and a cheer went up among the men working on the ships. Then, the sound of iron tools being put noisily away, followed by singing, reached Chipper and Paddy, as they continued their quiet solitude, leaning alongside the ship's rail with their shipmates and Bosun Belcher.

'How about letting some of us newer fellers off then, Chief? We promise not to run away.'

Belcher turned and stared at Chipper.

'If you'll wear the yellow sash and not go near the trees, I might consider it.'

'You're on, Chief,' said Chipper. 'Can Paddy come along as well? I'll keep me eye on 'im for ya.'

The bosun agreed, and the first party of six was let down into a boat and rowed ashore. Each man had a bright yellow sash over his shoulder to allow the regular men to know he was a pressed recruit, and had to be watched so he didn't escape.

As Paddy could see, though, this was hardly necessary as there was nowhere to run. Everybody was engaged in the navy's business, and apart from a few new houses that had been built in a double line down to the water's edge, most of the dwellings were tents or rough lean-tos. More significantly, there was not a tree within hundreds of yards. As the rowboat drew nearer, Chipper pointed out that all the nearby trees had been felled during the time of good Queen Bess.

'It was the bleedin' Spanish that time, Paddy. Then the French, the Dutch and anybody else who fancied a go. All had to be sent on their way. Then we 'ad a bloke called Pepys. 'E came over off a turn abroad and saw all the things goin' on in the navy. It was in a right state. Anyway, 'e persuaded the nobs to cough up some money, and the buildin' started. The ships we 'ad then was all out of date, and in a right mess. Also, the captains were all on the take. Bad crews and bad conditions. 'E changed it all and much of the change started 'ere. The best builders in the land came down 'ere, to make the best ships in the world. Come on, let's 'ave a look round.'

The boat landed on the soft well-trampled bank and the men jumped out. There was music in the air as fiddles were bowed and fifes were blown. Men were sitting around the fires that were sending their fumes up into the clear air. One or two women were around, too, but they were of the homely mature type. Paddy felt relieved.

There were a couple of taverns that attracted the newcomers. In them, for a few coppers, they could drink robust ale and enjoy some roasted rabbits. Chipper had some money on him, so he was able to float Paddy for the few pence necessary. As it was nearly the end of the week, there was a light-heartedness in the atmosphere, and a number of the craftsmen called out to them as they wandered around the settlement. The yellow sashes obviously were known to many, and a few people called out, 'Hey, canary!' as they passed.

Strolling across the back of the encampment, they would not have wandered too far towards the edge of the forest except that they heard a cry that was impossible to ignore. It was coming from some low bushes halfway towards the trees. Running across the short turf, they saw some movement and plunged towards it. Even though he was quite small, Chipper was several yards ahead of Paddy as they reached the scene of activity. He pulled up short and Paddy crashed into him as he stood staring. There in front of them was Chief Gunner Sande, with a lascivious grin on his face, pulling the wretched Reilly to the soft earth. Sande was wearing vivid rouge on his cheeks, and Reilly was twisting helplessly in the strong man's grip.

Chipper tried to lead Paddy away, but the spectacle of the bullying, and the unnatural reasons behind it, were too much for the simple Irishman. He pushed Chipper out of the way and shoved the big gunner aside, grabbing the unfortunate recruit with his large farming hands. Sande let out a growl and turned on Paddy. He brought up both fists and swung dangerously at the Irishman's head. For all his passive existence, Paddy was used to dealing with farm animals and their quick reactions. He automatically treated Sande like a dangerous bull. He circled the man, keeping out of reach of his lunges.

Sande, for his part, was the veteran of many a ship's brawl, and knew how to fight hard and, occasionally, lethally. Feinting to his left, he dived for Paddy's unprotected side and brought up his gnarled fist into the area under the ribs. Seeing the hand flashing towards him, Paddy turned towards the blow, bracing his hard stomach muscles. Had he turned away from Sande, the fist would have buried itself in his kidneys, causing terrible damage.

As it was, Paddy staggered under the force of the onslaught, and the chief gunner was onto him. Leaping forward and using his head as a battering ram, the navy man bore his opponent down to the ground. There was an audible thump from the soft earth as the two bodies connected and fell, like two giant trees in a forest.

Chipper and Reilly stood helplessly aside. Chipper knew his slightness would be brushed aside if he tried to intervene. However, had Paddy been in a position to see his friend, he would have noticed that Chipper's hand was clutching at his belt buckle, and the hidden Madonna. Reilly, his normally pale face looking more wan than ever, hopped impotently from one foot to another, as the combatants rolled around on the damp deforested earth, their efforts being broadcasted by grunts and the sucking of air into strained lungs.

Having gotten his attacker on the ground, Sande was doing his best to maneuver him onto his back, where he intended to cause as much damage to Paddy's face as possible. Within the fleet, it was known that anyone who dared to get in Sande's way was a marked man, and would carry the signs visibly for the world to see the cost of such effrontery. However, Paddy had been brought up in the company of sturdy countryboys, and was not ignorant of the ways of the street fighter. Lulling Sande into believing he was tiring, he allowed the big man to position himself over his prostrate body. Then he brought up his head sharply, and struck his forehead into Sande's nose. As the grip on Paddy's arm lessened, he brought up both hands simultaneously onto Sande's unprotected ears.

During a fight at Murphy's saloon some years ago, Paddy had received such a combination. He remembered his hearing was affected for days after, and he couldn't smell anything either for the amount of dried blood that was clogged in his nose. By the way that Sande fell back, he knew the chief gunner would suffer a similar fate. Not wanting to continue the fracas, Paddy rolled out from under the reeling man to join his stunned companions.

'Fuckin' 'ell, Paddy,' exclaimed Chipper. 'Where did you learn to fight like that? I've never seen the like of it. That Sande is a wicked bugger, killed several men in 'is time I 'ear.' Showing the thin ivory-handled knife in its protective skin sheath, he continued, 'I thought I might 'ave to bring the Madonna 'ere into play.'

Turning, the three men left the chief who was spitting out blood and cradling his head in his hands. Paddy told his two friends that he had learned wrestling in the fields and alehouses of Ireland. He had always had an aptitude for it.

They went back towards their ship, passing through the lines of men who were eating and drinking after their day's work. It was a quiet scene but there was an unhealthy warning in their minds. They knew that in spite of Paddy's and Reilly's escape, they had not heard the last from Sande.

They did not have to wait long. The next night as Paddy stood outside the entrance to their quarters, looking at the lights on the banks of the Beaulieu River, he half heard a sound behind him. Instinctively, he moved away. It was only a fraction of an inch, but it was enough to save his skull from being crushed by a falling billy club. As it was, he received a cruel blow on his left shoulder. Wheeling around, he saw a large figure escaping down the companionway. He could not be sure it was Sande, but the coincidence was too great to ignore. Nursing his bruised shoulder, he resolved to be more careful in the future.

Chipper saw him coming through the hatchway and knew that something was wrong. He noticed Paddy moving his shoulder and insisted on looking at the damage, although Paddy tried to wave him off.

'We've got a bleedin' big problem 'ere, mate,' he said, as he bent Paddy's arm around to make sure nothing was broken. 'That big bastard'll kill you if we don't come up with a plan. 'E's got time on 'is side and 'e's got a big edge with 'is position. I'll 'ave to give it some thought.'

So saying, he retired to his hammock, and Paddy could hear him clicking his knife in and out of its scrimshaw scabbard. His shoulder hurt abominably.

The next day, Sande started to pick on the two of them. It was quite blatant. Up to now, they had been largely left alone and, anyway, they were a good team with their gun. The drills were done efficiently, and the gun itself was in first-class order.

At first, it was little points about the way they were lined up. Then Sande found dirt around the well-greased axles. It was dirt that normally accumulated during exercises. In their case, however, it was turned into a major offense and called for additional drills, and also the carrying of cannon balls from one deck to another as punishment. Unfortunately, Chipper's lack of size let him down badly in this fruitless activity, which allowed the chief to create more difficulties. But worse was to come.

In the afternoon, a random inspection of the guns showed that Paddy's and Chipper's gun had a large lump of tar imbedded inside its barrel. This was a crime that might be construed as sabotage, as it would restrict the efficiency of the weapon, or even worse, cause it to blow up when fired. Sande made much of this crime. His loose-lipped mouth twisted into a sneer, as he accused the two men of a list of heinous acts destined to put all their shipmates in the greatest danger. The captain was alerted, and the two men were marched to his cabin.

Captain Merryview was a professional seaman. He knew Sande was a bad lot. But he also knew that, under fire, he was one of the best NCOs afloat. His discipline and routines paid off, and the man was fearless, as he stalked the gun-decks, shouting orders and commands through the din of battle. Captain Merryview also knew about the chief's perversions and his bullying. More than one new recruit had been savagely punished for not submitting to his whims.

He listened to the charges as relayed by Sande, and asked some questions about the spiking of the gun. He knew if it could be proved that the two new men had done it, it was a flogging offense. He decided to send for the senior bosun, Belcher.

Wiping his face free of the grease from the chicken leg that he was eating, the captain stood up and donned his blue frock coat while the two prisoners watched him with caution. The captain was a tall man with naturally silvered hair. His bearing and general appearance were of a well-groomed gentleman, with perhaps a touch of foppishness. This affectation immediately disappeared as Belcher came through the door and stood before him. He gave Sande no chance to repeat the charges, and bore straight into the bosun with a number of direct questions about the previous behavior of the cockney and the Irishman.

Being unaware of the circumstances, Belcher was unable to bolster up his fellow NCOs accusations, and merely answered that no, there had been no difficulty with them, and yes, they had buckled down to life on board. He even added that they had shown themselves the best team on the gun-decks, and could work alone without supervision.

During this discourse, Sande glowered and twitched, his eyes mostly cast down but occasionally burning into the tall Irishman standing meekly in front of the officer.

'Well, Sande,' Captain Merryview said, after his cross-examination of Belcher, 'it seems there is no actual evidence. It's all very circumstantial. Do you men have anything to say?'

'I can speak for 'im, sir,' Chipper spoke up. 'We never done nothin' to the gun, 'cept clean it and drill it and occasionally fire the bleeder.'

'Yes, quite. Well you had better be more careful about its innards in future. It's your responsibility to make sure it's safe at all times.'

'Yes, sir. Thank you, sir,' the cockney replied, and they shuffled out onto the deck.

With the disruption of their normal routine, most of the others in the gun crews had wandered off. Therefore, with a scowl, Sande indicated that work was over for the day. The two men went down below feeling lucky to have escaped. Paddy's shoulder hurt a great deal and this had not been helped by the cannon ball carrying that had been forced on them. He lay swinging on his hammock nursing the bruise. Chipper swung silently beside him, his face set intently as he stared at the bulkhead.

'Well, Paddy, we're in the ka-ka and no mistake. This big bleeder is going to do for you, and in the process, 'e'll probably do for me, too.'

'I don't know what to say, Chipper,' the Irishman replied. 'I couldn't let poor old Reilly put up with whatever that bastard, Sande, was going to do to him, could I?'

'No, no, it's not your fault. But if we don't come up with something, I'm telling you we've 'ad it. If we don't stop Sande now before it gets worse, Merryview will start to believe we're troublemakers. Christ, life in the navy can be a right bleeder and no mistake.'

The next few days of their stay at Bucklers Hard found no respite from Sande's bullying. He kept Paddy and Chipper at extra drill and complained about their apparent lack of ability, although they were particularly careful with their duties. Every session that was mustered on the gun-decks would end with the two of them carrying huge quantities of cannon balls from one area to another.

Every night, they stayed safely out of harm's way in their mess or in their hammocks. Neither of them desired another attack out in the open, like the one that Paddy had sustained. Then, on the last night they were in the port, with its activity and pleasant surroundings, Chipper swung his legs over the side of his bed and said, 'Well, sod this for a game of soldiers, Paddy, I've 'ad enough. 'Ow about you?'

Paddy looked up glumly from massaging his still sore shoulder. 'I've been better, Chipper,' he said.

'Well, I've decided to stop this lark before it gets any worse. I'll see you later.'

Jumping down, he strode out into the night, leaving Paddy in no doubt that he had some sort of plan. He lay quietly waiting for the Londoner to return and explain everything, but with the restful sounds of the ship, the slight swing of the hammock and the weariness of carrying all those iron balls around, he fell asleep. It was very early morning when he felt, more than heard, Chipper crawl back into bed and fall into a snoring slumber. It was nearly two hours later that the whistles began to blow, summoning them to their duties to make the ship ready for sailing.

Paddy tried to talk to his friend during their rushed breakfast of mutton stew, but the small man just silenced him with a wave of his hand and a wink. Then they were up on deck for roll-call, followed once more by their never-ending drills in the gun galleries. Initially, Paddy could see no difference in the chief gunner's behavior. There were still the same sneers, the same racial insults and the occasional swipe with his billy club, but by lunchtime, Paddy realized that there was no actual hardship. Sande did not find anything seriously wrong with their gun or their performance. He certainly never let up all day on his verbal attacks but at day's end, they had not carried a single cannon ball or toted the heavy gun on any needless trips across the deck. It was all noise and no action.

As they sipped their tea at Winston's scrubbed mess-hall table, Paddy said quietly to Chipper, 'I don't know how you've done it, but he's a changed man.'

Chipper smiled up at him and continued to cram his face with more hard tack. ''Ow's the shoulder, mate?' was all he said and continued with his eating.

Other men came and went as the business of the evening meal took its routine. There was a different atmosphere aboard now that they were once again under way. There was a more defined look in the experienced men's eyes. It was a look that showed alert concentration as each in his way took up a position of responsibility. The men on the rigging, once down from their lofty perches, constantly checked the set of the sails, and nodded approval or concern with every tack that the officers took. The watchmen scanned the horizon to keep their sea eyes sharp, and the gunners took note of the roll of the ship as she barreled down the Solent, once again on active duty. Even the pressees had now adopted a rolling gait as they developed their sea legs and began to identify with the duties of the senior service.

HMS *Distinction* was a serious fighting vessel, and during her next turn of duty, she was to patrol the southern waters around her country, looking for French men-of-war that would attack fishing and trading vessels without warning. Every man afloat secretly hoped to avoid real danger, but welcomed the opportunity to send some 'Froggy' running back to France with his sails in tatters and his scuppers leaking from some well-aimed shots.

The drills continued, and the efficiency of the ship

increased with the well-practiced discipline of centuries of seafaring. Each night, as they dropped anchor, as the predominantly south-westerly wind fell off, the men would fill their pipes, fill their bellies, and tell the tales of the sea.

Every night, Chipper would leave his hammock and disappear, leaving Paddy to worry about what was happening. Every morning as the crew swung in unison in their hammocks, supported by their plaited ropes, he would creep back and fall asleep until the bosun's whistles blew. Paddy tried to ask him what was happening, but Chipper somehow always managed to divert his questions by telling him he was about to do something, or by some other such ploy.

Eventually, five hours out of Falmouth, they were stung out of their drills and their prepared state of war by a set of sails beating across the southern horizon. The mainmast lookout saw it first and shouted down to the officer of the deck. He immediately uncapped his telescope and, grasping it alongside a spar, he focused the lenses on the vessel.

The captain was summoned on deck and he too extended his glass and stared intently at the boat, sailing innocently some five miles away. Merryview gave orders to come about and maintain the necessary course to bring the two ships within gun range. The gunners were sent below to their two decks, and the sound to action was beaten out on the drums.

It was a credit to unending practice that allowed all men aboard to be at their positions and ready to defend their nation within thirty seconds. Two minutes later, the word came round that the ship that had been sighted was indeed a French runner, attempting to sail too close to British waters in order to cut off valuable hours on the journey back to France.

Quickly, HMS *Distinction* broke out full sails and, with the crack of the unfolding canvas, the crew could feel the lurch as she accelerated towards the enemy. Paddy, standing next to his polished gun, felt a surge of adrenaline, as he peered down through the portholes at the wake ripping past the keel.

'Nothing to look at there, you dumb Irish farmer,' Chipper hissed, as he stood on the other side with his plunger ready. 'We 'ave to get within range, then we turn broadside and let 'er 'ave all barrels. 'Ere take this and stuff it in yer ears.'

He tore of a strip of rag and showed Paddy how to bind the plugs with a bandage to keep the worst of the blast out.

For an hour, the men stood in a state of readiness. Occasionally, one could not stand it any longer and would break discipline and peer out the gun's porthole. Such behavior would immediately affect the response by the chief gunner. Shouting to stand at attention, he gave the culprit a clout round the head with a knotted rope that he kept hanging at his side for the purpose.

The claustrophobia of the cramped gun lines bore in on the men and boys, waiting for the order to fire. Chief Gunner Sande strutted up and down the fat ends of the cannon as they rested on their stubby wheels. Each piece was primed and awaited the turn of the ship when the flares would be put to the touch-holes and the deadly shots would explode from the barrels. While the noise of the gunpowder died, the chains would rattle out and restrain the backward motion of the guns.

Sande's normal expression of disdain was replaced by an almost anxious stare as he, along with his shipmates, ran through his mind the possible consequences of today's action. He had been through over fifty naval engagements and lost two ships out from under him. Although he had sustained some injuries, he had been very lucky compared to others. However, being a gambling man, he knew his odds were shortening. He didn't like that. He scowled at a young boy sitting, fidgeting with a bucket of water at the foot of the steps.

'Leave it alone, boy, or I'll take the skin off your backside.'

Like most of the other youngsters on board, this one, whose name was Percy, had been the recipient of one of Sande's rouged assaults. Like most of them also, he had been protected by the other NCOs, who believed in their duty to look after the boys who were still innocents in this harsh and dangerous world. The NCOs knew that there would be plenty of time for sin later on in these young lives. For now they were there to help the ship, and although shouted at and kicked, they were not to be corrupted by Sande and his sort.

As soon as Sande spoke, Percy froze and sat stock-still. For a moment there was complete silence apart from the rushing of the water outside, but several pairs of eyes swiveled over to the bully close to the demure frame, and several fists bunched in anticipation of trouble. The danger passed, and Percy was left to his quiet vigil.

The sound of a crisply shouted order from above alerted the men that Captain Merryview was about to turn the racing ship into the wind. Within seconds, it was brought almost to a complete stop. At the same moment, a barrage of gunfire could be heard over on the starboard beam. It was some way off, but splashes could be heard around the *Distinction* as the French runner sought her aim.

Sande barked out his command, and the flames were touched to the charges. Twenty guns exploded, and flung themselves backwards. Twenty more on the lower decks barked an echo. Sande squinted through the smoke amidships to watch the flight of the ammunition, as forty balls, weighing over ten pounds apiece, hurtled towards the foe. 'Got 'er,' was all he said, and everyone stared across the three hundred yards of channel to the opposite ship. The guns were sponged and primed and then came the ordeal 'Reload.' The balls were rolled down the still-steaming barrels and the men stood waiting for the order to fire.

Ahead in the bow section a huge ripping explosion tore into the ship. A split second later another cannon ball burst through the side of *Distinction* as the French gunners finally found their range. Mercifully, the variance in the mass of the enemy's ammunition caused the other shots in the volley to fall short.

Distinction's guns roared back in defiance, and more of the French ship splintered both above and below the waterline. Peering through the battle, Paddy could see the frantic efforts of the French crew, trying to stem the flooding that must be occurring. Another enemy salvo arrived and all the men involuntarily ducked at the sound of the balls whistling across to them.

Cries could be heard on the top deck as the heavy shot crashed down on the unprotected wooden spars and masts. The ship shuddered as another group hit the stern of the ship, and men were heard to scream as flesh was ripped from bodies and bones were crushed beneath the falling yard arms.

Both ships were now positioned like prizefighters squaring off. The distance between them was only one hundred yards. Both opposing teams worked as if possessed to clear away debris, both human and naval, as they fought to help their vessel annihilate the other.

Sande stalked the gun-decks, moving his huge bulk skillfully up and down the narrow ladders that connected the two scenes of his responsibility. As he was stripped to the waist, the scars that decorated his battle-worn frame showed livid as the sweat poured over him. His tattoos ran with oil and grit as he wiped his face continuously on a rag that he wore on his arm. Sometimes screaming at the top of his voice, sometimes hitting men with both billy club and rope, he goaded all into keeping steady. He worked tirelessly, and even Paddy, who still nursed a wariness of him, felt that here, in his domain, he was the master.

Chipper looked even more like a drowned rat than normal. His was the job of dousing the cannon with his water-soaked plunger, ramming home the charge and then assisting Paddy to roll the loaded gun forwards. Paddy had to aim while Chipper tended to the supplies that the boys brought to them. Each gun had a pile of four balls in a box, together with some assorted other shot, like chain shot for stripping the enemy's rigging and grape shot for maiming and killing the opposition. Chipper would sometimes grab the flame and touch it to the gun, and sometimes Paddy would reach over, once he had assured himself that the back end was clear. The wheels were sufficiently well-oiled to allow the gun to move backwards at a very fast rate. Anyone within the range of the restraining ropes and chains would be severely injured.

The gun-deck remained undamaged apart from the first hits. *Distinction* had managed to hit the Frenchman sufficiently enough that it had developed such a pronounced list its guns were mostly ineffective. Their gunners fought to prop up the barrels, to be able to hit the *Distinction*, but the damage was done and the fight had gone out of the French.

'It's all over, men,' shouted Sande, as he made his way down the lines. 'Hear that noise?' There was a huge amount of gunnery activity, with no resulting damage on their own decks. 'They're making noise and not using shot. She's going to make a run for it, you mark my words.'

As if on order, the French captain could be heard shouting to his men who were running aloft amid the sagging rigging. The ship's helm came over and she began to fall away from the wind. Additional canvas flapped over the scarred yardarms, and the distance began to grow as

Distinction fired off a few more salvos. Most of these landed impotently in the sea, although one well-aimed shot crashed into the departing stern.

'Right up the Froggy's arse,' shouted Sande, and a huge cheer went up all around.

Since *Distinction* was on coastal patrol, Captain Merryview had no thought of chasing the beaten French runner. Men from all over the ship shouted to him to 'Get the bastard' and 'What about our bounty?' But he knew that he was already far away from his plotted track; furthermore, his ship was damaged and not about to sail towards the enemy coast. He sounded general quarters and assembled the crew below him on the main deck.

'Men, you have fought well; I am proud of you. You new men made a good account of yourselves and I am only sorry you cannot join in your rightful spoils of success. We have some damage in the stern and the bow that needs to be fixed. Sadly, we also have lost some of our shipmates, and the surgeons are working on the wounded below. May God help their ordeals.'

So saying, he dismissed all hands with orders to the bosuns to allow a double helping of rum, and the guns to be made ready before dark. At this, there was a general groan, followed by the swishing of the NCOs' ropes. Captain Merryview turned and looked down at the men.

'Now, my good fellows, this is a battle zone. We won the fight because we were better prepared and more on the lookout than our enemy. I'm not prepared to take a chance on another Froggy creeping up on us. Are you?'

There was a great shout from the men and Winston appeared on deck with his barrel and pump. One tot was dispensed to each man with the promise that the other would follow after the guns had been cleaned and made ready. As they went below to the gun-decks, Paddy caught Chipper by the arm and held him back at the entrance.

'What's up, Paddy, my old mate?'

'I want to know what's been going on,' the tall Irishman said, staring intently into the little man's face.

'What didya mean?' came the drawled reply.

'You know damned well what I mean. The nights you keep disappearing. I want to know where you go.'

There was a silence from the normally talkative cockney and he looked about helplessly as Paddy kept a firm hold on him.

'Come on, Chipper, I want to know. I'm not letting you go until you tell me.'

To give some credence to what he was saying he shook the thin arm that fitted easily in his farm worker's grasp.

'Okay, Paddy, I'll tell you. It's nothing to get yerself in a state about. I just went off to the chief's cabin five times. To pay off the debt.'

'What debt are you talking about?'

'Us duffing the bleeder up. You don't get away with that in the navy, old son. Not when you're just a couple of tars like us.'

Paddy had been getting some uncomfortable thoughts about Chipper's regular absences since that first night, and now those same images were becoming clearer in his mind. It was his turn to now look around and fidget.

'Look, Paddy, it's nothing all that bad. Sande's just an old queen. Once 'e's got his make-up on, 'e's easy. I can tell you.'

'God, Chipper, you're not letting him…'

His voice faded away as the image that he had been fighting came back firmly into his mind.

'Don't upset yourself, you daft bugger. I borrow one of Winston's famous drawings and it's mostly over from that moment on. Here,' he continued, as he saw the look of confusion replace the look of horror on his friend's face. 'Winston has this collection of dirty drawings. Uses 'em to shock some of his girlfriends. 'E says that it sometimes gets 'em going. Well, several of 'em show blokes getting it together. Nasty drawings they are, Paddy, but they're right up old Sande's street.'

Paddy's face became even more confused, so Chipper took him out to the side of the ship, and they both leaned over, staring at the sea passing gently beneath the hull.

'The deal was that I would 'ave to go to the chief's cabin five nights, yer see.'

Paddy nodded balefully but Chipper Johnson hurried on.

'Well, I'm not his type but a deal is a deal, so I eat a load of raw onions down at Winston's table first, and chew some baccy on my way up. Once I get in 'is cabin, he puts all 'is rouge on and also 'e wears some women's bloomers. Just about the time 'e's all ready, I pop one of Winston's pictures under 'is nose and he goes at 'imself.'

Paddy's face registered surprise once again.

'Look, you're straight out the bloody bogs ain't yer? 'E gives 'imself a wank and I'm off the 'ook. 'E usually 'as a fair bit of rum before I arrive, then 'e gets all excited at the prospect of dressing up and wearing 'is paint. By the time 'e gets to seein' the picture, 'e's close to the edge. I stink like a bloody polecat, anyway, and 'e does like Winston's art. It's bloody grim, but I let 'im keep the drawings, if 'e behaves isself. And that means keeping 'is bleeding 'ands offer me. I even feel sorry for the poor bugger. So don't worry, Paddy, it's all in 'and, so to speak,' he continued with a cheeky wink. 'Also, last night was the last, so we're in the clear.'

They left the upper deck's quiet and went below. Paddy felt shocked and alarmed at Chipper's news. He had led a sheltered life on his farm in Ireland, and the fact that men like Sande existed at all was still very bothersome to him. The fact that his best friend was now involved in such behavior was completely repugnant to him.

However, as they both worked on their gun and the surrounding area below decks, Paddy thought the matter through and, influenced by Chipper's cheery disposition, he began to realize that his friend's attitude was sensible and that they had both escaped from a very dangerous situation. Paddy rationalized that he had learned another lesson of life in this very different world of men cooped up for long periods. He accepted that Chipper had paid a great price for his continuing safety. He also realized that he was again in the little man's debt. He wondered if and when it would become time to repay that debt.

As the crew finally was dismissed from their battle-weary day, the bosuns told them all to prepare for another spell in port. This time they were to head for the deep-water harbor of Falmouth in Cornwall.

Chapter Eleven

Southern England, July 1992

Mitch was in no hurry to return to Northern Ireland. He felt he had managed everything well, both from the point of view of his own escape plans and also with the IRA mission with which he was charged.

He decided to drive the rented Audi north through the center of England, taking his time and thinking through the plans he needed to make. The rental company had a sister company in Manchester and so he agreed, for an additional fee, to drop the vehicle off there.

Using one of the coded numbers, he contacted headquarters in Ulster and let them know that the antiques they were interested in would cost over one million US dollars. There was a gasp from the other end of the line and he could visualize Taffy screwing up his face at the size of the amount.

The weather was hot and dry as he meandered through the small lanes of rural England. As he took his time, he set himself the job of rethinking all the years of hatred that he had bottled up inside him. He watched normal English people going about their day-to-day tasks, and it was hard to equate them with the monsters who had brought untold horrors to his own land and people.

Since arriving in Liverpool those ten days ago and being whisked around on the back of the Norton, he had no complaints about the way he was treated; yet, deep down, there was just so much hatred that it would not simply subside. Outside Oxford, he stopped at a small village church and decided to use the silence and coolness within to try and come to some sort of rationalization. Wandering through the sun-drenched churchyard, he gazed sightlessly at the tilted gravestones with their lichen-covered scripts dating back through the centuries. He read a number of the names that were still legible and was staring at one in the shade of a tall elm tree when a small croaky voice behind him said, 'Can I help you at all?'

Mitch jumped and spun around.

'I'm sorry if I startled you. But I wondered if you were looking for anybody's grave in particular.'

The owner of the voice was a small stooped man with a gray beard, and twinkling eyes behind steel-rimmed glasses. He had a rake in his hands and wore a shirt without a collar. Mitch realized the interruption had made his heart race, and he continued to stare at the man, who must have been over eighty.

'I'm sorry, you made me jump. I was miles away. Actually, I was just browsing around looking. I'm not trespassing, am I?'

The last remark, Mitch realized, was phrased rather too harshly, so he softened his voice as he added, 'I don't even know the name of the church, I'm afraid.'

'Irish, are you, then?' the old man asked.

'Yes, from Cork.'

'Funny, you sound more like an Ulsterman.'

'Born up there, but left when I was ten. I guess the accent still stays after all these years.'

'My mother came from Belfast, so I recognize the sound. I've never been there myself. It must be a worrisome place, with all the violence, isn't it?'

Mitch agreed it was a problem, but that fortunately there was no difficulty in the fair city of Cork where he resided now. He felt relaxed talking to the old man, although in some respects he was telling double lies.

'Come over here, then. You'll be interested in this stone. Oh, by the way, my name's Stan. Stan Hood. I try to help out a bit here. The weeds tend to get on top of one, and the vicar can't afford a proper gardener. The missus grows flowers for the church round the side. That's her, over there.' So saying, he waved to a stooping women of equal age, with an old-fashioned straw bonnet. She was bending over a bed of chrysanthemums. She waved back energetically.

Mitch followed along behind Stan, who had a pronounced limp. Eventually, they arrived at a large raised marble slab with severe Gothic lines. It had Latin words all over it and the name of the interred family carved deeply onto the headstone. It belonged to Joseph and Elizabeth Simmons, who apparently had died in 1847.

'See them?' asked Stan, pointing with his rake. 'Irish, just like you, but turned English. Those wild fellows up in the North – the IRA – would've liked to have got their hands on them, I can tell you. They would have been shot as traitors.'

Mitch leaned over the grave and fingered the still sharp lettering. The marble was obviously of the finest quality, and it was hard to believe it was over a hundred years old. Only the stylized script gave the age away.

Stan put his foot up on the edge of the stone.

'They were Irish, you see. Originally called Fitzsimmons. They had been an Irish family since the twelfth century, so they say. Owned loads of land all over Ireland, estates they had been given by several kings and queens. Well, they got into some sort of trouble, financial, I think, and they had to come over here and settle. They found a big house up there on the hill. You can just see it if you come over here with me.'

So saying, he grasped Mitch's arm with a bony hand that was blotched with brown marks, and drew him about six foot to one side.

'See it?'

Through the rich summer foliage, Mitch could make out a rather stark classical mansion with rows of windows reflecting the bright sunlight.

'Well, their fortune turned, and they managed to keep most of their land in their own country and buy a bit more. They dropped the Fitz from their name and began to pretend they were English. Eventually, after a couple of generations, they became English – maybe they had started out that way in the first place, of course, but who can tell?'

Mitch nodded wisely. He liked this little old man with his weathered face and raspy voice. There was an air of solidity about him that made the Irishman relax. There were little old men like this all over Ireland. One found them everywhere. They were thought of as wise and the backbone of the nation's culture. Mitch reacted to this one in a similar way – even if he was English. Or was he Irish, with his Irish mother?

'Pretty soon,' the old man continued, walking back to the grave, 'the family started running into problems with the overdue rents back in Ireland. They had been diminishing for years, what with the lack of contact and the many changes of collecting agents. Well, the Simmons family decided that, as they needed everything that they could lay their hands on for some overseas purchase, they would visit their Irish estates.

'By this time they were English, and thought of themselves as English. The two of them, Joseph and Elizabeth, sailed over the Irish Sea – notice that it's not called the English Sea, by the way – and made their way to their land. Unfortunately for them, they arrived about the time of the first serious famine. Their farms seemed to be among the first to be hit. In fact, the blight was in its second term, with the resulting death and disease everywhere.

'Once people began to hear who they were, the story goes, they propositioned them for help. In return, the Simmons tried to claim their backdated rent. The struggle went on, with both sides pleading their case, in a land that had no money, no food, no hope and no help. In fact, the only thing that was widely available was cholera. Know anything about cholera, Mr… er? I'm sorry, I don't know your name.'

'It's Mitch, er, Mitch O'Doule, actually.' Mitch couldn't believe he had used his real name. 'Please go on.'

'I saw cholera in action back in India, Mr O'Doule. Very nasty business. Once it takes hold it takes no prisoners. In an already weakened population, it kills in a few agonizing days. Well, the Simmons, or Fitzsimmons, if you prefer, were exposed to the disease while they tried to collect their rents. The agent had died, and there was nobody else to do it for them. Now, since they were only a generation or two away from being Irish themselves, you would have thought they'd show some mercy at the sight of all those starving tenants. But no. All they wanted was their money, and so they traipsed from cottage to cottage, witnessing first-hand the terror and starvation on the faces of men, women and children. Elizabeth had had two children of her own, but it apparently had no effect. She was as bad as her husband. All they wanted was their money. If the wretched tenant couldn't pay, they served the eviction notices themselves, and rode on in their pony and trap.

'Well, they ignored the disease at their peril. But it didn't ignore them. All the time they were there, they were becoming infected. One night, in the hotel, it struck Elizabeth and then, twenty-four hours later, he went down with the cramps. They were too sick to move, and the few doctors were overworked with the speed of the epidemic.

They were both dead within a week and they were buried in the town's graveyard along with their poverty-stricken tenants. Word was sent here to the big house, and their two children, by then in their twenties, were left to decide what to do with their estates and their much loved parents' remains.

'It appears that quite a long battle was fought over what to do. But eventually, the remains were dug up and shipped back here. This took over twenty-five years, and the family fortunes by then had fallen even lower. Some say it was a curse on them for the greed they showed at the end of their lives. There was no family in residence by the time the remains arrived. Only a caretaker who knew nothing about a family vault. The end of the story is they had no final resting place apart from the local parish church. So it was here the famous Fitzsimmons ended their days. No one to mourn them or see their homecoming. The final irony is they were a staunch Catholic family, and this is a Protestant church.'

Stan Hood finished his tale of woe with a totally undisguised grin. He leaned back and stretched his sides and, resting the rake handle on his chest, he put his hands on his hips and smiled up at Mitch.

'So this here would be a good spot to bring some of those IRA fellows, wouldn't it?'

'How do you mean? What would they learn here? I'm sorry, it's just another tale of horror to come out of Ireland. We have enough of them, you know.'

Mitch had a frown on his face, as the little man continued to smile up at him.

'Well, it's obvious, isn't it? Who do you blame here? For a start, were these people English or Irish? Even they became confused. Did they deserve their fate? They believed they were owed money. Their parents taught them it was theirs. The children couldn't work out where they should be finally laid to rest, and in the end there wasn't a proper place for them. Only Protestant ground. It's all so confusing. Just like the history of all the troubles over there.

'My mother started off hating the English and then ended up marrying one of them. My father couldn't understand any of it, and I've read all I care to without seeing where one problem ended and another began. I read somewhere the thinkers of the world end up laughing and the feelers of the world end up crying. I guess I've always been a thinker. Also, my mother's maiden name was Fitzsimmons.'

'You mean to say this grave covers your relatives?' Mitch asked with a touch of unplanned reverence in his voice.

'I don't know, frankly, but does it really matter? Sometimes I think they may be and other times I doubt it. It's kind of one of those unanswered questions that will probably never be known. I don't much care either way. I just like to tend the whole area. I like the peace and quiet here. The problems were none of our doing. I just wish we could all live in peace. But that's rather unlikely, I think. At least for a few years.'

As if to end the conversation, Stan began to rake some grass around the marble slab, and then to spread his strokes out along the well-kept paths.

'Church's open if you want to look around. Collection box is, too. We all need money. Even if it's not as much as the Simmons family. Oh, by the way, the house got turned into a hospital – for the mentally ill.' He cackled at that, and prodded some errant leaves at his feet.

Mitch bade him farewell and started towards his car. On an impulse, he stopped and, turning slowly, went back and entered the church. It was dark, cool and silent, with a heavy musky smell that had built up over several hundred years. Stan's words rang through his head. Something he said was gnawing at Mitch's thoughts. What was it he said about feeling and thinking? Ah yes, now he remembered. Thinking people end up laughing and feeling people end up crying. Mitch could see the wisdom in that. He had all these years been feeling the horrors of the past and feeling the vengeance of the present. It had all started changing when he started thinking about the present. Now Stan had made him think about the past as well.

The Simmons had caused their own end, Mitch mused, or was it their parents that had instilled the behavior? The end result was messy, with a fight over the remains in the wrong religion's graveyard. Finally, the only witness left was an old gardener who found it all rather amusing. And he had an Irish mother to boot. As Mitch sat there in the quiet, a big smile began to form on his face. He was beginning to think at last. As he stood up and made for the door, he pulled a five pound note out of his pocket and pushed it through the slot of the collection box.

That must be the final betrayal, he thought, as he strode back to his car. Bunging IRA funds into a Prods' collection box. Jesus, he laughed out loud. I'll be excommunicated as well as shot. There's no hope left.

As he drove through the lanes of Oxfordshire, he tried to see the people as possibly being as mixed-up in their heritage as Stan Hood's relatives. It made him feel much more relaxed, and he started to concentrate on how he was going to steal the money and the Mephistos from his ex-colleagues.

The round trip had taken Mitch nearly two weeks by the time he alighted from British Midland Airways flight 3546. He had eventually tired of his holiday, and now he felt the need to progress with his plans as soon as possible. The time had been well spent, and his contacts with ordinary English people, together with his revelations at the Oxford churchyard, had encouraged a change in him. He believed that, at the tender age of forty-five, he had become a thinker.

He occasionally felt the old knee-jerk reaction of so many years, particularly when he heard the upper-class English accent that was so synonymous with the ruling class. It seemed important to him to come to some rationalization of his early struggles. Without such an understanding, his former life would just be seen as a fruitless round of violence and terror. In fact, he had genuinely tried to make his people free from a recognized oppressor.

Over the years, however, these same oppressors had in themselves become victims of a false tradition that ruled them, rather than the other way around. In Stan Hood's words, it was all a mess, but at least he could now recognize it and feel good about his escape. Into the bargain, he would also come out with enough money to survive, and dash the hopes of the wilder elements. He just needed to hang on long enough.

As usual, as he stepped off the plane, it was raining. 'Welcome back, Mitchell,' he said to himself as he followed the line of passengers into the terminal buildings. Once again, there were several signs of the struggle that had been going on for so many years. Soldiers strolled around with guns on display, and barricades had been erected to stop any vehicle from crashing into the actual building. Also, Mitch could spot several one-way mirrors where hidden eyes, watched all the people as they moved from plane to terminal and back. He knew he had undoubtedly been spotted, but coming in meant that whatever he was doing over there had been done. There was nothing more that could be gleaned by the forces of law and order.

From the airport, he had to cover his tracks and so, as usual, on such a mission, he took a taxi and headed downtown to Belfast itself. Here, he could take a variety of routes to his home or to the new headquarters, which had moved once again since his departure two weeks before.

The countryside was as green and as damp as ever. Some of the early summer heat had gone, and Ulster had settled once more into its customary grayness. The fields had a more scattered look than in England and he could recognize the cultural difference in the two societies as his Vauxhall taxi sped through the roads towards the city.

Entering the built-up areas, Mitch caught sight of the bombed-out pubs and filling stations that seemed to be on most street corners. Long ago, they had been cemented over to cause eyeless memorials to the violence of two and a half decades. Compared to the orderliness of England itself, this place looked like a poor, tired and battered city. The population, too, looked stooped and worn out as they hurried from shop to shop or about their duties. Even the man driving the taxi had a pressed-down look as he slumped in his seat. It's great to be home, thought Mitch sarcastically.

The taxi dropped him at a large office block that had four doorways. Mitch hurried inside. Today, instead of rushing out of one of the other doors and taking a different street, he carried his tote bag up two flights of stairs to an unmarked office. It was here that a friendly lawyer allowed 'travelers' to sit for awhile, make phone calls or just be seen to be 'respectable'.

Mitch knew the secretary, sitting as custodian outside the glass door. He had taken her out a few years back. Her father had been killed by some RUC (Royal Ulster Constabulary) toughs, and she had been bent on revenge when Sean Ferguson, Esquire found her, and offered her a job as his assistant. Over the years, her anger had settled into a sort of dumb throb, and she had became a plump, rather matronly woman, in her late thirties, with a fondness for cream donuts and port wine.

'How's it going, Alice?' Mitch greeted her cheerfully.

Their union had not been successful, but neither of

them felt betrayed by the lack of passion. Anyway it had been what? More then ten years ago, he thought. Alice smiled up from her typewriter.

'Just the usual, Mitch. How about you?'

Mitch noticed that she had put on some more weight and her complexion was not as fresh as he remembered. No doubt the donuts were taking their toll.

'He's on the phone at the moment.' She gestured with her head towards the fluted glass door, where Mitch could see the slight movement of the lawyer pacing around near his desk.

'It's okay, Alice, I just need to use the phone.'

She pointed with a pencil at the instrument that sat between them, and Mitch dialed the line that would connect him with their central command.

'O'Doule,' he said sharply to the voice at the other end of the line. 'Send the truck to Fergy's. Right.'

As he put the phone down, Alice looked up again.

'You don't waste a lot of time on pleasantries, do you?'

'You never know who's listening, Alice,' he replied. 'Look after yourself,' he called to her, as he went back into the corridor.

She waved absently to him, while continuing her lawyer's work.

Nice woman, thought Mitch as he went out of the office. Too bad about her dad. Just another damned casualty in this nonsense.

He climbed down the stairs and stood inside the door looking through the smeared panes into the street. It was ten minutes before the dark green windowless van pulled up outside. A back door opened, and Mitch carried his bag into its anonymous interior.

Taffy O'Brian was at the wheel. Even though it was only eleven, there was a strong smell of whiskey in the vehicle. Taffy obviously did not care if he was stopped by the police.

'So you're back with the boys again, are you?'

Taffy was his normal friendly self, but then he always was, even when he was shooting suspects in the legs.

'We missed you. These new young fellows just don't have the same ideas. Always wanting to step things up. Cause a bigger shock to the system. Doesn't suit my old bones, I suppose.'

'Come on, Taff,' Mitch replied round the Players that he was attempting to light in the bumping van. 'You're only thirty-eight or nine, aren't you?'

'Thirty-nine it is, Mitch, but I feel a hell of a lot older. I think it must be the struggles I've been through.'

Mitch exhaled a chestful of smoke and stared out of the rain-streaked windscreen. Taffy was probably the laziest member of the war council. He rarely did much apart from sit, sipping his Bushmills and dispensing advice. Still, on the surface, he was easy to get along with, and not a direct danger to Mitch's seditious plans.

'Where we going, Taff?'

'The new place. You'll like it. It has what you might call real ambiance.'

'What do you mean by that?'

'Don't worry, you'll find out. We're almost there.'

The van was now in the section of the city near the docks. Mostly it contained warehouses and distribution centers. It was run down, and had few people about, as Taffy pulled into a yard, climbed out, and slammed the door closed behind him. Mitch followed him inside the stark building. There was a strong smell of fish.

'What the hell is this place, Taffy?' he asked. 'Smells like a herring boat in the summer.'

'We were overdue to move, and this was all we could get in the short term. The other one fell through. You get used to it eventually. It's been closed for a year too. Just imagine what it must have smelled like when it was active.'

They climbed some iron stairs and entered into a small room that was crammed with their usual table, chairs and charts. As far as that went, nothing had changed. Matt was even on hand to wave them through into the inner sanctum. Mike Ryan was sitting in his noisy chair as usual and glared at Mitch as he entered.

'So, how's the holidaymaker? Good time with the Brits then?'

'I'm fine, thanks,' Mitch replied, curtly. 'How's it going here. Any action?'

Mike lit a cheroot, and pointed at the map in front of him.

'Caught a couple of Prods the other night. Right here, near Doughalls Farm.'

He pointed with a yellow-stained finger at the map in front of him.

'They were trying to smuggle some plastic over from the Republic. We beat the shit out of them, stole the goods and sent them on their way with stained trousers. Apart from that we've been fairly quiet. So tell us about the visit with the mysterious woman. Did you fuck her, then?'

Mitch found Mike's tone and general attitude to be as offensive as ever. He had steeled himself for the sort of reception that he would get and the sort of tasteless comments as well. God, he thought. Was I ever as bad as these idiots?

'Sorry to report she was not quite my cup of tea.'

'Not many of 'em are, from what I've heard.'

'Just what does that mean, Mike?'

Mike stared out of his squeaking chair and mumbled, 'Nothing, nothing.'

Mitch gave a report on the way the system operated. That the woman – whom he kept nameless, for some unfathomed reason – made all the contacts. The buyers would meet their opposite numbers as soon as the arrangements were down to the final part. The money would be handed over in two chunks, half when they were satisfied that the goods were what were required and in working order, and the second half on delivery. All the details would be agreed beforehand. Delivery would be anywhere the customer wished.

Matt came in with a tray of coffee and tea. There was a Bushmills provided for Taffy, who took it gratefully and swallowed down half. He looked as if he would have swallowed all of it if there had not been no one else around.

'You do realize the amount they want is going to pretty nearly wipe us out?'

Mike Ryan sat back, recalling the hurried phone conversation of a couple of weeks earlier. He looked at Mitch through half-closed eyes.

'What about some funding afterwards?'

Mitch gave the analogy of the bankers only lending the umbrella when it was sunny, and everybody nodded in agreement.

'It was not my idea to go this route, I might remind you all. You don't have to do it. But if it's still on, then I don't think we have too much choice. Without Mephistos, you'll never compile enough explosive to do the job. In order to affect the entire population, you need to hit every center. That will take about a hundred units. That's a lot of stuff, and the price is one million dollars. That's all there is to it.'

There was a pause while Matt came in and took out the tray for refills. Then Taffy and Mike began with the questions about how, what and when. It was all pretty predictable – including the suggestion that the complete council reconvene the next day to make a final decision. With little else to discuss, the meeting then broke up.

Matt had arranged for Mitch's Fiesta to be brought over to the new headquarters, and it was mid-afternoon when he settled himself into its damp interior, for the drive back to

Ballyhean. His flat was still in its same lonely situation, and Mitch was again aware of how much he was looking forward to leaving this whole scene. It was empty, pointless and disturbing.

After he had unpacked his few belongings, he called his Aunty Kate and told her that he was well. He also told her he would like to have the letters that had come from his ancestor. She agreed to put them in an envelope and post them to him that evening, before the last collection.

It was an odd sensation giving his address to anyone. Once again, he was reminded of how even simple things had passed him by. The only mail that ever came to his various addresses were of the canvassing nature. The other stuff, mostly bills, was forwarded automatically to Ferguson in the city.

Having put the phone down, Mitch tried to think of when he had last used his own address. He couldn't think of a time. He hoped that it would not be long before he could enter the normal realms of society and behave like everybody else – have parties, a listed phone number, maybe even a business card.

The next day, the whole war council met in the fish-tainted premises down at the docks. Conny Fitzherbert sat staring ahead with his maniacal grin, Bryan Flynn looked moodily at the map in front of him, Taffy drew little marks on the table with the condensation off the glass of Bushmills, and Mike Ryan gave off his usual malevolence.

'God, what a crowd,' Mitch thought, as he came through the door.

Smiling broadly at them all, he asked Matt for a cup of tea and sat between Taffy and Bryan.

'You've all heard the terms, I suppose,' he began. 'So are there any initial reactions apart from the fact that it's a hell of a lot of fucking money?'

Connie and Mike both began to speak at the same time.

Mike won out and played the part of the elder statesman, no doubt to impress his importance on the juniors there.

'We don't have a lot of choice, do we? If we're going to go this route, then we have to have the bombs. Apparently, if we make a success of the missions, and we're good little boys, the sand jockeys will float us for a few more dollars. That's always assuming that the funds in the States dry up. Which the senior colonel here believes.'

The last comment was made with his customary sneer. Connie broadened his grin and shuffled around in his chair.

'When can we do the jobs?'

Bryan Flynn shook himself out of his customary silence and looked balefully at Mitch.

'That's Mike's side of the operation, Bryan. I get the bombs, he places them.'

For the next two hours, they all pored over maps of the various cities across the sea that would receive the fury of the oppressed people whom these five men felt they represented. Mitch played his role on automatic pilot. He found it fairly easy. After all, he had been playing the part and believing it all his adult life, so to continue was very natural. Of course, the inner belief had now completely disappeared, and he was left with the realization that these men were all, in their own ways, psychopaths. Again, it gave him a chill.

At one o'clock, Matt brought in a huge pile of ham sandwiches and several bottles of beer. The talk began to refocus on the old stories of the heroes of the movement. Jobs that had been accomplished, escapes that had been engineered, and explosions that had caused millions of pounds of damage were all picked over for the umpteenth time. Mitch noticed that Bryan and Connie played little part in these discussions.

Yes, he thought, you boys are just in it for the violence

aren't you? Not for you the glory of shaking off the colonialist's yoke, or for proclaiming freedom for your land. For you, it's just the violence and the joy of horror.

Once lunch was over, Mitch suggested some firm arrangements be made to acquire the Mephistos. He suggested they try to arrange viewing of the devices as soon as possible, explaining he had left the matter up in the air until they had all reached agreement. Mike Ryan, being nearest the door, called for Matt to bring a phone with a speaker attachment.

'You'd better make the call, Mitch. You've no problems letting us here know what goes on, I suppose.'

'I'll be glad to drop out of the whole thing if you feel a better deal can be struck,' Mitch shot back. He knew apart from Taffy, who seemed to have sold his soul to a distillery, there was no experience among the group at dealing overseas. He let the question hang in silence for a long time. No dissenting voice was heard, so Mitch dialed the first of the numbers that Margitte had given him.

There was an atmosphere of anticipation as the connection was made after the customary clicks and silences. A tinny ringing sound came over the wire, and it rang for about fifteen seconds before it was picked up. Margitte's voice sounded breathless. Maybe she had been outside, maybe sunbathing naked. Mitch tried to take the image out of his mind and concentrate on the conversation.

'I'm with my friends. We need to see the items we discussed. When can we do that?'

'It will take some fixing. There are many people to contact. Also a lot of arrangements.'

'Can we cover most of it over the phone, right now?'

'That's not possible. If you have the funds, we need to meet.'

Margitte sounded very businesslike. There was no room for misunderstanding and, out of the corner of his eye, he could see the other four, leaning intently towards the small black box as it amplified the sound through the battered room. He let another silence ensue, and then said, 'Hold on a minute.'

Disconnecting the sound box, he held his hands over the mouthpiece of the handset.

'I think I can get this moving along, if you want. I'll go back over. This woman is greedy, and she trusts me.'

Mike Ryan was about to make one of his distasteful comments but Mitch turned his pale eyes full bore on him and the remark stuck in the other man's throat.

Lifting the receiver to his ear Mitch said, 'I'll come over if it's necessary.'

Margitte's tones through the regular earpiece sounded more her normal warm self, and the sunburnt image came through to Mitch's mind once again. It was not unpleasant.

'I think that would be good. Do you have the other number I gave you? Well, come to Truro and call me the day after tomorrow. Understood?'

Mitch agreed and hung up.

'She wants to meet down in Cornwall, the day after tomorrow. Anybody fancy a trip?'

As he expected, there were no takers, which was a relief, as he had the germ of an idea forming, the execution of which would depend on the absence of any witnesses from here.

The next day, Mitch received his package from Aunty Kate. There was no note inside, just a wrapping of tissue around the six yellowed letters inside the envelope. He sat down and once again examined the writing from the men whose fortunes were somehow so tied up with his future.

The coincidence of his having visited Bucklers Hard was one thing, but the proximity of Truro to the second letter's location of Falmouth was too close for comfort. Mitch was not a superstitious man, apart from throwing salt over his shoulder and not walking under ladders, but there was something eerie about his following in his great-great-great-grandfather's footsteps. Also the fact that he was going to try and escape to Australia, where the last letter had originated, caused him to read the thin script again with even more interest.

In view of the importance of his visit, Mitch was flown back to England on a private plane. It was a small American-built twin-engined machine that pitched and yawed horribly on the journey over to Bristol. There, another hire car had been organized and, once in front of the wheel, he turned towards the south, taking the M5 in the direction of Plymouth.

The heatwave seemed to be over. There was a streaking of mackerel skies as his Ford Escort ate up the miles. It was still holiday time and there were numerous caravans being pulled to their destinations by cars crammed with bored-looking occupants. Far off in the distance, the light gave hope that the summer was not yet over, and Mitch settled back to enjoy the passing scenery.

As it was a Sunday, the church bells were in evidence by the time the Escort pulled up at the Trust House hotel in Truro. It was a quiet town, and the tolling of the bells seemed to create an even quieter atmosphere. Mitch took a quick shower and made his way to the cocktail bar. Giving his room number to the barman, he carried his drink to the small wooden box that served as the payphone. The bare light bulb made it hot inside, as he sat on the wooden bench and dialed the number. Margitte answered straight away.

'I was waiting for you, Mitch. Are you tired?'

'Not really, but the journey was not the best I've ever had.'

He thought back momentarily to the buffeting that he had received, and the bouncing landing that seemed to take at least four lurches before the plane came under control.

'I assume you're on your own. I'm sure I could hear all those heavies breathing around you last time we spoke.'

Mitch assured her that he was on his own, with no heavies, as she called them.

'Good, I was looking forward to seeing you again.' The accent seemed heavier once she came out of her business-woman role. 'Do you want to meet tomorrow? It's a bit late tonight.'

Mitch said that would be fine, and where would be a good spot? Margitte suggested her hotel once more.

'It's called the Trethawnton, in St Mawes. It's rather exclusive, and quite difficult to find unless you happen to know where it is.'

'It would obviously appeal to your sense of mystery, Margitte. Why don't you give me the details?'

She explained how the hotel sat back from the main road going down into the little town. It had a doorway in the wall that was easy to miss. The car park was way around in the back, so it would be easier to park in the village and walk from there. She suggested eleven o'clock.

'I can't think where this Saint Mawes is,' Mitch said. 'This is not a part of the country I've ever been to. Can you give me directions?'

'Oh, you can't go wrong. It's across the harbor from the port of Falmouth. 'Bye.'

Mitch hung up and swallowed his drink which had become warm. Falmouth. Immediately, he saw the name written in spidery writing on the yellowed parchment wrapped in tissue paper back in his flat.

He left the telephone box and went back into the bar. He decided not to dwell on the coincidence. This was a very small part of the country anyway, so the name of Falmouth was certain to have come up, if only on a sign-post somewhere.

What was really more important was the scheme he had been turning over in his mind. If he could bring it off, he would accomplish several things. He would steal enough money to start afresh, put a serious dent in the plans of a bunch of pathological killers, wreck their future plans to draw in the other maniacs in the world, and start a new and normal life for himself. It was a big list, but he knew if he could make one small connection, he would be able to pull it off. He needed an accomplice.

The following morning, Mitch dressed in a casual outfit of jeans, plain green T-shirt and a windcheater. With a pair of well-worn sneakers, he looked like any of the scores of tourists who were emptying onto the streets of the small town of Truro.

The town was waking up and going about its normal business at the start of the week. The drive to St Mawes was only going to take about half an hour so he had plenty of time to look about. Shops were full of those slightly unfashionable garments that seemed to be popular this far away from the capital. The weather had turned cooler, and shoppers seemed to take less time as they went from business to business on their various errands.

Mitch found himself near the Anglican cathedral, and hearing the comforting strains of the organ, he decided to go in. He took a small booklet from the dark mahogany case at the door and sat quietly at the back on a padded chair. He smiled at the realization that this was the second time in a few days he had been in a Protestant church. I'll be converting at this rate, he thought ruefully.

The sounds of one of Bach's preludes rolled around the stone recesses. It gathered itself like waves and poured over the surfaces of harsh masonry. Scanning the information sheet, Mitch was amazed to find that the cathedral was modern. It was only completed in 1920 rather than back in medieval times. He found himself approving the style, as he hated attempts to modernize something as traditional as a place of worship. Years ago, he had visited the Catholic cathedral in Liverpool and thought at the time that there was nothing right about it.

He, himself, was a traditionalist. As he sat, letting the organ's inspiration wash over him in the empty cathedral, he once again had the feeling that his whole life had been a lie, based on untruths and empty political statements. He wanted out so badly that if he could have escaped, he would have walked out of the cathedral and out of this life now. As it was, he needed the money to escape, and he needed the knowledge that he had stopped the killing of many thousands of innocent lives.

He checked his watch and decided to hear what the organist would play next. He had a little knowledge of music, having been an altar boy when he was very small. Part of his duties was to assist around the parish church, and he was often there during the organ practice of the good Mr Perigrine Walters. He remembered the fat little man who would roll about on his seat, while pulling out the stops and dancing his plump feet across the slatted pedals.

With a crash, the cathedral's organ stopped and the silence grew as the last notes echoed into oblivion. Mitch could hear some words up in the loft where the invisible player no doubt turned the pages of his score. A random few notes were played and then the quiet sound of 'Sheep May Safely Graze' came filtering through.

The remembrance of Mr Perigrine Walters was complete, as this was a piece he had often played. As he sat there, Mitch was transported back to his childhood, to a time when things were so much easier to understand. He closed his eyes and reveled in the luxury of his memories. He forgot for a moment the strain of the last few weeks, and the dangers of the future. When the music stopped, he had to force his eyes open and accept once more the responsibilities and the problems of his situation.

Wearily, he stood up and began to leave. With no more music, he could hear his own soft footsteps as he left the nave. Once again, he put some money into the collection box and replaced the information sheet in the rack.

'It's all right, you can keep it.' A small woman in a black outfit spoke from behind the display. Mitch had not noticed her before.

'She's a wonderful organist, isn't she?'

Surprised, Mitch smiled. Somehow, he had not thought of the music as emanating from a female. Just one more change in the world to adapt to, rang through his mind, as he headed back to the hotel.

At ten thirty, he drove down through the Cornish lanes towards St Mawes. Many of the roads were sunk below the level of the fields, so that it was impossible to see over the banks. There was no rain but there was a grayness about the sky that looked uncertain.

God, I hope it's sunny in Australia, he thought, as he negotiated the wildly turning roads.

Eventually, he arrived at the outskirts of his destination. There was a small round castle that stood sentinel over a large expanse of water. No doubt put there by the English authorities, to guard what Mitch realized was Falmouth harbor.

'So Paddy,' he said quietly, 'our paths cross again. I wonder what you and your friend, Chipper, were up to all those years ago?'

He drove down into the little town and saw the doorway that Margitte had spoken of the previous night. Parking, he could see, was at a premium. He tried several side streets, but each one had been decorated with infamous double yellow lines, and lacked even one courageous motorist to start a trend. At least it kept the traffic, such as it was, moving. Returning once more to the main street, Mitch could see a red car backing out of a spot. Accelerating, he pushed in front of another motorist who was intent on pushing in front of Mitch for the same place. 'Screw you, feller,' he mouthed, as he raced across the other man's front fender.

'Even down here, it's all push and shove,' Mitch mumbled to himself. He slammed the door, noting that there was only parking for one hour, and walked back up the hill.

One or two businesses were modern tourist-type shops, but St Mawes looked as if it had not changed much over the centuries. The pubs that stood discreetly back from the twisting, steep, little side streets looked down on mostly local people. Apart from their outerwear, Mitch felt the people must have seemed the same to Granddad Paddy, if he had made the journey across the bay from Falmouth.

A clock struck eleven o'clock as he reached the doorway that led to the discreet Hotel Trethawnton. At least he gave the appearance of being efficient with his timekeeping, Mitch thought, as he entered the plush reception area. He asked for Ms Ledenfeld and was shown the house phone so he could call the room directly. As before, Margitte answered the call immediately. She told him to wait a few minutes, and then she came down, somewhat out of breath.

'It's a long way from the rooms here,' she said, 'but it's a wonderful hotel.'

She was wearing a short top in her customary yellow. Like Mitch, she also sported a pair of faded jeans, and she carried a large purse over her bare shoulder. Her tan was again very evident. Mitch got up out of the chair and she kissed him lightly on the cheek. Putting her arm through his, she turned him towards the door, acting the part of someone going out on a day's date.

'How have you been, Mitch?' she asked, as they went

out into the street. She disengaged her arm as they were forced to lean into the wall to allow a screaming, under-powered motorcycle to pass them.

'Oh, the usual routine of blowing things and people up,' he replied with a heavy sarcastic tone. 'Nothing much changes where I'm from.'

'Let's have a drink, shall we?' Margitte suggested, and they turned up one of the small side streets, where a hanging sign proclaimed a pub called The Standard. It was cramped and dark inside, although the management had tried to modernize the place by resorting to the now all-pervasive plastic and Formica.

They both ordered some whiskey and accepted the Scottish type when the publican could not locate any Irish. There were a couple of old men at the bar talking in beery gulps, so they took their drinks over to the small bay window that shared the daylight with the houses across the narrow divide.

'So, this is another of your haunts, is it?'

'Yes. I love Cornwall, and particularly this area. It's completely different from anywhere else in England. But you probably don't like anyplace this side of the water at all, do you? No doubt it reminds you of the struggle against the oppressor.' Her tone was flat and lacking in sarcasm.

'In fact, I like the countryside very much,' he replied. 'After I left you the last time, I toured for about ten days. I saw a lot of wonderful places and learned a lot.' He was about to tell her about his lesson on Anglo-Irish affairs outside Oxford when the two men let out a loud laugh. He thought better of it and sipped his Scotch.

'You've not been down here before, then?' she asked.

On hearing that it was his first time, she told him a little of the history as they sat in the dark pub. They ordered another round, and she suggested that if he were not in a hurry, she could show him some of the other places round about. The two old men were joined by a third and then a fourth. It seemed from the comments that this was a regular meeting point for them. Silently, Margitte and Mitch finished their drinks, feeling like the outsiders that they most certainly were. As they left The Standard, she held him back for a moment. The street was deserted and there was no sound of traffic around them. There was just the soft noise of the water lapping at the edge of the small harbor at the bottom of the street.

'This is a very old place, Mitch, and when it's quiet like this, you can almost imagine the smugglers riding through the town, can't you? There is an old poem about them: Four and twenty horsemen, riding through the dark / Brandy for the postman, tobacco for the clerk. / Them that ask no questions never hear a lie, / So watch the wall my darlings, while the gentlemen ride by.

'It's all about the smuggling that used to happen here. Apparently, everybody was at it, so the children were told never to look at the men riding by; they might see the squire or the priest or anyone. If you got in the way, you were dead. It was the big growth industry, until the Customs and Excise men managed to get control of it all.'

They reached the Escort and Mitch peeled off the parking ticket that had become affixed after his one hour was over. It would be another problem for Mr Ferguson to have to solve.

Margitte directed him out of the town through the one-way system and into the countryside. He asked her about the harbor at Falmouth, and she told him it was the deepest berthing in Europe, much used by shipping in the old days.

'The resort is not worth visiting these days, though. Just another industrial backwater. I never go there. Always stay this side.'

As they sped along the narrow lane, Mitch physically began to unwind in Margitte's company. She was an ideal, glamorous companion, and the confusion of her femininity, mixed up with his present mission had already faded as they immersed themselves in the local scenery.

'If you look through the trees there, you can see some of the ships in storage.'

Mitch nearly lost control of the vehicle, as he saw some huge funnels through the foliage right next to the road.

'Careful,' Margitte said, as he wrestled the small car back on course.

Involuntarily she put her hand over his on the steering wheel. Her touch was warm and dry.

'They do look out of place, don't they. They've just been left there until someone wants to buy them, I think. I always think they look so sad. Like great landed birds with their wings cut.'

Mitch had to agree that seeing such large ocean-going vessels moored inland like that was a pretty unusual sight, and he made sure that he kept his wits about him as he negotiated the winding route. Margitte slowly removed her hand from his. He missed its presence.

Eventually, they arrived at a small inn. It was covered in roses and had white metal tables and chairs in its neatly trimmed garden. The sun had begun to break through, and so they agreed to sit outside. Margitte knew the place quite well, and the little dog behind the bar recognized her and demanded to be let out.

'You really are a regular here, aren't you?' Mitch said, as they took their drinks back out through the door. 'Even the old man at the bar gave you a smile. The one with the big side-whiskers.'

'Oh, you mean the captain,' she said. 'He knows me because I took his chair one day. He always sits at that same place, and I inadvertently took it when he went to the bathroom. The landlord was off that day; otherwise he would have warned me. When the old man came back, I thought he was giving me the eye. It turned out that he always sits there, and he was upset. One of the locals had to put me right. It's funny how these little traditions stay in a place like this. Times come and go, but people like the captain seem to go on for ever. It's the same back in Holland, particularly around the seaports. Perhaps it's the tradition of the sea that keeps things from changing.'

A tall young man with a bobbing pigtail came out with two plates of smoked mackerel. He put them down on the table and asked if they needed anything else. Mitch cocked an eye at Margitte's whiskey glass and she indicated that a refill would be fine. After it was brought and Mitch had paid, he began to ask her questions about their business together.

Between mouthfuls of fish and salad, she explained again that the money had to be paid in two parts. She would contact the necessary people who would agree to make the shipments of the goods wherever requested. Half the funds would be required on examination of the items, and the remaining half on shipment. There would be no negotiation.

Margitte and Mitch must have looked like any other couple out for a day. Her tone was demure, and his interest focused, as she explained it all again to him. Her contacts had huge resources behind them, and asked few questions. She had made an initial inquiry, but so far she had not indicated to them where her other party was from, or what the nature of their business was. This was just in case Mitch and his organization changed their minds.

Mitch found it unsettling to be hearing these types of plans coming from such an elegant and innocent-seeming woman. The waiter returned several times and on each occasion replenished their glasses. Since their visit to The Standard, they had consumed quite a large quantity of Scotch, and Mitch's eyes were beginning to follow a split second after his head turned. Margitte seemed to be unaffected, but he couldn't really tell.

There seemed to be little else to discuss in regard to the plans. Mitch's team had to present half a million in cash, at the appointed time and the appointed place, as yet to be decided. Margitte's people would, in their turn, provide working samples of the Mephistos, for demonstration. Delivery would be agreed, then the second payment would be handed over at the point of departure, or possibly the point of arrival. Nothing else was needed except money, and the fate of thousands would be sealed. What a ghastly business, he thought.

Mitch drank the last of his Scotch and caught the waiter's eye for more. In spite of the macabre circumstances, he was feeling good.

Margitte declined another, saying, 'I think you'd better leave the driving to me this afternoon. I know these lanes pretty well. There are virtually no police in this area, but it wouldn't look well to have the colonel caught at the wheel of a car, imbedded in a Cornish lane, would it?'

Mitch agreed he was most certainly the worse for wear, but he didn't get like that very often. In fact, he thought that what he wanted most was a cup of strong coffee. Margitte said that she knew just the place and she would take him.

She handled the car well. The bends were sharp, and Mitch's head lolled around as she turned the wheel firmly to and fro. He found the movement somehow sensuous and soporific. He allowed his head to rest against the window, and his drooping eyes would catch glimpses of the miniature Cornish countryside. The lanes again were often sunk below the level of the fields and showed the great age of the area. It was even smaller than his homeland, and once again, Mitch found himself wondering about the conflict between the two peoples. It no longer made sense from the swaying car.

He must have dozed off, as he came to with a jerk when Margitte put the handbrake on. They were in a small car park.

'Come on, you look like you need that coffee,' and slipping out of the driver's seat, she came round and pulled on his arm, kicking the door shut behind her.

They walked down a narrow path and through a glass door. It was only then that Mitch realized that they were back at her hotel once more. In spite of its obvious upper-class air, there was a musty smell about the place, that even air fresheners could not hide completely.

Margitte led him up a flight of stairs and into a bright airy room that overlooked the harbor. The furniture was light oak, well-upholstered and expensive.

'I'll make some coffee for you,' she said. Kicking off her shoes, she filled a kettle from the bathroom, and set it on a small table that was loaded with tea and coffee things. 'You looked all in after lunch, so I decided this was the best place for you. I hope you don't mind.'

Mitch stood up and looked out of the window at the bay. It was a big piece of water, and off in the distance he could hear the sound of a mechanical hammer clanking its rhythmic message. Margitte came and stood beside him. Without her shoes, she seemed a little less imposing.

'You like the view?'

'Yes, I was thinking about someone.'

'A woman back in Ireland, no doubt?'

'No, there isn't one of those. No, I was thinking about someone I never met. He was my great-great-great-grandfather. I have a letter from him mailed from somewhere around here.'

'What was an Irishman doing way down here? I assume he was an Irishman?'

'Oh, yes he was Irish all right'

'What was he doing way over here?'

'I don't really know. He was in the royal navy. Maybe he had been captured. Nobody knows.'

The kettle began a high-pitched whistle.

'Let me turn that off. Do you want coffee or tea? You can see, they really spoil you here.'

'I think I prefer tea.'

'You're in luck. I actually have Irish breakfast tea. It's a bit late in the day but let's try it.'

Mitch returned his gaze to the view as Margitte bothered with pouring water into the china pot.

'I have to let it stand for a bit, I think,' she said and came back to him at the window.

Her perfume rose and, quite without thinking, he put his arms around her and kissed her strongly on the lips. Her arms came up around his neck and they stood kissing in front of the window for long enough for Mitch to remember that he had been drinking. The combination of that and her perfume was making him feel unbalanced. He wanted to lift her up, but doubted that he could accomplish the feat without causing damage to himself or dropping her, or both. He therefore pulled her gently over to the bed and lay down.

The tea was virtually stone cold when they finished. As she rose up from the bed, completely naked, he could see that, apart from a small pale line around her hips, her tan went all over her. It was a marvelous sight. He lay back luxuriously and watched her empty the teapot and start a new process.

'Are you happy with the view?'

'It's even better than the one outside.'

Margitte showed no trace of embarrassment as she went about the large room. Having made the tea once more, she came over to the bed and settled back, plumping up some cushions behind both their heads.

'So how long had you been planning that little move, Mr Colonel in the IRA?' she asked slyly, as she sipped her hot tea.

'I never planned anything at all,' he answered guiltily. 'I might ask the same question of you.'

'Well, I won't deny that I took more than a professional interest in you from the moment that we met, but it was you that started it.'

'Why is it that women always seem to want to know who started what?'

'I expect that you've had more than enough experience to know women's ways, so I won't get into an argument.'

Mitch tried to drink his tea, but it was much too hot.

'Look, I really am not the ladies' man that you think. To prove it, I'm going to do something so gross you'll realize that I'm straight out of the bogs.'

'Oh, so you know even more little tricks, do you?' she purred.

But in answer, he merely poured his tea carefully into the saucer and proceeded to blow on it.

'Real working-class, you see.' Gently he poured the tea back into the cup and began to drink it. 'But not lower working-class. Lower working-class would drink it out of the saucer. My mam would never have stood for that.'

Margitte watched the whole operation with interest.

'I've never seen anybody do that before. But why is it working-class? It seems very practical.'

'I can't tell you why precisely. I just know it's wrong. Sort of one of those things that one is born with.'

'Like why the Protestants hate the Catholics, and the Irish hate the English, I suppose.' She said it with a smile but the subject made Mitch visibly stiffen. She noticed and pushed herself closer to him. 'It's okay, Mitchell. I was only joking.'

'I'm sorry, but some things run very deep, you know.'

She pulled the cream-colored sheet up, and tucked it over her tanned breasts. Mitch deeply resented the loss of view and was about to say something, when her next words stopped him dead in his tracks.

'So exactly when are you going to tell me the truth about all this?'

Mitch said nothing. He just lay still and stared ahead.

'Well?' she continued, 'I know something's wrong, so you better tell me what it is.'

Mitch got up from the bed and went over to his jeans, lying in a twisted knot on the floor. He fished around for his packet of Player's, and then started the hunt for the matches.

'Look, Mitch, I know who you are and what you stand for. Or rather what you should stand for. Maybe I should explain who I am, and why I think something's wrong. Very wrong. And do stop fiddling around with that cigarette and come back into bed with me.'

Her voice had a commanding ring to it, and Mitch found himself complying with little resentment.

'You know I am Dutch and that I put deals together. All of that is true. Also, you know I am not very involved with causes and other foolish reasons why men fight each other. I just act as a mediator. Well, that was not always the case.

'I was brought up in a standard middle-class home with a private education. But until the age of fifteen, it all took place in Indonesia. My father was a business man spending half his time with the Dutch and half with the Indonesians. He was a trader and did very well out of those relationships.

'Unfortunately, he put all his money into real estate and bought a lot of land in Molucca. Somehow the title to the land was transferred, and we lost everything. It was supposed to be sorted out by the Dutch government but by the time we arrived back in Holland, almost penniless, my father fell sick and died. I've always believed it was the strain, but it was probably one of those tropical diseases the West never fully understands.

'Some months later, my mother contracted pneumonia in the damp climate, and after a spell in a nursing home, she too died, leaving me alone with a host of bills, and no way to pay them.'

Mitch poured them both another cup of tea and said, 'It's the sort of story that many an Irishman could tell. Different locations, of course.'

'Well, your people don't have the exclusive rights on tragedy, you know. It happens everywhere. So, anyway, there I was, orphaned, sixteen and broke, when a man called Julian arrived at my door. He was half-Moluccan and half-Dutch. He was about twenty-three, very potent, very sexy and a terrorist. I fell in love with him within half an hour.

'He had come to call, as he wanted to persuade my family to donate funds to his movement. They were in the process of trying to force the Dutch government to accept responsibility for the territory and help the people whom they had once controlled. Sort of the reverse of what you are trying to do. He wasted no time, and took the only donation that my impoverished family still had left – me!

'I was whisked out of my middle-class colonist upbringing and plunked down into a world of dope-smoking, free-loving, violent, crazy anarchists. I loved it. Julian was the top guy and I was his woman. I was respected by the group and loved by him. It was romantic and exciting and I wanted it never to end.

'Well, after two years, Julian decided to trade me in. I never suspected anything, but obviously I was getting too old and too self-opinionated. Also, he was rather immature and needed the adulation of someone very young to flatter his ego. I found out later I was the oldest he'd had in years. Normally, they came in around fourteen and only lasted about a year. So I had had quite a few good innings.

'I didn't know I was being traded in for a newer model. I was still quite naive. However, over the previous three months, we had struck up a relationship with some Arabs, and I was being used as a courier. I had to fly out regularly to the Persian Gulf – or should I call it the Arabian Gulf now, to be politically correct? Anyway, one day in Bahrain, I was taken to a desert party.

'I had been to them before, but this one was wilder than usual. There was a lot of marijuana and camel racing, and I got caught in a bet that I would win ten thousand dollars if a certain mangy beast won. If I lost, I had to spend the night with a particular prince, who was anything but mangy. I knew him quite well, and I had always quite fancied him.

'Of course, the camel proved to have three legs and a blind jockey. The quiet prince claimed his prize. In the morning, sitting on raked sand, over a beautiful breakfast of grapefruit and strawberries eaten off English bone china, he gave me a letter from Julian. It said he was sorry, but it was over, and he hoped that I would enjoy the climate more in the Arab kingdom than I had in Holland. It's funny. I distinctly remember the taste of that breakfast and the sight of the camp with its raked sand, miles away from Manama. But I don't remember if I cried.

'Ali Mohammed Kalish spent several days comforting me. He taught me how to hunt with falcons, how to ride a camel and how to shoot a rifle. He was not a real prince, of course. He was a Palestinian. But everybody played the game and pretended that he came from royal blood. I expect he was really from a refugee camp rather than a palace, but he was kind to me, respected me and in every way was just a normal guy. Except when he started thinking or talking about Jews. Then he became irrational, violent, and almost psychotic.

'I worried that one day he would find out my last name

was Ledenfeld. I was always called Maggie Ednas or Maggie the Dutchie. After I witnessed his Jekyl and Hyde transformation, I used to lie awake worrying about him finding out I was half-Jewish and killing me in my sleep. In fact, for a period of some months I tried never to sleep when he was around me. But he never harmed me and he treated me well. I knew it wouldn't last, of course, but I was young and having a good time despite the danger.

'After a couple of years, Ali decided it was time for a change in his life. I found out he was spending time with a large Turkish dancer. Initially, I was terrified and then outraged. One evening, I stormed off to the club where she danced. When I saw her, I couldn't believe he could be interested in her. She was at least one hundred and eighty pounds. But apparently that's what he liked.

'It was time to move on. Again, he made it easy for me. He started sending me away, just as Julian had done. This time, I decided to make my own move. I found a member of the German Red Army Faction. He became my husband of seven years. Well, after a year, my husband in name only.

'By that time I had become a sort of terrorist's moll or groupie. I knew how it all fitted together, how the money and power circulated within the various organizations, and how the 'soldiers' were dealt like hands of cards. My husband was one of the chief soldiers. He didn't need an enemy to be violent. He was like that all the time. It was the killing he loved. It turned him on. He was respected because he was feared, and it was that respect that attracted me. It was also his need for violence that eventually got him killed.'

Mitch finished his tea in one swallow.

'I've met a few like that. An almost pathological need to be in some sort of permanent danger.'

Margitte nodded.

'Yes, that's it exactly. Well, I lived through that

unaffected, because by then I had grown to hate him. The process only took a few months. We stayed together but lived our separate lives. Have you ever noticed how "respectable" terrorism is within its ranks? The leaders look for the same qualities of stability and controlled morality that leaders of industry insist on. Nonetheless, as in most corporations, what goes on under the guise of respectability would make a good soap opera for American TV.

'During my life with Gunther, or rather my lack of life with him, I traveled everywhere as a courier. Sometimes I carried cash, sometimes drugs. I never got caught and I met a lot of people on both sides of the law. But I knew it was bound to come to an end. I was getting disillusioned and scared. So I looked around at what I could do.

'I could speak several languages, I was well educated and I could take shorthand, which I had learned at school. I saw an advertisement one day for stenographers for court service and applied for a training course. I passed with flying colors and became my own boss. That was three years ago. I kept up many of my old contacts, however, and although I worked in a respectable job, I offered to put some occasional deals together. They worked. For the most part.'

She got up and put on a yellow floral dressing gown. Refilling the electric kettle from the tap in the bathroom, she plugged it in once more, and then sat cross-legged on the end of the bed. Her make-up was smudged and her blonde hair was askew, but Mitch thought that she looked even more striking than the first time that he saw her. He lit another cigarette and worked hard at not interrupting her.

'During the years I was "married" to Gunther, I mixed with maybe ten or more men in the movements. I'm not proud of that, but I'm not sorry, either. After I got out, my new job meant I spent a lot of time watching people in court, studying their behavior and their voices, watching their body language, and hearing their intonations. What that experience and my earlier life have taught me is to recognize the terrorist type. I know the truth when I see it, and I also recognize an untruth. Since sixteen years of age, I have lived with, and among, men of violence and men deeply committed to terrorism. I know the type, and, Mr Colonel in the IRA, you're not it.'

The whistling of the kettle cut through her accusatory tones, but she sat quietly watching him, her eyes boring into him. Mitch felt very exposed.

'Are you going to turn that damned thing off then, Margitte?' he asked, and slowly she dragged herself off the bed, and her eyes left her quarry.

'Okay,' he said quietly, 'it's a fair cop, as they say. I better tell you my story.'

As she washed out the teacups, and performed another tea-making chore, Mitch allowed the missing piece from his plans to fall into its inevitable place.

As the sun dipped further towards the sea, turning the room into a soft pink and orange confessional, Mitch told Margitte his life story. He began with how he had lived in the north of Ireland and how he had lost his friend. He told her about the camp at Loch Neagh, and how he was weeded out as being a likely recruit by the gatherer, Brendan Murphy.

The similarities to her own experiences were really quite noticeable. There were different scenes, of course, but the excitement coming out of the loneliness of their existences was parallel. She was silent throughout the telling, but she nodded from time to time, as she recognized the paths that they had both trodden.

He told her how the movement was coming under the control of the younger element. It was an element that wanted action faster than he and his colleagues had provided before. He told her of his disillusionment and how he wanted to leave. He told her that he needed to escape without trace, or he was a dead man. And then he stopped.

The room was now becoming quite dark and Mitch put his hand on his forehead where the whiskey had left a band of pain behind the eyes. He lay back on the pillows and watched her stand up and take off the yellow wrap.

'So, now, you just need me to help you steal the money, and you'll live happily ever after.'

He rose up from his position but she was already on him.

'It's not the most original idea, you know. You fellows always forget there has to be an end to it all. And the job doesn't come with a pension. Let's talk about it over dinner. It's delicious here in the hotel, and it's not served for one hour yet. I think I can find something for us to do until then.'

Mitch forgot the pain behind his eyes.

Margitte was right. The dinner they served in the Trethawnton was delicious. It came from the tradition of the best food in most expensive English hotels, in that none of the dishes originated in England. The service was silent and unobtrusive, with a tall head-waiter directing the traffic of the serving waitresses who glided around the white linen-covered tables. There were some two dozen other diners spread around the restaurant, and Mitch and Margitte had to delay their discussion, since one couple nearby sat listening to their every word. They obliged them with a perfectly ridiculous conversation of a fictitious holiday spent touring France – a country that Mitch had never visited.

They consumed a bottle of Saint Emilion with the course of rack of lamb, and then enjoyed a half-bottle of Sauterne with a plate of éclairs. Feeling rather full but in that glow of contentment that only the newly attached can feel, they left the hotel and walked through the town. It was a perfect night for the stroll of two lovers, beside the gently splashing water, lapping across from Falmouth. Having reached the far end where Mitch had originally parked his car earlier in the day, they turned around and climbed back up the hill. Here, looking across the small Elizabethan fort and the great bay that had given safe haven to so many ships in the past centuries, Margitte broached the subject of what they both had to do.

'You won't be able to do it alone, Mitch, you know.'

'I had come to that conclusion myself a couple of weeks ago. There are too many problems in getting hold of the money. The IRA have quite a lot of funds spread around, but no one person gets to ever carry all of it. Also I have the feeling that some of my former colleagues are not as trusting as they should be. I was the one who was against their plans, after all. Then I came around, perhaps just a little too easily. Maybe they're bred suspicious where I come from.'

'Well, I think that I can solve your problems for you. I will need help from some others, but I've earned plenty of favors. Also, not all my friends come from terrorism, thank God. The method usually chosen is the way I told you at our first meeting. The bombs would be shown to you. They would be tested at some remote site, or at least a couple of them, to show they were the real goods. Then the rest of the shipment would be offered for inspection, after half the money had been handed over. The final amount would be given as the shipment leaves.'

Mitch listened intently as he watched the progress of a small fishing boat, chugging its way towards the open sea.

'So we have to grab the money somewhere along the route?'

'Yes, and we'd better make the route as complicated as

possible. Particularly if there will be more than just you.'

'I'm pretty sure you can count on that. I'd never be allowed access to half a million dollars without an escort.'

'Okay, then. Here's what we should plan for. Tomorrow we need to buy two identical briefcases. Give me two numbers where I can reach you, one official and one private. In two weeks, I will arrange for you to view the "bombs" in Holland; then the rest will take place somewhere else. You won't see me until it's over, and your friends won't know they've been had, until we've escaped. Where are we going to escape to, by the way?'

Since the final piece had dropped into place this afternoon, Mitch had known that he would have to tell her where he would be going, eventually. But having spent nearly all his life in deceitfulness, it was not hard for him to tell a convenient lie, driven as he was by such a fear of discovery.

'I thought that Spain would be a great place to visit,' he said evenly. 'Although, one wouldn't have to stay there for ever.'

The small fishing boat had disappeared from view, its dim navigation lights swallowed up by the darkness of the night, and its puttering engine still echoing across the bay.

'There's something else that needs to be in the formula, Margitte. I hope that it won't make the plan too complicated. I want the cause's new direction embarrassed. Really embarrassed, Margitte. The new order frightens me. If they continue along this new path, with new world wide partners, the next weapons could very well be nuclear. Somehow, we have to stop this and put a rift in anything that might get cooked up with potential allies.'

'That's even easier, Mitch. Right or wrong, the Irish still have a less than serious reputation in the world of international terrorism, where many are Moslem fundamentalists. The Irish reputation for strong drink frightens the purists. I think I can handle it all. But you have to get me away afterwards. I'm using up all my credit. Frankly, it's a little scary.'

The boat's engines finally gave way to complete silence and the two conspirators stood holding hands in the cool sea breeze.

'When it's over, could you ever go back to Ireland, Mitch?'

Mitch stood up and taking her hand he turned towards the hotel once again. A feeling of loss swept over him.

'No,' he said, 'never.'

Chapter Twelve

Falmouth, 1786

HMS *Distinction* limped into the port of Falmouth. As she passed under the small fort above Saint Mawes, she sounded a single gun in greeting. The fort returned her salute with one of its own, although it was no longer strictly required by the captains, who recognized the need to conserve ammunition during this time.

Distinction's recent exploits with the routing of the French runner had been reported back, and several men came out onto the battlements to watch her slow passage into the Sound of Falmouth. Captain Merryview had had all men piped up on top to present a fighting company to the citizens of the county of Cornwall. Ever mindful of his duties and also his reputation within the royal navy, he also took great pride in displaying his success.

Paddy too took pride in his efforts. He couldn't be sure that any of his shots had landed on target, but Chipper stated unequivocally that several had smacked through the foe's sides, and he was now prepared to believe it. They both stood in line with their colleagues, all enjoying their arrival with the accompanying noise and excitement. It was a grand sight drifting slowly across the open water of the harbor towards the berth and safe haven of the royal docks.

The light shone strongly out of the west as they eventually tied up at their allotted place and made all safe and secure. With the damage yet to be assessed, Captain

Merryview refused permission to all hands to go ashore that night. He again gathered everyone to congratulate them on their efforts and to warn them to be ready to assist in any help that might be necessary to prepare *Distinction* for active duty again.

'Men, there seems to be a deal of damage caused by the scurvy French, but our shipbuilders will soon make short work of the repairs and we shall be afloat again in no time. As soon as I know that we are on the right track, I will allow the normal shore leave. Oh, and Mr Belcher, no more yellow sashes for the newer recruits. They performed like professionals in battle, and I think they've earned the right to be treated like regulars.'

A small cheer went up, and the rum ration was broken out again. With the jolly sound of a fife on the upper decks, the battle-weary crew watched the night drawing in around them.

Paddy sat looking ashore as the surrounding fields gradually darkened. 'You know, Chipper,' he said, 'it looks a lot like Ireland here. I thought it was going to make me feel homesick, but after the fight this morning, my blood's up and, so help me, I'm starting to enjoy this life afloat.'

'Gawd help us,' the lively cockney replied. 'I knew it would 'appen. Gets 'em all in the end it does. Even the softest bugger starts to get a light in 'is eyes, when they've fired those big guns in anger. Well, good for you, shipmate. Still, we mustn't forget the folks back 'ome, must we. 'Ows about you get back to normal for a bit and drop yer missus a line?'

So saying, he produced a small piece of paper and a piece of quill. Using the same small cup that he had used for his rum ration, he went off to the purser's office and returned with some ink in the bottom. Paddy looked blankly at the materials and shook his head.

'Okay, mate, don't worry about it. Most of 'em 'ere can't

write either. I'll do it for you. I guess she'll get someone at the other end to read it for 'er. Same sort as we done the last time, Paddy?' he asked, and Paddy nodded in a rather distant way. He watched as Chipper put his tongue out of the corner of his mouth, and began to write.

Dear Kathy,
I am well and I miss you and all the children. I think of you always.
All my love, Paddy.

'There you are, mate.'

Chipper handed over the small strip of paper for his friend to examine, saying, 'Short and sweet.'

Paddy looked at the thin ink-blotted writing with suspicion. 'Do you think you could ever teach me to do that, Chipper?' he asked. 'I would feel a proper toff if I could write.'

'Shouldn't be too 'ard Paddy,' the little Londoner replied. 'I learned it myself off poor old Charley. He'd been taught by the monks, Gawd rest 'is soul. It's the bleedin' ink's so 'ard to get 'old of. But we'll see if we can get somethin' else.'

With the success of the ship's company, Winston had produced extra rations for the evening meal. The different sittings of men gorged themselves on pork, chicken and potatoes, washed down with beer. To follow, the ever enterprising cook had produced one of his famous puddings. It was made with flour, lard, currants and jam. He called it roly-poly and several of the men burned the roofs of their mouths as they shoveled in the sticky layers hot from the boiler.

That night, Paddy slept soundly from the moment he swung up into his hammock. It was the first time Katherine's face and the children's voices had not haunted him. In the morning, he was too busy to notice the absence, but it dawned on him slowly throughout the day. Then, he felt as if in some way he had been unfaithful to his loved ones.

After munching on some hot biscuits for breakfast, he began to help with the repairs. His job was to help one of the shore-based carpenters cut away the damage in the forward section. It was cramped and hard work. His carpenter was called Joe, and his thick Cornish accent was almost impossible for Paddy to understand. Nonetheless, in spite of the difficulty in communication, they worked happily together, engaged in a task which both understood.

Chipper joined them for their lunch and all three bit into the round pasties that the local men had brought on board. Even the cockney could not make out everything that Joe said, which surprised the Irishman. But it was very pleasant sitting staring out across the bay eating the pastry-covered peppery meat and vegetables.

Chipper had been working in the captain's stateroom during the morning, and he had some gossip to pass on. Provided they could finish the repairs inside four weeks, the *Distinction* was going to sail for the coast of Holland. There were plans to cruise outside of Amsterdam, which was allowing enemy shipping into its port. Chipper could not be sure exactly what the plan was, as the captain and his lieutenant stopped talking as soon as they realized that he was in the room.

'I tried to act dumb, like you, Paddy, but they shut up like little clams, they did.'

'I've never set foot outside of the county,' said Joe, swinging his legs over the side. 'But I suppose them foreign parts wouldn't agree with me. I don't envy you all this traveling.'

Chipper winked at Paddy and Paddy smiled.

For two weeks, the ship's company and the local artisans

worked day and night to refit the ship for its next voyage. Nothing further was heard about their duties once afloat. Slowly, as the work became more routine, men were allowed ashore to enjoy the delights of Falmouth and its little sister town of St Mawes across the bay.

Joe lived near the docks, and he had invited Chipper and Paddy to his home whenever they were allowed off the ship. So far, this had happened twice, and both sailors had enjoyed some happy times with their new friend and his plump wife, Martha.

Their house was built of wood and was very small, but it was cozy and neat. They had no children and, although they were both only thirty years of age, they behaved more like sixty year olds. Their lives were ordered, with everything in its place and no occurrences out of the ordinary.

Everything would have remained so, had it not been for the night that Martha brought out her jug of apple cider at the end of the meal. She brewed the mixture four times a year and was very proud of its potency. She and Joe called it scrumpy, and there was a twinkle in their eyes as they boasted how strong it was. Joe was used to it, of course, but even his mouth pursed up at the first taste of the thick brew.

'By God, Martha, m'dear, you've done a proper job this time. Don't you think, boys?'

Both the visitors nodded over the tops of their china mugs. A warning sounded in Paddy's head, but he was feeling good and relaxed in this happy home. It was so different from his own damp house back in Ireland, with its draughts and squealing children.

The men finished the jug, and Martha brought another. They finished that, too. It was only seven o'clock and they had at least four hours before they needed to return to the ship.

Chipper said, 'What's it like across the bay, Joe?'

Martha spoke up. 'It's a lot smaller than Falmouth, but it's pretty, isn't it, Joe? Why don't you take them across on the ferry?'

'Oh, it's getting late, m'dear. They're probably too tired—'

'No, we're not, Joe. We'd like a run out, wouldn't we, Paddy?'

Paddy smiled up as the two men started from the table.

'Take 'em for a quick one at The Flag, Joe, but don't be too late back. You've another early start tomorrow morning.'

They left the house, standing in its little patch of garden, and headed down to the dock area once more. A small rowboat was tethered to its mooring place with two men standing at the side. Already there were a couple of customers sitting in the waist of the boat, urging the men to hurry up and get on with it. One of them was Chief Gunner Sande. He was with Welch, and they looked up as Paddy, Chipper and Joe jumped down to join them.

'Evenin', Chief,' Chipper greeted the senior NCO with a smile. 'Goin' over to the other side, are we?'

Sande grunted in recognition and stared straight ahead.

'You'd better behave yourselves over there, you men. They don't appreciate rough behavior.'

He stared hard at Paddy. The Irishman felt a chill and also a passing moment of recognition at what his friend, Chipper, had endured in order to keep him from harm. Apparently, the debt had been paid, but Paddy knew that he would always have to keep well away from the malevolent gunner with his appetites and harsh ways.

Feeling otherwise content, the three friends sat in the bow of the boat while the ferryman dipped his oars into the darkening water of Falmouth Sound. It was just a few weeks before that Paddy had found himself rowing for the first time. He now appreciated the work that was being undertaken by the man at the oars. The fee was a penny, and his earnings were sufficient for the job that he held. Like everyone in the small community, outside of the squire and the priest, his life was centered around either the sea or the soil, in this gentle corner of rural England.

He spoke occasionally to his passengers, pointing out this sight or that feature of the landscape, but he kept his main concentration on heading the boat towards a bright lantern that marked their point of landing at St Mawes.

Avoiding Sande's eye, Paddy, Chipper and the carpenter, Joe, jumped ashore and joined the crowd of other seamen and women walking around the little coastal town. The streets were twisted, but were kept very orderly. Cobbles covered the hilly ground, and the sounds of laughter and song echoed off the cramped stone and wooden houses.

Joe guided them along the sea wall and up a side street. Here, the houses were so close together that they almost touched at the top, forming an arch. Halfway up, a sign swung creakily in the seaborne breeze. It showed a picture of the royal standard, and Joe said, pointing, 'This here's The Flag. I hope you like it.'

They entered a bright smoke-filled room, which was crammed with villagers and sailors, both from the navy and from the fishing fleets that operated locally. A fiddle, a fife and flute were being played in the corner of the room, and people around the players sang the shanties that made up the repertoire.

Joe, who was recognized by a few of the locals, pushed his way through the throng to collect three foaming tankards of local ale. It was strong and heavy, but took no time at all to drink; soon, another round was in the newcomers' hands. They were feeling very much at home. Chipper had even been on the receiving end of a favorable glance or two from some of the prettiest women.

Feeling flushed with *bonhomie* and good cheer, Paddy

offered up a couple of Irish songs, and many of the revelers joined in the simple choruses. It was all very happy and homely with good friends and a warm atmosphere. But, then, the door was thrown open, and a black-clad figure stepped into the room. He wore a cloak, even though the evening was far from cold. His face was dark and his deep piercing eyes traveled the room, searching out the occupants. One by one the singers stopped, and the music stuttered to a halt. Some of the merrymakers closest to Paddy said, 'It's the man.' And, reaching for their belongings, they began to leave.

After two or three minutes, the figure withdrew into the night and, eventually, the bar became almost empty. Only a couple of old men were left with the three friends from across the harbor. After watching the exodus, they too finished their drinks, and made for the door.

Chipper, feeling the night had hardly started, leaned across the bar and asked the landlord what was going on. The man ignored him and continued his work of clearing away tankards and mugs. 'What the 'ell 'appened?' Chipper continued, undismayed by the lack of response. Again there was no reply apart from a mumbled, 'Pub's closing.'

Although the landlord was quite a large man, Chipper vaulted over the counter and took him by the arm.

'We're in the royal navy, mate, so you'd better not play that game with me. I'll 'ave a couple of 'undred of the boys round 'ere in the morning if I've any more of this silent crap.'

The landlord recognized he was not dealing with someone who gave up easily, so he pulled three pints and placed them on the bar top.

'These are on me, lads. Sorry, but we don't talk much about things in these parts. But you'll be gone soon, and I guess none of you are excisemen, are you?'

The three lifted their mugs in unison and declared that

they were just ordinary seamen, serving King George. Also, they had no love of the Customs and Excise officers, who usually carried out their duties in a more than zealous way on poor sailors coming home with a few paltry trinkets from abroad.

The landlord settled back with his arms folded and his damp cloth hanging at his side.

'Stuff gets brought over from France, usually. Brandy, tobacco, silks. All kinds of things. Lands in one of the local coves and then gets brought through by horse. No one talks about it, but it probably brings in more money than farming or fishing. It's a way of life down here. The point is, everybody's in on it, you see. That way nobody can be an informer. If the excise found out too much, they'd have to arrest the whole town. The only true innocents are the children, but then you often find them playing games of customs and smugglers, so I suppose they're a part of it as well.'

They finished their beer, and thanking the landlord for his hospitality and explanation of the local ways, they went out into the steeply sloping street. It was very dark outside away from the warm glow of The Flag and they stumbled over the uneven cobbles, as they made their way back to the water's edge. Linking arms, they started up a verse of one of Paddy's earlier songs and were thoroughly enjoying themselves, when they noticed a commotion up ahead.

There was a light on the ground and they could make out some figures grouped around what seemed to be a pile of clothes. As they came nearer, the pile turned into a man, and when they were almost upon the group, the man stood up, and they could see it was Sande. There were four other men holding pistols pointed at his heaving, bloated stomach and Paddy could hear his rasping breath across the night air. The pistoled four shrank back into the shadows as Sande stared at the three men.

'Thank God, you're here,' he wheezed. 'These bastards were trying to rob me.'

Paddy could see there was none of the rouge on the chief's puffing cheeks, but his eyes were staring wildly from their sockets as he tried to regain his composure.

'Now, that's not the truth, and you know it.' A voice came out of the shadows and a tall man came forward, holding his pistol loosely before him. 'I caught this sailor trying to attack one of our young men.' He gestured at Sande, who looked truculently ahead. 'We were out on some business when we heard the noise. We found the two of them here and released the young fellow. It's all right, friends,' he continued. 'I'll take over here. These seamen can help me. There'll be no more trouble. And we don't want to bring out the excise tonight.'

There was a shuffling sound as the man's friends moved off silently into the night.

'So, you men, let's get this one off across the bay and we'll say no more about it. There's no evidence to bring against him, so there's nothing anybody can do. Just don't let him come back. The people here don't take kindly to robbers.'

He uncocked his pistol and put it into his belt. As he turned away, Sande leaped onto him. It was so sudden that the three friends standing in front of him were taken completely by surprise. They were standing immobile as they saw the glint of a blade, as, without warning, Sande stabbed the man in the chest. As he fell to the ground, Paddy rushed forward to help the man, but it was no good. His eyes had rolled up and his breathing had stopped by the time that Paddy and Chipper reached him. 'Leave the bastard where he lies,' shouted Sande, 'but let's see what he's got on 'im.'

Horrified, Paddy saw the burly chief start going through the man's pockets, pulling out a watch and some letters. In his turn, he still could not believe that he had witnessed murder in front of him, and pulled the dripping knife out of the dead man as the body lolled over him. Chipper spoke to them. 'We've got to get away from here, or we'll all be in the soup.'

But Sande continued to search the man for spoils. Had they not delayed over this, they would probably have all escaped from the scene, and the corpse, whoever he was, would have ended up as another casualty of the night. However, this night was a night of especial activity along the Cornish coast. Smugglers and excisemen were out in full force. As the group of witnesses stood in horror while the chief ransacked the body, they were confronted by the sudden appearance of lanterns belonging to the authorities. A group of officials, armed to the teeth, in search of import duties owed to the crown, faced the confused men grouped around the corpse. With lanterns held high, the leader shouted to them not to move.

They must all have looked guilty as hell, Paddy reflected later on. He was standing holding a dripping knife, and Chipper stood with his hand on the chief who was examining the watch and the papers that he had stolen. Only Joe looked to have no part in the tableau, and the leader of the excisemen reacted accordingly. 'I know you, don't I?' he asked roughly. 'Carpenter, aren't you?' Joe nodded meekly. 'Did you have anything to do with this murder?'

Joe shook his head vigorously and was about to speak, when the man in charge interrupted him.

'Well, you get along, my lad. You're an honest local, and I'll not have you involved. Be off with you now.'

Paddy had a sinking feeling in his stomach, as he saw their new friend do as he was told and turn off quickly toward the ferry mooring. The excisemen stood silently in a circle looking at the scene before them.

The leader turned towards Paddy, the nearest, and said, 'What's your explanation here?'

Paddy was about to begin, but the chief started up immediately.

'Now listen here, my man, you've got all this out of order. These two scallywags were robbing the corpse when I came on the scene. The big one here is a known trouble-maker, and his friend likewise.'

'You can shut up for a start,' the exciseman said. 'I'm not getting into what happened. You'll have to tell that to the magistrate in the morning. As far as I'm concerned it's murder and robbery and you'll all hang before the week's out. Round 'em up,' he commanded, and the troops pushed the three protesting sailors forward towards a dark building at the end of the small town.

All the glow of the evening's alcohol consumption vanished instantly from Paddy and Chipper, as they were herded along by the soundless men. For the second time in his life, Paddy felt the cloying helpless yoke of capture. He tried to walk erect but his feelings of alarm and depression made him keep his eyes down, as their way took them closer and closer towards incarceration.

Chief Sande, by comparison, kept up a running stream of banter to any that would listen to him. In particular, he directed his speech towards the tall officer, who was responsible for their arrest. It seemed to matter little to the senior NCO that there was nothing in the form of a reply to his remarks about mistakes, and no hard feelings, doing their jobs, and similar comments.

As they passed along the dark streets, figures scurried from doorway to doorway, engaged on the activities that the landlord of The Flag had alluded to earlier. This atmosphere of furtiveness added to the overall feelings of fear and foreignness that Paddy experienced. Even his small companion, Chipper, seemed unable to lighten his mood with his customary personality. Like Paddy, he also seemed struck dumb by the appalling consequences of their plight.

After five minutes, they arrived at their destination. It was a round fort, standing on the hill overlooking the harbor. Paddy could see that it was old enough to have been standing on its bleak spot for several hundred years. The soldiers on guard waved the party through into the courtyard.

Sande's protestations must have had some effect on their captors because he was taken off separately under the watchful eyes of four heavily armed men. Paddy and Chipper were taken to a large cell, made out of iron bars and strongly fixed to the outer wall of the fort. The three sides of their prison gave no opportunity for escape, as they were bolted to the floor and the ceiling. The wall that provided the fourth boundary was solid granite. There was dry straw on the floor and a guard was placed outside the bars, with instructions not to enter the cell. Four rough benches were fixed on the stone wall, and the two friends sat dejectedly on two of them, blinking in the half-light from the guard's lantern that bathed their confinement in its sallow gloom.

'We're in a right fix 'ere, Paddy,' Chipper said. 'I don't know 'ow we're going to get out of it.'

Paddy silently shook his head, having no solution to their difficulty.

'Our only 'ope is Joe,' continued the small Londoner. 'If 'e gets to the captain, and tells 'im what 'appened, we might get off. Otherwise, we could 'ang, and no mistake. We're outsiders, and the authorities are looking for blood, with all this smugglin' that's goin' on. I reckon we could be a couple of good scapegoats. And I don't like the way that queer bastard, Sande, got put in a different cell either.'

Paddy could see that his normally irrepressible friend was not able to find a vein of comfort anywhere, and this abnormality added severely to his distress. In the last few weeks, he had come to rely so much on the guidance and direction of his new friend that he felt lost and totally vulnerable without even a word of encouragement concerning how they could successfully protest their innocence. Following Chipper's lead, he fell sideways onto the rough bench and tried to sleep.

The quantity of alcohol they had consumed during the evening allowed both men to sleep through most of the night, in spite of the general discomfort and difficulty of their surroundings. Paddy had to rouse himself once in the night to take advantage of the tin bucket in the corner of the cell. At that time, a feeling of dread overcame him, which deepened with his rehashing of the circumstances leading up to their arrest. The dawn was slow in coming as he lay on his bench, reliving the stabbing and the resulting looting of the bleeding corpse by the fat gunner.

He decided there was little else that he could do but protest his innocence and accuse the guilty man. If Joe would turn up, or even better, bring one of the officers from the ship, they might be released. It was a slim hope, he knew, but it was their only chance. Chipper turned fitfully on the next bench, grumbling in his sleep. Paddy envied him his insulation from the horrors of reality.

How long they remained in their respective states, Paddy could not tell, but some considerable time later, the sound of jangling keys alerted him to the approach of jailers. The guard who had stayed in the outer area all night had been changed, and the new man, hearing the approach, stood up stiffly and faced the door. Three official-looking military types entered, and looked cruelly at the tousled prisoners.

'All right, you, get yourselves cleaned up. You're to go before the magistrate in half an hour.'

Chapter Thirteen

St Mawes, 1992

The following morning, Mitch left Margitte with more regret than he would have believed. He knew that he had reached a point in his plans where the next move would mean total commitment, and this added to his feelings of vulnerability as he took his leave of her.

They had spent a night of passion that had left them drained and soaking wet. The expensive sheets that the Trethawnton Hotel provided its elite and gentle guests were a tangled and twisted rope as the two lovers finally fell into an exhausted oblivion.

They had wakened to the screeching sounds of swooping seabirds. The morning's brightness stung their eyes as they lay naked in its glow. Ever practical, Margitte reached across the stretching form of Mitch and yanked the phone off its cradle. A tinny voice chattered in her ear as she gave the order for breakfast in the room.

Mitch made no secret of his continuing lust for the statuesque Dutchwoman as she wandered naked in and out of the bedroom and the bathroom. He reached for his packet of Players, but knowing her dislike of the habit, withdrew his hand, and decided to try giving up the weed, at least until he had a cup of coffee.

They shared a luxurious hot bath, and when a knock at the door announced the arrival of the meal, Mitch insisted on staying in the hot water. He had already been 'volunteered' to the tap end and also he wanted to look at her getting in and out of the tub all wet and glistening. He was happy that she gave in with little more discussion. He was also happy with the cup of coffee that she brought to him and, of course, the view.

'The best view,' he said, 'this side of the Irish Sea.'

They settled the outstanding bill at the hotel and drove to the middle of the little town. Following Margitte's suggestion of the previous day, they visited an expensive tourist shop and selected two aluminum Samsonite briefcases that were identical in every way, including the combination locks alongside the snap fastenings. They declined the offer of wrapping, and each carried a case out into the quiet street, looking like commercial travelers representing the same organization. Mitch and Margitte sat in the car with the cases on their laps.

'What number would you like for the locks?' he asked her. 'I don't have a lucky number or anything like that.'

She frowned at him.

'Neither do I, but from your suggestions over dinner last night, we better have a number that we know in case these get locked and need to be opened.'

He thought for a moment.

'Let's use my birthday, the second of April nineteen forty-eight.'

He peeled off the lining and, using the end of a ballpoint, inserted the numbers 2,4,1, on the left lock and 9,4,8, on the right-hand one.

'I'll have to remember that it's the English way, sorry Irish,' she said quickly. 'I guess I'm always going to have problems making that distinction.'

'I guess I better stop worrying about the distinction myself, in view of what we're planning.' So saying he leaned over and kissed her tenderly. Then, swapping over the cases, he entered the same number in the locks of her case.

They sat for a moment or two at the end of the town, looking out over the peaceful water. The scene of gently bobbing sailing boats was quite at odds with the turmoil that seeped into their minds. Eventually, Mitch drove back up the hill to drop her off once more at the hotel car park. He had to return to London and fly back for the last time to Ireland.

As they reached the top of the hill, Margitte took his hand and said, 'Mitch, pull into the castle again, and let's say our good-byes there.'

Swinging into the little area designed to drop off passengers, Mitch got out of the car and held her close. They stood for a minute in the soft breeze that came across the harbor. Neither of them wanted to leave the other, and yet neither of them could find the words necessary to communicate the feelings of sadness and trepidation that they felt at the prospect of leaving this little Cornish town that had come to mean so much to them.

During the night, between bouts of passion, they had planned out their scheme. It was simple in the extreme except that it relied almost totally on Margitte and her 'friends', whoever they might be. She had only volunteered the scantiest details about who they were, and Mitch had not asked for names or backgrounds, as there was little point.

'Everything will be done through Hans Muller,' she had said late into the night. 'He will be your chauffeur and guide. He owes me many a favor and he will play the part I ask.'

Mitch had felt her confidence and accepted that he could do nothing about her end. He was only required to follow the simplest of instructions.

As they stood sharing their last few moments together

next to the castle, Mitch said, 'You know, it's a funny thing, but that relative I told you about?'

'Your great-great – I don't remember how many greats – grandfather, you mean?'

'Yes. Granddad Paddy, I should call him. I told you, I think, that he was here. I've sort of been following him around. A hell of a long time later, but I've been to all the places he went to. Looking at this old fort makes me think of what it was like for him back a couple of hundred years ago. It probably didn't look a lot different from now. No cars or modern dress, of course, but still a high view over a big waterway with the seagulls swooping and the grass shining green and new. It's almost as if we seem to repeat the things of years ago, don't you think?'

'Now you're just trying to make me believe all you Irishmen are poets, aren't you?'

'Maybe we are, Margitte. Maybe we are at that. But all the years I've been trying to blow up things and change the world, I've never thought much about the past, except the way we've been controlled and cheated by the English.'

'So, perhaps, you should start thinking of history a bit more positively. Maybe you should look at it like a road map. You know, it shows you where you've come from and tells you where you're going. Maybe Paddy would have liked to think that you O'Doules could have made some progress since the days he was here. I wonder what he would have thought of his ancestor if he had known your reputation. Maybe, if our plan works, he will be really proud, because your outlaw friends are going to have a hard time with their ambitions after all this.'

Mitch shook his head silently, the images of the past deserting him for the feelings of the need to depart. He gave her his aunt's phone number in St Mary's as well as his flat in Ballyhean. In return, she produced a piece of paper, with a number in Holland where she would be from the next day onwards.

He took a last look at the view and kissed Margitte fondly before returning to the Trethawnton and dropping her with her new briefcase at the hotel. He felt a sensation of loss as he maneuvered once more along the Cornish lanes towards the main road that would take him back to the world from which he felt more estranged with every mile he covered.

After the usual changing of cars and addresses, he arrived back in war-scarred Belfast. All pretense of gaiety had disappeared with the sodden weather conditions which darkened Mitch's mood as he entered his dismal flat over the barn. The prospect of his forthcoming ordeal with the war council, plus a thorough buffeting in the air, as the BAC111 fought its way through the approaching depression, had exhausted him.

Although it was only seven o'clock in the evening, he dropped his bag and lay down on the unmade bed and fell instantly asleep. It was pitch-black as he was awakened by the strident ringing of the telephone. Disoriented, he stumbled over a chair in the darkness, scraping his shin as he groped to find the instrument. Eventually he grabbed the shrieking handset, and after first putting the wrong end to his ear, he found the mouthpiece and croaked, 'Hello.'

'I just wanted to see that you were safe.'

The accent once again was amplified by the wire. Mitch felt a warm glow at the sound of her voice.

'Yes,' he answered, 'I fell asleep. I'm glad you called. I have to get going, otherwise people will wonder what's become of me.'

'Well, take care of yourself, Colonel. Call me when you can.'

'Yes, give me a couple of days—'

The line went click as she broke the connection. He lay back on the bed and lit a Players, half seeing the dismal room illuminated with every draw of the glowing end. 'Jesus, this is a miserable place,' he said out loud. Margitte's presence, albeit at the end of the phone, had seemed so incongruous here. He regretted that he had been so stilted with her, but he had been caught completely off guard. There was little doubt that she felt the same attraction for him that he felt for her. He smiled at the recollection of her as he lay smoking in the bare room.

After stubbing out his cigarette, he made some tea and checked in with his control number. A voice he didn't recognize answered and said he was expected. There was a pause and the line clicked as a phone was picked up further down the line.

'So you're back from the crumpet, are you? Did you dip your wick this time, then?'

Mike Ryan managed to portray his unpleasant nature just as effectively down the telephone as he did in the flesh. Mitch sighed inaudibly.

'I'll see you when?' he asked.

'Do you want to meet tomorrow or tonight?'

'It's all the same to me,' Mitch said, 'but maybe I'll get some kip and see you in the morning.'

'Okay, that's fine. We're all anxious to know how you got on. Goodnight, Colonel, call me when you can.'

There was a snigger as Ryan hung up and Mitch stood impotently holding the phone. The bastard had heard Margitte's call. 'By Christ, this is getting to be bloody dangerous,' Mitch swore to himself. Suddenly, it occurred to him that the flat might be wired. His every sound could be amplified. He put all the lights on and began to go through the scant premises, looking behind every item, turning back mats and pushing furniture around. I could have blown the whole fucking thing wide open, he thought silently to himself. All it needed was some sort of 'Oh Margitte, darling, I miss you' and the party would have been over in a big way.

Severely shaken by the realization of his vulnerability, but satisfied there were no hidden microphones, Mitchell O'Doule began to pace around his dismal flat. Deep in thought, he found the need to repeat the routines and drills that he had enacted so many times when about to undertake one of his many missions. Going to the locked cupboard over his bed he took down a bundle of oilcloth. Turning on an angle lamp, he focused the light on the bundle and carefully unwrapped it, revealing two revolvers of German manufacture, four clips of ammunition and two ancient British army hand grenades. He also uncovered several lengths of electrical wire, a packet of plastic and some detonators.

It was quite a small arsenal for any law-abiding citizen of the land, but as he gazed at the dully gleaming metal, he could see that, although it would be a dangerous collection in the wrong hands, it offered little protection in the fight he was about to undertake. He stripped the guns, oiled and checked them. He discarded the other items and returned them to their hiding place. Then he put the small automatic behind his back, tucked into the belt, and the other revolver into a thin steel box together with the additional ammunition. It was not normal for any of the senior officers to carry arms but the gun pressing into his back gave him a feeling of security, even though he recognized it as false.

At one o'clock in the morning, he made some more tea and then took out his atlas once more. Sitting down at the scuffed table, he turned his smoke-reddened eyes onto the areas of the world he hoped he would be visiting. They were places that, until just those few short weeks ago, had only been names with very little identity. He took comfort from the fact that his unfamiliarity was also shared by his soon-to-be ex-colleagues in the movement. He was banking on that fact. He turned the pages until he reached the projection that showed Western Europe. There, in the middle of the page sat the small dot of Amsterdam, Margitte's home. He wondered what it would be like. Would all the women be as statuesque as her? Did people actually wear clogs? Did they eat cheese all the time?

He knew without a doubt that he would find the answers to such childlike questions soon. Margitte had a stability and dependability about her that made him accept that whatever she said would happen, would happen. He only hoped to God she didn't call him again. It only needed one word to blow the cover off his treachery. The thought of such imprudence worked away at his mind and only left after he had taken a screwdriver to the small black junction box and disconnected the wire.

Eventually, deep into the night, Mitch turned out his light and lay down for a restless sleep, secure at least in the knowledge that no phone call would now disturb him.

In the morning, after a hot bath and a champion's breakfast of two Mars Bars, he left the flat to drive to the meeting place. It was to be held in the old fish warehouse which still served as the present Ulster headquarters. He affected a smile and cheery greeting to the various 'soldiers' who stood around either waiting for instructions, or just guarding the inner sanctum.

He was the first to arrive and he settled down at the table with some of Matt's coffee and a ham and cheese roll. Like his flat, this was a dismal place, but at least it had the appearance of being shared by other human beings, male ones at that. Matt's stewardship, however, did not run to overt cleanliness. The evidence of Mike Ryan was there, with the stubs of cheroots in the tin ashtray, and there were rings on the table top where Taffy's whiskey glass had been repeatedly positioned.

The coffee tasted good in Mitch's tobacco-tainted

mouth. He felt a tightness in his chest, sitting and waiting for his role of fellow terrorist to begin. He knew that he could turn on the act, but he did not know if it would withstand the pressure of too many questions. His treachery was so unlikely, however, he was sure he would not be suspected, provided he remained calm and in full possession of his familiar role of a senior colonel.

He could hear laughter downstairs. That will be Taffy arriving, he thought. He was such an unlikely person to be mixed up in this business. He came from a middle-class background with a father who had been an assistant bank manager. To the outside world he just seemed to be a jovial drunk who ate too much. But Mitch had seen him in action and knew him to be cold-blooded and ruthless. Mike Ryan was treacherous, but woe betide the unhappy soul who ended up in the sadistic hands of Taffy.

'Hello, Taffy,' Mitch said, as the plump misnamed man almost fell into the room. He was clasping a big mug of coffee in his damp white fist. Mitch could smell the whiskey that had been poured into it by Matt. 'I was just thinking about you.'

'Good thoughts, I hope,' replied Taffy, perspiring as he drank.

It is funny, thought Mitch, how fat drunks always seem to be leaking from their pores. It is as if the booze had no other exit but the skin.

'Oh sure,' continued Mitch with a reassuring grin. 'Just thinking about the old days when we were out and about, instead of sitting inside, like a bunch of old women, gossiping.'

Taffy nodded his head sagely and took a long pull from his mug. They sat in silence for a few moments as the Bushmills snaked its way into Taffy's system. Mitch could see him relaxing with every moment.

'I'll just get a top-up,' Taffy said, and squeezed his way out from the table. As he left, his battered clothing bunched and tugged round his fat waist, exposing a loose roll of waxen stomach.

Mitch sat patiently for a few moments and then heard the clatter of thick soles on the hard steel stairs. Mike Ryan came in, looking fierce. He was followed by Conny Fitzherbert and Bryan Flynn. They sat down and stared at their ambassador. Ryan was about to start, no doubt with his customary sneer, but Mitch took the wind out of his sails.

'Since when has it been the policy to bug the phones of senior officers?' he asked directly of Ryan, whose seat was directly opposite him at the big table.

'Well, it was done by accident, Mitch,' Ryan replied, his reptilian, unblinking eyes showing that the question had not fazed him in the least. 'I was completely taken aback when I heard your voice on the squawk-box last night. There you were, twice as loud and twice as lovely. With your mystery girlfriend, too.'

Mitch leaned forward and pointed his finger at Ryan's face.

'That's enough out of you. I've had about enough of your sly insinuations. If you want to go off and handle this side of the deal, that's okay by me. I don't particularly enjoy all the difficulties and risks getting in and out of the country, while you and your mates sit around here dreaming up a lot of nonsense. This was your scheme from the start. So far, I haven't seen too much activity, apart from the usual snide comments.'

'Okay, okay, calm down, Mitch,' Ryan said and leaned back in his chair away from the force of Mitch's words and threatening gesture. 'Our turn will come soon enough. Then you can guard the fort here, when we're laying the charges underneath all those fat English arses.'

Mitch continued his pose of aggression and said nothing to reduce the tension that had sprung into the air. Taffy blundered back into the room, and everybody looked at him as a way of easing the atmosphere. However, Taffy assumed he was the object of their disapproval, and mumbled an apology about being late and needing more coffee.

Mike Ryan, not missing anything, said that Matt probably had had to open another bottle of Bushmills since Taffy had polished off a full one the day before.

'So are we going to hear the plan, Mitch, or are we going to fuck about here all day playing games?'

'Everything's fixed. We just need to come up with the money and check the merchandise.'

'Just like that, eh?' Ryan drawled. 'We hand over most of our money, and a bunch of unknowns hand over stuff that may or may not work? There's got to be more to it than that.'

'It can be as easy or as complicated as you like, Mike. They seem the genuine article but I guess it all comes down to trust in the end, doesn't it?'

'Well, I trust nobody. Never have and never will. So you better remember that.'

'That's why I suggest that you take over from here, Mike. I'm sure that you'll make the best final arrangements. I've had it with flying around all over the place. While you're gone, maybe I'll get a tap on your phone line – just by accident, of course.'

He leaned back feeling the uncomfortable, yet reassuring, bulk of the Luger pressing into his spine. He allowed his anger to show around the table, and he waited for the first suggestion from his fellow council members.

Ryan quietly requested he tell them everything that had happened before they decided whether to change roles in the matter. Mitch reported the contents of his trip, at least, the parts that were relevant to his and Margitte's plan. He told them how they would be expected to give half of the money on completion of a successful test. The balance would be arranged at the time of delivery. The date and place had to be agreed upon after the testing of the Mephistos. He had a number in Holland, where the woman would make the final arrangements. Thereafter he planned to fly to Schipol, Amsterdam's airport, check the merchandise, and arrange withdrawal of the final amount.

'How do we get the stuff into the UK?' Brian Flynn asked. His normally bland, rather bored expression did not change, as he continued to look absently around the room.

'They will arrange for delivery wherever we want,' Mitch replied.

'That's easier said than done,' Taffy spoke up between sips from his mug of doctored coffee. 'The drug traffic has made the Customs and Excise people more on the alert than ever. One of our shipments got caught the other day, coming over from Blankenburg. We lost the lot, including a couple of reliable men.'

'Don't worry about the men, Taffy,' Ryan said. 'We'll get them out in a couple of years. They're safe where they are for now, and we've plenty more since Eastern Europe fell apart. This little shemozzle is going to give all the fellows a chance to make a dent in the Queen's crown, God damn her.'

Mitch looked at them each in turn.

'I suggest we take the first half of the money over, and arrange for a Swiss bank to transfer the remainder, once we're satisfied. Assuming that you all still want to go through with bombing the living daylights out of the cities, and, I should warn you again, choke the life out of the Yanks' support for some time to come.'

He felt that there was little enthusiasm around the table. It was definitely not like the old days, when they would all have been raring to go and make their respective marks for the glory of the old country.

'Well, assuming your lady friend is the real McCoy,' Ryan spoke up, 'we'll be in with the Libyans and the other groups. That's supposed to be the bloody deal, isn't it?'

'There's a hell of a lot on trust, Mike.'

Mitch played his role of senior officer with the concern that would be expected of him. After another hour's discussion, they were all in agreement that the next step should be handled by him. The foreign aspect of the operation still created a feeling of difficulty for most of his partners. Nearly all of their experience had been within the cloying atmosphere of terrorist Ireland. There were few opportunities to escape abroad. Their general inhibitive attitude towards leaving their borders made him think that he was going to get away with it all, but Taffy, damn him, made a joke about letting Mitch 'elope with his paramour' with all their funds.

In response, Mike Ryan said that, for overall security, it would be best if one of them accompanied him. The group's assent to this and their overall subservience to Ryan needed no clarification that he should be the one to perform that role. Mitch smiled grimly in agreement, silently thinking that even the bad aspects of the plan seemed to be working perfectly.

After a late sandwich lunch and a session of ideas on the planting of the Mephistos deep in the fabric of English society, the group broke up to adjourn until the next day. Mitch agreed he would make contact with his associate in Holland and report back regarding the next step.

The evening had turned out fine as he left the warehouse. The streets still had a sheen on them as he walked along beside the darkening buildings. There was no suggestion on anyone's part to accompany him, and this only made him feel further distanced from the group and its ideals.

All his life he had been aware of the struggle for independence. As he reached adulthood, he had welcomed the excitement of the IRA and its lore and heroes. His friends were all in the movement, and yet, here he was in middle age, disillusioned, friendless and a traitor to his previously deeply held beliefs. He wore his present dual role with difficulty, because he had to keep switching from one aspect to another. Intellectually, he understood his new direction, but emotionally, he still had a large part of his psyche committed to rebellion.

Earlier, back in the war council, he was horrified to feel himself entering into the enthusiasm of the moment, as he gave suggestions and opinions on the planned bombing of countless innocent civilians. However, even the grim realization it was all for nothing did not dampen the comradeship of his fellow conspirators that had always been the crux of his former life.

Now, out in the fresh air, he felt like an unfaithful husband about to unleash his infidelity on an unsuspecting wife. Divorce would be inevitable, along with some accompanying guilt, but after that was over, he would begin a new life without having to tolerate the pretense that had been growing, undiagnosed in him, like a cancer.

Looking around him at the desolation of the war-torn city of Belfast, he was the first to admit that the struggle so far had produced nothing for the citizens hereabouts. They seemed to have become immune to the twenty-odd years of bombing and civil unrest, which were only the most recent upheavals of a century's long conflict. They merely wanted to get on with their lives, be they Irish, English, Protestant or Catholic. There were young married people with children of their own who had known nothing but war, with its bloodshed and casualties of innocent men, women and children.

Regimes in Westminster had come and gone. Stormont, with its facade of local rule, had been disbanded two decades earlier. The Irish government to the South continued on its merry way, getting deeper and deeper into European debt; it was uninterested in unification and fearful of the added responsibilities of more mouths to feed without the English taxpayers' subsidies.

And still, the likes of Mike Ryan, Taffy O'Brian, Conny Fitzsimmons and Brian Flynn continued to play the game as if they really understood the wants and needs of the people. Politicians the world over were the butts of everybody's jokes, but far, far worse were the terrorist movements that purported to fight for freedom for whole groups of unwilling people. These were the real maniacs.

'And God help me,' Mitch mumbled, 'I was one of the best.'

A lone phone box stood at the end of the street. Sticking out of the corner like a sentry on duty, it allowed a view of both streets simultaneously. Mitch, on impulse, decided to try Margitte's number. The lines could not be any more public than his own, and he still did not feel comfortable speaking out loud in the sparse flat. He used a credit card booked out to the long-suffering attorney, Fergy. The buzzing noise at the other end proclaimed a 'foreign' destination. There was a click and Margitte's voice saying, '*Met* Ednas.' Mitch felt a slight twinge in his stomach and almost hung up. '*Met* Margitte Ednas,' the voice said again with a touch of annoyance.

'It's me. We need to talk.'

'That's okay. I'm alone.'

It had never occurred to Mitch she would be otherwise, although she undoubtedly had a life outside the world of court reporting and terrorism which she had turned her back on. Somehow, he could not imagine her situation in a foreign country, talking in a foreign tongue.

'It's all going as I suspected. I will be accompanied.'

'Don't worry. I have made some of the preliminary arrangements. It will all be fixed in principle by tomorrow evening. Can you call me then?'

'Do you know when the meeting is likely to take place?'

'It could be in another two to three weeks. There may be a delay for the final shipment, but I'll know that tomorrow.'

'I'll call you at the same time tomorrow then.'

'I'll be looking forward to it.'

'There may be others with me on the line.'

'That's okay. 'Bye.'

There was a soft click and she hung up. Then Mitch stood for a while in the metal and glass box. The image of her had been real, as they shared their few words, but now that image was vanishing rapidly. He looked around at the dismal outside world and realized that, in a couple of weeks, it would all be over for him here. He didn't feel upset. His footsteps had a purposeful ring on the pavement as he strode away.

Chapter Fourteen

St Mawes, 1785

In the early morning, feeling disheveled and cowed, Paddy O'Doule and Chipper Johnson were marched roughly into a bare, stone and wooden room. At the far end was a long table behind which sat a hunched figure, swathed in a black gown and wearing a grubby tousled wig. As they were herded along, the figure pushed a tattered ringlet aside, raised a rheumy eye at their progress, and stared, unblinking, as they approached an iron rail before him.

There were five or six official-looking types on the figure's side of the barrier and some ten or so military personnel and guards on the prisoners' side. Paddy looked around desperately, hoping to see the face of their friend, Joe, or any of the ship's crew. But they were alone. Not even the bulk of Sande was in the bare room.

The party came to a halt in front of the judge, who continued to stare.

'Disgraceful,' he mumbled under his breath.

From behind the prisoners, a voice began to drone. It relayed the crimes of which the two men were charged, robbery, murder, mayhem, smuggling and tax avoidance. As the last words faded into the gloomy atmosphere, Chipper turned round and said it was all a lot of bloody nonsense. At this the judge banged a carpenter's wooden mallet on the table, and mumbled, 'Disgraceful' again.

As quietness once again descended on the proceedings,

the judge, whom Paddy estimated to be at least eighty years of age, reached into his robes and, with his clawlike hand, pulled out a black hood. He was attempting to place this on his head, when an usher moved over to him and spoke rapidly into his ear. Looking somewhat annoyed, the judge threw the hood on the table and glared at the two prisoners before him. 'Disgraceful,' he said once again. Slumping down further on his seat, he appeared to nod off for a few moments but, after a second or two, he jerked up and, glowering, said, 'Is there anything you want to say before I pass sentence?'

The usher ran up to him again. The judge looked even more disapproving and said, 'Is there any defense?'

Chipper couldn't stand it any more and said, 'Look, Sir, we are completely innocent. We were just coming back from shore leave—'

'Disgraceful,' the voice said once more.

The usher produced a piece of paper and put it under the judge's watery eyes. There was silence as he proceeded to read the words before him. Looking up at the usher, he spoke sharply, 'Does this change things then?'

The usher nodded grimly and withdrew. Chipper made as if to repeat his outburst but the judge stared malevolently at him, and the small cockney shrank before his gaze. A bubble of snot began to form underneath the right nostril of the judge. Paddy watched its progress, fascinated, all the time horrified at his impotence to affect whatever outcome there might be from these alien proceedings.

The judge sniffed loudly, with the sound of another 'Disgraceful' escaping from his lips.

'The other man who was brought here before me seemed to have some authority over you men,' the judge began again. 'I sent him back to his ship for discipline, with a strong recommendation for hard punishment. I won't have this sort of drunken behavior in our community. Now it seems that recent acts of parliament have removed my power of sentencing from such cases. Had you not been caught red-handed with the spoils of your crime, we could have strung you up at daybreak tomorrow, a lesson to all of the results of ignorance of the Lord's commandments.'

A pious look came over the waxen features, and was only broken by the movement of the clawlike hand to the offending nostril.

'However, it seems that now, adding theft to that of murder, the authorities require that I turn you over to the assizes for sentencing. I find the whole thing disgraceful.'

So saying, he banged his mallet once more on the table before him and shut his eyes, no doubt to blot out the image of such sinners. For one final time, Paddy noticed the bubble of snot escape once more from the pinched nose, as the guard closed in on the two men and removed them from the proceedings. As they descended to their cell, Chipper seemed to have perked up since he was away from the awful authority of the judge.

'So what's the drill now, then?' he asked, as they were returned behind their bars. The soldier in charge said that they would be taken to Truro immediately for the assizes that took place there.

'The judge wants you out of town this afternoon. Murderers aren't liked here, and we don't want a crowd of lynchers stampeding the castle.'

He was as good as his word. Within two hours, Paddy and Chipper were given a late breakfast of water and hot bread with some bacon fat, and then they were ordered out of their cell and into an open wagon, standing in the grounds. A pair of mismatched, stocky farm horses twitched at their bridles as the prisoners were manacled and chained into the crude seats. Two unsmiling uniformed guards climbed up front, and with a jerk of the reins, the party moved out of the castle and onto the top of the hill.

Paddy looked over his shoulder at the bay of Falmouth sparkling below them. The ships on the other side moved sluggishly at their moorings, and he could see The Widow among the throng. He could not understand why, but he found himself feeling unutterably sad at this sight of what had been his home for the last three months. Chipper stared sullenly at the same view, seeming less affected by the realization that he was saying goodbye to His Majesty's ship *Distinction*.

As they rocked in the back of the cart, Paddy found his emotions confused that he should be concerned at the loss. He had been, after all, a virtual prisoner of one situation, and here he was a prisoner of another, and neither of them had been his fault. Surely, one incarceration could not be so very much worse than another.

The journey to Truro took more than a day. When they ran out of daylight, the party had to seek shelter for the night in a barn. There seemed to be no lack of chains to secure the two seamen, which added greatly to their discomfort, but the farmer's wife brought them some food which was good and wholesome. The farmer himself came by to see everything was in order for the night. Unfortunately, his accent was so broad that neither of the two friends could understand more than a few words, which left all of them feeling frustrated.

The following morning, cold and stiff from their night in chains, they set off once more through the tiny twisted fields of Cornwall, and reached the small town of Truro at noon. It seemed to be market day, as, all around, stalls had been set up, with country people bustling about buying and selling food, animals and other items necessary for their lives in this sleepy, and often forgotten part of England.

Chipper turned his nose up at the country ways, mumbling 'Stubble-jumpers or, Swede-bashers' under his breath. For Paddy though, it was all reminiscent of his own visits to the small towns back home in Ireland. There was the same frenetic energy and good humor of the people enjoying their weekly or monthly visit, with the chance to catch up on gossip. The memories flooded back to him and, with them, the mortifying realization that his life in Ireland was now almost certainly over. He suppressed a sob, building deep in his chest, and coughed into his hand.

Once again, their temporary home was another gray-stone castle. Soldiers pulled them down from the cart and marched them to a cell where they were to spend more uncomfortable days and nights, waiting for their turn to come for trial. At least they were kept together. However, although they could hear other prisoners in the vicinity, they were visited by no one, apart from their personal jailers, nor were they given any account of what was to befall them.

'Bleedin' typical, that is,' Chipper said. 'Always the same, when you break the rules. Down the sewer you go, my ol' mate. Nobody cares, jus' so long as you gets punished, ev'rybody else feels good. The toffs always act the same. Kick the poor bleedin' workin' bastards up the arse as 'ard as they can. I don' mind tellin' yer, we are goin' to get it, an' get it real 'ard.'

He made this little speech to Paddy three or four times, and then he would lapse into a silent shaking of the head. No amount of reassurance, albeit false, from Paddy would take him out of his withdrawal. Even on the lonely forced exercise walks out in the yard, nothing would remove the little man's depression.

About the only other words that he spoke in the whole time were, 'I've faced the rope and the bullet several times, Paddy, and I've never let it bother me, but now there's something worse lurkin' out there for us. But I dunno what they've got lined up for us, and not 'nowin' is drivin' me potty.' Then he lapsed into his silence once again.

The end of their wait in the drafty cell came one dark rainy afternoon. They were taken out and across the drenched yard to a flight of steps. At the top was a long room with people sitting, crammed together on both sides. These were not country folk in working clothes but members of the middle and upper classes. Their combined disapproving stares made Paddy feel terribly guilty, although he fought to remember he had done nothing wrong.

A high mahogany bench rose up like a wall in front of the two men. They looked dwarfed beneath its monolithic authority. This was altogether a far more opulent place of trial than the simple place they had been in before at St Mawes. There was a babble of conversation around the long room's balcony, which eventually sputtered to a stop as a door to the side swung open.

A tall slim figure entered, wearing red robes and a white powdered wig. Before taking his seat behind the bench, he raised a bejeweled lorgnette to his piercing gray eyes and looked around at the gathered throng. He smiled, obviously pleased with the day's turnout. He removed both his smile and his lorgnette as he lowered his eyes to the two wretches beneath him. With an affected wave, he bade the proceedings to commence.

A disembodied voice read out the same list of crimes that they had heard previously in St Mawes. The judge continued to look around at the people and seemed to be smiling at various women who returned his greetings by enthusiastically waving back. The two prisoners before him not only seemed superfluous to the proceedings, but looked completely incongruous in a setting more akin to a royal court with the monarch smiling at his various courtiers.

After the voice stopped its droning charges, the red-cloaked judge allowed a few moments of silence to reign over his presence, while he massaged his temples with his thin fingers. Then, throwing back his false locks, he spoke with a sardonic lilt, in his high affected voice.

'So, it would appear that we have yet another case of wuffians descending upon us poor countwy folk, and wobbing us. I must say that these two chaps look particularly unwholesome specimens to me, too. Now, we're just simple countwy folk here, and we weally don't like all the twash of the world wunning amok. It has simply got to stop. Now, as the good people of Tworwo know, I'm not a vindictive man. I weally hate putting on the old black hat.'

At this, there was a considerable chuckling around the court, which seemed to please the judge greatly.

'Unfortunately, the black hat has seen quite a lot of work wecently, but still, the cwiminals continue their cwimes. It's simply not fair. So, fortunately, our good and gwacious majesty the King, and his servants in parlyment, have come up with another solution.'

For effect, he stopped and gazed around the room once more. Several of the prettier women made no secret of their adoration of him, and waved their gloved and beringed hands to encourage his favors.

'Now, before we get onto the best bit of this twial – namely the sentencing, followed natuwally by the gwovelling for mercy, which we all so enjoy – I suppose we'd better go thwough the borwing business of you chaps pwotesting your innocence. But huwwy it up, please, as we'd all like to go out for some tea. It's been quite the most exhausting afternoon's work.'

Paddy and Chipper stood downcast, realizing that they were caught in a spot from which there was no escape. Neither said a word. The judge leaned forward and tapped an ebony and silver horsewhip on his bench.

'Now see here, you chappies, this is where you blubber on about being innocent, d'you hear? So just get on with it and we can all get some tea, or whatever it is they give you chappies down there.'

More giggling followed this witty riposte, during which the judge preened himself and gazed around looking through his lorgnette. Paddy decided to try and set the matter straight.

'With due respect, sir, I'd like to tell you what happened.'

'Oh, delightful,' crowed the judge, 'one of the bog people, I believe, if I'm not mistaken. One of Saint Patwick's own. Absolutely pwiceless. Pway cawwy on, my good fellow.' He chortled to himself, and smiled benignly down from his vantage point.

Undaunted, Paddy had another go at it.

'We're sailors, sir, and we were coming back from shore leave when we saw the body lying on the ground. Begging your pardon, Sir, but we'd had a few to drink.'

'Oh, this is pwiceless, evewybody, a pissed Iwishman and his fwiend notice a dead body just lying awound, and no doubt were just checking for identification when they were disturbed by His Majesty's officers. Oh, it's all so pwedictable.'

'And so are you, you pansyfied fucker,' piped up Chipper, who had seen more than enough. 'Let's jus' get this 'ole act over, shall we? Then we can dismiss and 'ave our tea in peace.' The last few words he uttered in an imitation of the judge's affectation.

A look of supreme annoyance passed across the judge's brow and he stared down at this affront to his dignity.

'Very well. The sentence it shall be. Twansportation.'

Both Paddy and Chipper looked up with the same bemused expressions on their faces. This was a word with which they were unfamiliar. Transportation. What did it mean?

'Quite so,' the judge continued. 'As you can see, the lack

of a pwoper education has left you chappies somewhat innocent of the world, hasn't it? I don't suppose Van Diemen's Land means anything to you either, does it?'

The two unfortunate men looked at each other and shook their heads.

'Well, you are going to have the opportunity to visit a bwand-new land, initially for seven years.' A loud 'Ooooh!' followed this pronouncement at which the judge smiled and raised up a slim gloved hand. 'Courtesy of His Majesty,' he continued. 'Wather disappointing for us here, of course, as we were hoping to stwetch your cwiminal necks for you. Still, as you so carelessly were caught wobbing the body, we can tweat you as thieves and send you away to help the cwown build up the empire. Personally, I think His Majesty is altogether being far too lenient by pwoviding what will no doubt be a sort of extended holiday. But then he's in charge, and I'm just his humble local servant. I'm sure you'll have a jolly super time. We wish you both *bon voyage*.'

As they were led away, several of the women could be heard to echo his farewell, '*Bon voyage*.'

'Fuckin' loonies,' was Chipper's parting shot over his shoulder, as he was led out of sight. Paddy found the whole experience bewildering and as degrading as he was sure it was supposed to be. He felt as if he had been put in a pit to be baited and laughed at by those who were supposed to know better. If this was the English upper class at work, they were obviously headed for disaster.

He had heard about what happened to the French nobility fifty-odd years previously, and he had always thought it was a terrible thing. But then, he had never had any contact with the aristocracy before. If what he had seen moments ago represented the cream of the English crop, then they were asking for a similar fate. Paddy no longer felt as outraged by the behavior of his French cousins. If given the opportunity, he would be in the forefront of such a revolution. The whole court had been populated by fools and poseurs of the very worst sort. And they were supposed to be the upper class!

The guard marching close to him could see the look of puzzlement on his face and, no doubt feeling sorry for the Irishman, said, 'The Right Honorable Clancy does carry on, doesn't he?'

Paddy nodded gloomily.

'You're to be sent away for seven years, lads,' the guard continued. 'You're lucky. There's people who gets fourteen years or even for ever. He's not always in such a good mood. No doubt he got lucky with one of the farmers' wives last night. Quite an appetite for the ladies has our honorable Judge Clancy.'

'Is he Irish?' Paddy asked.

'I suppose somewhere along the way he must have been, or at least his family, but he came to us from Bath about five years ago. They say he used to be at court before he got tangled up with a royal lady and the monarch decided to get rid of him.' So saying, the guard gave them a mournful smile and walked off, jangling his keys beside him.

Both prisoners sat down on their bunks and gazed gloomily at the dirty floor. The sentence meant little to either of them and only caused confusion. They had both expected to be hanged. The terrifying feeling of banishment, which was to strike terror into the hearts of those similarly punished, was slow to reach out and grasp them. They both knew they were to face a dangerous and unknown future, but being already prisoners of the royal navy, such an uncertain life did not seem too harsh.

Chipper was a hardened seaman, and Paddy, over the last months, had been subjected to both harsh and effective discipline. More importantly, he had heard many times the stories told around the mess room table. Loose tales of monsters and cannibals, repeated by the sailing professionals in the late eighteenth century, were known to be only for simple-minded landlubbers. Therefore, they were to start their great adventure with an advantage over their fellow convicts, even though they shared with them what was to be for English Georgian society the 'final solution' to the problem of increasing lawlessness. They and their fellow transportees were to become a living embodiment of the saying, 'out of sight, out of mind'. It was a perfect punishment, with no accompanying guilt associated with the death penalty.

Chapter Fifteen

Ballyhean, 1992

Mitch had to spend a waiting period of three weeks before he was to escape from the clutches of his former life. It was a time of mixed emotions that swung wildly from fear and depression to relief and anticipation. Unfortunately, these feelings crowded in on him and fluctuated from one extreme to the other in bursts of minutes or seconds.

During the first days after his meeting back at the war council, and his subsequent phone call to Margitte in Holland, he smoked too much and consumed vast quantities of strong coffee. Neither drug gave him any real relief and only contributed to his lack of sleep, so much so that, when he visited his Aunty Kate, she assumed he was dreadfully ill. His fellow members of the war council seemed not to notice his sickly pallor, as they were all accustomed to looking grim beneath the buzzing, flyblown fluorescent tubes in their inner sanctum.

Eventually, Mitch came to terms with his dual role by browsing through the well-thumbed paperback autobiography of a Hollywood movie star that had been left near the coffee pot outside the war room. Most days, he had to wait for his colleagues to arrive, so he had begun to dip into the book. Soon he came to the realization that he was, after all, only doing what any two-bit actor could do – he was playing a part. Except, of course, in his case, a bad performance would mean not a drop in ratings or fans, it would mean losing his life.

Nonetheless, the reading of the book gave him a direction. He tried to enter into the play-acting aspect of his existence with more enthusiasm. He knew the plans for the carnage of countless innocent people would never occur if he could pull off the plot to scare off the IRA's intended allies and at the same time escape with the money. Margitte had given him every reason to believe that what she had in mind would put a severe dent in any future plans.

During the three-week wait, he had called her from the war room twice. He had used the speakerphone, and Taffy, Mike, Conny and Brian Flynn crowded round to hear the low, guttural accents from across the sea. She sounded strong and highly efficient, as she reported to Mitch in guarded tones that everything was going ahead as planned, and the new allies were gathering sufficient test material for their approval.

Four times, in the evenings, Mitch had called from a public phone near Ballyhean to a bar in Alphen aan den Rhine where she had set up the call. On these occasions, her voice lost some of the hard edge and, although still guarded, they were able to inquire after each other's well-being. After the wire-taping that had been instigated in his flat, Mitch was still too paranoid to relax enough to make any remarks that could be misinterpreted as other than those between war mongering colleagues.

On the last of these planned calls which Margitte referred to as *stikem*, apparently meaning secret, she told him the events had gone through more smoothly than she had expected. They were to be met by her old friend, Hans Muller, when they arrived. Via a courier, she would send him final plans which would spell out the arrangements.

Mitch gave permission to use the second of the two addresses that he had left her when they were back in England, and they finally hung up knowing they would be unlikely to meet until it was all over. Either rich and free, or very dead.

The daily planning sessions at the old fish warehouse became more and more exacting as dates for the planting of the explosives were written into a large desk planner. Each location was meticulously chosen, with each team's ingress and exit to the targets logged into a separate file. Mitch could see that, if the bombs were ever to arrive, this team of assorted fanatics was quite capable of carrying out hideous devastation. It would be hard to fail, using such well-planned precision and such terrifying explosives.

Mike Ryan, as the accompanying officer, was given the responsibility of arranging the trip for himself and Mitch. They checked schedules for arrival at Amsterdam's Schipol airport, which Taffy always jokingly referred to as 'Sheep-Hole'. A date was chosen, and they decided to travel separately via England. Mike would go by British Air out of Heathrow, and Mitch would travel by ferry from Dover over to Ostend, and then drive, using the Belgium and Dutch motorways.

A few days before the intended departure date, Mitch received a call from his aunt. For what would be the last time, he drove the short distance to collect the details which had arrived. Margitte and he had spent nearly an hour on their last night together discussing how the final arrangements would be given to him. They had talked about using coded messages but realized that, until she knew all the aspects of how her friends intended to set up the deal, there were altogether far too many parameters. They had ruled out both telephones and faxes during the final stage because of the danger of taps.

Finally, Margitte had insisted that the instructions be written and that they be delivered by hand. As the first licks of dawn had come across their curtains at the Trethawnton, Mitch gave her his own farm address and that of Aunty

Kate. It only remained for him to say which one was the most suitable. In his present nerve-jangled condition, the second of the two had been no choice at all. It had been a necessity.

'I don't know what games you're up to, Mitchell O'Doule,' his gray-haired aunt said to him as she swung the front door open at his knock. 'But you'd better come on in, and take this packet away from me before I'm tempted to steam it open.'

As if in response to her words, the old enamel kettle on her kitchen hob began to sing at the top of its cracked voice.

'I'll make you a cup of tea while you look at your letter in peace,' she said and pointed at the overstuffed armchair he had come to think of as his own over the last few weeks. 'It came by some uniformed girl. She knocked at the door and wanted me to sign for it; tried to make out she was a proper courier, but I think she was an air hostess. I've seen them around. Still it's none of my business, as you've told me before.'

With a sniff, she busied herself with the tea things, and Mitch tore open the manila envelope and shook out three smaller ones that were inside. One was typed, another blank, and the third was written in Margitte's hand. The funny Continental characters seemed so out of place in this traditional Irish kitchen.

He looked firstly at the typed envelope. Inside, on one single page, was the plan to be understood by Mike Ryan and the others. These same plans would be dictated at the final phone conference. He and Mitch would be collected at the Sheraton Hotel, Schipol, on the morning of the twentieth. They would be driven to a secret destination where they would be introduced to all the parties. At a suitable time, they would be shown the effectiveness of the goods. Following that, they would be escorted back to the airport, where they would be given the necessary tickets for their next destination. It would be here they would take delivery of the final shipment.

The letter closed bluntly with the statement that half the money would be handed over in cash in Holland; the other half would have to be transferred electronically to an account to be disclosed later. Payment for the first half would be acceptable in pounds, dollars, or Deutsche Marks. They were to indicate before departure which currency. It all looked too easy, but nonetheless, it sounded very organized and professional. The Irish could pull out halfway through, if they were unhappy with the goods or their performance. Supposedly, they could pull out later, if they desired, except they would probably have some difficulty regaining the first half of the money. Obviously, these people play hardball, thought Mitch, as he sat motionless in the chair.

He opened the second envelope, and nodded stiffly, as his aunt put a steaming cup next to him, with the customary plate of ginger cookies.

Darling Mitch,

I thought for several moments before I decided to use that form of address. I hope that you will forgive it. Also, I was worried this might fall into the wrong hands, but then, if it did, we would already be under suspicion and, if that were the case, we could not carry out the plan, which relies on complete trust by your colleagues. So far, I hope, like you, they are bewitched by my foreign ways. Well, they haven't seen anything yet!

You must bring the money in your briefcase. A swap will occur. Do not be alarmed if it happens without your knowledge. My friends are very good.

The arrangements should all fit together well, but just to be sure, please mix the contents of the small blue envelope with your traveling companion's drink the night before Hans collects you. The other brown envelope is to go into either his food or drink the day before you go to the next destination. There will be no taste and it won't kill him!

Once it's all over I will be in touch, and then it's up to you. I can't wait to see you.

Love,

Margitte

Mitch opened the third package and shook out the two smaller envelopes, one blue and one brown. He wondered what devious chemicals they enclosed. But, as in every other aspect of this whole business, he was forced to leave all the details to Margitte. He tried to gain some comfort in the knowledge that at least the concept of the plan was his, even if he was a somewhat silent and impotent partner at the moment. The two small envelopes he put in his outside jacket pocket. The hand-written note and the typed instructions, he read twice more.

Aunty Kate was bustling around the kitchen doing heaven knows what menial task over and over to try and seem occupied. Mitch had to smile at her apparent innocence, which was barely enough to cover her bursting curiosity. It is funny, thought Mitch, how people behave. Once they know you are involved in dangerous business, they become attracted to it. This, in spite of initially protesting their desire not to know what it is all about. It is probably a question of familiarity allowing one to become easy with the situation. Still, this was something he could never divulge to anyone. He was almost at the point of no return.

Swallowing the last of his tea, he pulled himself out of the chair and carried his cup into the kitchen. He reached for the teapot and, shaking it, removed the lid and poured some more water in from the kettle. Replacing the kettle, he pushed the iron handle into the slot on the black stove.

As he threw Margitte's notes onto the glowing coals he thought how convenient the old household equipment was. A modern electric cooker would never do the same job.

The paper caught immediately and he used a poker to stir the ashes around within their last resting place. He hoped his actions would be missed by his aunt, but she, ever watchful, could not let the circumstances pass without comment.

'I thought all you types used invisible writing,' she sniffed. 'It must have been pretty important for the fire treatment.'

Mitch replaced the cover and looked around for some milk and sugar. His aunt stared at him as she produced a matching willow-pattern jug and bowl.

'Sorry, Aunty, no can do,' Mitch said quietly, as he went back to his chair. 'Just pretend you never saw me and we'll all be fine. Rest assured that no one is going to get hurt,' he added.

He spent a few minutes more with Aunty Kate, and would have stayed longer, except the covert nature of his visit now made it difficult for them both to remain without speaking of it. So they endured some silent moments before Mitch made his excuses and left.

As he walked down the small neat path to the street, he was very aware this would be the last time he would ever see his Aunty Kate again. He was surprised at how upset he felt at this realization. Without a backward glance, he turned the wheel on the small Fiesta and drove away.

The final meeting of the war council took place the next day. In the intervening time, Mitch had a haircut and allowed the two-week stubble on his upper lip to continue its snaillike progress towards mustachehood. The haircut was clipped down to almost a similar length at the back and sides of his narrow head. The barber left more length on top. Mitch liked the new appearance as he felt it gave his thin sallowness an air of distinction.

Since they were quite used to regular changes, none of the other members bothered to comment, as they all took their places around the battered table for the last time. Mitch outlined his and Mike Ryan's role. Mike, in turn, produced the tickets supplied by Ferguson, the lawyer. Mitch's were for a private airplane to Southampton airport, a car-hire reservation and another ticket on board the Sealink ferry from Dover to Ostend. Ryan skimmed the fat envelope across to Mitch, who pocketed it without comment. Mike's own arrangements were for the normal Belfast/Liverpool crossing, a train to King's Cross, a tube to Heathrow and a British Air flight direct to Schipol. The journey times were almost the same and so they agreed to meet at the Sheraton Hotel two nights hence.

Matt brought in the telephone and placed it in the middle of the table with instructions that the call would be coming through in ten minutes. Leaving a pot of coffee, and a glass of Bushmills for Taffy, he quietly withdrew.

'So, gentlemen, we are down to the short strokes,' Mike Ryan said, as he reached for the pot and filled his chipped mug. 'Does anybody have any second thoughts or suggestions, before Mitch and I go off "on the piss" in Holland. Maybe he can fix me up with one of his new girlfriend's pals.'

Mitch forced himself to smile.

Taffy sat back and looked glassily at his colleagues.

'I still think it's a helluva lot of money.'

'We all know that, Taff,' Conny spoke up, grinning his usual inane grin. 'But we can't do the job without the Mephistos, and they seem to come a bit expensive. Can't we just get on with it, so we can move to the planting stage? Then to the best bit – the blowing-up stage. That's the bit I like.'

'Brian, what do you think?' Taffy asked the quiet

member almost hiding behind his coffee mug.

Brian tore his gaze from the curling maps on the wall and answered in almost a whisper. 'I agree with Conny. Let's just get the goods and blow the Brits to kingdom come.'

'You're right, I guess,' Taffy sighed. 'It's just that I hate to see so much of our money disappearing. You know how long it takes us to accumulate it.'

Throwing back his head, he emptied his glass and then looked embarrassed, as if he was in some way undermining the plan. Seeming unconcerned by the tense atmosphere, Ryan leaned forward.

'Mitch and I will take the money in separate lots. It has to be a cash transaction, if we agree to do the deal. And that depends on the results of the tests. There should be no problem in carrying the money. It is the Common Market after all.' He smiled at the rest of them.

'Has Fergy drawn it all out?' Mitch asked.

Ryan lit one of his cheroots, and in an exhale of pungent blue smoke, replied, 'It's on its way here in the van. There's four of the lads riding shotgun with it. We don't want any mistakes over here, do we? The patrols are always on the lookout. Providing there's no sudden roadblock, it should be a smooth ride.'

The phone in front of them buzzed and they all stared at it. Mitch switched on the loudspeaker box next to it and gestured for Ryan to take the handset. Instead, Taffy picked it up.

'Hello,' he breathed into the mouthpiece, 'and a good day to you.'

Margitte appeared unconcerned at the sound of the newcomer's voice.

'To whom am I speaking?' Her accent was just a trifle heavier than usual.

'This here is Colonel O'Brian, a colleague of your initial

contact. I just wanted you to know we are taking this financial aspect very seriously. So I don't expect anything to go wrong, do you hear me? We've worked hard for it and I shall hold you personally responsible if there are any mistakes.'

Taffy's true nature came through in the tone that he used. It was threatening and unpleasant. Mitch knew that Margitte would be unfazed by it, but he was grateful once again to witness Taffy in full flood. At times, even he could be fooled by the plump, drunken exterior. Hermann Goering, Mitch thought, as Taffy leaned back and stared into the bottom of his empty glass. Just like Fat Hermann. Somehow overweight people seem less menacing than thin ones, like Ryan, me, and the others round this table. There were Goebbels, Himmler and Hitler also, he was forced to remember.

Margitte's voice ignored the threat and began to read down the short list of demands, including the currency denomination.

'We're ready to go as instructed. It's in dollars.' Ryan added, 'I assume that's okay?'

'That will be acceptable. The amount is as agreed?'

'As agreed,' Ryan replied in a clipped tone. 'I look forward to meeting you.'

There was a click as the connection was broken at the other end.

'Not too friendly,' Ryan said.

'I told you all along, very professional,' Mitch replied, pleased to be able to make some comment during the proceedings.

Taffy slumped back in his chair, looking more like a sack of lumpy vegetables. He mumbled and looked gloomily around the group. The others sat staring at the bare surroundings, waiting for the news that the money had been driven over from the lawyer's office. They did not have to wait more than half an hour. A call came in to announce that the vehicle had left its destination, and they all checked their watches, knowing the approximate time it would take to cross the Belfast traffic. Eventually, there was a clattering of steel-studded boots on the metal stairs, and the faithful Matt brought in a rain-slicked cardboard box, tied up with string.

'Fucking hell,' Conny Fitzsimmons, exploded, grinning wildly. 'Is that the best old Fergy could come up with? It looks like a box of old clothes on its way to the Salvation Army.'

Ryan winced and mumbled, 'Precisely.' He then glanced back at Mitch and mouthed the words, 'Thick as shit.'

Ryan undid the string and counted out the bundles of five-hundred-dollar notes. They were neatly bound, but had the look of the used currency that was preferred, whenever suspicious financial transactions took place. He pushed over the pile to Mitch.

'You take it across in that flash case of yours, Mitch. I can't face those immigration boys.'

'If you're sure, Mike. They don't worry too much about money.'

Taffy's bleary eyes watched the proceedings warily.

'Cheer up, we're using it for the cause, not for a booze-up,' Mitch said and smiled across at him. Taffy slumped further down.

Putting the five hundred thousand dollars into a plastic bag, Mitch pushed the buzzer and waited for Matt to come in. He wanted to get the hell out of here now the game had most definitely begun, but he felt he should delay as much as possible. As soon as Matt arrived, he ordered a sandwich and tried to relax. Thank God, they're not mind-readers, he thought.

Mitch felt a wave of relief wash over him as he bade his comrades farewell and returned to his flat. The bag of money that he clutched to him felt extremely conspicuous, as he walked the three blocks to where his car was parked. He stopped at an off-license on the way home and bought a small bottle of Scotch whiskey. He felt it was time to wean himself off the local brew. It would probably not be too easy to obtain down under.

Now he was under way, his fears of capture were diminishing rapidly. He was at heart a loner and felt claustrophobic playing a role around the war table, with the four others who were so anxious to blow the world apart with their false dreams. Now he was in his element again. He was out on his own, controlling his own movements and, he hoped, his own destiny. He smiled at the realization that most of his future, however, was in the long, well-shaped hands of his Dutch lover. He had to admit that for him to feel as relaxed about the situation could only mean his normal life-preserving instincts were either completely fooled, or he was totally correct in his view that he had found a soul mate.

He spent his last night in Ireland sipping his Scotch, listening to some soft rock music, courtesy of the BBC, and thinking about Margitte, before falling into a dreamless sleep.

Chapter Sixteen

Truro, 1787

Paddy awoke from his dream with a start. He had dreamed he was lying in bed with Katherine, and little Becky was tugging at his arm. He just wanted a few more minutes of peace before he went out to work on the farm, but Becky would not let him rest.

'Get away from me you little devil, or I'll tan yer little backside for you.'

'You do that, yer great mick, and I'll kick yer in the balls.'

Chipper Johnson's harsh London tones shattered Paddy's subconscious. As his eyes came awake, a great feeling of sadness swept down on him, as he recognized the same dreary cell that he had been confined to for the last two months. He was cold and stiff, and the sleep-induced images of his life back home were now replaced with the stark reality of prison routine, as they both awaited their banishment from the shores of the British Isles.

'Back 'ome was yer?' Chipper asked, smiling.

Paddy nodded and rose up from the hard bench that served both as bed and seat.

'I gets the same dreams. They can't take them away from yer, even if they wanted. Still, we've got somethin' on the go today, me ol' mate. The screw tipped me the wink earlier that we're on our way.'

The time had hung heavy for the two of them. Each day

was a replica of the last, with only Sunday holding any difference. Then, they would be chained to an outside wall along with the other inmates and allowed to say their prayers in unison. After this, a local minister would preach at them for the better part of an hour. Such sermons were usually a diatribe of the effects of sin, and how they would all be forgiven if they would only repent. Occasionally, someone would shout out some witty remark during this lecture. Such behavior would have no effect on the preacher, but it would attract the attention of one of the guards, who would stand in front of the offender and threaten him with a thick nightstick.

As a Catholic, Paddy felt confused by his emotions during these Sunday services. He knew what he was listening to was the work of the devil, although so much of the proceedings were like his simple services back home. Eventually, he decided he would try to concentrate on what he was familiar with and ignore the rest.

Chipper liked the Sunday service, because it allowed him to sing the few hymns that were permitted. He had a light baritone voice and apart from the odd dropped aitch, his London accent did not show through.

As Paddy left his bed and stood over the night bucket, he calculated that it was Thursday. New Year's Day had come and gone with no effect on their lives. Well, if today was the day they would be moved, so be it. There was no comfort here. He would be happy to be off to Van Diemen's Land, Australia, or wherever the hell these damned Englishmen wanted. His life was over anyway, so he might just as well accept whatever fate had in store for him. At least with Chipper beside him, he would not be alone.

It was mid-morning when the jailers came for them. They were taken outside and put aboard a covered wagon, and with no more ceremony than a rough shout to 'Get on' from the driver, they left the confines of Truro jail and bounced out into the countryside.

There was a small grilled window on the side of the wagon, through which they could see the passing view of the same small fields and hedgerows that they had witnessed on their way into the Cornish town. Again, they were the only passengers. Their crime was seen by the authorities to be most heinous, hence the special punishment that had been pronounced for them.

After four days' uncomfortable traveling across Devon and Dorset, they were deposited in a wooded area and pulled out into the cool spring air.

'This is it, lads, you get out 'ere.'

The senior jailer who had been with them since Truro, was not unkindly and stood back to let them leave the dark confines of their mobile home. A giant of a man, he was called Ben, and although he was known to have a wicked temper, he had always treated Paddy and Chipper with decency.

He had been a farmer until a blight had poisoned his land, making his already stretched finances unable to support him and his family any longer. His cousin worked for the mayor and so he was able to obtain a job at the prison. Paddy felt Ben's years on the land had given him a more reasonable attitude to broken rules than those others of his colleagues, who constantly took a holier-than-thou attitude to their brothers outside the law.

'When you're out in the fields, Chipper,' Paddy had said, 'you have to remember nature doesn't always do what she's supposed to. Ben's lived with all the late summers and early frosts for many years, so he knows that things don't always go as planned.'

Chipper preferred to think of all jailers as screws, and even though he begrudgingly said Ben seemed okay, he still kept close-mouthed whenever any prison staff were around.

'So what's up here, Ben?' Paddy asked the large ex-farmer.

'We've been told to bring you as far as this, Paddy. We have to wait until some others join you, then we turn around and we're back to Truro.'

The jailer sat on the ground a few feet away from his charges and lit a small pipe he kept in his waistcoat pocket.

'I think you are due to go round to Southampton. That's another day or two from here, I think. I don't know, 'cos I've never been this far away from home before.'

Chipper was sitting on Paddy's other side, so it was unlikely Ben could hear the 'Stubble-Jumper', the little cockney greeted this news with. Ignoring the remark, Paddy confessed that, although they had not been to this precise part, they had been to Southampton Water before. This was strange, he added, because, until just a few months earlier, he, like the farmer sitting on the ground and relaxing in the sunshine, had never been further away from his home than a few miles.

'Now I've been all over the South of England. And none of it my choosing. I tell you honestly, Ben, I was knocked on the head in Ireland, woke up on board the *Distinction*, made to work like a dog, then punished for a crime I didn't do. Chipper's innocent, too. We were coming back to the ship and ran into the problem.'

'Save yer breath, Paddy, 'e's just a screw,' Chipper snarled.

'I guess I am to you,' Ben replied, tamping the tobacco down in his pipe with a gnarled finger.

The horses between the shafts of the wagon shook their heads in their nose bags as Ben's colleague dozed up on the platform.

'Those of us at the bottom of the heap have a lot to contend with,' the jailer continued. 'I'm not doin' this job because I like it. I lost me farm and all me money, so I took what I could. It's not the best job in the world, but you do meet some interesting folks at it.'

He smiled at the recollection, and looked hard at the pair before him.

'Everyone says they're innocent, you know. It's all the same to me. Apart from 'angin, most evr'ybody gets off eventually. Some sooner than others. If it wasn't for that other one, you might 'ave stood a better chance, I 'ear tell.'

'What do you mean by that?'

Chipper sat up straight, the chains round his ankles and wrists rattling, as he stared round the bulk of his Irish friend to look at Ben. The big man stood up with a grunt and paced about, under the trees, the dappled light shining on his florid face.

'It's what I 'eard,' he said in his rich Cornish burr. 'The other one they arrested that night, he turned King's evidence and they sent 'im back to 'is ship.'

'The bastard,' was Chipper's only comment.

Paddy sat quietly, the thought of the betrayal sinking in slowly. He knew things with Sande looked suspicious when he had not turned up that first morning when they were put before that old black-robed judge. Even he had alluded to the fact that the NCO had been sent back to his ship. Paddy had taken the words at their face value. It had never occurred to him Sande had managed to put the blame for the murder on both of his shipmates.

'So you're telling us Sande confessed to his involvement but put the blame on us?'

'So I 'eard,' the jailer continued. 'Of course, there's lots of rumors running round any prison, but this case was a bit different. They say that Sande, if that's 'is name—'

'It's pronounced "Sand",' Paddy interjected,

'Well, whatever 'e calls 'imself, he got put into a cell different from you, right?' Ben came and sat down once more in front of them.

'Yes, that's right. You remember, Chipper?'

'The bastard claimed officer rank as I remember,' Chipper replied.

'Well, that night there was only one other cell available, and who should be in there but a drunken character called Sir Anthony Black, sleeping off a night on the town.'

'So what did that have to do with us?' Chipper asked belligerently, his face showing signs of anger at the mention of the chief's part in his present predicament.

'I don't know what 'appened,' Ben continued. 'But in the morning, this Sir Anthony asked for an interview with the judge, who happened to be a cousin of his. Sande got brought before the beak and sent back to 'is ship. Then you get sent up to Truro to the assize. A copy of Sande's confession arrived before you and so it was all over before you even knew it. You see, Sir Anthony is an old drinking buddy of the Right Honorable Clancy, the popinjay that sentenced you. Whether you were innocent or not, you never stood a chance.'

'I wonder 'ow the bastard got away wiv it?'

Paddy felt a return of the same emotion that had struck him when he and Chipper were taken from Clancy's court to the derision of the powdered and perfumed audience. It was a feeling of helplessness, a feeling of losing control of your life. There was a terror about it that struck the normally placid Irishman with such force that a blinding anger welled up in him and made him shake. To think such people could tear your world apart and walk away from the scene as if nothing had happened. He had felt this same anger before, when he had that run-in with the chief. What was it about that man that caused such a feeling?

'Perhaps you should know why Sir Anthony was in jail,' Ben began again. 'He's quite well known in the county. Likes to flirt and drink and dance and all kinds of stuff. A regular rowdy toff. Unfortunately, 'e 'as been known to be a little careless who 'e goes with, if you get my meaning.

Everybody has to watch out for him.'

'Another one of them?' Chipper exploded. 'And you put Sande in the same damned cell? Bloody marvelous. And in the morning, the toff says he understands. Christ, I'm surprised they didn't call for a vicar, and get hitched while they were at it. They both must have thought they'd died and gone to 'eaven.'

'Sir Anthony had been found drunk down by the harbor, they say,' Ben continued. 'He was wrapped in a cloak but, as they took him out of the way, it fell open, and 'e was wearing a full set of women's petticoats underneath. That don't set well with us countryfolk, you know. So they flung 'im in jail to sort it out.'

Paddy's catatonic state had begun to disappear and so he turned to the jailer and said, 'Look, I know it makes no real difference to you, but here is what really happened.'

He explained the problems that he had had with the chief on the voyage, and his threatening behavior. Then he told Ben how they had spent the evening in St Mawes, culminating with the discovery of Sande with his victim, and how they were arrested by the Customs patrol. Ben shook his head and looked sadly at the two men who had been his charges during the journey from Truro.

'It's a bloody dreadful shame,' he said. 'I wish I could do something about it. But you know that once the likes of us are put to carrying out orders, there's nothing we can do about it.'

Chipper began to make the suggestion that perhaps he could let the key to the chains drop and sort of look away, but one look at the jailer's face caused the words to quickly dry up. Ben might be sympathetic, but he was not sympathetic enough to risk the consequences of aiding and abetting an escape by two dangerous men on their way to transportation.

'I feel real sorry for you both,' the jailer said, 'but I can't do nothin' about it. Try and look on the bright side though. Maybe this new place will be better. You've not made much of a life here. Maybe Australy's better.'

He stretched his arms and stood up. Then he slowly walked over to the wagon and reached up next to the sleeping driver. He pulled down a bundle of cloth and carried it over to the two men sitting with their chains draped around them.

'They say it's going to be a long voyage. This may keep you company and keep the rats at bay.' So saying he unfolded the cloth and pulled out a small ginger cat that had been sleeping inside. 'This 'ere's Marmy. I've been wonderin' what to do with him.'

The cat opened up its bright blue eyes and stared at them with an annoyed expression.

'It came into my room one day back at the jail. The mother had deserted it and it sat on my bed for several days, even though I kept throwing it out. Obviously, it likes human company. Its color reminded me of the marmalade that my old mother used to make back on the farm, so I called it Marmy. Here, take him, if it is a him. Kind of hard to tell with cats sometimes, isn't it?'

Paddy took the little animal in his big hand and turned it over on its back. It squealed in protest.

'It's a him all right,' said Paddy, and turned the cat the right way up again. It stared up into the Irishman's face and blinked its eyes. 'It's a looker, isn't it, Chipper?'

The cockney reached over and rubbed the cat softly under its ear. It leaned against his finger.

'Yea,' he said, 'it's a pretty one. Real kindly of you to let us 'ave it, Ben,' he added as an acceptance of the jailer's new status as one of his friends.

Paddy stroked the little cat, which purred contentedly and then put him inside his shirt, next to his stomach. 'I hope we get enough food to feed him,' the Irishman said.

'Don't worry too much,' Ben replied. 'He's caught nearly all his food so far. He may be small, but he can run down most rats and mice he wants. I'm glad you like him. Maybe he'll bring you some luck. God knows you haven't had much so far.'

The wait for the other convicts lasted a whole day. Watched by two guards, the prisoners, bound in their heavy chains, spent the time lying around under the rich foliage of a small cluster of trees. A local farmer provided a basket of fresh food for which the jailers paid with a signed voucher.

There was a pail of milk with the evening meal, and Paddy pulled Marmy out from his shirt and let him drink from the pail's upturned lid. There seemed to be a bond between the two of them from the start, but this luxurious offering cemented the whole pact. Sensing this, Paddy allowed the little animal to play around on the ground afterwards, and saw that it was happy to stay in his immediate vicinity. As darkness descended, Paddy returned Marmy inside the shirt where he nestled, a ball of orange fur.

In the morning, through the mists of the forest, they saw a rider approaching their camp. He was wearing the uniform of the royal navy, but with some insignia that Chipper did not recognize. He reined in his horse and banged on the side of the wagon where all four men had elected to spend the night, jailers and prisoners both.

Ben climbed over the others and went out to see what the commotion was about. Dismounting, the officer reported in a high officious voice they were to be ready for immediate inspection and departure within the hour. The party they had been waiting for was three miles away and was anxious to be off.

Pulling the horse's head up from the grass where it had been grazing, the officer rode off once more, and left the men to prepare themselves. Marmy had wriggled out of

Paddy's clothes in the night and seemed to have found some small shrew to breakfast on. His paws were bloody and his eyes had a narrow look as if he had been squinting into the dark for a long time. Mewing softly, he followed the men about as they performed their ablutions.

Ben shook the hands of both his charges, saying he felt it would be best to say their goodbyes now before the others arrived. He told them that they had been model prisoners and that they didn't deserve their punishments. But come what may, they should not give up hope and should continue to trust in the Lord.

Before much longer, a sound reached them through the trees. First, it was just a soft rustling, but within a few moments, the noise grew and took on the sound of a small army with its armor and swords clattering and its horses trotting. The four men stood up and peered through the trees, half expecting to see a medieval force burst through the cover of the forest.

The farmer had told them they were within the area where King William II had been assassinated in the eleventh century. The red-bearded monarch had been shot by an unseen archer and the spot was marked by the Rufus Stone, less than a mile away. The gathering noise through the morning's stillness played on the minds of the men and took them to that time of Norman knights and caparisoned steeds.

The first men who finally came into the clearing shattered any further imagery of high ideals and grandeur. What emerged before them was a jostling ragbag of the most awful specimens of humanity they had ever seen. Shuffling under the authority of their many guards were some hundred prisoners, manacled and chained together and dressed in mud-splattered and torn clothing. Their eyes were downcast and their hair matted on their heads and faces. Thin arms and legs jutted out from badly fitting clothes, and many of the men had no shoes on their blackened feet.

'Dear God,' muttered Ben under his breath, as the column approached the wagon. Paddy and Chipper both stiffened at the sight of this group of human debris, half-trotting and half-staggering towards them. There was not a glimmer of life in any of the glances that were stolen their way.

'Prisoners, halt.' A harsh voice barked through the clear air and the throng of heaving men stopped and threw themselves on the ground, panting.

'Well, where the bloody hell are the rest?'

'Beg yer pardon.'

Ben stepped forward, looking for the owner of the voice among the sea of humanity before them. A small man, with a fierce mustache and mutton chop whiskers, dismounted and bustled over to him. He was wearing a faded uniform that had seen better days and he was carrying a thick stick. This he swished about on anyone who happened to lie within his path as he came briskly forward. The objects of his administration merely cowed under the glancing blows, and paid no more attention to them than if they were being buzzed by flying insects. It was obvious to the stunned onlookers that this man's charges were blunted to whatever harshness might be doled out to them in their captivity.

'Well, speak up, man, I 'aven't got all bloody day.'

The small officer peered up into Ben's benign face, with an intensity that others might have felt intimidating. With the stolidity of his type, Ben merely stood his ground and asked politely whom he might be addressing.

'Captain Charles Constantine, of the special service, bound for His Majesty's penal colony in Australia. And again I say, where are the others?'

'This is all there is,' replied the jailer. 'How many were you expecting?'

'They said at least another fifty.'

The captain glared at the taller man.

'Well, I guess you'll be coming up four dozen short then, won't you.'

It was clear Ben was not impressed with the man's attitude nor, judging by the disapproving look he gave around, with the miserable specimens crouching on the ground.

'Now, listen here, my man. I've marched this bunch of assorted dregs down from Andover, and I'm expected to swell their ranks by half before we get to Southampton.'

'That's your problem then, isn't it, squire,' Ben said firmly, as he turned to his own charges with a poorly disguised wink. 'You'll just 'ave to ask for some volunteers as you travel along.' So saying, he took hold of Paddy's and Chipper's chains and walked them over to the edge of the group where he let the links fall to the ground.

Captain Constantine rushed over and grabbed the chains up.

'Are you crazy? These men are convicted felons of the worst sort. They could have run away. They look very dangerous to me.'

Ben slowly walked back to his partner, who was waiting with the reins in his hand, ready to begin the return to Cornwall. He turned, as he climbed up alongside, and said, 'While they were in my charge they never tried to escape, but then they weren't half starved to death by a sadistic bastard like you, were they, Captain?'

'I'll report you for your damned insolence.'

Without another word, the wagon moved forward slowly and Paddy and Chipper were left to their fate. As they found out, the condition of the rest of their new colleagues was not due to Captain Charles Constantine. It was more the fault of the penal institutions from where the group had originated and the state of the men's minds.

These poor wretches came from all over the southern Home Counties. They represented a quarter of the seven hundred souls who were destined to form the unwilling passengers of the famed First Fleet. This was to be under the command of Captain Arthur Phillip, who had volunteered to command the long and dangerous voyage to Australia.

Paddy and Chipper stood staring at the wrecks who were to be their companions and shook their heads slowly. They felt strong, healthy and relaxed, compared to the troop that shared their chains.

A bucket of tea was sent around and the newcomers were silently appraised by the group who looked as if they had been born laced together and dragged up from hell.

The 'army' had been marched in columns of three, and Paddy and Chipper were chained to a man who introduced himself as Edgar Smithson. He had long, bedraggled, white hair and a layer of grime on him that must have been the result of months of neglect. Nonetheless, he had a cultured air about him, although his immediate neighbors giggled at his introduction and insisted he was really called Prof. Apparently he had studied at Oxford. His knowledge of the world had initially been viewed with suspicion by the others, but then was finally respected and eventually sought after. He had a slow relaxed way of talking, and his bright gray eyes showed an intellect that was missing from most of the others in this assortment.

Prof was also very tall, which meant that the first choice of his immediate companion was not good. Chipper hardly measured five foot three and Prof must have been over six foot four. It took a moment before the guard assigned to the task accepted the suggestion that Paddy would make a more suitable neighbor. As they finished the tea break and rose up for the journey, the graduating height of their heads made the three of them look like the sloping roof of a shed.

The troop walked along towards the east, and the goal of Southampton. Prof told them his story. He had been unable to complete his studies at the great college of Oxford, because his father, a man of the cloth, had fallen victim to the sinful temptation of gambling. In order to pay the debts he had run up, he had sold everything and left the family destitute, running away to Scotland where he had never been heard from again.

Prof was forced to leave his comfortable life of academia, and wander the small towns to the South, looking for work at various churches and the libraries of stately homes. Unfortunately, he fell in love with the daughter of one of his employers. The couple were caught in a full embrace, red-handed, and the girl was sent immediately to Switzerland. Prof was effectively banished from the county as being an undesirable.

Eventually, he headed off towards London, sleeping rough and living off the land for several weeks. Unfortunately, he neglected to care for himself too well and his appearance began to suffer. This meant he was seen as indistinguishable from the other con men that traveled the roads, preying on the gullibility of the public. Although he lacked the innate skill of these petty criminals, he looked like them and was treated accordingly.

He spent every penny of his money and was forced to take a job digging graves at one of the parishes situated on the London Bath road. It was exhausting work and he earned so little that he could only just manage to feed himself, during what was to be one of the most unhappy periods of his entire existence.

Relief from his wretched plight finally came when he was walking past a line of clothing, hanging out to catch the drying winds. There, at the end of an assortment of women's things, was a large woolen cloak. It fluttered enticingly at him, just beyond reach. Its promised warmth reminded him of the cold nights he spent shivering on the ground of the gravedigger's hut. In his weakened condition, he forgot what he was doing.

Like a tiny child drawn by a bright object in his mother's hand, he reached across the hedge and stumbled through. He took hold of the cloak and wrenched it from the line. Had he been more careful and quietly lifted the garment, he would probably have got away with his crime. But he made two mistakes. By pulling hard he shook the line and caused it to attract the attention of the resident, who was enjoying a cup of lemonade at the window of his cottage. His second mistake was in choosing the home of the local Justice of the Peace to perpetrate his crime. And crime it was considered to be. The householder ran out and grabbed Prof's arm, as he attempted to make his getaway through the hedge. Pulling him back into the garden, he wrestled him to the ground and performed the indignity of tying him up with a pair of damp women's drawers.

'Light pink they were in color,' reminisced the tall stooping convict, as they trudged along the country road.

'I was in court the next morning, sentenced by my very own captor, and sent off to Newbury jail that afternoon. Transportation for fourteen years was the sentence and I never even got the chance to protest. Apparently, transportation is all the rage here in the South. Since I've been locked up for more than six months now, I've had the chance to learn all there is to know about it.

'With the Americans turned against us, we've got too many people looking to feed themselves. Too many old soldiers back from the colonies, with no skills apart from fighting. The jails are full to bursting and they've even filled up a line of old hulks moored in the Thames.

'It seems Parliament decided to solve several problems at a stroke. They say we need to protect our Far East trade route, sailing down from India. The French are always causing problems with raids on our ships, carrying spices, and we have to look after our interests carefully. Apparently, we've borrowed money from the Rothschilds to subsidize our trade out there, and so now we need to set up a base from which the royal navy can freely sail out into the Indian Ocean.'

This brief economic and geography lesson was delivered in measured tones to his two pupils, and both of them found themselves listening with interest. Affairs of state were not often understood by the likes of Paddy and Chipper, but the explanations of the events surrounding their own miscarried punishment were fascinating to them.

'There's also hope we can find some new forests of tall trees for the royal navy's masts. To fight the French, we need fast ships with many guns. The only way to do this is to catch more wind. This means we need either more masts and sails per ship, which means more clutter on the decks, or we need taller masts.'

'We know a thing or two about that, me ol' mate,' Chipper spoke up. 'We've come from the navy only a few weeks ago. There's enough crap on a ship's deck to almost sink it.'

'So you can attest to the need to put more sail higher up,' Prof continued. 'Well, seventeen years ago, Captain James Cook – you must have heard of him?'

Chipper nodded enthusiastically, but Paddy looked blank and said he didn't think he'd ever come to Ireland; leastways, not his part of it.

'I'd be surprised if he hadn't,' said their new friend. 'He's been virtually everywhere else. Well, to continue, Captain Cook found this new place that he claimed for the Crown. Some say that a Dutchman called Van Diemen was there first, but the Dutch didn't do too much about it, being as it was so far away. So there you have it. Four solutions in one. The Establishment gets rid of the overpopulation of criminals, establishes a new base for the royal navy, and builds a new land that will never have the independence that those rebellious Americans build up. Then, as a little bonus, we get to harvest the tall trees that Captain Cook's botanist reported, fix 'em to our ships, and chase the French off the high seas. Brilliant, I call it.'

He swung along easily beside them, his loose chains gathered in one hand, while the other waved around, stabbing the air to make a point. He seemed, to all intents and purposes, to be on a stroll round the campus of his college, outlining some thesis to his favorite students. His flowing white hair and long beard swept around with the agitation of his speech. There was a broad smile of contentment on his face.

''E's fuckin' barmy, yer know,' one of the prisoners from the rank in front mumbled over his shoulder.

'Now don't you start your grumbling, Ackers,' Prof good-naturedly pushed the man in the back. 'You were all right when we talked the other day. What's happened. Are you missing your mum again?'

The man Prof had called Ackers turned around and said, 'I always miss 'er when it gets to dinner time. I can't seem to forget 'er pies. Can't get 'em out of me mind.'

Saying this, the man shook his great shoulders and began to sob. He gave the appearance of having once been a big man, but now, as he placed his hands over his crying face, one could detect that he had somehow shrunk during his incarceration. The three colleagues walking behind him were moved with compassion at the sight of such despair.

'See if this little chap can cheer you up a bit.'

Paddy reached into his shirt, took out Marmy and handed him across the gap to Ackers. For a moment the man was too upset to realize what it was and merely continued to draw in on himself. But, after several attempts, he grasped the small animal and held it to him.

'Cor, 'e's great,' the man said, and held him up to his face. Ackers seemed to straighten up at the feel of Marmy's warmth, and although Paddy worried the cat might try to escape, he was pleased to see that, while Marmy kept a steely eye on his new master, he was happy to submit himself to this new duty.

'None of this seems to worry you too much,' Paddy said to Prof, surprised at the relaxed attitude that the academic had exhibited.

'Frankly, it doesn't, Paddy. I may call you Paddy, mayn't I?'

The Irishman smiled in assent as, since he had been in the company of Englishmen, he was called that by everyone without thinking.

'Look here. In my case, I was nearly starving, certainly destitute, and about to commit my first crime. I was going nowhere, had no ambition and couldn't find one. Here I now am, being looked after by His Majesty, fed and soon to be clothed, I hope. I am part of a great adventure to the other side of the world, playing a part in England's glory. Compared to what, eh? Living on the floor of a mud hut, digging holes for uncertain wages. I think it's a great opportunity. I'm convinced fate has given me a tremendous chance.'

'You'll be callin' it a bloody 'oliday next,' Chipper spoke up. ''Ere, you don't know a poncey fucker called Clancy, do you?' His pinched face clouded over at the recollection of their day in the assize court.

'Clancy? No, I don't think I've had the pleasure. Is he Irish like you, Paddy?'

'No, Prof, he was the judge that sentenced us down in Cornwall. Don't mind Chipper, he was rather upset by the experience.'

'Well, being sailors, I expect that you at least are less frightened than most of these poor souls. Nearly all of them are absolutely terrified. They can't eat or sleep, and believe that they are going to a sort of hell on earth. It's mostly just ignorance. Nothing can be done about it, I'm afraid. Still it was certainly providential that we ended up together. I'm sure that the shackles will come off soon.'

The shackles remained on for all of that day and most of the next. Captain Constantine set the pace of the party at about four miles per hour. Unfortunately for the captain, his wards were not capable of marching any faster than two to three miles per hour, which meant that he had to constantly ride backwards and forwards, chivvying his herd. The thick swagger stick was regularly used on whomever he felt was holding the party back, but it had no overall effect.

Through the village of Totton they shambled, ignoring the children, running out to see the procession, and the sly looks of the populace, who had the wholesale opportunity of witnessing those more unfortunate than themselves. Country living in those parts was very routine, with little variation. Therefore, to see at first hand a large band of acknowledged sinners on their way to a deserved punishment was too much fun to pass by.

In spite of the depressing circumstances of their bondage, a few brave souls tried to strike up a song as they continued on through the thin woods of Millbrook, but their hearts were not in it, and the effort soon petered out. Up the hill outside the first environs of Southampton they staggered, like a beaten army returning from massive defeat.

A break for lunch was taken, and as the prisoners lay on the warm grass, bread was handed out, together with cheese and some apples. Many of the men ate little, but Prof, Chipper and Paddy ate their full share and whatever they could scrounge from those with smaller appetites. Marmy was generally handed round. This gave a great deal of amusement to all the men who had been starved of any interest, apart from their own uncertain future, for so many months. His antics were particularly cheered when he always ran back to Paddy after being inspected by a new fan.

'Even better than a little 'oming pigeon,' Ackers said.

The strong friendship between Ackers and Marmy was apparent to all. However, on one occasion, Paddy caught the stocky redhead using the cat's coat as a handkerchief and he had to be treated to a push in the back in the manner shown by Prof, with a demand for the animal to be returned. It was well into the afternoon before Paddy agreed to hand Marmy back to this latest member of his immediate family.

They were well into the center of the town when it came time to stop for the night. As they were to sleep out on the ground, they were lucky that the weather remained fine. A couple of fires were needed, however, and around these the guards and the prisoners clustered, taking small comfort from the flickering flames.

In his normal way, Prof found out what the plan was, and passed on the information that the next night would be their last on English soil for many years. They were to be ferried over the River Itchen in several parties. After this they would camp close to the eastern bank of Southampton Water, before joining the boats, moored close to the shore. Prof seemed to glean all this intelligence from various guards who escorted him to assorted clumps of bushes. He had what he called 'convenient diarrhea'. He explained it was convenient every time he needed new information. As the warders were not too bright, on a mission of mercy they could be tricked into releasing data that was normally very difficult to obtain.

The night was uncomfortable as none of their bindings were loosened; this was an effort to appease the paranoid Constantine's suspicion that an escape attempt was being plotted. He had no intention of being the man to allow a single one of these hardened criminals to abscond. He circled round and round the group at night, checking the chains, which only further disturbed each man's shallow sleep.

In the morning, there was a foolish roll-call which showed that either the good captain was correct to show such concern, or that there had been no plot to begin with.

Another meal, consisting of apples and bread with milk, put them all in as good a shape as could be expected for the remainder of their march.

The ferry was a waterlogged thing that was pushed through the turgid river by two stooped men with long poles. They kept their eyes downcast as each load of beaten humanity was pushed aboard their craft. Ropes, which passed through eyelets on the sides, ensured that they were not swept downstream, but the journey across the hundred yards of Itchen caused everyone's feet to become wet, adding to the general misery.

Only Prof and his two new friends stayed reasonably cheerful, as did Ackers, whenever he was permitted to look after Marmy. When they were deposited on the far bank, there was a final march to their staging post and a merging with more convicts in a similar plight. Away to the side was a small group of female prisoners. Their presence caused considerable excitement among the men, most of whom had not been that close to a female for months. Whistles and catcalls were sounded out with cries and soprano trills returned across the rough ground. Captain Constantine ran about officiously banging heads right and left, all to no avail.

The nearness of so much femininity, albeit in a dreadful condition, was too much to bear. Eventually, the senior guards conferred and agreed they should seek permission to have the women put aboard their own vessel before the men.

This order was agreed to by the navy officers who had left the seclusion of the floating prisons to inspect the situation. The women were shepherded off down the shallow banks to the edge of the dock and ferried out to their ship, waiting in deep water. A groan rent the air at their departure, and as if in acknowledgment of the general wretchedness, a light drizzle settled down on prisoners and jailers alike.

Spikes had been driven deep into the ground as permanent fixings for the transportees. Ten men apiece per spike were shackled to the spot for the night. Such an arrangement was not designed to cater to the convicts' comfort, and with the constant downpour, it was a wonder that illness did not become rampant.

In the morning, they were wakened from their wet night and sent without ceremony down to the waiting boats. Their last view of England was to be of the hillside that would become known as Spike Island by successive generations of people born in the immediate area.

The group that had traveled together for the last twenty-five miles stayed together through the final hours. Paddy, Chipper, Prof, and Ackers stumbled into the boarding vessel to be transferred to their new quarters aboard HMS *Falcon*. Ackers sobbed as the shore receded before his gaze, but Prof slapped him on the shoulder and told him to think of the opportunity that fate had given him. Were it not for this providence, Ackers would be faced with a life of living in the gutter and spending all his time trying to steal the ingredients for his mother to make yet another pie.

The reference to Ackers' mother only caused the convict to begin his sobbing again, which made Paddy get out Marmy to take the red-bearded man's mind off his unhappiness. Chipper showed no emotion as they left English soil, and Paddy only felt relief the marching was over, as he had developed blisters. They both sat together watching the ship ahead loom closer, aware they were entering a new phase in their lives. They were alone with these private thoughts when Chipper stiffened.

'For God's sake, look up there, Paddy,' he said between clenched teeth.

The Irishman looked to the bow of HMS *Falcon*.

'No, you daft bugger, there, in the stern.'

Paddy's eyes traveled back to the blunt rear of the ship. There, leaning over, was Chief Petty Officer Gunner Sande.

'They got the bastard, too, then, Chip?'

'I don't think so, Paddy. He's 'olding a billy club. We're as good as dead men.'

Chapter Seventeen

Ballyhean, 1993

The big day for Mitch's departure broke dramatically for him. All the day before, the thick Atlantic clouds had been building up from their breeding ground out over the gray western ocean. By mid-afternoon, rain had begun flooding in, and leaves had swirled around in miniature tornadoes out in the deserted farmyard.

He had made a few visits to local businesses in order to buy the few supplies he felt necessary for his journey, wherever it might eventually take him. His credit cards were paid up to date, and he had even arranged for an additional five thousand pounds to be available on both his Visa and MasterCard.

He kept his two guns handy at all times. The large Mauser was still in its tin box. He was confident the metal covering would allow him to transport it through the airport security systems, provided it remained in his checked-in luggage. Within the same box he stashed the two potions that Margitte had sent him, being careful to remind himself which one should be administered on each day.

His journey out to Holland did not require using public airlines, so he did not expect any problems with keeping the small pistol in its now familiar position at the small of his back. He knew very well the circumstances into which he was going would almost certainly preclude him from using a handgun effectively, but its presence gave him a gratifying feeling of security.

The war council had had another session, with Taffy being ever more suspicious about 'all their money going out of the country'. The reaction of the rest of the group to his slurred implications was such that Mitch managed to keep out of the argument, thereby giving him the appearance of an innocent bystander. His regularly thrown psychological switch worked its well-worn magic, and he kept apart from the melee, waiting for peace to reign once more. Nonetheless, it was a nasty moment that came out of the blue.

As his start was an early one, Mitch had packed his few belongings the night before. With the rain beating in waves on the windows of his flat, he ate a lonely final dinner of eggs and bacon, washed down with the Scotch that he had bought at the end of the meeting at the fish warehouse.

*

A crack of thunder almost directly overhead woke Mitch from a troubled dream. He had been crawling across a wet field, avoiding lights that were skimming across its surface, when the explosion entered his consciousness.

In a confused state of half-dreaming and half-waking, he believed he was being shot at and started to run. As he jerked awake and realized the events were less dramatic, he reached for his clock with the blood pounding in his head. 'Come on, Mitch,' he said to himself, 'it's only thunder and a dream. It's not the real thing yet.' Feeling almost guilty he had spoken out loud he got up and took a swig of orange juice out of the carton in the now almost empty fridge.

It was only five o'clock, but there was little point in trying to go back to sleep, so he turned on the radio and listened to what he considered a wildly optimistic weather forecast. Over the next hour, however, the rain lessened, and when he finally left his dreary home at seven thirty, there were patches of clear sky mixing with the dark clouds that were headed for the same destination as Mitch.

He was glad to be off. He now felt in charge and less a victim of circumstances. He was to drive to a small airfield in the south of Belfast and take a flying lesson that would include a very short stop in the Isle of Man. Here the instructor would report some engine difficulty and ask for a mechanic to be on hand. The plan would then call for Mitch to have a 'double' return with the small plane to the flying school, while he would take another aircraft on to Southampton. Mike Ryan would take the more normal commercial routes into Heathrow and thence on to Schipol. Due to Mitch's use of private flying facilities and a simple boat, Ryan had declared himself happy to pass on the responsibility of the money. Nonetheless, Mitch knew there would be watchers along his route to report the safe passing of both messenger and briefcase. He smiled at the notoriety that this expensive package had already gained. 'Mitch's yuppie bag' was how it was known among his colleagues.

The first leg of Mitch's journey presented no unexpected difficulties except for the nervousness of the pilot. Undoubtedly, this was one of the first 'errands' that Freddy, as he asked to be called, had undertaken. He was no doubt working under the threat of some dire punishment if the mission was upset. His hands on the joystick were wet with sweat as they trundled down the grassy strip and the little plane lifted into the air.

Mitch said to the man, 'Relax, Freddy. This is one of the easiest lessons you'll ever have to give. I'll not even touch the plane. You can do it all yourself and I'll just close my eyes until it's time to get out.'

He was aware of some stilted conversations with the ground control stations as the flight took them out over the

Irish Sea. But during the half-hour trip, Mitch did as he promised, and kept his eyes shut as he tried to concentrate on the details of the plan that had been left up to him.

The sudden drop in altitude caused his ears to pop and a glance at Freddy showed that he seemed to have loosened up somewhat since he took control of their destinies up in the sky.

'I've reported a problem with the fuel line, as I was asked. The original flight plan has been changed to Douglas, so you'll be able to do whatever you have to do there.'

His voice carried a tone of disapproval, but Mitch did not rise to the challenge and merely watched the ground coming up fast to greet them as Freddy pointed the nose firmly downwards. After a short taxi, the aircraft came to a stop in front of a dilapidated hangar, reserved for private flights. Mitch slumped down in his seat, waiting until the few spectators lost interest in their movements. Once the chocks had been put under the wheels, Freddy jumped out to talk to the mechanic who was standing at the ready.

Mitch silently waited while the two men walked inside the hangar. Grabbing his bag and briefcase from the tiny space behind the two seats, he pushed his way out of the cockpit and jumped to the ground to follow the two men inside. Here the mechanic was stripping off his overalls. Mitch walked past them and out into the street where a blue van, painted with the message 'Manxman Pies', was cruising around the car-parking area.

Mitch spent the next hour inside this van while Freddy and Mitch's mechanic 'double' took off once again towards Belfast. The van was under the control of a small Irishman called Blacky. He gripped the steering wheel with grubby fingers, and sniffed energetically as he told his disinterested passenger about the many fish he had caught on a recent angling expedition in the Lake District. Mitch found the whole episode unnecessary, but he recognized security for the higher echelons was taken very seriously, so he had no justifiable complaint.

Eventually, he was deposited back at the airport by Blacky, who had run out of Lake District memoirs and was now starting on a particularly crafty bass that he had caught off the coast of Stornaway. Mitch said it had been a pleasure and removed himself from the constant harangue.

A trim, twin-engined craft, with the letters VW on the side, was waiting for him, with the passenger door open. Mitch climbed aboard and accepted the headset that was offered by the mustached pilot. Through this, he listened to the procedures as they were given permission to take off on runway 42 South.

In contrast to the effusive Blacky, the pilot was completely silent throughout the hour-and-a-quarter journey. This suited Mitch, who was never at his best during a buffeting. The departing storm had left big patches of unstable air, through which the small plane traveled on its way to the South of England. Mitch knew there was little that the pilot could do about it. Although reference by the air traffic controllers to smoother air at higher altitudes was given several times, unfortunately, it was far above the reach of his airplane.

Through breaks in the clouds, Mitch could see the green rolling scenery of England, five thousand feet below them. His knowledge of the countryside's geography did not help him identify the various towns and villages they passed over. He thought he recognized Oxford and then Reading, but it could just as easily have been High Wycombe and Andover.

The flight plan took them over the New Forest and in a wide arc towards the eastern location of Southampton's airport. Mitch could see the edge of the forest and the gleaming reflection of Southampton Water with the River

Itchen flowing into it at the north-east end. Mitch could spot the bridge that he had crossed four weeks earlier on his way to meet Margitte for the first time. Houses were packed up to almost the very edges of the water, but here and there small clumps of grass showed through where man had yet to put his permanent stamp.

They crossed over the city and swept down onto the ground, where their arrival solicited no more interest than if they had been one of the many seagulls that were settling on the grass all around them.

The rental car was ready, and when he had locked the briefcase in the trunk, Mitch drove out onto Hampshire's road system and headed towards the ancient port of Dover. The sun was coming in over his right shoulder and he found it uncomfortably hot. 'At last, on my final day, they get the bloody weather forecast right,' he groaned and then regretted once again speaking aloud. One can never be too careful, he thought. After all, there was no way of knowing where this car had come from. There were spies everywhere. He grinned stoically and continued on his way, grateful for the occasional cloud to take the heat off the window.

His embarkation aboard the Sealink *Seaspray* passed uneventfully, with hardly a glance from the black-trousered and white-shirted officials who lolled at their posts, no doubt dreaming of their index-linked pensions. Lifting the briefcase of money out, he locked the blue Escort on B deck and climbed up to the main passenger floor to watch the departure for Ostend; he had a last glimpse of the British Isles, perhaps for ever. Mitch could find no regret in his heart for the moment, only a certain numbness mixed with apprehension.

Once the ship had cleared the harbor, he decided to treat himself and booked a cabin. Then he went into the restaurant to order a good lunch, even though it was somewhat late.

The Belgian staff spoke a mixture of Flemish to themselves, French to the upper-class British, who were distinguished by their old-fashioned clothes, and English to the rest.

'And what would you like?' a sneering waiter asked Mitch, thereby passing on his opinion of the customer's heritage.

Mitch ordered a steak – medium – mixed vegetables and French fries. Before leaving, the waiter plonked a large bottle of tomato sauce noisily on the table.

'And fuck you, too, Jack,' Mitch mumbled under his breath, extending his middle finger out of sight, beneath the table. 'You'd sound a bit different, if you knew what I had between my feet, you insolent bastard.' He gave the Samsonite a comforting nudge with his knee.

He drank three bottles of Grolsch beer with his lunch, enjoying the foreignness of the china-stoppered packaging and the strength of the brew. It really is a civilized way to travel, he thought, as the food and drink settled in his stomach. The engines far below throbbed their rhythm throughout the vessel.

He had a feeling of freedom growing inside. He knew that in truth he could just disappear right now; he could get off the boat at Ostend and drive south into France and vanish, avoiding whatever watcher might be at the other end. But the need to bury his former colleagues' maniacal dreams of wholesale slaughter was proving stronger every day. He ordered a cognac from the waiter, who had perked up once Mitch had decided on 'foreign' beer. Obviously, he was not totally lower-class.

The cold English Channel rushed past, separating Mitch further and further from his roots of hatred and violence. He did not care to dwell on his past. He had done enough of that during the nearly four weeks of inactivity before his departure. He sat quietly enjoying the warmth of the brandy and the pleasant contemplation of Margitte somewhere in his future.

His cabin was solidly built in wood and aluminum. A small round porthole looked out across the gray water and allowed the rushing sound of the sea to act in counterpoint to the throb that pounded beneath him. Mitch lay down on top of the blanket and fell fast asleep, until, some two hours later, a knock at the door warned him that disembarkation would be in fifteen minutes. He splashed some water on his face and rushed upstairs on deck to see the ferry in the process of turning around, about half a mile from the coast.

Belgium looked flat and uninteresting at first sight, but however unimposing it might seem, it was the starting point of Mitch's freedom. He tried to retain his previous feeling of relaxation, but a tight ball of apprehension had begun to grow in his stomach.

The engines turned the water into a froth as the captain put the *Seaspray* into reverse, and they moved backwards towards their berth, passing alongside a wooden pier at what appeared a dangerously fast rate.

Mitch began to consider that the captain had fallen asleep at the wheel, or had suffered a heart attack. The people on the pier, however, took very little notice of the ship, and continued with their dozing, reading or conversation, as, finally, at the last moment, the engines reversed again, and the *Seaspray* settled gently at her dock. Loudspeakers announced in three languages that motorists could now remove their cars, and Mitch joined the others in the slow crawl up the metal ramp, off the ship.

With the briefcase again locked away in the trunk, the blue Escort attracted no more than a cursory glance from the immigration officials. They seemed far more interested in a mobile home driven by a long-haired student type who was ahead of him in the queue. Nonetheless, Mitch stared stonily ahead as he left the docks, pleased to have escaped another border crossing with no trouble. He was pretty sure that in these days of the European Community, he would not be stopped for any reason other than a tip-off. And apart from the revolvers, he had nothing of any interest to customs inspectors, who these days seemed only on the lookout for drugs.

Ostend had a quaint Continental look about it. Mitch was in no hurry, so he decided to wander into the town. After parking next to some fish stalls, he walked around, watching the activity of the market. The weather was fine, and the day was coming to an end for the beachgoers returning from the shore.

Tea was being served in numerous establishments, and women in expensive outfits were working their way through rich dark-chocolate cakes with an abandonment that would have shocked their British or Irish counterparts. There was a smell of opulence and relaxation that added to the air of sophistication that was around. Mitch could not help feeling out of place here, and also a little lonely. His situation strengthened his belief that holiday resorts could be very bleak places when one was alone. After perhaps an hour and two cups of strong coffee, Mitch checked his watch and calculated he would not be in Amsterdam until nine or ten that evening, which served his purpose admirably. He had no wish to spend longer in Mike Ryan's company than was absolutely necessary. So, stiffly, he returned to the car, climbed in and pulled out towards the route headed north.

His journey was uneventful. His adaptation to driving on the other side of the road was easy enough, although the first major roundabout outside Ostend did make him think hard. He found some music on the radio coming out of Rotterdam that pleased him, and after only one stop for some more coffee at a roadside cafe, he picked up the first sign for Schipol at ten o'clock.

Several jets on a parallel path overtook his progress as he searched for the Sheraton Hotel. It was just past the entrance to the airport, and after a slight tussle with a farm vehicle loaded down with turnips, he negotiated the overhead ramp that branched off the motorway, and located the Sheraton's car park. Taking his briefcase and bag, he shut the car and entered the cool interior of the hotel. He paused only to use the hotel safe for his briefcase.

There was no sign of Ryan, which pleased him enormously. He was allotted room 236 and, as soon as he shut and locked the door, he turned on the television and lay down on the bed. He must have been dozing for about half an hour, when the telephone rang stridently in his ear.

'I won't be there until tomorrow afternoon. 'Bout two o'clock. Can you meet me?'

Ryan sounded in a very bad mood.

'Do you have the flight number?' Mitch replied.

'No, there's been a screw-up this end. It's the BA flight that gets in from Heathrow at one fifty-eight or thereabouts. Should be pretty easy for you.'

'Okay, I'll see you tomorrow.'

Mitch wondered what the screw-up was, but felt at ease in the knowledge he was out of the country and to some extent already out of their clutches. On impulse, he called Margitte's number, but there was no reply. 'Nothing for it,' he said to himself, 'but to spend the time by yourself. And talk out loud,' he added with a grin.

After a small sandwich downstairs in the coffee shop, with no diversion other than the discreet ministrations of a tall and very plain waitress, he slept well. The distant rumble of the early jets taking off from the airport opposite only disturbed him. He called room service for some breakfast and then, tiring of the repetition of *Headline News*, decided to check out Schipol, and then Amsterdam.

At the British Air desk, he found the flight Mike was due in on, and then took a good look around the airport. It was run with European efficiency with the usual assortment of business travelers and trippers milling round in a confused state. With his dark jacket and gray trousers and once again carrying his businessman's briefcase, Mitch hoped that he fitted into the former category.

Uniformed and heavily armed policemen strolled in pairs throughout the jostling melee. The public announcements, when they came in the Dutch language, reminded Mitch of Margitte and of how much he was looking forward to seeing her again. He was disappointed there had been no reply from her number.

His trip into the city was fraught with difficulties. He constantly found himself lost. Every street seemed to have a church, a canal, and some trees. The buildings had a sort of squashed look as they gazed down at the green, thick water. For all that, Amsterdam had a charm which Mitch found very attractive.

Making sure he could find his way safely out of the city to collect Mike Ryan, he parked the car and looked around for something to eat. Walking down a narrow cobbled street, he found a shop selling small appetizing rolls. He went in and pointed at the food piled up in rows under glass counters. '*Brotgers*' was the sound of the word the young girl used to describe what he wanted.

She was very tall, well over six foot, and she had a solid look about her. Her English, which seemed completely fluent, had the same accent he had found so attractive in his Dutch contact – a sort of softer German, he thought.

Munching his way through two rolls containing minced raw steak, which made him feel as if he really was abroad, he deliberately began to shake off his mood of separation, which had been with him since he left. When he met Mike, he would have to be all business and well on his guard. He welcomed the return of the tightness in his gut, as a constant reminder to be ever watchful.

Swallowing the last of a very strong coffee, he wiped the soft flour off his fingers and smiled goodbye to the shop girl. As the drive to the airport took only thirty minutes, he was right on time. So was the Irish colonel, who still seemed to be in a very bad mood.

'That bloody fool, Taffy,' was the greeting that he gave to Mitch as he came through immigration. 'Got as pissed as a rat on his way back from Fergy's, fell over in the street and had to be sent to hospital. Had my damned ticket in his pocket. Took us nearly six hours to find out where he was. The drink is going to kill us all if he doesn't take more care.'

Once safe in the confines of the hire car, Mitch suggested that Ryan should use the yuppie briefcase to store his valuables in. His passenger said he shouldn't be so bloody daft, as he didn't have any. They headed for the hotel in silence, where the newcomer was checked in with crisp efficiency. Like Mitch, Ryan was traveling light so he literally flung his bag into his room and joined Mitch at the bar. It had the dark-cornered, pseudo-English look that had become so popular all over the world and it sold Guinness.

They had two each, which must have kept Mike Ryan's level of alcohol well up since no doubt he had been drinking since leaving Ireland earlier that morning. As he fingered the small envelopes in his pocket, Mitch prayed that he would continue in the same manner later in the evening.

He needn't have worried. Mike Ryan had shown a general state of tenseness back at the airport when he realized that Mitch was carrying the money around with him. Mitch had great difficulty in assuring him it was the best place to keep it. Mike had even suggested they should sit in one of their rooms and guard the precious hoard until it came time to hand it over. Mitch shrugged off the idea as being beneath their dignity. Eventually, however, the wary Irishman began to relax into the state of being abroad.

'It's all pretty easy from here on, Mike,' Mitch said, as he leaned the briefcase up against his leg in the darkened bar. 'This fellow, Muller, comes for us in the morning, and then we're treated like VIP customers the rest of the way.'

To give himself a break from his enforced company, Mitch complained of a headache and left Ryan at the bar for a couple of hours. In truth, he was feeling tired, but also he could not face a complete afternoon and evening with his fellow colonel. Their relationship had never been close, outside of their mutual business. They both disapproved of each other's moral values and only shared the common goal of 'Ireland for the Irish'. Even the way to achieve such an end had always been widely varied, although the fight seemingly had now gone out of Mitch O'Doule.

On entering his room, he lay down on the bed and stared blankly at the TV, which flickered its way through endless pictures of supposed entertainment. There was still no reply from Margitte's number, and Mitch began to accept her insinuations that she would appear after the event. He felt a slight regret once more at the loss of power, and napped his way through his rest.

The evening was as stilted as Mitch had feared. Mike Ryan had continued drinking in the bar while Mitch slept upstairs. He was alternatively aggressive and then depressed. It took a great deal of talk and persuasion to steer him to the dining room for some food, which was then followed by more time at the bar, where Ryan insisted on mixing his alcohol by drinking brandy.

The plan had called for Mike to consume copious quantities, and he had certainly done that. Mitch was sure that, even for a normally heavy drinker, the level of booze in his colleague must have reached the desired high mark that had been called for. Around ten o'clock, he surreptitiously emptied the contents of the blue envelope into a warmed glass of Hine that was left unguarded on the dimly lit table, during one of Ryan's many pit stops. It was less than a teaspoon's worth of white powder and dissolved immediately. Mitch waited with damp palms, as the bleary-faced Irishman, on his return from the restroom swigged it down.

There was no immediate effect. Mike was well into his cups already and obviously tasted nothing odd about the potion. He continued to stare ahead glassily with the snifter hanging loosely in his hands. Mitch attempted some conversation but it was like talking to a dummy.

For the umpteenth time, Mitch took a trip to the men's room, more from boredom and tension than from any real need to go. On his return, he found Ryan fast asleep in his chair. It took Mitch and the burly barman a good quarter of an hour to drag the comatose man to bed. Having rolled the unconscious man in the bed's counterpane, Mitch returned to the sanctuary of his room, worrying that whatever had been in the powder might have been too much, but also slightly envying Ryan the sleep that would no doubt elude himself.

He needn't have concerned himself about the former. Mike Ryan was not permanently damaged when Mitch called round to his room at ten the next morning. However, evidence of his over-indulgence was obvious.

Mitch had slept very badly, which was fully expected. He had tossed and turned all night long, listening to the unaccustomed noises of Amsterdam's airport until he fell asleep only an hour before the first jets of the day began their work. Then he watched satellite TV and ordered breakfast from room service, which he couldn't finish. The time from five-thirty to ten hung heavily and he had begun to fear what he might find when he collected Ryan at the appointed hour.

A haggard sallow wreck of a man opened the door. The bed looked as if it had not been slept in. There was just the outline of the body that Mitch and the barman had laid on top of it the night before. Ryan had bloodshot eyes sunk in a face that looked as if he had been on a bender for a lifetime. He had always drunk alcohol, but he had never been in Taffy's league.

'Jesus,' he croaked. 'What the bloody hell do these Dutch bastards put in their booze?' he mumbled, as he swayed across the room into the toilet.

Mitch sat on the edge of the bed and felt a smile form on his face. He quickly removed it as Ryan lurched back into the room.

'What time is this bugger coming for us?' he asked.

'In about an hour,' Mitch replied. 'You look pretty grim, Mike. Can I get anything for you?'

'Just some orange juice, and some bloody aspirin, too.'

Mitch slipped out of the room and went down to the reception area. Here, he purchased two bottles of Sunkist and some Advil from a vending machine, and returned upstairs.

Mike was in the shower when he got back into the room, and a cursory look round proved there was no weapon amongst the belongings still packed haphazardly in the carry-all. The noises from the shower consisted of a series of groans and curses, proving that Margitte's powder had certainly given the Irishman a real world-class hangover.

As he emerged from the steaming bathroom ten minutes later, there seemed to be no improvement in his appearance. Although much of the croaking had disappeared from his voice.

'Why, in God's name, did you let me drink like that?' Mike asked accusingly, still trying to focus his red-rimmed eyes. 'And turn that damned television off. I can't stand the noise.'

Mitch had switched on the news from CNN, which he had seen several times already that morning. He concluded he needed the flickering distraction to reduce the tension that was ringing throughout his entire being.

'It was none of my doing, you silly bugger,' he replied as good-naturedly as possible. 'I had a hell of a time even getting you to eat any food. You seemed hell-bent on drowning your sorrows. There was nothing I could do. It was one heck of a job getting you up here with the barman's help. You'd passed out like a light downstairs.'

'I'm sorry. But I feel terrible.'

He had drowned the orange soda out of both cans in huge gulps and swallowed several aspirins. The gas in the drinks had caused him to develop hiccoughs, which shook his limp body with every surge. Mitch actually felt sorry for him slumped on the side of the bed.

'The barman said it happens to a lot of Brits. His words, not mine,' he added, at a withering look from Ryan. 'He said the percentage in their beer is much higher than we're used to. Maybe they should tell you that before you start. You only had about six or seven pints before the brandy, after all.'

The strident ringing of the telephone interrupted his explanation. Ryan clutched his head as the sound echoed round the room. A soft Germanic accent announced, 'There is a small delay. Your car will be ready at four o'clock and I will be waiting at reception. Please to remember to bring the payment.'

Mike Ryan staggered to his feet and lurched once more into the bathroom to splash his face with cold water. He needn't have bothered, as he looked just as ashen when he came out.

'Thank God I've got a few more hours to get over this

hangover,' he said, as he sank back once more onto the crumpled sheets. Mitch accepted that the wait was inevitable, although he had endured more than enough of this particular hotel's hospitality.

Chapter Eighteen

Sholing, 1787

As they came up under the side of the ship that was to transport them to the other side of the world, Paddy O'Doule and his friend, Chipper, lost sight of the man who had struck terror into them throughout their earlier times together. His bald, jutting head vanished as they came alongside and tied up ready to embark.

'What's the matter with you two?' the professor asked. 'You both look as if you'd seen a ghost.'

'Far worse than that,' Chipper replied, grimly. Turning to Paddy he said, 'You don't think we made a mistake, do you, mate?'

'Not the same mistake from both of us,' was the almost whispered reply.

Marmy, the ginger cat, stirred sleepily inside the Irishman's shirt. Paddy patted him unconsciously as he thought helplessly about their situation.

'Stand up, prisoners,' came the shouted order, and shuffling under the weight of their chains, the men made their way unsteadily up to the main deck. They were lined up in the gray light and then, one by one, sent below to the cramped quarters where they were to live for the next eight to nine months.

Paddy and Chipper hardly noticed the dark unsanitary area, as their minds were still full of the shock of seeing Chief Sande on the same vessel. And it seemed he was in some form of authority as well. What could it mean? How long could they last with his malice? The questions turned over and over in their minds as they sought out a place to sleep and stay.

Ackers, who had never been on a ship in his life, was fascinated by all he could see of the structure of the vessel. Chipper pulled himself free from his preoccupation, and busied himself with finding appropriate berths for the friends. He found four, located close to a tiny air vent and with a strong bulkhead nearby.

'Adds more stability than being out in the open,' he said, making a determined effort to force the normal grin back on his face.

They stowed their few precious belongings around them and then waited for more instructions. As it happened, they were to wait, locked below, for the next day in the places Chipper had selected for them. The authorities considered their situation too precarious to allow them up on deck.

These were dangerous men, who were being deported from their homeland for vicious crimes against the property of Georgian England. No chance was to be given any of them to escape the sentence of banishment for the prescribed duration.

With only occasional visits from the crew to supply food and water and to remove the waste buckets, the prisoners below deck were left alone in near darkness. Only Marmy found ways to roam around the ship at will, often returning from a trip with evidence of food, both hunted and gathered, sticking to his grubby face.

Two long days after joining their floating prison, the captives were shaken out of their bored reveries by the sound of shouted orders and running feet. The clanking of the anchor chain indicated their journey was about to begin. A wave of apprehension swept over many prisoners, including Ackers and Prof, but Paddy and Chipper smiled at the prospect of once again getting under way. Their good humor helped sustain them from the fear that lurked within their other two friends. With no further evidence of their joint nemesis, Chief Sande, they both made the determined effort to try and help their inexperienced colleagues.

The ship lurched and creaked its way out of Southampton Water and along the Solent, turning south at the eastern end of the Isle of Wight to head for the first leg of the journey. By now the curious route to Australia was known to all. Instead of traveling due south down the west coast of Africa, Captain Phillip had elected to take the longer route of crossing the Atlantic twice, via Rio de Janeiro.

The prisoners lay on their rough bunks in the cramped quarters, telling stories – some true, some false – to pass the time. Prof began to lose much of his normal *joie de vivre* in the dark well that was their home. He withdrew into himself and would go for hours without moving or speaking.

'Don't worry about me,' he said once to them. 'It's something I learned to do years ago. I can shut myself off and live in another place. I find it helps whenever I'm unhappy or ill at ease with my lot. Let's face it,' he said with a tired smile, 'this is not the most cheerful situation at the present. But we must look to the future, lads, for a new beginning and a new hope.'

Soon the routines began. The men were fed twice a day from buckets suspended from the opened hatch, during the first two days; this was the only brief snatch of fresh air they were permitted. Eventually, however, they were allowed up on deck for short periods to exercise. Initially, as HMS *Falcon* swayed her way across the easternmost reaches of the Atlantic, the guards were wary of their charges, and only small groups of two or three were permitted out of the dark hold. Groups of marines on the upper decks would stare stolidly along their gunsights, aimed at the men as they walked around in circles. Eventually, as each man became known to the officers in charge, it became evident that, far from being the desperate brigands they were purported to be, most were simply poor petty criminals, scared to death about their unknown futures.

After nearly two weeks at sea, the jagged shapes of the Canary Islands began to form on the distant horizon. The prisoners were once again considered to be potential escapees and were consigned below decks for the duration of their visit in port.

The boredom of their existence had become a common plight. Most of the stories had been told and retold, and then retold over again. Small handicrafts had been practiced, with materials scrounged from every nook and cranny of the ship. Everything had a use. Glass fragments were ground into small stones to make jewels; splinters and chunks of wood were formed into models, representing everything from animals to angels; pieces of string and wire were cut and formed on many a bunk to while away the empty hours. The slim secret knife in Chipper's belt buckle had been used to make a Christlike statue from some wood found floating in the bilge water. The figurine achieved almost mystic significance on Sundays, as even committed felons of the worst sort had strong recurring mystical needs.

At the sound of the rattling anchor chain, the stories of planned escape started up once again. They were either the bravest or most stupid who voiced ideas of how they could rush the hatch cover and jump overboard. These well-worked and completely impractical plans had been listened to and rejected by the four friends, who had spent this first leg of the journey building their friendship and a quiet reliance on each other.

Prof had become more and more silent with each passing day, preferring to spend the time deep within his own form of meditation. In the evening, though, after the food had been consumed, he would talk to them about the various subjects on which he had been ruminating during the day. His education at first proved too eclectic and academic for the others to fully understand. However, he took it upon himself to try to pass on his knowledge to any that would listen.

It was his belief that, in order to fully enjoy life in its many forms, one had to know all the options.

'Oh, yes,' he would say, 'I know learning is hard work, but you try the alternative – ignorance.'

He helped Paddy with his reading and his letter forming, using an area of the dusty floor as a slate. After each sentence, more dust was sprinkled around, until Paddy could trace his fingers through the covering, in the quest for more and more perfection.

Prof taught geography, history, and mathematics. He tried to explain some of the great paintings that he knew about, and even tried to hum some of the music he was familiar with. But it was during one of his discussions about theology that he and Paddy had a disturbing disagreement.

It started one quiet evening, about a week and a half out from Southampton. He had been leading a lively discussion on the teachings of the Bible, which dealt with the Holy Trinity.

'Of course, the church would have us believe that three forms of God exist in one overall body,' he said. 'But there is no evidence for such a manifestation anywhere else in the known universe. This is why I cannot accept it.'

Paddy, who in spite of his hard life and his present circumstances, had always remained a staunch Catholic, crossed himself at the sound of such blasphemy. Instead of letting the moment pass, Prof smiled at him.

'You might want to repeat that for me, Paddy, as I'm sure I'll need all the help I can get from such superstition.'

The Irishman bridled at the taunt, and stared threateningly at his tutor.

'What do you mean by that?' he snarled at his friend.

'Well, Paddy, I have to confess to a total lack of belief in the whole subject,' Prof replied.

'You're not telling us that you're a damned atheist?'

Paddy had trouble in spitting out the hated word, for, where he came from, there was no worse label. In fact, he could safely say he had never known anyone who would admit to such a terrible sin.

'My dear friend,' Prof replied, with a good-humored smile playing through his gray beard, 'we are each of us free to draw our own conclusions in our lives if we are given sufficient evidence. After all, with the taking of the apple from the tree of knowledge in the Garden of Eden, did not our ancestors choose enlightenment over ignorance?

'I began as a Christian like all right-thinking Englishmen – oh, and Irishmen too, of course – but during the years, I have simply come to see it all as symbolic of the ways of nature and not to be taken literally.'

'But you teach the Bible to us, and you join us in prayer,' Paddy blurted out. 'How can you do that and not be a believer?' Paddy was confused and outraged. He was beginning to see this man in a different light and it was worrying him.

'I believe there is a difference between a man who chooses not to accept the literal interpretations of Christianity out of ignorance, and one who makes an informed decision. I teach the Bible because it is a rule book for life that has served men well for thousands of years. It uses stories and situations to help us understand our faults and how to deal with them. Without that knowledge, we are ignoring our pasts and living in the same darkness that savages are forced to live in.'

'But that's the most dreadful sin we know of,' protested

Paddy, his face set in a mask of disbelief at what he was hearing.

Chipper smiled at the argument as it wafted back and forth between the two bunks. Neither of the contestants, however, was prepared to give any ground, and Paddy seemed to be getting more and more distressed with every turn, until Prof finally said, 'Look, Paddy, what I have told you about my own beliefs is really only just that, my own beliefs. I don't want to convert you or ask you to change your faith. What works for me may just not work for you, and vice versa. And I'm sure you'd be the first to admit I'm one of the best teachers of the faith you have ever met. Isn't that right?'

Paddy screwed his face up and looked at the prematurely aged man. He tried to look on the Prof as a sinner and a doomed man. Everything in his background demanded he treat the older man as a pariah, but the words Prof had used carried no hint of malice. They merely sounded hollow to his ears. Recognizing all men had doubts, his balanced disposition allowed him to see the Prof as a heretic, and he said he hoped that one day he would see the error of his ways. After all, he would be having plenty of time for reflection over the next fourteen years of his sentence. Paddy's facial muscles relaxed and, although he failed to turn them into a smile, the crisis was obviously over. The other two friends, who had watched the exchange, leaned back, relieved.

Once the ship had begun its rolling movements, Ackers was horribly sick. For hours at a stretch, he was forced to either lie completely motionless on his bunk, or kneel crouched over the unsavory buckets which served for communal purposes. His normally pale face took on a greenish tinge that clashed unpleasantly with his stubbly red beard.

With their previous experiences to draw on, Paddy and

Chipper were better off than most, having served aboard a royal navy ship. They talked about their respective lives, and busied themselves in keeping as groomed and as fit as possible. They took every advantage of the exercise periods allowed above. After that first shocking sighting, neither of them had seen their arch-enemy.

Within a few days, Chipper had made friends with a guard, a fellow cockney whom he vaguely remembered from a previous spell of duty. He offered the man a bribe of a piece of polished metal, in the shape of an anchor, that he had won in a game of cards. Accepting this payment, the man told Chipper that the big bald ex-gunner was not a part of HMS *Falcon*'s crew. He had been sent for by the captain to assist in a final check of security before the prisoners arrived on board. Apparently, the 'chief', as he liked to be called, had a reputation as a disciplinarian, and was to serve that purpose both on the voyage and when they reached their destination in Australia. He had spun a yarn to the authorities and been accepted to watch over both convicts and men. So far he had caused no trouble, although many of the older hands were wary of him.

Chipper told Paddy his news, as he gleaned it from the rating up on deck. They were both very relieved to know that they were apart from their sworn enemy, if only for the duration of the journey. However, they remained highly apprehensive concerning their future, once the chief found out about them.

On the morning of the second day in the port of Santa Ana, an opportunity presented itself to Paddy. The hatch had been opened and the ladder removed, to allow the inmates to enjoy some sunshine without fear of escaping out of the ten-foot-deep hold. Two armed guards lolled in the hot midday sun as a group of goats were herded up the gangplank. Perhaps sensing their future role as fresh meat for the *Falcon*, the animals were skittish in the rising heat, and pranced about, as they were encouraged upwards in their mandatory embarkation.

Paddy was standing beneath the hatch opening, when, in the crush above, one of the goats jerked sideways, and fell through to land on top of him. Which of the two was the most startled was hard to tell, but at least there was no damage to Paddy. Unfortunately for the goat, things were not so good. She tried to stand and, from the bleating, it was obvious that she was in pain every time her right front foot touched the deck.

A rating swung down a makeshift rope and took a look at the beast, pronouncing it unfit for travel. Paddy, out of curiosity, examined the goat and disagreed with the prognosis. The rating then held on to the rope while his colleagues hauled him upwards, and that would have been the end of the matter except for the cantankerous nature of the local Spanish farmer who had made the sale to the fleet. He argued he was not responsible for the animal's welfare once it was on board. That responsibility passed immediately once all four feet were on the royal navy's gangplank. There would be no refund. This conversation reached Paddy down in the hold through the thin faltering translations of one of His Majesty's clerks at the embassy who had been brought aboard for the precise purpose of dealing with the local merchants.

The Spaniard knew he had a good strong point, mostly because he had his bag of gold in the pouch at his waist – payment on delivery at the dockside. He had no intention of returning any of the money, or producing another animal, simply because of these foreign seamen's poor ways. His black eyes darted from one to another and his head shook vigorously from side to side.

Paddy looked carefully at the bleating goat at his feet and shouted up to the arguing parties above him, 'I think I can cure the creature, if it's important.'

A lieutenant, sweating from the tropical heat, in his thick uniform and tight collar, peered over the edge to see who was shouting.

'I'm a farmer, you see,' continued Paddy. 'In a few cases, you can mend a fracture, if you're quick about it.'

The lieutenant's head disappeared and one of the more senior ranks stared down.

'I'll need some canvas, some strong thick thread, and a needle to do the job. It'll take three weeks to heal and the animal should stay down here with us, away from its fellows.'

The head disappeared from view, and beneath, Paddy stroked the goat and sang quietly to it. The men, who had leaped up to see the fracas, gradually lost interest in the small tableau being played out in front of them and went back to their boredom. Paddy hoped that his words would not prove false, as he really had little experience in veterinarian matters outside the normal sort of events that occurred on all farms. Once anything major happened, the 'cure' usually was to kill the creature immediately. There had been something about these circumstances, however, that had made him feel lucky with the situation, and he now had to make good his boast.

After about ten minutes, a bundle of canvas was thrown down to him, as he sat with his charge in the heat of the midday sun. Inside were a spool of sail thread, and a sailmaker's needle – long, thick and curved.

'No knife, you artful buggers. We don't trust you that much!'

Paddy beckoned hastily to Chipper and his other two friends to come over and help him. Ackers arrived with Marmy in his arms.

'He'll have to go, Ackers,' Paddy said. 'I need the goat to be as calm as possible. I don't think Marmy's going to help us to do that.'

With some coaxing, the ginger cat wandered off with its tail swishing around it.

Prof was in one of his dream states on his bunk again and showed no sign of hearing the request, but Chipper, bright as always, came over to help in the operation.

The canvas was too big to use, and so Chipper removed the famous Madonna belt buckle, for Paddy to cut a slice of canvas, about two foot long by ten inches across. At a word from Paddy, both men then held the goat firmly to the deck, allowing the Irishman to bind the leg with the stiff fabric, from the shoulder to the hoof.

'It's very important to get the tension right,' Paddy said to both of them. 'Too tight and the leg will turn gangrenous. Too loose and the fracture won't heal.'

He felt all around the bandage and then invited the others to do the same, after carefully exchanging places with them. Both men declared that it seemed tight enough to them, although it would have been easier if the goat could say a few words.

A small area was then made for the injured animal to spend the next few weeks, and everybody went back to what had become for them all, a normal existence. Each day the pattern was repeated – sleep, food, daydreaming, and occasional exercise.

The rest of the stay in the Canaries had passed without event. Soon, they were pleased to hear the familiar rattling of the anchor chain, as HMS *Falcon* took her place in the line for the long trip across the empty reaches of the Atlantic Ocean to Rio de Janeiro. They had lost two men to illness and all felt tired from their enforced incarceration in port, but otherwise, they were intact and ready for whatever fate held in store for them. Paddy ruminated that now he had not only a small cat, but a medium-sized goat to look after as well.

The prospect pleased him, for although he had grown

mightily fond of Chipper, Ackers and Prof, he missed his life with the animals on his farm back home in Ireland. His long-lost family's image still stayed with him, although he tried to force such thoughts out of his head. With little activity, this proved a Herculean task for him. Therefore, he was glad of the routine of another soul, albeit a dumb one, to look after.

Each day, he would check the goat's damaged leg, and ask for green leaves to be thrown down to nourish the creature. As the discipline of life afloat returned once more, he was once again allowed on deck. Up in the fresh air, he soon found a number of the sailors and marines interested in the condition of the ship's mascot, as it had become. Often, heads would come over the hold's opening and peer about for the goat as it lay in its pen or stood three-legged next to Paddy's bunk, getting its ears scratched. After two weeks, it would put its foot down from time to time, although it took another three weeks before it could fully transfer its weight onto it.

Several of the officers also showed interest in the progress of the goat, and soon Paddy's opinion was sought out with regards to possible cures for the ailments of other animals aboard. At first, he modestly denied that he had any real knowledge at all. But then, one night, when he happened to mention to Prof that an officer had asked him about a swelling on the back of one of the pigs, Prof delivered one of his lectures.

'You know, Paddy, let me tell you a little about our situation. We are just units to the men above us. Dangerous crates with appetites is probably how they look at us – all the same, like peas in a pod. Now most of us are exactly like that. And don't care otherwise. But you, well, you're starting to have an edge. Something that gives you some identity.'

The gray-bearded face peered intently at him. Rather

than shrugging off the well-intentioned advice, as he had done many times in the past, he listened carefully to the Prof, respecting the older man's knowledge and knowing that his words were intended to do him good.

'So, Paddy, when they come to you for advice, always listen carefully, and give a measured reply. Keep it as vague as possible, but always try to pretend that you are the expert. Most of these fellows are townies and wouldn't know one end of a cow from another, so you be the one who has the knowledge.'

'That's all very well, Prof,' the perplexed Irishman replied. 'But what happens if my advice causes one of the animals to die? It will be my fault and I'll get the blame.'

'Now, don't get carried away, Paddy. The creature would almost certainly die anyway, wouldn't it?'

'Out here? In these circumstances? Oh yes, the odds are very much against any sick animal recovering. When they're ill, they're very delicate, even under the best of conditions.'

'Well then, you've already caused one miracle of healing with the goat. It would have been dead long ago. And dead meat we did not need back in port, right?'

'I guess you're right,' Paddy said, seeing straight away how being the ship's animal doctor was going to benefit him. At the very least, it would take him out of the hold from time to time.

'Just put on a righteous face and say you'll look at the animal, then do what you can for it and hope for the best. I promise you, Paddy, it will serve you well over the next few months.'

Paddy did as he was asked and during their voyage across the Atlantic, he was often called to look at an animal with a tick or a swelling or some other malady that he had no idea how to treat. However, with the help of Prof and one or two others below decks, he managed to cure nearly half the ailments. Soon he began to feel at home in this role. Particularly when he realized he seemed to be having as much success as all the vets he had ever met back home. Paddy's nickname even began to change to Doc by the time Rio's shoreline came into view. He nearly always frowned at such use by ranks lower than officers. He felt happy to fool the privileged class, but no one of his own status.

The goat that had suffered the fractured leg was now completely cured, except for a tendency to stand on only three feet. It was looked upon as a pet by all aboard and was even called Paddy's goat. In spite of all the success of his work, however, when they dropped anchor close to the shoreline of Brazil, Paddy was still locked away below decks along with all the other prisoners. His new found status immediately vanished with the imagined prospect of escape.

Chapter Nineteen

Amsterdam, 1993

Mitch had to feel sorry for Mike Ryan. He looked like death, and the reeking smell of Hans Muller's untipped cigarettes wafting through the compartment of the black Mercedes was not helping him at all. The roads at least were completely flat so Mike Ryan was spared the added problem of up and down movement to add to his considerable discomfort. Mitch could not tell how much of the damage to Mike's system had been caused by Margitte's unnamed potion and how much was self-inflicted. The end result, however, was a wreck of a man, with a sallow, sweaty skin and a serious case of the shakes.

Muller, their driver and escort for the day's proceedings, was a heavy-set man, with tortoiseshell-framed glasses and thinning, cropped blonde hair. His accent was thick and throaty and he spoke rapidly, with the stresses on his words coming in many of the wrong places. After he had collected his charges at the Sheraton's reception, he herded them into the car and whisked them out of the driveway and onto the motorway that swept through the outer suburbs of Amsterdam.

'We're in for a bit of a drive,' he said around the stub of cigarette in the corner of his mouth. 'It's up near the resort of Zandfoort. You know, where the motor racing takes place?'

Mike looked stonily out of the window. Mitch said that

he had heard of the place, but it didn't mean much to him.

'Well, it's past the season now, so it will be quiet enough for what we have in mind.'

'And exactly what might that be?' inquired Mitch, frowning at the Dutchman's attempt to light another cigarette from the stub of the previous one. He found himself feeling smug at the realization that it had been at least three weeks since he had smoked.

'Just a small demonstration of the power of the merchandise. It should be enough for any doubting Thomases. But you'll see.'

There were one or two attempts by Muller to start a conversation, as the big Mercedes ate up the kilometers, but neither Irishman showed much enthusiasm for talking, and preferred to stare out at the passing flat countryside. From his appearance, it seemed that Mike's condition was improving.

They pulled into a roadside café for an early dinner. Mike refused and remained hunched in the car. He was fast asleep by the time Hans and Mitch returned, but he still looked pasty and drawn. Mitch left him alone in the back seat and sat in front with Hans, his briefcase held tightly between his ankles.

They left the motorway at long last and began traveling north, along carefully tended roads lined with houses made from the small flat bricks so favored by the Dutch. The further they traveled, the more expensive the houses became. Eventually, they were impossible to see, as the hedges became larger and the distances from the road increased. It was in this type of prestigious locality that the car turned into a driveway. They swept through two wrought-iron gates that opened mysteriously at the sound of two blasts on the Mercedes' horn. A long overhung path led to a dark red house with many lead-lined windows looking gloomily out onto the grass that bordered the drive.

After parking the car, Hans led the two visitors through the studded wooden front door and into a dark reception room hung with curtains redolent with pungent tobacco smoke.

Sitting on well-creased, brown-leather chairs, were two men in identical gray suits and two Arabs in traditional thobes and headscarves. The Arabs also found it necessary to wear sunglasses, although, with all four smoking heavily and the overall lack of light in the room, it was hard for anyone to make out too much.

One of the gray-suited individuals, a man of about fifty, stood up stiffly and said, 'I hope your journey was comfortable.'

'We were fine. Thanks,' Mitch added the courtesy almost as an afterthought as he gazed through the thick atmosphere.

'My name is Pieter Kirkdorp,' continued the host. 'I'm responsible for gathering us all here today. This is Alan, my assistant.'

The second gray suit stood up and bowed slightly to the two newcomers.

'The other two distinguished gentlemen represent our allies on the other side of the Mediterranean. Mohammed Eldi and Prince Ali Hussein.'

The two Arabs swiveled their heads towards Mitch and Mike Ryan, and their sunglasses glinted through the smoky haze. Mitch couldn't help wondering which, if any, of these men might be in on his and Margitte's secret.

Mitch introduced himself and waited for Mike Ryan to do the same, but there was only a silence from the man who, Mitch noticed, was swaying slightly next to him. With a gesture of his hand Mitch said, 'Colonel Mike Ryan.' Then he led his gaunt-faced companion to a vacant sofa and sat down, his aluminum case tucked carefully next to him. Pieter Kirkdorp rang a small bell beside him; almost immediately, a door opened in the wooden paneling and a white-jacketed manservant entered, carrying a tray of tea things. After pouring out a cup for each man in the room, the servant silently withdrew, allowing the conversation to begin once more.

'Let me explain our procedures to you, if I may,' the elder Dutchman continued, reaching for a cube of sugar with a small pair of tongs and then elegantly stirring the cup with a silver-plated spoon.

'We have the facilities here to explode two devices which you may choose at random. You may not have realized it, but this house runs down onto the beach which is quite private. In about fifty minutes, there will be several explosions from a nearby sculptor's studio. He casts bronze behemoths, and explosions happen regularly due to some faulty equipment that was purchased in a cheap sale outside the country. Therefore the local residents will not be unduly alarmed if they hear a couple of little bangs.

'After we have detonated our two devices, we will be able to show you the extent of the likely damage. You then have the opportunity to make your decision. If you are satisfied with the demonstration, you will hand over the first half of the money, and we will proceed further with delivery instructions. If you feel you wish to call a halt to our arrangements up to that precise moment, then we will return from whence we have come, and the matter will be forgotten.

'I must say that I think the latter situation to be extremely unlikely. I assume you have the money here with you?'

At a nod from Mitch, there was a silence during which the two Arabs smiled at each other and Mike Ryan noisily cleared his throat. Mitch noticed that he had not touched his cup of tea, no doubt due to the fact that his hands were shaking too much to grasp the fine porcelain handle.

The robed man, who had been introduced as

Mohammed Eldi, beamed at Mike Ryan and said in perfect Oxford English, 'Would you say that the climate here is the same as in your own country of Ireland, Colonel?'

Mike stared at the blank sunglasses and stammered, 'N-n-n-no, it seems a bit sunnier, I th-th-think.'

He sounded as bad as he looked, Mitch thought. The Arab leaned back in his chair, apparently satisfied with his contribution to the proceedings.

'Well, then, if everybody is ready,' Kirkdorp announced, 'let us get ready to show you what you have come all this way to see. You can leave your case there, Colonel O'Doule. It will be quite safe, I assure you.'

Mitch wavered at the thought, but felt it would look odd if he were to insinuate anything might be questionable in this large house, with all its implied gentility. Nonetheless, he moved the case around to the very back of the sofa, out of immediate sight.

They walked to the rear of the house, passing rows of portraits staring blankly down from paneled walls, until they emerged out into the fading sunset. There was a wide long sweep of sand beyond a well-cared for lawn. Off to one side was a large garden shed with just one frosted-glass window.

'Alan, why don't you take our two guests in and let them choose their weapons?'

The younger man led Mitch and a still shaky Mike into the garden shed, which was far more luxurious inside than it appeared from outside. There was a lowered floor and soft tapestries on the walls, with a long upholstered bench running the length of the wall. What was incongruous, however, was a green metal rack in the middle of the fitted carpet, with about three dozen sinister-looking canisters, painted in military camouflage, stacked on each shelf.

'Here is our small stock, gentlemen. Please choose whichever two you would like.'

Mike Ryan had sagged against the upholstered bench and did not look too steady, so Mitch pointed out two of the octagonal Mephistos, which Alan lifted down onto a plain deal table that had been placed there for the purpose.

'As you can see, these latest devices are modular. It is possible to remove each of the eight charges, if required. Also, as you can see, the design allows one to join several containers together, using the clips at the sides. We have dug two fairly deep holes down on the beach with metal plates placed at various locations, in order to test the range of both explosions. Holland is a very congested country, gentlemen, and so I am going to suggest that we do not use the full charge for the test. With your permission I would like to remove three modules from one and four from another. That will give you sufficient indication of the effectiveness of the variances. We can provide you with some written data to take with you that will substantiate the tests.'

Mitch indicated his agreement after looking over his shoulder at Mike Ryan, who was staring, motionless, out of the window at the empty beach before him.

Alan expertly set about removing the explosive modules from one Mephisto, and then realigned the remaining one. Weighing the Mephisto in his hands, he encouraged Mitch to pick up the other. Mitch was surprised at how heavy the bomb weighed.

'With this particular model, our most modern version, you will find it hard to carry more than four,' Alan said. Mitch thought that even on a good day, he would be hard pressed to manage two.

The Arabs and Pieter Kirkdorp were in deep conversation as the Mephistos were carried out. They did not appear to notice as Alan led the small party down towards the cold North Sea. The water was so far out at low tide it was almost invisible in the now deepening gloom. After some hundred yards, Alan stopped and drew Mitch's attention to two iron covers, twenty feet apart in the sand. Mike eventually caught up and tried to follow the directions.

'We will put the first, lighter charge down the hole on the right,' Alan said. Lifting off the cover, he began to pull on a rope that snaked into the sand. 'This goes down fifty feet, and the device will be underneath three inches of high-stressed steel. That means the charge will be exploded outwards.'

He lay the bomb on a tray, which fitted into two grooves. Half the shaft was covered in the same high-stressed steel, which gave a measure of protection to the house side of the intended explosion. He took the other container from Mitch, and repeated the procedure with the heavier charge. Both devices were linked to thin electrical wires that ran up to the shed from which they had come.

'All we do now is to lower away and get clear. Colonel, if you please.'

He indicated for Mitch to start lowering the bomb on the right, as he began feeding his own rope back down into the sand. He then replaced the covers and beckoned them further out towards the receding water. As they walked across the sand, he stopped every ten feet to pull up a plate that had been lowered into the beach. Each one was of polished aluminum and shone dully in the darkness. In all, there were perhaps thirty of these test plates buried around in various locations.

'After the explosion, we can check the effects of distance on the aluminum. It's fairly crude but it will demonstrate the extent of the charge.'

They returned to the group of observers, and together they entered the garden shed. The Arabs were beaming behind their dark glasses, and there was an electric air of expectancy around. Mitch, who was aware of trying to ensure that none of his treachery showed through, kept a watchful eye on Mike Ryan, who looked as if he was liable to throw up at any time. Pieter Kirkdorp checked his gold Rolex watch and gestured for everyone to take a seat.

'We have about five minutes to wait for our artist friend, and then on my signal, perhaps one of the colonels would like to push this button here.'

He gestured to a bell push, similar to the type that one would find on any suburban door.

'There is a small delay between the Mephistos you have selected for us.'

A silence descended on the group as they looked through the window onto the deserted beach.

'You have decided to join the overall struggle against the oppressors of the world then, Colonel.'

Prince Ali Hussein addressed his remarks directly to Mitch. His voice had a thin reedy texture to it and Mitch was reminded of scraping fingernails. A thoroughly unpleasant character, with some nasty habits as well, he thought. An uncomfortable, unhealthy aura surrounded the man.

'It seems our methods have been failing for the most part. The war council therefore felt we should explore the world outside for more effective methods.' Not bad to the ear, Mitch thought, as he continued to affect the posture of a zealous patriot.

'Quite so,' agreed the Prince. 'A wise choice. We hope that our initial support meets with your committee's approval so that we can join in future operations. The British Isles have long interested my brothers.'

'We have about one minute before the diversion begins.'

The host checked his watch and inclined his head, listening intently.

Mitch could hear Mike's labored breathing in the silence and then a series of bangs shattered the air. Counting off with one hand, Pieter Kirkdorp beckoned Mitch with the other and pointed to the button. On his signal Mitch pushed down and was rewarded by a vibration under his feet that carried very little sound. A moment later there was another explosion, somewhat more forceful than the first. Outside on the beach the two lids had blown off and were now rolling down towards the sea. A few puffs of sand shot up into the night sky, but otherwise, there was no great disturbance. The sculptor's explosions were certainly far more disruptive to the citizens of Zandfoort, who were, no doubt, now enjoying their cold Geneva gin aperitifs before the dinner hour.

Alan, the evening's orchestrator, held the door open for Mike and Mitch to accompany him to view the evidence of the experiment.

'The covers were not supposed to blow off,' he said, as they quickly covered the ground to the first aluminum plate. 'Mr Kirkdorp will not be pleased with that. I shall have to devise a better safety hatch, if I ever have to repeat the test. But let's start with the furthest plate away, shall we?'

Mitch did not know quite what he expected to see, when the plate was pulled out of the sand. By the light of a small flashlight, he could see the aluminum was bent outwards and away from the explosion. It also had several gouges on its bottom edge.

'This is through dense sand, gentlemen,' Alan explained. 'About fifty feet on half a charge. You can imagine the effect if there was only normal dry wall and wood. And with a full charge. Anything or anyone standing in the way would be cut to ribbons.'

Mitch could tell that, in spite of his damaged condition, Mike was showing more interest than at any time that day.

They walked slowly back towards the epicenter, pulling up the aluminum plates as they went. As was to be expected, with every step, the damage to the metal became more and more severe, until, ten feet from the bombs, nothing remained of the metal or its heavy anchoring chain. Knowing the dampening effect of tightly packed sand, and its use for that purpose behind firing-range butts, Mitch could see how devastating these Mephistos could be if they were strategically placed among people's unprotected lives.

Pieter Kirkdorp and the two Arabs came strolling down the beach, smoking large cigars. They beamed like relieved expectant fathers on their way to the viewing ward. Picking up a shattered aluminum plate, Pieter handed it over to the two robed men. They turned it over in their bejeweled fingers, and handed it back to him as if it was something rather distasteful.

'Shall we all return to the house, then?' the host inquired. He turned back up the beach, dropping the plate back down into its hole.

The noise from the neighboring studio had stopped, and now a peace had descended over the Dutch seascape. There was no evidence of the deadly business that had been demonstrated there. An innocent eye would merely have seen a group of men strolling back to their residence, having taken in the dark evening's air.

The moment Mitch entered the reception room, he knew his case had been touched. He remembered the warning, to be prepared for such an event, so he merely sat down next to the case and waited for his host to begin the next stage. Nonetheless, he felt exposed and highly vulnerable. Putting all his trust in an unseen person who knew the rules of the game when he didn't, made him feel as uneasy as his poisoned colleague looked. He leaned back against the sofa's thick covering, in order to feel the comfort of the revolver in the small of his back.

'So, Colonels, you have seen the power of the merchandise,' Kirkdorp began. 'I hope that you're impressed. I must say that I was. It's the first time that I have seen that big a charge.'

Neither the Arabs nor Hans Muller had returned to the room, so Pieter and Alan faced Mitch and Mike Ryan across the atmosphere that had temporarily cleared of its tobacco haze.

'Do you have any questions?' Alan asked, as he handed both of them a folder packed with information. Mitch spread the papers out on his knees. They contained the technical details of the Mephistos, as Alan had promised earlier. Mike idly flipped through the information and deferred to Mitch to carry on.

'It was a good demonstration. I think we understand the power. How do we progress from here?' Mitch asked.

'Hans is to take you to the next point. The delivery section. We will relieve you of the half-payment here and then, at the other end, we will ask for release of the funds on a bank of your selection, once you have made the count. I trust these arrangements meet with your approval?'

He looked quickly at Mitch's briefcase, and for a split second Mitch felt that Kirkdorp knew. He was the one that was in on the undercover deal he had hatched with Margitte. The impression was fleeting, however, and Mitch did not allow himself to dwell on the thought as he looked across at Mike Ryan sitting bolt upright on the sofa next to him.

'Any last minute questions, Mike?'

In reply, the Irishman shook his head with a brief movement and continued to remain his immobile self.

'In that case, Mr Kirkdorp, we'll be glad to proceed.'

He handed over the case and Kirkdorp quickly lifted the aluminum Samsonite onto his lap and sprung open the locks. He briefly scanned the contents and then closed the lid once more.

'Well, that's in order, then, I will hand this to our two

colleagues. Can I offer you anything before you leave?'

Mitch was about to suggest that a beer would be nice, when Mike Ryan spoke for almost the first time since he had arrived.

'We'll be off directly, if it's all the same to you,' he said, standing up unsteadily and moving to the door.

'Very well, gentlemen. Hans will take care of you from here. Here is the number to reach us should you need it.'

He handed over a scripted card with a telephone number on it and shook hands with Mitch. Mike was already out of the door and walking towards the car park with Hans Muller in pursuit. Mitch turned round and nodded at Kirkdorp. The Arabs were nowhere in sight.

The Mercedes pulled out of the driveway once more and both men relaxed in the plush leather seats, glad in their respective ways that the ordeal was over.

'You okay?' Mitch inquired.

'It's taken all my strength to keep from throwing up.' Mike replied. 'It's been a nightmare. In fact, pull over there will you, Hans, or whatever your name is.'

Muller brought the car to a standstill, and Ryan hurtled out.

Over the sounds of his retching, the Dutchman said, 'He doesn't seem in the best of shape, Colonel. Did he have a bit too much to drink last night?'

'More than was good for him, evidently,' was Mitch's reply.

Mike Ryan climbed back in the car once more and their journey recommenced.

'How long is the journey, Hans?' Mitch inquired of the blonde-haired man at the wheel.

'The first part, to Schipol, is about an hour and a half. Then tomorrow at ten thirty, you'll have a flight of about three and a half hours. After that, I really don't know much more. You'll be taken care of at the other end.'

'And where might the other end be?'

'A little climatic change for you. The Canary Islands. Tenerife, to be accurate.'

A shiver ran through Mitch at the sound of the place name. Into his mind came the image of the faded note with the shaky, looped writing from his great-great-great-grandfather.

'Been there before, have you?' Hans Muller inquired, as he maneuvered round a large truck, barreling down the highway, shedding dust and grit.

'No. But, of course, I've heard of it. What's it like?'

'Never been they're myself. A friend of Mr Kirkdorp has a villa there, I believe. Bit like Hawaii's big island they say, all volcanic and black. Still, you won't be there long, I think. Oh, if you want to offload that gun in your belt, Colonel O'Doule, now would be a good time to do it. The Dutch airport authorities don't take kindly to armed passengers.'

Mitch O'Doule stared at the tortoiseshell glasses smiling at him in the driving mirror.

'Oh, it's my job to spot things like that,' the Dutchman said.

Mitch pulled out the revolver and put it on the passenger seat beside Hans, who promptly covered it with a newspaper.

'I didn't know you were packing, Mitch,' said Mike Ryan, sitting up straighter. 'Taking a bit of a chance, weren't you?'

'I wasn't sure what we were getting into. Just wanted to be on the safe side.'

It was only later that Mitch realized that his action would confirm his caution and help remove suspicion from him. He turned his face to the window and thought of the expression, 'The devil looks after his own'. At the same time he hoped the metal box would protect his other gun from the prying eyes of the scanner. His understanding of checked baggage gave him some confidence.

Hans reached into his pocket and passed back two tickets wrapped in the red and orange colors of Iberia Airlines.

'You'll be met off the flight.'

They arrived back at the Sheraton at ten thirty. Mitch realized he was starving hungry and had a blinding headache. Hans stopped the car long enough to let them off.

'I'll be back at nine o'clock tomorrow morning. I would recommend a quiet night. You've a busy day tomorrow.'

He gave a cold look in the direction of the stooped Mike Ryan. Hans needn't have worried, as Ryan didn't even acknowledge Mitch's invitation for a sandwich and a beer at the bar. He merely trudged across the carpet towards the elevator and the quiet darkness of his room.

Chapter Twenty

Rio de Janeiro, 1787

Paddy's new-found status as the animal doctor vanished once the HMS *Falcon* arrived at Rio de Janeiro. Like all the other captives, he was considered far too dangerous to be allowed sight of land. Therefore, he was once again consigned below decks; only the occasional square of sunlight filtered down to him and his incarcerated colleagues when, three times a day, the creaky hatch was removed. Such confinement lasted for only a short time, however, as the demands of illness in the remaining animals soon allowed him more and more access above decks. He remained under strict guard, of course.

During the voyage from the Canaries, his three friends had formed an even tighter bond. Ackers had overcome his seasickness, and Chipper had instructed them all in matters of seamanship that he felt were necessary for them to survive such a long voyage. It was only Prof who did not seem to have weathered the journey well. He became even more emaciated and drawn, spending longer and longer each day deep in his thoughts.

He maintained he was very happy doing this, but Chipper made a point of getting Paddy to relate whatever occurrences he could, at the end of every day, to the silent man. As he had about ten assorted animals that needed his attention, there were little anecdotes and events that he could pass on to Prof. But now that they were all locked below decks, there was less to talk about. During the day, Prof lay motionless on his bunk and let time pass silently by him.

Each evening, though, he would continue instructing his friends, and they benefited from his extensive knowledge, imparted as it always was with patience and good humor. Paddy's handwriting became quite proficient, and he could even have written his own letters back home, rather than have Chipper carry out the task for him. However, he quite enjoyed Chipper's enthusiasm for the task, and was happy to allow the practice to continue.

One of the guards, whose pet parrot had benefited from Paddy's attention and ministrations, carried the latest missive off, promising that it would find its destination in Ireland if he had anything to do with it. Although Paddy could have no way of knowing if the message would ever reach his home, he was pleased to have the ability to send such little notes. They gave him a link with his former life, the memory of which was steadily diminishing.

Paddy's general mental condition had changed quite dramatically in the ten months since he was captured at the docks in Belfast. He was still quiet and introspective, but hardness was developing around his eyes. And it was a different hardness than that of the usual sailor's stare, which was brought on by hours of exposure to the elements.

Away from his rustic ordered life, Paddy was now facing a structured future based on men's hierarchy. There were those who were in control, and those who were used. Beneath these two levels, in his present environment, were the convicts. They too had their own structure: the predators and the preyed upon.

His size, which he had always rather taken for granted, had stood him in good stead. The convicts with whom he shared his sleeping moments generally stayed away from him; he was, after all, part of a small effective clique with Chipper, Ackers and Prof, all of whom seemed knowledgeable and confident within their floating world.

Paddy also had the ear of a number of the officers and shiphands. On the long journey across the Atlantic, he was often seen above decks, ministering to various animals that were in need of attention. These he kept penned up at the stern of the ship, as it dragged its way across the endless wastes of the Atlantic Ocean.

As he was almost free within the confines of the *Falcon*, he had the space and time to contemplate his life. Looking back, he found Paddy, the farmer, almost unrecognizable. He seemed like some long-lost brother left behind on the distant shores of his beloved Ireland. Paddy found increasing difficulty in remembering Katherine's face. His four children, too, were vanishing from his memory. At first, this had alarmed him greatly and he would try at night to force each one's features into his mind. Eventually, he found the exercise created such pain in his heart that he put it off for longer and longer periods.

Back in Ireland, he had always accepted life as it came to him. It was hard, but outside of the normal pestilence and natural pitfalls of the farming life, he had few difficulties. His family, compared to everybody else, had seemed normal. They were poor, but they were generally happy. They lived their lives as thousands of their fellow farmers did. There was an evenness and balance to everyone's existence. The priest, the landowner, the agent and the magistrate all had some authority over them. But each of these dignitaries shared a similar viewpoint and culture, and understood there was an order to the simple life on which each of them depended.

Since he had been taken away, however, he had had to face a new view of the world. Here each day's events were dependent on the wishes of others. Discipline was harsh, and the majority had little control over it. Every man knew his destiny was totally outside his own making. Even if one complied, circumstances could easily alter, and authority would often punish with little interest in a fair hearing.

Paddy had long hours to ponder his new life. The desperation and sadness had long since subsided, thanks due mainly to Chipper's guiding hand and the Prof's philosophical teachings. Now, Paddy accepted that his life was beginning anew and he had been given a tremendous gift. He had the trust of the ship's masters and a steady hand in dealing with his animal charges. What Prof had said was true. The more authoritative he sounded in his diagnoses, the more the officers were convinced he knew what he was doing.

When his charges died, as they did with some regularity, it was accepted he had done his best. When the animals returned to health, he was considered to be a very good vet indeed. Paddy took everything that came his way with a quiet smile and a slight inclination of the head.

His evenings generally were confined below decks with his colleagues, except for the occasions when he had to visit the pen above to administer some care. When he was below, he would continue with Prof's training in the mysteries of the world, and also would spend time playing board games with Chipper and Ackers.

Marmy had transferred his principle allegiance to Ackers, who continued to be totally bewitched by the small ginger creature. Marmy would visit Paddy and all the others who showed interest in him, but it was to Ackers he would regularly return to spend the early night. He would lie close to the top of the stocky countryman's bunk so it was impossible to tell where the cat's ginger fur ended and Ackers similarly colored locks began.

Chipper still acted as the unofficial guide to seamen's ways and for 'fiddles' as he called them. These were small acts of disobedience that generally resulted in some material gain, a good laugh, or both. As Chipper regularly remarked, 'fiddles' kept everyone alert and full of fun, and although they often amounted to small games, they did keep everyone on their toes.

Paddy began to notice, however, that, without his regular attendance at the routines of convict life, the other three began to form alliances with some of the other men aboard.

He watched these alliances develop, blossom, and mostly lose much of the early enthusiasm, as the ship continued its steady track across the sea. Although he was very often apart from them, Paddy was careful to never lose touch with his friends. He knew well that, once the journey was over, they would all need each other to survive the challenges of a new land.

However, the long hours he spent isolated from his colleagues allowed him to think through the fate that had befallen him and assess where he stood in the order of things. The result of this pondering began to create in him a feeling of the injustices that existed in the affairs of men and society. He would sit with his dumb charges, watching the turns of the drills and routines of shipboard life.

He could see that, without discipline, nothing would be accomplished. However, he saw there were so many privileges at the top of the chain of command compared to so few at the bottom. This was something he could neither accept nor understand. The officers, like those in the strata below them, shared their common home. However, they had a luxurious mess to spend their off-duty time in, and they had the pick of the food, or so it seemed to Paddy.

They seemed to saunter around the decks looking bored and uninterested in what was going on. Nonetheless, their eyes were everywhere, picking up details and savoring the pickings they collected. These were then whispered to the disciplinarians for action. The sergeants at arms, bosuns and other non-commissioned officers were then expected to rectify whatever fault was found.

Paddy watched these power games and the torment they would wreak on the shiphands' lives. He stored away in his memory the injustices, and the events that created them, to think on at his convenience. Unwittingly, he was becoming a student of simple politics, and his viewpoint, from the lowest rung as a convict, would be considered communist by his great-great-great-grandson, Mitch.

Two nights after mooring off the South American coastline, one of the friendlier seamen, Varcoe, stopped by Paddy's cramped pen. Paddy had received permission to come above decks to care for a sheep that was suffering from an attack of lice. He was soaping the twitching animal's back with a solution of tar and paraffin, when Varcoe sidled up to him. A man as slender as a string bean, who seemed to spend his life suspended in the top rigging, Varcoe had an odd habit of speaking out of the side of his mouth at the best of times, but whenever he was in a confidential mode, he would accompany this trait with many head jerks as he glanced around, to see if the coast was clear of unwelcome ears.

'Your mate, the cockney,' he began with a soft Cornish lilt.

'You mean Chipper?' Paddy asked, leaning his head towards the words, which disappeared on the Brazilian air, as the *Falcon* bobbed at her moorings.

They were completely alone, apart from a solitary guard posted some thirty feet away at the top of the gangway where the jolly boat would berth after her trips ashore. Nonetheless, Varcoe's head rotated, his eyes swiveling in their sockets as he sought security for his words.

'Yes, him. Chipper. I don't like the looks of 'im.'

'What do you mean?' Paddy replied, catching the surreptitiousness of the man's tone, and looking about in the same furtive way.

"E's got that pallor about 'im. I've seen it many times 'afore. If 'e's got a touch of a gutser, it can be fatal out 'ere. I've seen better men than 'im drop like flies. You better check 'im over 'afore it's too late.'

Paddy watched the man depart into the night, his elongated figure still looking around as if he expected some awful apparition to jump out on him. Reflecting on the few times he had spent with Chipper over the last day or two, he could not recall that there seemed something about his friend that alerted him to any sickness.

There had been a number of bouts of illness above and below decks during the voyage so far. Considering the cramped conditions and the poor sanitation, it was surprising there had been no deaths, or serious incapacities. The medical attention was at best limited, and, at worst non-existent, so men were left to lie on their hammocks and bunks to cope with discomfort as best they could.

A number of primitive cures were practiced on those who became ill. Leeches, kept in glass jars, were applied to areas of the skin to draw out the poisons that circulated in the patients' veins. If more concentrated reduction of pressure was needed, it was brought about by the barber's knife, with the blood being drained away into a bowl. Any resulting infection was 'cured' by more applications of the same method. Certain herbs and purgatives were also administered by the surgeon, who shared other duties with the junior officers, as well as shaving the faces and cutting the hair of the seniors.

In common with all countrymen of the age, Paddy had a general overall knowledge of cures that would clear up minor discomforts, but outside of these, he also shared a horror of unknown plagues and pestilences. Since the Black Death had reduced the population of Europe by nearly two thirds so many centuries earlier, he, like all those who had inherited the dreadful tales, prayed constantly for protection against such terrors coming out of foreign parts.

As soon as he could finish his duties with the sheep, he signaled to the guard to lift the hatch so he might descend into the dark murky air of the hold to seek out his friend. His practiced way through the lines of hammocks and bunks brought him swiftly to Chipper. At first, he thought the Londoner was sleeping peacefully, but as he stared down at the still form, he could feel the heat rising off his friend. He placed his hand on Chipper's forehead and felt the fever raging beneath him.

Chipper stirred restlessly and Paddy said quietly, 'You all right, Chipper?'

'Not in the best shape, me ol' mate. Must've eaten some of that queer food we're always 'earin' about.'

The talk at mealtimes was often that the authorities would try to poison them once they were safely out to sea. It would be cheaper in the long run and save everyone a lot of trouble. Prof had tried to explain the Georgian mentality regarding death in the face of strong Christian belief, but rumors still persisted.

'How long have you had it, Chip?'

'It's been about four days now. But don't tell anyone, Paddy. I don't trust their medicine. Particularly that butcher with the knife.'

Paddy put his hand back on Chipper's brow. It was not a normal temperature, Paddy could feel. His experience with his children and close relatives was enough to tell him that Chipper was a sick man. With the shifty Varcoe's doom-laden words ringing in his ears, Paddy decided to act. He waited for two or three hours, watching over the troubled Chipper. Then, as the dawn began its golden red wash across the hull, he tapped softly on the hatch.

A new guard lifted the edge and, after seeing Paddy's

confident grin, lifted it all the way and lowered the ladder.

'I need to check on one of the sheep. It's been bad for several days.'

That was all the explanation needed to justify the guard letting Paddy up onto the empty deck. Moving aft toward the animals' pen, Paddy began to work out his plan. Chipper was very sick. He needed help desperately. At the same time, quite rightly, he feared the only 'doctor' on board.

Among his charges Paddy had a large cat that had suffered from a nasty ear discharge. The effect of this infection and the cowslip wine that Paddy was using to treat the complaint was to make the animal even more soporific than usual. Taking hold of the creature, Paddy stroked it and offered it another draft. Fortunately, the cat liked the potion and sucked away on the bottle that was offered, until it was drained.

The cat was called Percival and belonged to Captain Jenks, the master of the ship. It was a renowned mouser and had traveled aboard all the captain's ships in the past ten years. He was extremely fond of Percival and asked after his progress every time he could.

Paddy waited with the sleepy cat in his arm as HMS *Falcon* came to life. Fortunately, Percival was responding to Paddy's home-brewed cure even though at the moment he was in a deep sleep. The last thing the Irishman wanted was to lose the captain's favorite, but at the present, he was grateful for the animal's pathetic appearance, lolling in the morning light.

Jenks appeared on deck, bright and early as usual. He was fresh from his morning shave and his face glowed from the sea air and sunshine of the voyage. He made his rounds, with a watchful eye on Percival who snored softly through the proceedings.

'How's he doing, O'Doule?'

Paddy did not stand up. He sat crunched up, hoping that the cowslip wine would continue to keep the cat sleeping.

'I'm sorry, Sir. I don't want to disturb him. He's very weak, I'm afraid.' This was hard to justify as the animal had put on considerable weight since being under Paddy's care.

'If we don't get some proper medicine, I think he might die in a day or two. I can get him well, sir, but it'll need a pharmacist.'

Captain Jenks looked crestfallen. He was devoted to Percival, and with so few personal things in his mariner's life, the potential loss of such a companion was a bitter blow. Paddy looked suitably depressed. Percival, in keeping with his role, allowed a milky inner eyelid to peek drunkenly out at his master.

'I'll bring a man aboard right away.'

'That could take too long, I'm afraid, sir. These foreigners are a difficult bunch, and it would take a visit from several, before we found the right man who knew what the right formula was.'

The captain had more than enough experience of such foreign difficulty and concurred.

'But we can't let him die without an effort,' he said rather sadly.

'Perhaps, if you and I could go ashore together, we might manage to find someone who we could trust to prescribe safely for Percival, sir.'

Paddy watched as the captain turned such an unorthodox idea around in his orderly mind. It was strictly against orders, but there was poor Percival with his blindlike eye staring balefully at him. Paddy sat hunched over the cat waiting for the verdict.

'Marlow,' Captain Jenks called, 'bring over a set of light irons for O'Doule.' He turned to Paddy, who was gently laying Percival down in the hope the animal would not wake up and look healthy. 'I'm going to send you ashore with Marlow. You're to scout out a chemist, and return here within two hours. Any attempt to escape, you'll be shot. Do you understand?'

'We shouldn't be too long, sir, and I'll have old Percy back in your cabin in a couple of days. I'll need some money and could I also have your man, Varcoe, come along as well? He's got some of the lingo. That would help a lot.'

The captain agreed to his requests, and after handing over a written draft, exchangeable for the King's money, he bent down to stroke Percival behind his ear.

'Don't do that, Sir, he needs all the sleep he can get. It's best if he just rests quietly in his pen until I get back with the medicine.'

Putting out his hands for the manacles, Paddy ensured his expression was sufficiently serious, as befitted his mission. With a final backward glance of great concern, Jenks walked silently away.

The jolly boat tilted dangerously as Marlow, Varcoe and Paddy climbed aboard. A two-man crew pulled steadily over the still waters of the harbor, dodging the other vessels that plied their trade in the busy port. Varcoe kept his shifty eyes on the wooden hull, but Marlow, the younger man, had his face fixed in wonder on the docks as they loomed closer with every pull.

As they mounted onto the first dry land Paddy had experienced since his embarkation back in Southampton, Varcoe said to Marlow, 'Look, lad, this is the first bit of "foreign" you've 'ad a chance to see, isn't it?'

Marlow gazed around and said it most certainly was.

'Well, then take the opportunity of a look see. I'll keep 'old of Paddy 'ere. 'E's no problem. We'll be back in a couple of 'ours, so be waitin' for us.'

Looking elated at the thought of getting into some mischief, Marlow escaped off towards the shanty-type bars that were the Mecca for all seafaring men with big thirsts and roving eyes for the type of femininity that lay in wait.

'So you don't 'ave to tell me this little jaunt is not just for the sake of old Percival, is it? Could it be that your mate's taken a turn for the worst, then?'

Paddy nodded slowly.

'It was the best I could think of at the time. But Chipper's real bad, he needs medicine.'

'And not the bleedin' bowl either,' Varcoe concurred. 'We've all 'ad enough of that.'

They pushed their way through the crowd milling about. Paddy tried his best to hide the chains that bound his hands and feet. He needn't have worried as everyone was far too interested in the wares that were on sale at various stalls, shops and doorways. In fact, every spare inch of space was taken up with someone selling something, usually something that looked bright, or smelled strongly. And overall, there was the overpowering odor of humanity that washed across the waves of people who pushed and shoved through the tiny packed streets. It was a hot feral smell that differed from the damp musty odors of the Irish markets and the English alleys. Those thoroughfares were almost completely devoid of garlic, which seemed here to be the base from which all other scents grew.

A split second before his eyes saw the danger, Paddy's instincts put him on full alert. Pushing down through the throng was a tall bulky shape. At first glance, the uninformed would have thought they had seen a big woman with excessive rouge and paint applied to thick lips which added to the permanent sneer that played upon them. But moving along with the press of people, Paddy immediately recognized ex-chief gunner, Sande, bearing down on him only some hundred yards away.

He pulled hard on the chain that bound him to Varcoe and pushed them both into a startled woman's stall. She looked accusingly at Paddy, as he shrank beneath the bales of striped cloth she was selling, pulling Varcoe in a heap on top of him. He clamped a strong-gripped hand over his guard's mouth and, putting his own mouth down next to his ear, said, 'Sorry to pull you about, but we were just about to run slap bang into a very dangerous type, name of Sande. It wouldn't do you any good being seen alongside me either.'

Varcoe looked wildly at Paddy and nodded to let him know that he understood.

'I've heard about him. Bit of a queer type, they say.'

'Dangerously so. He's the reason I'm in this position. But that's a long story. Keep your head down and I'll take a look-see out there.'

Poking his head above the countertop, Paddy could see Chief Sande had passed their hiding place and was charging ahead towards some unknown goal. As he pulled himself and Varcoe to a standing position, he felt the rigidity begin to leave his body. The woman stall owner also began to take stock of the situation, and left her customer to attend to her two uninvited guests. Varcoe silenced her developing harangue with a withering look, accompanied by some colorful language, which had the desired affect, and she withdrew from them as they departed up the street away from the market area.

'Do you think we might get a drink before we carry on, Varcoe?'

Paddy was beginning to feel a light-headedness take hold of him, since the adrenaline rush that had caused his quick reaction. Also there was an almost primeval effect that even accompanied thoughts of the man who had so dominated his destiny since he had been snatched from his life back in Ireland. It was a completely new experience for him and he felt stranger than he had ever felt before.

'Well, we're in luck, Paddy. There's an apothecary right

next door to a café. What do you fancy first? Business or pleasure?'

'You're a good sort, Varcoe. I really could do with a drink, but let's get the medicine first.'

Crossing the street, they entered a cool dark room, smelling of spices and fruits. There were glass-fronted cabinets along three sides, with a long table running down the center of the shop. A tall stooping man, with a dark robe that reached to the floor, smiled quietly from a stool he was perched upon by the door.

Varcoe pointed to Paddy and stumbled through his attempts at the man's language. The chemist at first looked confused and then amused. He raised a hand and spoke to them both in a halting form of Latin. From his years at the altar of the Roman Catholic church, Paddy recognized many of the words and smiled back. Varcoe, not wishing to be outdone, entered the conversation and between the three of them, they were able to conduct the business Paddy had come for.

Senhor Fermin, as the apothecary was called, understood Paddy urgently needed medicine for a colleague on the boat. He diplomatically ignored the fact that Paddy was chained to his partner, and carried out a series of questions, using a mixture of Latin, Portuguese, Spanish and, above all, gestures.

He was able to understand Chipper's illness had left him shivering and that, above all, bleeding was not needed. If anything, the patient needed something to help him build up some strength rather than to continually weaken him. He inquired if others had suffered from the same problems, and if a supply would be of benefit for future doses.

Paddy told Varcoe to show *Senhor* Fermin the paper that Captain Jenks had given them. The chemist produced a pair of thick-lensed spectacles from the folds of his robe and carefully scanned the sheet. He paid particular attention to the signature, and nodded wisely that he would be happy to accept the paper.

Paddy said he was pleased, but the paper also had to serve another purpose, that of buying them a drink next door. He did this by pointing through the wall and using the time-honored gesture of raising his curled fist to his lips. The chemist smiled acknowledgment and moved to the end of the table, taking a pestle and mortar out from underneath, and some boxes from one of the glass-covered cabinets behind him.

For a quarter of an hour, he selected, mixed and ground an endless succession of ingredients. He bent over the bowl and worked steadily, hissing a mournful dirge through his gapped teeth in accompaniment. Paddy and Varcoe looked on as the work came to its fruition, and two medicines were placed in paper bags and then into an oiled cloth to protect them from the sea's dampness.

Reverting once more to their unusual eclectic form of language, *Senhor* Fermin explained that the medicine needed to be mixed with a little water and given in a small glass. The other mixture should be taken three times each day until the patient was able to settle into a normal routine. It would take about four days, he felt, for this to happen. Then, gathering his robe around him, he escorted the two men next door, and with considerable flourish arranged for their needs to be met. Then, following a deep bow, he swept back to his business.

The small barkeep placed a pitcher of red wine on the bar top. Paddy was fascinated by the atmosphere of the place. A sound of music filtered through from a back room, and several men sat at round tables, talking and laughing. Both he and Varcoe leaned against the bar and sipped their wine from small pottery mugs. It warmed their insides like nothing they had experienced since leaving their own lands far to the north.

'It would be so easy to stay here and forget the past, wouldn't it?' Paddy remarked.

'It would at that, Paddy. But it wouldn't be the past that would be a problem. It would be the immediate present. The crime for desertion is bad enough, but for an escaped prisoner it would be far worse.'

'Oh, I know. But it's so peaceful here. Just look at the way people are so happy. No one to push them around like we have back on the boat. In the navy, everybody is always telling you what to do. If it's not the officers, then it's the NCOs. That bastard, Sande, really made me think. How could we live with that kind of injustice?'

'It's just the way of the world, Paddy,' Varcoe nodded sagely, his head jerking round in his constant quest for prying ears. 'I'm sure it's really just the same for these people. Right now they're taking it easy, but in a while I expect they'll probably have their own NCOs kicking them up the backside. I've been all over the place with the navy, and I've never seen it different.'

Paddy finished his mug of wine and said, 'Perhaps we'll have a chance in a new land to make something different. Once we're free, perhaps we can make a new society where no one has to live in fear.'

'From your lips to God's ears, old son,' Varcoe replied, banging his empty pot down. 'It's a beautiful thought, but I have my doubts. As long as there are people like your friend, Sande, in the world.'

As the level of wine inexorably sank in the jug, Paddy lost the warmth that had flooded him with the first draft. He must return to his life on the *Falcon* and whatever his sentence in Van Diemen's land would bring him. Right now, the realization of the need for curing Chipper and being with Prof and Ackers meant he had to leave what was, after all, only a small glimpse of another life – one he could never join.

Grimly, he turned for the door, and with Varcoe alongside, he trudged heavily back to the quay where from a distance they could see Marlow fidgeting beside the jolly boat's painter.

Chapter Twenty-One

Amsterdam, 1993

Some of the color had definitely come back into Mike Ryan's face. He opened the door at Mitch O'Doule's knock and wandered back into the room.

'Want anything to eat?' Mitch inquired. 'They've a huge buffet downstairs. It's obviously built for the Americans. It's got that funny bacon that's all brown and burnt.'

Mike Ryan shook his head and stuck a cigarette in his mouth, lit it and picked up his coffee cup.

'Bloody room service takes its time, I can tell you. I only wanted a coffee, for Christ's sakes, and they took half an hour. No bloody tip for them, that's for sure.'

'You look a hell of a lot better. Sleep well?'

'Not bad. I've still got a slightly dicky belly. But that's the price, I guess, for all that rot-gut. I'll be as bad as bloody Taffy with the booze at this rate. I can't understand it, Mitch. I can't remember being as sick as that since I was a boy.'

'I tell you, you'll have to watch out for this foreign stuff. It's a lot stronger than you think. You ready to go then?'

The room was pretty bare and there seemed to be no evidence of packing.

'Yes, I shoved it all in the bag in the wardrobe. That Hans is likely to be on time, I guess. Damned foreigners. There's something about 'em. What about those bloody Arabs yesterday?' Ryan pronounced the term A-rabs, with a sneer in his voice. 'It's coming to something when we've got to go to the likes of them for help. What did they look like in those dresses? All very dodgy, I think.'

'Each to his own, I guess.'

Mitch tried to take a non-confrontational side. Underneath, he was feeling very apprehensive, and was in no mood to get into Mike's large repertoire of racial theories. He was always likely to trot out a long list of tired epithets which Mitch had heard many times over the years.

Ryan threw on his jacket, stubbed out his cigarette, grabbed his overstuffed bag, and walked down the long corridor towards the elevator. As expected, the Mercedes was parked outside the main entrance with Hans reading a local newspaper and filling the cabin with his own mixture of cologne and smoke.

'And how are you this morning, Colonel Ryan?'

Ryan grunted and turned towards Mitch.

'You got the keys to that Escort?'

Mitch nodded.

'Well, leave them at the reception. Fergy's got some fellow picking it up tomorrow. He's after watching the pennies, as always.'

Mitch did as asked, and saw the keys to the hire car disappear behind the entrance desk. Trust Fergy to cover all the angles. Too clever by half, he thought.

Mike shoved himself into the back next to his bag, squeezing Mitch against the far door.

'Okay,' he answered brusquely. He was obviously in no mood to be reminded of the previous day.

'So what's the attraction of the Canary Islands, Hans?' Mitch asked as the car swept out of the car park.

'Mr Kirkdorp likes the spot. You know, we Dutch don't get enough sunshine—'

Hans let out a curse that sounded like *hotfordommer* to the ears in the rear as a large farm truck, stacked full of manure, weaved in front of the Mercedes as it tried to exit into the airport.

'Sorry about that,' Hans said, and returned to the topic of the Canaries. 'Our weather is very damp here and all Dutch people dream of unlimited sun. Rich ones, in particular. In Mr Kirkdorp's case, the Canaries fit the bill. He has other places, but the location of the islands allows easier access to the coast of Africa.'

The traffic into Schipol was already stacked up and they were stationary for several minutes in the flow. Since he had awakened in the early darkness, Mitch felt very nervous at the prospect of another big part of this whole scheme being enacted without planning from him. He really hated not being in control like this. Still, as he stepped out of the big German car, he put on a stoical face and went through the motions of thanking Hans for his help, before going off with his grim-faced friend.

They pushed through the same throngs of assorted business people and tourists who always seemed to congregate in such places, and who appeared to find it necessary to communicate at the top of their voices in every language known to man.

Mitch apprehensively put his bag containing the metal box on the scales, and smiled at the Iberian ground attendant. Mike tried to use the small amount of charm still remaining in him to plead the case for an upgrade into first class. It was politely ignored as a poor joke. As they collected their boarding cards and turned to leave for the gate, two Dutch policemen strolled past with slung automatic machine-guns and steel-wary eyes. Mitch felt Mike stiffen at his side and then relax as they continued their beat.

'I tell you, Mitch, the sight of policemen with guns always scares the bejasus out of me. Good job that the bloody English don't behave that way; we'd never get any of the lads to do anything.'

Mitch, who had his own private nightmare of being caught shipping a handgun, merely nodded in agreement.

Flight 382 to Lanzarote was late in taking off. Air traffic delay was the excuse given by the heavily accented pilot. But after they sat at the gate with their seat belts fastened for the obligatory twenty minutes, they were on their way. They were sitting close to the front and had very few other passengers around them.

The flight attendants smiled efficiently as they dispensed food and drink, and both Irishmen dozed their way across the western part of Europe. Mitch waited for a chance to slip the contents of the remaining packet of goodness-knows-what before the plane landed. So far, apart from an orange juice, Ryan had shown no interest in alcohol. Mitch waited patiently.

Eventually, Mike, who was sitting next to the window, pushed himself up and said, 'I'm off to the lav.'

Mitch seized his chance and said, 'How about a quick whiskey before we land. I could really fancy one. Not too good going up or coming down, I'm afraid.'

Mike raised his eyebrows at the admission of weakness, and said he could manage one, if they had a decent brand like Bushmills available. Climbing over Mitch he made his way down to the back of the 737. Mitch also walked to the back a few moments later, and returned with two Carlos Primero brandies with ice. Sitting down, he opened the last of the two of Margitte's envelopes, and shook the contents into Mike's glass and stirred it round. The ice was seriously melted by the time Mike returned.

Mitch said, 'I got you a drink, but they only had brandy. It's okay, though.'

For a moment, Mitch thought that Ryan would not take the potion. He had suggested Bushmills; otherwise, he might have declined. Then, because Mike was such an expert, he could not risk letting him drink a doctored glassful. His palate might well have detected whatever the poison was.

As it happened, Mike sipped the drink and then swallowed it. 'Good stuff' was all he had to say about the brew, and Mitch felt the needle on his dials coming out of the red danger zone once again.

The landing was bumpy, and even on the ground, the pilot seemed to enjoy throwing the plane from side to side as it careened down the runway towards the terminal building.

Mitch felt his insides bunch up as they deplaned. If his pistol was detected he would have some explaining to do, and his planned excuse of needing protection seemed flimsy at best. He needn't have worried. The bags appeared on the carousel with no accompanying alarm bells and running policemen. On the first pass, he deliberately let the bag travel past him and watched for anybody to show an interest in it. There seemed to be nobody looking, and everyone else was trying to struggle with their possessions. The two of them circulated in front of the tourists who were standing with anxious faces and outstretched arms.

A cursory glance was given to the baggage slips as they passed out of the hall and through the customs green channel. Mitch had a nasty moment as an agent stared over at him. But once again, as in the case of his arrival from the boat in Ostend, there was a student type ahead, who attracted the attention of the clerk and upon whom the full majesty of authority descended.

As they passed through the frosted glass of immigration and customs, they were immediately greeted by a small man in a black suit and peaked hat. 'Mr O'Doule and Mr Ryan?' The voice was soft and projected through a mouth that lacked teeth. The little man turned and walked away with a shuffling gait. The two colonels followed behind at a short distance, both smiling at the apparent energy of this small man of very late middle age.

Parked quite illegally at the curbside, was a large Seat – the Spanish version of the Italian Fiat. A female meter attendant was in the act of sticking a ticket under the windscreen wipers. The small man snatched it out and tore it into little pieces right in the woman's face and threw them on the ground. The woman totally ignored this behavior, and continued on down the line of cars, writing as she went.

The door catches popped, and the three climbed into the roasting interior.

'My name is Rafael, but you can call me Ralph, if you wish. I am to take you to the villa. It will be about half an hour. Please not to smoke,' he added as Mike stuck a cigarette in his mouth.

'One of the things I hate about leaving the ould country,' Ryan allowed his accent to roll around the ancient term, 'is the fact that you can't ever get a decent smoke when you want it. What happened to you, by the way? Have you given it up for good?'

There was the tone of a sneer that all dedicated smokers tend to deliver to those of their number who try to desert their addictive club.

'Thought that I'd give it a try,' was the bland reply.

The ride was smooth and without incident. Ralph was an experienced driver, and apart from an occasional remark about a passing point of interest, he remained quiet at the controls. Both Mitch and Mike remained watching the scenery from opposite sides of the Seat. Mitch wondered what, if any, effect the potion might be having.

After twenty minutes, the main road turned inland at an almost ninety-degree angle. However, the car continued straight, passing two high wooden gates bleached almost white from the clear sunshine. The road took them over a steep hill, scorched golden brown through lack of rain, and eventually through another open gate.

'Security is tight, *señores*. Please do not be alarmed at what may seem a lack of it. When we left the main road, every move is on television in the villa.'

Ralph looked through the mirror at the two passengers, who had never doubted the arrangements, since they had been recipients of Peter Kirkdorp's hospitality and opulence at his home in Holland.

The road now twisted violently from side to side and began a sharp drop downwards. They could see that the ocean swept round into a bay, overlooking which was a large pink house with a first-floor balcony that went the entire length of the building.

'Mr Kirkdorp owns this whole peninsula. We have been on it for the last five minutes. Anyone who strays from the highway and makes it through the first gate will be turned back by a guard. Mr Kirkdorp hates to be disturbed when he is here. The authorities were, how do you say, reluctant to allow the purchase of the land, but it went much smoother after some money passed over. Mr Kirkdorp called it a grant for their new town hall. As he said, everyone came out a winner. That is Mr Kirkdorp's way.'

Mitch noticed that Mike Ryan was twisting around in his seat while looking out of the windows. He also seemed to have again developed his white pallor of the previous day.

'You okay, Mike?' he inquired.

'Just need the bog,' was the answer, delivered from the side of the mouth.

Eventually, the car turned a corner and began a slow sweep up to the front of the house. Ralph brought the car to a dusty stop and jumped out with a speed surprising in one so elderly. The two passengers climbed out into the heat of the midday sun and were duly shown into the large, spacious hall of the imposing house.

Standing ready to greet them, as Ralph went back for the bags, was a tall white-haired man of about fifty, dressed in a white cotton safari suit with a red neckerchief. Beside him stood an equally elegant woman, some twenty years younger.

The man introduced himself as Derek Ossman, and with a gesture, indicated Diane Stacey, 'my assistant, companion and confidante.'

Mitch put his hand out and was about to take Ossman's when Mike spoke out loudly, 'Where's the toilet, please?'

'Diane, could you show Mr er, are you Mr Ryan or Mr O'Doule?'

As Diane Stacey led Mike away, Mitch explained who they each were, and that Mike had been suffering from some sickness for the entire trip.

'Yes, Mr O'Doule, we had heard all was not well with your colleague.'

He pointed the way into a room at the side of the hall, sat down on a plump sofa covered in a rich silk of intricate design, and indicated to Mitch that he should take the chair to the side.

The room had windows from floor to ceiling along one wall, which looked down on three sizable yachts clustered round a small jetty. The other walls of the salon had been decorated first in pale pink silk, and then with paintings that even Mitch recognized as French Impressionist. A gas 'log' fire flickered behind a glass door in a huge Spanish fireplace; not a hint of heat escaped its vastness. The whole room was straight out of *Architectural Digest*, *International Design*, or *Lifestyles of the Rich and Famous*.

In spite of his complete lack of familiarity with such opulence, Mitch found it impossible not to relax in these surroundings.

'As you can see, Mr Kirkdorp likes to live well when he

visits us here. I am his partner and general manager for those business interests which are run outside of Holland. At the back of the house, there are three offices and a full secretarial staff. They have all been given time off during your visit.'

Mitch was aware that Derek Ossman had a slight accent and assumed that he was also from Holland. He was about to inquire further about the situation when his host's 'assistant, companion and confidante' came into the room and sat down.

'Your friend didn't seem to be vacating the bathroom, so I left him to it. I'm sure he'll find us here eventually.'

There was something familiar about Diane Stacey's voice and her mannerisms, but Mitch couldn't quite put his finger on it. He'd been with too many 'foreigners' over the last few days; they were all beginning to confuse him.

'I do hope Mr Ryan is not seriously indisposed; we have the sheik arriving for an early dinner. I think he'll expect you both to be present.'

'What are the arrangements exactly, Mr Ossman?'

'Call me Derek, please. It will go more smoothly if we are informal. But to answer your question, we expect you to accept the wares we will show you; then we will ask for the money to be transferred. The sheik will tell you the bank and the full amount. Once the transfer is complete, we will load one of those vessels that you see down there, and you can dictate its destination. A crew will be available for the purpose. Once they depart, you may take your leave.'

'So this sheik is the main man, is he?'

'As far as the financial transaction is concerned, yes. He has not been here before, but the arrangements were made by Pieter and he never slips up. The merchandise arrived early this morning, and was unloaded down at the jetty. At present it's under guard in the launch on the other side of that yacht.'

Mitch had not noticed it on his first glance, but now that he looked more carefully, he could see a sleek green bow that pointed out to sea and foretold a powerful vessel.

'As you can see, Mitch, we are very well organized here, and very secluded. Provided all is acceptable between you and the sheik, we can have you out of here by lunchtime tomorrow.'

Just then Mike Ryan appeared at the door. He had a most unhealthy pallor, and he clutched at the doorway for support.

'Sorry about that,' he said. 'Must have been something I ate.' He threaded his way through the furniture and sat down on a hard chair with his back to the windows.

'We've been going over the final stage, Mike,' Mitch explained to him. 'Everything seems to be well organized. We have one other visitor to arrive, and then we can complete the deal.'

Mike's eyes were very glassy and Mitch could see he had not fully understood what had been said. He was about to repeat the statement when Mike staggered to his feet and weaved back out of the room.

'Poor fellow, he seems to have an attack of "Canary tummy", except that he's hardly been here long enough.'

Derek's face showed his concern.

Mitch was well aware that once again, Margitte's mysterious packet had done the damage. He realized that turning Mike Ryan into a sweating, confused and decidedly unhealthy link in the chain was all part of the plan, but he could not help feeling sorry for him.

Through the door, Ralph could be seen bustling about with their bags. Mitch stood up abruptly, as he remembered the concealed weapon in his holdall. He did not want it to somehow be discovered.

'Would you mind if I freshened up a bit? It was an

uncomfortable journey.'

Derek pulled himself to his feet saying, 'I'll show you your quarters. Hold on for Colonel Ryan will you, Diane?' He led the way out and up a staircase, which divided into two at the top. 'As you can see, all the rooms are designed to face the water, with the exception of those for the office at the back. But then, the poor worker bees are supposed to have their heads down working.'

Bloody typical, thought Mitch, It's the same everywhere one goes.

Derek Ossman opened a door and showed Mitch into his room. It, too, was spacious and airy, with more paintings on the walls and an unrestricted view of the jetty.

'I hope you will be comfortable here for your short stay,' his host said, and left Mitch alone with his incongruous bag which had been placed on a small table at the foot of the bed.

Mitch looked around the room, lifting table lamps and peering under paintings. He checked under the pink and blue rug in front of the fireplace, and along door and window frames. There seemed to be no wires or devices that could be used to snoop on him. Nonetheless, he removed just a change of clothes and his wash kit, and put his bag, with its steel box and gun, in the closet. There was a small key in the lock and, with his back to the room, he turned it and put it in his pocket.

He felt the warm water of the shower relax him, and, putting on a new shirt and slacks, he went down to join the others. Almost at the bottom of the stairs, he heard the crunch of tires on the gravel outside. Ralph – now clothed in a butler's black jacket with a waistcoat across his small chest – opened the front door, and Mitch could see the gleaming shine of a white Rolls Royce. As he stepped into the hall, Derek Ossman, together with Diane, came out of the salon with wide smiles and smoothing their already elegant clothes.

'Ah, Mitch, you're just in time to meet our VIP,' Derek said, as he stepped forward to greet the figure emerging from the dark interior of the Rolls.

Like Ossman, he was dressed in a white suit, but one that had the unmistakable mark of London's Saville Row. There was a bulk to the shoulders and a tightness to the sleeves and the material was obviously silk. All this outer splendor was designed to hide a somewhat bulky man of about forty. With a white silk shirt and matching tie, he had the appearance of a squat vanilla ice cream, with a chocolate topping provided by his dark complexion.

'Welcome to our villa, Sheik. May I present one of our honored guests, Colonel Mitch O'Doule. Colonel, His Excellency, Sheik Idi Bin Sulad Al Mohammed. I hope you won't mind if we merely call you Sheik. Arab names are rather difficult for us to get our tongues around.'

'I am delighted to meet you.'

The voice was accented and deep, and the sheik seemed to beam goodwill from behind his dark glasses. Ralph was scurrying around taking expensive-looking suitcases from the back of the Rolls. Derek led the way into the salon and seated everyone.

'Did you drive yourself from the airport, Sheik?'

'Oh no, arrangements were made for me to be collected and the car will return and come back for me when I call. As you may know, I am here officially as a special representative of the United Arab Emirates, and they have very good facilities on these islands.'

'But I thought you came from the Libyan leader,' Derek said, in a tone that showed that he was not expecting early misunderstandings.

'Yes, you are right. I am here at the master's personal request. That's unofficial, of course. But tell me, are there not two gentlemen from the Irish Republic?'

'My fellow colonel is suffering from a slight stomach upset, but I am sure he will join us shortly.'

Mitch tried to be as businesslike as possible, but with the combination of the sheik's bonhomie and these opulent surroundings, it was hard not to fall into the overall feeling of relaxation. He knew he had to stay on his guard for this final stage of the plan.

After pointing out the jetty with its impressive collection of boats, Derek suggested that they all eat, although it was rather early. Assuming agreement, he led the party of four into the dining room across the hall. Five places had been set around the Spanish oak table, and there was a buffet laid out on a long sideboard at the end of the room.

The guests busied themselves selecting from the various platters and sat down with the minimum of conversation. The quiet continued during dinner and well into the coffee stage. Ryan remained absent throughout, and, as the talk began to start with a repeat of the routines that had been given to Mitch earlier, Diane decided to go and see how the absentee was progressing.

When she eventually reappeared, she was accompanied by Ryan. Mitch was shocked by the look of the man. All the color was missing from his face, and he was hunched over as if he was suffering from a very severe stomach-ache, which in fact he was.

'You don't look too well, Mike.' Derek had risen to his feet and gone round to greet him as he shuffled through the doorway on Diane's arm.

'I'm feeling a bit better now, thanks.'

'Come and sit over here, Mike.'

Mike gave Mitch a small glance, and it was obvious that he was in some considerable discomfort.

'What's the plan then, Mitch?'

The voice was as weak as the appearance of the Irishman.

'We have to view the merchandise, and then agree payment with Sheik Idi er, er… I'm terribly sorry, but I can't remember all your names.'

'"The sheik" will do nicely, Colonel.'

The smile was all-encompassing and swept around the table.

'How do you do, Sheik.' Mike Ryan pronounced the word SHEEK, and at the same time bent over as a spasm gripped him. 'Sorry about my condition, but my colleague will keep a lookout for things. It's been a rough trip for me so far.'

'Yes, my partners in Holland told me you were not too well on your visit there. When was it now, two days ago? Our end of the business is very simple. You view the packages, then we arrange the payment. Once that is done, we can send you both on your way. I think we have airline tickets for our friends, do we not?'

Derek Ossman nodded that everything had been taken care of.

'Are you all right to visit the jetty, Mike? Or would you prefer to wait until later?'

Mike requested that he be allowed to rest for an hour and they agreed to meet in the salon two hours later at seven thirty. Diane helped the sick Ryan away, and Mitch, too, said he would take a nap until later. As he entered his room, Mitch checked around, but could not detect anything unusual. He was only concerned that his bag could have been looked at and his gun detected. He deliberately did not open the closet door, and lay down on the bed, hoping to sleep for awhile.

Blissfully, he dropped off almost immediately and slept until a starting motor from the jetty rumbled into a roar and disturbed him. A glance at his watch showed him that his sleep had lasted barely ten minutes. He tried vainly to return to his previous state, but there were too many things going through his mind to make that possible. He was so deeply into this whole thing he was having difficulty in remembering what was real and what was false. For instance, who in this house was real? How many were Margitte's contacts, and how many believed that they were about to provide the IRA with the means to blow up huge numbers of innocent people?

In the few days that had passed since he left his dingy flat in Ulster, he had passed through Belgium, visited Holland, and now here he was in the lap of luxury with a fresh set of strangers on this volcanic outcrop off the coast of Africa.

The smiling Sheik – was he genuine? How about Derek and his 'confidante'? The chemicals he had put into the unfortunate Ryan – what were they and what sort of permanent effect would they have?

As he lay there, he felt waves of insecurity sweep over him. When he first decided he wanted out, he had never imagined his route would be so complicated. Initially, he had felt he could just get out and disappear. Everything had taken on a far more exotic tone, once he had met Margitte. What had happened to him from then on was almost a miracle. He had never felt as drawn to anyone as he was to her. Where was she? He'd had no contact at all since he was back in Ireland. And yet, things had gone flawlessly. He was exhausted and wanted this last part of the plan finished quickly, so he could get away.

He lay on his side and let his mind wander. Those faint letters from his great-great-great-grandfather that Aunty Kate had shown him; it seemed they were somehow dictating his movements. The fact he was here on the island the long dead Paddy had once visited: what sort of coincidence was it that brought him here?

With a start, Mitch woke up. He was shocked to see he had slept for over an hour and a half. For a blissful moment, he had no idea where he was; then the insecurity returned, with the realization of the time and the next stage of his escape.

After splashing some water on his face and cleaning his teeth, he went downstairs and found the four organizers of the forthcoming exchange sitting gazing out at the sea, which was sparkling in the early evening sun.

Mike Ryan still looked ghastly, and Mitch went over to him with a nod at the others.

'How's it going, Mike?'

'Bit better, thanks. The kip helped a bit, I think.'

Mitch was reminded that, even when ill, Ryan was a dedicated man, and seemed to be completely unaffected by the richness of his surroundings.

'Are you up for a look at the stuff, then?'

Mitch automatically assumed the same clipped and businesslike tone.

'Let's get on with it,' Ryan announced to the room in general, and pulled himself shakily to his feet.

Derek and Diane escorted the sheik out of the salon and through a side door to a long flight of steps leading down to the jetty. Mitch and Mike followed in the rear.

'Christ, I hope there's a bog down there, Mitch,' Ryan said, as he clutched at the rail for support. 'This is the worst case of the shits I can ever remember. Keep an eye on that Arab. I don't trust him. Bloody white outfit. I prefer the frocks his mates were wearing up in Holland. At least they looked the part. This fellow looks like something out of a comic opera. For Christ's sake, watch him, Mitch. I just don't trust any of them.'

'Come on, Mike, I think you're being a bit over-suspicious. After all, we approached them with this idea.'

'They came after us originally, remember.'

'That's been going on for years, Mike. This recent business was our approach. What we're after now is fairly small beer, and there's no point in any funny business.'

'I just don't trust the buggers. All that smiling and the damned dark glasses. Shifty bastards, the lot of 'em. Oh God.'

Ryan doubled over and grabbed at his stomach. A sweat broke out on his forehead, and he lolled against the rail. The three others ignored his condition and continued down the steps. Eventually, the spasm passed and the two fellow conspirators could join the others at the cliff end of the jetty.

'Do you have a toilet down here?'

Mike's glassy eyes swiveled around the bobbing boats at anchor. '*Capitan* Rochas, *el lavabo por el señor, por favor,*' Diane called to the open doorway of the closest yacht. A dark-bearded head came out and stood to one side as Mike Ryan hurried up the gangplank and disappeared inside.

The high-speed launch whose engines had disturbed Mitch's rest earlier had been brought round to the side of the landing stage and sat low in the rippling water. Its two-man crew busied themselves with polishing cloths that seemed unnecessary in view of the pristine condition of the vessel.

'It's packed from stem to stern with Mephistos, Colonel,' the sheik said, grinning conspiratorially at the thin Irishman. One false move, and there would be enough of a bang to be heard by the master back in Tripoli.'

'They're safe as houses without their detonators, Sheik, I can assure you.' Derek spoke in a soothing way. 'Still, one never totally believes that, does one?'

Mitch felt like saying that if they had spent as much time around explosives as he had, they would know the difference between a primed bomb and a safe one. But he stood quietly and said nothing.

'Pedro.'

Derek spoke to the nearest man in the launch, as he guided Mitch to the boat. Pedro held out a hand, and Mitch climbed over the transom. Once on board, Mitch could now see that all around the floor and along the sides of the launch were tarpaulins dyed the same dark green as the craft. The boatman pulled back one side and showed that underneath were the same boxes that had been on show at Pieter Kirkdorp's beach house in Holland.

'The full consignment's packed and ready to go wherever you decide. We have a trawler on hand about halfway to the UK for refueling purposes. The covers should hide the cargo from all but the most serious binoculars. But, fortunately, this little boat will outpace anything a Customs and Excise department could send.'

'Very impressive, I'm sure.'

Mike had emerged from the yacht and rejoined the party.

'I'd like to have a look at the goods if I may. Give us a hand, will you, Mitch?'

He didn't look a lot better, but at least he had stopped sweating and seemed more agile as he came on board.

'Let's get a couple of these babies out, then.'

Mike grabbed at the tarpaulin and pulled a bomb onto the deck.

'How about one from down in the hold. Mitch, can you grab one?'

Mitch went through the hatch and pulled one of the boxes to the floor. Opening the container, he saw the same brooding octagonal shape, holding its different compartments of deadly explosive in place.

'How does it look, Mitch?' Ryan's voice came through the open doorway. 'Bring one out here and let's compare them. Mitch carried the bomb out into the fading light and laid it down next to the other.

'They're all the same, Colonel Ryan, I assure you.' The sheik's tone was comforting.

Ryan looked up from his examination.

'This is a very serious business to us, Sheik. Our funds are limited. Colonel O'Doule and I represent a struggle that's been going on for hundreds of years. There must be no mistake.'

'I assure you that everything is in order. In fact, the master has increased the quantity that you ordered by ten per cent, at no additional cost. He is anxious that you understand his enthusiasm for your cause.'

The deep voice positively oozed concern. Mike Ryan seemed oblivious to the generosity of the offer and the good wishes of his new ally.

'Well, we'll see if this one can make as big a bang as the ones in Holland. I sort of missed that, being under the weather.'

'That's not too easy, Mike.' Derek spoke up. 'The Spanish authorities are not overly enthusiastic about loud explosions around one of their best tourist spots.'

'Well, that's really too bad, Derek. Because I want to see how good this can be. You and your friends here are wanting to get a lot of our money. I'm not keen to part with it until I'm sure these are the same as the others. They look the same, I know. But I just want to be sure.'

'Okay, Mike,' Derek answered. 'We'll arrange a demonstration for you. I'd like to suggest early tomorrow morning. Fewer people around. We'll take one out to sea and let it go there. Will that do for you?'

'I guess so,' was the terse reply. 'Excuse me a moment.'

Ryan climbed back onto the jetty and moved rapidly towards the yacht that he had first entered, and once more disappeared.

'We had not expected this, Colonel O'Doule,' the sheik said quietly. 'The master is not used to being doubted.'

'There's no need to make more of it than it is, Sheik.' Derek's comment was calm and placating. 'We're just dealing with rather cautious people. Let's arrange all the other matters and then perform a small demonstration in the morning.'

Eventually, Mike Ryan appeared again, and after he indicated to Pedro, who had returned to his incessant polishing, that the device at which he had first looked should be put to one side, they climbed back up to the house. Seated once again in the salon, the sheik removed a piece of paper from his jacket and spoke directly to Mike.

'As agreed, we have provided you with one hundred and ten of the most recently designed high explosives, which you call Mephistos. In return, we expect payment by electronic transfer to our account. Is this agreed?'

Mitch noticed the sheik's tone had lost all of its bonhomie and had been replaced with a cool directness. He could see that Mike pulled himself up a little straighter.

'That's the deal as I understand it.'

'And where would you like the launch to deliver the goods?'

This part of things was quite new to Mitch, since the final details had been worked out after he had left. He knew his ex-colleagues wanted the explosives sent to the UK, but as they had no idea of the delivery method or the direction from which they would come, they had to make some fairly flexible plans.

'We thought that we would have the goods sent over to a part of Suffolk. But I guess that we're too far south for that.'

Derek assured the two Irishmen that, if they wanted the consignment sent to Suffolk, they could have it sent there.

'We have another site, if you don't mind,' Mike said. 'It's not so remote, but provided the tides are right, we can put into an area off the south coast. I'll call a number and set it up.'

'Please feel free,' Derek said and pointed to the phone on a side table. 'Or would you prefer some privacy?'

'That's not necessary. But first, tell me, have you got

some sort of communications on board the launch?'

'But, of course.'

'The sort that can tap into a normal phone number? We'll want to call when we're close enough to land.'

'We?' Derek's tone showed a certain surprise. 'Are you intending traveling with the shipment?'

'Too bloody right. I'm not parting with our cash and sending the goods off into the wild blue bloody yonder, captained by a bunch of Dons, thanks very much.'

The sheik smiled behind his glasses.

'You have every right to be cautious, Colonel. I admire your resolve.'

'We have a small problem, however.' Derek's tone sounded a little nervous. 'Our launch is already rather full, and it needs two people to work it. I am, like you, reluctant to send it off into the wild blue yonder,' he said, his tone warmed by a smile he allowed to come through, 'But I'm afraid only one of you can travel with the boat.'

'Have you got a toilet on board?'

'Yes.'

'Then if you've no objection, Mitch, I'll travel in the boat. You can find your own way back, I'm sure.'

Mitch nodded his acceptance.

The sheik handed Mike his piece of paper.

'The bank is the Sovereign, in Liechtenstein, Colonel. This is the agreed amount and the number of the account.'

Ryan winced as pain hit him again, but he ran his eye over the paper.

'I didn't count the boxes. Did you, Mitch?'

'I can assure you the number is correct, including the additional ten per cent that I spoke of earlier. We are men of honor, Colonel.'

The sheik's tone underlaid the fact he seemed to be tiring of Ryan's attitude.

'Look all right to you, Mitch?'

Ryan handed the paper over and Mitch could see that there was no variation from the agreed deal: exactly five hundred thousand dollars.

'Let me call this information in then, Derek.'

Mike went to the phone, and after being told the dialing sequence for England, spoke rapidly into the handset.

'Site number three, sometime late the day after tomorrow. Keep this number open. The account number is 354267-754, Sovereign Bank in Liechtenstein. The amount is as agreed. Wait for my call early tomorrow before transferring, got it?'

He hung up.

'What time's the demo, then?'

Derek looked at his watch, a slim Cartier, and said, 'How about seven o'clock sharp? Then, provided everything is to your satisfaction, we can ask to make your call by eight o'clock, which is nine o'clock Vaduz time.

'I have arranged for them to fax us here as soon as the payment is through, which should not take more than an hour.'

Ryan, too, looked at his watch, an old Ingersol, and thought for a moment.

'How long will the transfer take, do you know?'

Derek thought for a moment and said that two hours should be sufficient, if the bank was organized.

Ryan leaned over to Mitch.

'Assuming bloody Taffy's okay, they should be ready.' Then to Derek, he said, 'With the time differences, you should have the fax by twelve.'

'And you can be off immediately.'

Diane, who had been watching silently, said, 'Anybody fancy a drink?' She rang a small bell on the coffee table and Ralph appeared as if by magic.

'Nothing for me, thanks,' Mike said and stood up. 'I'll leave you, I think. I hope you don't mind.'

Derek stood also and said, 'I hope you feel better in the morning. Rafael here will wake you at six. Goodnight.'

Mitch and the others stayed on for close to an hour. The conversation dragged in spite of heroic efforts on the part of Derek to lift it. The day's events, and Mike Ryan's change of plan, had obviously annoyed everyone who up until now had prided themselves on a smooth operation. Mitch felt joined to Ryan in his perfidy, and therefore seemed an outsider in the small group lolling on the opulent seating in the Spanish salon. After a small drink, he wrestled with himself over the extreme need for a cigarette. At ten thirty, he excused himself, and retired to his room to run through the arrangements of the following day, along with their inherent dangers.

Chapter Twenty-Two

Rio De Janeiro, 1787

Paddy felt a great feeling of despair descend over him as he was helped over the side of HMS *Falcon*. In spite of his respite ashore in the port of Rio de Janeiro, he was far from relaxed, and he faced his onward journey with even more trepidation than when it started back in Southampton, several months earlier.

The small packet-boat had been rowed expertly back from the jetty as a bleary-eyed Marlow leaned back with a contented look on his young face. Varcoe had nudged Paddy with a knowing wink at the boy's condition. The two older men had wandered back to their agreed meeting point at the jetty, their thoughts on their two unique forms of imprisonment.

Varcoe's imprisonment was the regulation and routine Paddy had known once he had been 'pressed' into the royal navy over a year ago. At least, Varcoe would eventually earn his honorable discharge, and barring accidents of war or the daily danger of shipboard life, he would find his way back to his beloved Cornwall. However, he kept talking softly about the little lanes and fields with such adoration that Paddy had to ask him to stop. Up until then, Paddy had been successful in keeping his memories in check, but Varcoe's description was starting to make him feel home-sick for his own land.

'Please,' he said, and Varcoe stopped immediately and

asked for Paddy's forgiveness. 'I surely know the feeling, old son. My mistake.'

Paddy's future was somewhat different. His future was out of his control. He faced seven years in a land of monsters that nobody had ever lived in before, always providing he and his friends could keep out of the clutches of Sande. And after seven years, what then? At least he only had half the sentence of Prof.

With the medicine provided by the chemist, Fermin, tucked inside his jerkin, Paddy remembered the trumped-up reason for his trip, and once on board, he made his way to his small pen where Captain Jenks's cat, Percival, lay sleeping where he had been left. The small quantity of alcohol Paddy had slipped him had done the job and had ensured Percival would remain in a stupor long enough. Stooping down, Paddy reached inside his clothes and pretended to take a pinch of medicine for the cat. Picking up the animal, he put his finger inside Percy's mouth; the cat immediately woke up and grumbled. Then, he stretched and blinked at the face in front of him. Paddy almost laughed out loud, but contained himself as the captain hurried out of his quarters and over to his pet.

'So, O'Doule, you found something, did you?'

The captain was watching his favorite closely.

'He hasn't moved from where you left him. Started snoring an hour ago. I was quite worried. Thought it might have been a death rattle.'

Paddy continued to stroke Percy, who was in all probability suffering from a hangover.

'He came round pretty quick, Sir.'

Percy was now exercising his claws into Paddy's forearm and the Irishman was trying to remove the offending sharp points without letting the animal escape.

'I'll keep him on the medicine for a few days, Sir, if you don't mind. It's best to let him rest as much as possible.'

'You've done a good job, O'Doule. I'm very fond of Percival. Please keep tabs on him and let me know if he needs anything else.'

Varcoe gave a sly wink as the captain walked away, and then in his normal out-of-the-corner-of-the-mouth style, said, 'Let's hope your miracle laying on of hands works with your mate down below.'

Then he led the prisoner to the hold and waved him down into the depths.

Being berthed in port, the captives were back into their slothful ways once more. Paddy squeezed his way towards Chipper's bunk past several sleeping men. Many of his fellow travelers made inquiries about his adventure, most of them with emphasis on the females ashore. Paddy smiled and shook his head. As he reached Chipper, Prof looked over and said, 'Thank God you've come back. He's been really sick. It's taken all my patience not to have to call for the ship's doctor.'

'That would not have helped. He's a butcher. Where's Ackers, by the way?

'Don't know, he's been gone for ages.'

'Well, I suppose we'd better see what this stuff is like. The chemist seemed to know what he was doing.'

All the time, Paddy was looking at Chipper and was alarmed to see that he was shivering and seemed to have turned a dreadful yellow.

'Has he been here all the time? Any runs to the bucket?'

The prof had climbed down from his bunk and stood alongside Paddy.

'No, he's just lain there asleep.'

'Okay, Chipper, my lad.' Paddy's voice was gentle. 'Let's get you sitting up a bit.'

With difficulty, they managed to get the sleeping form into a sitting position, and propped him against the bulkhead.

'Prof, can you get me a cup of water? We need to mix this stuff up for him.'

Prof hurried away and returned with his own well-worn mug. Paddy took out the mixture and poured some into his hand, then tipped it into the water and stirred it with his finger. Chipper's eyes were open by this time and he was watching the scene in front of him.

'How you doing, Chipper?'

Chipper didn't speak and just smiled weakly.

'This'll probably taste pretty terrible. But the man said to drink it in one go.'

Chipper put a hand on Paddy's as the mug was raised to his yellow lips. It obviously tasted as bad as Paddy had promised, as Chipper shrank back from the medicine once it was in his mouth, but Paddy kept raising the vessel and Chipper didn't have the strength to resist.

As he sank back on his bunk, Chipper managed to let one word out of his mouth, 'Jesus.'

'Knowing Chipper's complete lack of religious beliefs,' said Prof, 'I can only assume that his statement was in confirmation of the vileness of the potion's taste.'

'We have to keep him warm, and then he could find that he's got to get to the bucket pretty quickly. The chemist told me whatever was in him needed to come out. It was probably too long inside to come out through his mouth. So the other end it will be.'

They sat on Chipper's bunk talking quietly and watching the sleeping form. Paddy told Prof all about his visit and the near miss with Sande. He also described the feeling of freedom that came inside the café, how bad it was coming back over the side of this floating prison, and how he envied Varcoe his certain freedom.

'Ah, there you may be wrong. Varcoe and his friends are not really any freer than we are. He's at the beck and call of the officers, and his grub's no better than ours is.'

'I know, Prof, but at least he's got some sort of future to look forward to. What have we got?'

Prof was about to start on one of his talks about the general uncertainty of life, when Chipper groaned and his eyes started to open.

'You all right, Chip?'

Both men peered down at the waking man who was struggling to get out of bed.

'Well, here we go. The chemist said that the medicine worked pretty quickly.'

Paddy and Prof hooked their arms around the small man and rushed him to the bucket that served as the latrine for half their deck. They helped Chipper to remove his belt and trousers and then lowered him over the bucket. Chipper hung limply down and both his supports turned their faces away as whatever had been inside him came out.

It took all their strength to get him back into his bunk again, wrapping the blankets tightly around him.

'Not too tight, Paddy, he may need to go again.'

'I don't think there's anything left inside the little bugger.'

Chipper had lapsed back into a deep sleep, and the two men watched over him as the light faded from the small portholes along the sides of the hold.

The morning brought a renewed activity from aloft. The sound of shouted orders and bosuns' whistles betrayed the fact that HMS *Falcon* was again to start her voyage towards the unknown. Paddy had slept badly and had been aware of the still, sleeping form of Chipper, wrapped like a cocoon, across the cramped aisle from him. However, he must have slept deeply enough, since he saw, for the first time, above the sick man's bunk, the form of their other friend, Ackers, with Marmy curled up into a ball on his chest. Prof seemed dead to the world.

Paddy climbed down and sat next to Chipper. At once

he could see that the dreadful yellow color had almost disappeared, and although pale, his friend was looking much better. There was a movement from the bunk above, and the red face of Ackers swung over the side.

'You're back safe and sound then. Where were you last night then, Ackers?'

'Down in the bilges. There was a game of cards that I was into. I won a bottle of Crusty Kent's booze.'

Crusty Kent was a small, active man, sentenced to a double term for stealing what he considered the necessary equipment for distillation from one of London's premier hospitals. He was a helpless alcoholic, but he wore the illness with pride. He was caught red-handed with a selection of retorts, tubes and glass receptacles as he was climbing out of the window onto the street.

The authorities were outraged that a man could be callous enough to steal from the sick and also rob the exchequer of its just revenue – hence the sentence of fourteen years. The length he would be away from his beloved London should have made Crusty a chronic depressive. However, it seemed he had decided to accept his lot, and he had put his mind to finding a way to prop up his regular dependence on alcohol.

It seemed at some time in his forty-one years on earth that Crusty Kent had learned about the making of, as well as the consumption of, strong drink. He first had made friends with the cook on board, so he had access to many necessary ingredients such as yeast, water and vegetables. His brews were of a particularly lethal concoction, and usually left the tippler with the most dreadful hangover.

From the clear look in Ackers' eyes, Paddy could tell that he had not indulged in one of Crusty's mixtures.

'Kept off it then, did you, Ackers?'

'Yea, but I got it 'ere. Thought it might warm old Chipper up, if your trip didn't work out.'

'Nice thought, Ackers, but I reckon in his state it could well polish the poor little sod off. Thanks, anyway.'

'I had the best run at cribbage that I ever had.'

Ackers stroked the stirring Marmy as he spoke. The little ginger cat now believed himself to be the exclusive property of the big redhead and would rarely visit others. Paddy did not mind, as he was now constantly in touch with the other animals aboard.

'How's the patient coming along then?'

Ackers swung down, leaving a disgruntled cat above scratching at the rough blanket.

'Well, you can see he looks less like a Chinaman this morning. We had to hold him over the bucket last night. Not a pleasant experience, I can assure you. I managed to visit a chemist ashore, and he made up this medicine. I couldn't make out much of what he said but it seems they have a different attitude to Chipper's type of sickness.'

Chipper groaned slightly and turned over to face the wooden wall. At the same time, the anchor chain rattled into its housing and the ship lurched as the wind tugged at its sails and took them away from land.

Both men fell silent at the movement and looked towards the bow end of their cramped quarters, judging the roll of the ship. They knew any real lurching would begin once they were outside the harbor that had been sheltering them for the last two weeks.

Paddy forced his mind away from the long voyage ahead and once more concentrated on his new patient.

'Yes, the man said, as best he could, that his people believe in getting such poison out of the sick person as quickly as possible, but not through our primitive method of bleeding. So I guess, whatever it was that he mixed up worked. Old Chipper had to get up within half an hour, and he's been back here ever since.'

'It's bleedin' bad enuf, 'avin to go thru your bloody so-called cure, without 'avin to listen to it.'

The sick man turned round and fixed them with a staring eye and a slight grin.

'I don't know wot you did last night, but I had a feelin' that I'd shat misself. Very nasty business, and me guts hurt too.'

Paddy was delighted to see that his friend was at least sounding as if he was getting back to his old self; his color was definitely better, too.

'Let's see if we can get you some tea. I'll try and get Varcoe to help me. He's sort of got an interest in you. But now you must drink this.'

Chipper eyed the next medicine warily, but he drank it down with no fuss. Paddy made his way to the hatchway, and, using the time-honored method of attracting attention from down below, he threw his drinking mug up against the cover. After several goes, the top slid open a couple of inches.

'What do you bloody want?' the stern voice shouted down to them.

Paddy asked if Varcoe was on deck, and the man's head withdrew. Varcoe appeared in a moment, and after inquiring how things were below, took Paddy's request away and returned with a canister of tea.

'Oh, by the way,' he shouted after the handover, 'old Percival's right sprightly this morning. Caught a bloody great mouse. The old man was pleased as punch. Took the mouse away and nailed it to the mast for good luck. Can't say as I see the point of the good luck.'

Eventually he withdrew and, with a wave at Paddy, pulled the cover on top once more.

As soon as HMS *Falcon* had left sight of shore and had her bow set towards the coast of Africa some four and a half thousand miles away, life settled into the normal routine for both crew and captives.

Chipper's condition improved with every draft of the apothecary's medicine, and his friends ensured that his diet would help his progress. All their meals were pooled, and the better nourishing things were put onto Chipper's plate, swapped for those things that were just for filling up the bellies of hungry men.

Paddy's sick animal charges often died, but many miraculously recovered. Paddy's knowledge grew, and so did his confidence in treating his patients. No one blamed him for his lack of professional knowledge when a creature expired. In fact, whenever a plump sheep or pig was handed over to him, men would suggest that he helped them pass away quickly, so all that good flesh could end up on the cook's cutting board before it wasted away.

With the huge empty tracts of the Atlantic Ocean all around them, the difference between the jailed and the jailers became less marked. The hatch stayed permanently off, and a rope ladder swung in motion with the *Falcon*'s progress, never to be removed, even at night. The days blended into one another, with only the Sunday service to mark the passing of every week. Food deteriorated and water became an obsession on everyone's mind, with the fear that the trip across might have been miscalculated.

Paddy's regular position on deck caused no more comment than that of the coxswain or the bosun. Everyone on board had time on their hands and thoughts to brood upon. Paddy's little animal hospital regularly brought visitors for something to look at and something to discuss. Such callers were a welcome relief for all from the emptiness of their surroundings and the emptiness in their souls, as the ship carried them relentlessly towards their bleak futures. One regular visitor to Paddy's charges was a young lieutenant named Jeremy Blackman. A short fair man of twenty-two, he was a career officer who took no trouble to hide his dissatisfaction with his current posting. His daily visits usually took place at the change of the morning watch. Initially, he made the various animals the focus of his inquiries, but eventually he began to talk to Paddy about their respective lives.

Lieutenant Jeremy Blackman claimed to be Irish, although he certainly did not look it or sound it.

'Nonetheless, it's true,' he protested, seeing Paddy's disbelief. 'My family goes back to the Normans. They were granted their estates by King Henry the Second in 1169. So I'm as Irish as you.'

Paddy kept his eyes downcast as he frankly could not accept the heritage that was being told him.

'Of course, none of us were actually born over there,' the young officer continued, 'but we're as Irish as you, I tell you.'

Paddy raised his eyes and looked at the earnest young man.

'No, Sir, I think not. You may consider yourself Irish but not as I am, and that's a fact.'

The lieutenant turned at this denial and took his place up on the forecastle with his gaze on the unfolding ocean.

The next morning they were all battened down through a rough squall that had man and beast hanging on for grim death. However, the following morning, as the watch changed, Lieutenant Blackman sauntered over to Paddy, who was trying to repair the damages to his charges that had been caused by the weather.

'I've given your remarks some thought, Paddy. And I've an apology for you.'

'Quite all right, I'm sure, Sir,' Paddy replied politely.

He felt odd being on the end of an apology from someone who he normally would have considered well above him. However, there was a youthfulness about the man that gave Paddy a feeling of superiority, even though they were obviously from very different ends of the social spectrum.

He felt this way even though he was considered a common criminal, and Lieutenant Blackman was one of the chosen of His Majesty's royal navy.

Blackman looked awkward and leaned against the dipping rail, trying to find the right words.

'I know I wasn't born in Ireland, but my father always taught me to believe I was Irish. I took many a licking at school for it, as well, I don't mind telling you. The other boys didn't think it was something to be proud of.

'I know the history of the English in Ireland, and I know how most of you view us, but we're not all evil people, you know. My father and his father before him put back into the land far more than they ever took out. He's buried over there. My mother didn't want it, but it was clearly written in his will. So there was no argument. The trip across with the coffin and my mother and brother was the first time I can remember ever going there, although they had taken me over when I was a baby. It was a small boat with a rag of a sail and only a couple of crew. I wonder how we survived.

'My mother cried all throughout the ceremony, and I broke down as he was lowered into that cold damp ground. I looked around and there was nothing familiar. Just dark cold weather and a barren land with dark soil turned over to receive his remains. I knew it was destroying my mother, because she knew she would never come back to visit him. She was from a French family, and didn't even like living in England very much. Ireland might have been on the moon for all she cared about the place. And here was her beloved husband, the love of her life, being interred in this cold, damp land across the sea.'

The ship shuddered as it made a tack. With a crack the sails repositioned themselves, and a spume of foam covered both men as they grabbed on to a handhold.

'I comforted her as best I could, but she just wanted to be alone. She sat up in her room at the tiny inn for nearly a week, only leaving it to visit the grave and stand there desolated. She would not even allow me to accompany her. It was very hard for me.

'I took long walks around the place, in the rain. It never stopped raining until the day we sailed away. The walks lasted hours, and I usually arrived back sodden and exhausted. But they made me think about the place, and eventually I began to see a beauty in the richness of the land.

'During my wanderings, I was also made very aware of the dreadful poverty of the place. Such terrible simplicity. Women and their children, huddled from the rain, wrapped in threadbare shawls, were around every bend. Men, out in the fields, were digging with primitive spades and mud-caked implements.

'I was only eighteen at the time of my father's death, and I had very little knowledge of the world. I was the younger of two sons, so my elder brother inherited our estates in Ireland. At the time of the funeral, he became locked in all kinds of difficulties with the lawyers. Apparently, my father left several debts. But as the truth dawned on me that many of the problems of Ireland were directly attributable to the absentee landlords who owned so much of the land, I decided to try and do something about it.'

Jeremy Blackman's eyes had taken on a faraway look as he leaned on the rail, braced against the roll of the ship. Paddy could see the young man was troubled, so he sat on the deck among his few charges and let the story unfold.

'I met up with my brother a day before we were due to return, to plead with him to consider offering the people round about some of their land back. I knew enough to know they were really just peasants, working for a pittance of the true value of the land. At the ripe old age of twenty, he knew far more than me. He assured me it was the very fact the English owned the land that had stopped it from falling into the hands of the unscrupulous French or even worse, the Spanish.'

The ship lurched again, as the captain called for another course correction. The young lieutenant continued with his tale, his eyes focused on the distant horizon.

'We had a very bad row, and it caused my mother even more distress to see her sons falling out. We toned it down a bit for her, but the essence was he truly believed the English had saved the Irish from themselves, and I believed that the Irish had been enslaved.

'Mixed up in it all, of course, was the fact that my father had for years instilled in me pride of my Irish heritage. It was very difficult to be proud of the poverty that I had witnessed, and there was no evidence of the poetry and the grace my father had always talked about.

'Perhaps, though, my words had some effect. Within a year, my brother began to visit our estates. At first it was for a week or two, then for a month. Finally, he decided to live over there, and he now has an Irish wife. He never turned Catholic, though, so I imagine there could be some difficulties with that.

'Forgive me for going on so. It's a bit of a hobbyhorse of mine. I imagine I would have remained happy and content in my ignorance if my father had not insisted on his burial site. But those walks in the rain brought a great sadness on me and showed me how a system can ruin the lives of so many people. Although I did not feel very pleased at this particular posting aboard the *Falcon*, I think maybe a new land could make for a new system and greater justice. But I've bothered you enough. I hear good reports about your character and your work with the animals. Let's hope this new land will be kinder to you than the old one. Good day to you.'

As he turned brusquely away and walked towards the upper deck, Paddy felt his words hit him in the chest, 'A new land and a new hope.' But then how could that occur when the rules of the new land would be exactly the same as the one they were leaving. The strong would be in control of the weak, and the sick would be administered to by the callous.

The anger in him that he had first experienced during his confrontation with Chief Sande came back to him. It was an uncomfortable anger, deep in the pit of his stomach. He knew it was a dangerous emotion, and he feared it. Forcing it down deeper and choking it off, he hugged close a small lamb with a bad case of colic. Looking up at the approaching sky, he could see it was turning grayer with rolling waves of blackness. Another storm was on its way.

They were to experience many such storms during that long empty trek across the Atlantic. It seemed everyone became sick. Prof, Ackers, Paddy, had their turn, and even poor Chipper caught another bout of illness. Mostly it was some form of stomach trouble or a cold or the flu. All the medicine that Paddy had acquired in Rio had been used up in curing Chipper, but fortunately, none of the turns were as bad as Chipper had experienced that first time.

Their entry into Cape Town was much as the others had been. All the convicts were sent below under guard, and even Paddy was not allowed up on deck for more than three days. Apparently, with English being the common language there, the authorities once again feared an organized escape.

It was very hot, but now, after nearly six months afloat, the men were used to the discomfort and lapsed into their stupors as the *Falcon* bobbed idly at her moorings. Each man was left to his dreams, or his nightmares. In Paddy's case, the words of Lieutenant Jeremy Blackman often came back to him with the promise of a new beginning in a new land. Only time would tell.

Chapter Twenty-Three

Canary Islands, 1993

Mitch had left his two hosts and the other guest, the mysterious sheik, for a lonely and restless night. He had tossed and turned, and even left his opulent bed to sit in the tall armchair, but he only actually slept for a few brief moments before he heard the house begin to stir with first light. He could hear steps and voices, and a look at his watch showed that it was only five fifteen. 'Damn and blast,' he muttered, and steadfastly turned his face away from the window. He dozed for another hour, feeling that he needed to get as much rest as possible. Then he went through to the shower, dressed and went down to meet the day.

A small breakfast of rolls, coffee and cold meats was placed on the long sideboard. The others had obviously eaten and were engaged in their respective duties. Mitch sat down and watched the boats below him. There seemed to be a lot going on around the fast cruiser they had inspected the day before. A movement at the door caused him to turn round, his face half-full of croissant. Mike Ryan was standing there, white and shaking.

'I hope you're feeling better than me this morning,' he groaned.

'You don't look right. Have you been ill all night?'

'That's the funny thing. I slept pretty well. Then this morning I got up and came down here. The three of them were sitting around the table, talking in Dutch, it seemed. Well, I sat down, too. I was feeling a lot better. Bit sore in the guts but getting up to speed. The girl – Diane, isn't it? – she got me a glass of orange juice and some aspirins. I drank it and said I'd go upstairs and shave. Diane said there was no rush, as we weren't due to get breakfast until seven thirty – it was only five thirty or so at the time – so I went back up and lay down. Must have dropped off again, and when I came round, boy, it was back with a bloody vengeance. I must have spent the last half-hour on the bloody bog.'

Mitch genuinely felt sorry for him, as he sat crunched over at the table.

'Can I get you anything, Mike?'

'Glass of water. Hope that's not bloody poisoned.'

Mitch poured one from the jug and felt a twinge of guilt run through him. Mike had to leave the room twice before Mitch had finished. As a clock in the interior of the house struck the half-hour, Derek and Diane came in, looking hot.

'We've been down at the boat getting everything ready for your test,' Diane announced. 'Did you both sleep well?'

'So so.' Mitch replied. 'But Mike here is still bad, I'm afraid.'

'This has been going on too long. I'm going to send down to the pharmacy for some medicine.'

Derek looked concerned, and rang a bell pull on the wall. Rafael appeared almost immediately and Derek spoke rapidly to him in Spanish. Mitch heard the term '*medicina*' several times, and then the servant disappeared. Turning back to Ryan, Derek said, 'Would you like to hang on here for a couple of days, Colonel Ryan? Just to get yourself right?'

'No, thanks. I'd prefer to get on with it. I've been sick since I left. So it's better I get home, where I'm used to things. Must be the water or something.'

Involuntarily, he looked at the glass that Mitch had poured him and smiled.

'Well, if you're sure, here's what we've arranged.'

Derek sat down next to Ryan and pointed down to the jetty.

'As soon as you're ready, we'll go down and let Pedro and his colleague do their thing. That is, they'll take the sample that you chose, sail out to the horizon and drop the charge. It's only half the amount. I hope you don't mind, but we would not like to alarm our Spanish authorities. To explain the noise, we have taken the liberty of warning them that Mr Kirkdorp has asked to test a new security device,' he finished with a raised eyebrow cocked in the crouched Irishman's direction.

'Well, if you're happy, I guess I'll have to be.'

Mitch thought the normally terse Ryan was certainly not made any more benign with a bad case of Canary tummy or whatever it was he had now.

'I'm sure your arrangements will be fine, Derek. Can we get on with it?'

Leaving the few breakfast things, they all left the dining room, and were joined by a puffing sheik as they began to go outside.

'I wish you'd put an elevator onto those steps, Derek,' he commented, as they began to go down.

Much was made of the selection of the Mephisto Ryan had chosen yesterday. Also he was invited to remove half of the charge. However, he lolled against the cabin doorway and waved Mitch to do the job for him. Then everyone disembarked and watched the launch turn out to sea with a roar of its powerful engines. As the boat swung around parallel with the horizon, it slowed and then began its return to its base. Halfway back, a huge spout of water appeared, accompanied, a few seconds later, by a dull boom. The sound was more of a feeling they could feel in the soles of their feet. The spout turned into a perfect circle of water and they could see the wake of the explosion spreading out towards the racing launch.

Mitch looked across towards Mike. He had stood up straighter than he had seen him since they arrived, and he had a fixed glassy look in his eyes. What shook Mitch more, however, was the smile of complete ecstasy that was across his cruel mouth.

'Jesus, that's beautiful,' he whispered.

Mitch, of course, had always known his erstwhile colleague was a driven man with more than his fair share of mania. But it was standing there he realized fully for the first time the amount of bloodlust that was present in him.

'I hope you find the material of satisfaction, Colonel?'

The sheik had finally stopped panting and seemed as engrossed as his customer by the sheer force of the blast.

The four spectators watched as the launch returned and the captain and his assistant expertly brought it alongside. The water seriously dampened the effect of the blast but still the waves came in after some few minutes. It was as if a large vessel had passed across and caused a wake. The group was largely silent, but Mitch could not help realizing once again, as he had done in Holland, that such force would be devastating against an unguarded civilian population.

Derek gathered everyone together and guided them once more up to the house. Following at the rear, Mitch tried to rationalize all he had been through. Who were these people? He was starting to feel confusion coming down on him. Rationally, he knew that Margitte had arranged everything, but it was all going in the direction of mass murder. Ryan, in spite of his stomach ailments, was in it up to his big Irish boots. Where was the flaw? Something didn't seem to add up. Nonetheless, Mitch could do nothing but play his role. He seemed a complete passenger, being secondary to Ryan in the matter of the financing and also the final arrangements. He joined the others in the salon and sat quietly at the end of the room in an ornate chair with an accompanying footstool. Diane had disappeared at the top of the steps and now returned with a cup of liquid.

'Mike, I want you to take this,' she said and handed over the medicine. 'It'll taste pretty brutal, I'm afraid. But you must take it down in one go.'

Ryan looked suspiciously at the potion.

'Go on,' she urged. 'It's not poison. It's a very old Spanish cure, some salts that will purge your system. You've some time before you have to make the calls, and you should be okay within two hours. Hurry up, drink it while it's still warm.'

Ryan started to swallow and stopped immediately. 'Jesus,' he said.

'I know it's bad, but honestly it will cure you. Now drink it all down.'

Diane's tone showed she would take no nonsense, and Ryan obliged, almost choking on the mixture.

'If I didn't trust you, I would swear that that was poison. But I realized you would not do me in until you'd got your hands on the bloody money, would you?' Ryan said, smiling grimly. 'But that was the worst thing I've ever tasted in my life.'

'I'm sorry about the taste, but I promise you that whatever was in you will not stay there long. Could I suggest you walk about for a little bit? It's supposed to help.'

The sheik started to repeat the instructions regarding the banking arrangements, but watched Ryan closely as he ambled about the spacious room looking at the pictures.

This went on for about twenty minutes as they listened to the sound of the crew below, tuning the launch's engines and preparing for the imminent trip. Derek was telling them all about some of the Impressionists hanging on the wall when Ryan turned quickly for the door and disappeared.

'Medicine's working,' smiled Diane. 'It's a different philosophy out here. Northern Europeans believe in holding the poison in and trying to neutralize it. Down in the south, they believe in getting rid of it. Poor Colonel Ryan is in for a little discomfort and then he will be fine. Weak, of course, but fine.'

It took Ryan half an hour to recover, but when he appeared once more in the salon, he was definitely better, although, as Diane predicted, he was decidedly weak.

'I don't know what that stuff was, but by God, it worked. I feel as if I've been run through with a steel rod.'

'Just sit still for awhile, and you'll get better and better. Before you go, we'll give you a big pot of yogurt. Sounds funny I know, but it will set your stomach right.'

Diane seemed to enjoy her role of party nurse, and she sat next to her patient with a look of concern on her face. Derek paced the room, and eventually left to collect a remote telephone.

'We need to start the phone connections as soon as you're able, Colonel Ryan. Liechtenstein has already been open for maybe an hour, and I'm sure we all want to complete the deal as soon as possible. No need for you to spend more than one night on the boat.'

He thrust the handset into Ryan's hand, and repeated the international dial numbers he had done the day before. Ryan leaned forward and made the call. His voice was so quiet they could not hear the rapid instructions, murmured across the miles of sea to the waiting contact.

He looked across at Mitch and said, 'Any messages for Taffy?'

Mitch shook his head, and Mike broke the connection.

'He sounded sober, for a change.'

The sheik sat up straighter.

'I'll make a call as well, if I may.'

Derek collected the handset from Ryan and passed it across.

'Well, Colonel Ryan, do you still wish to travel with the merchandise?'

'I've told you, the movement considers this a most important deal, and it's my duty to stick with it.'

'Very well, we should hear from Vaduz in about thirty minutes. They promised to fax me as soon as the transfer was complete. In the meantime, Colonel Ryan, might I suggest that you pack. And as for you, Colonel O'Doule, where do your plans take you?'

Mitch assumed he would somehow go back to Amsterdam, but decided the best plan would be to suggest an immediate return via another city in Europe.

'I'll take a flight to Madrid, or Paris, whatever is most convenient out of Lanzarote. Just get me to the airport.'

Ryan and Mitch went upstairs. Mitch felt even more unreal than ever before. The call had been made, the money was apparently on its electronic way. He was still in a trap, of course, if anything went wrong at the last. He walked up the wide staircase alongside the sick Ryan, thinking, Just play out the hand, Mitch. Just play it out.

'You're okay with all this, are you, Mitch?'

Mike gestured for him to enter his room, at the other end of the passageway from Mitch.

'Everything seems to be on track, Mike. Although I don't think they were too happy about the extra demonstration this morning.'

'Well, they can get stuffed, can't they? I don't know any of these tossers, with their fancy paintings. And as for that fat little Arab, he's as artful as a wagonload of monkeys, with his talk about the master, and his generosity. I'll believe it when we've let a few of those babies off at full strength. A couple in the Channel Tunnel for a start would be a good bet. Need a suicide fellow for that, though. Wonder if the master would like to donate one of his?'

As he was talking, he was shoving his belongings into his bag and looking out of the window at the launch below.

'You didn't tell me about the delivery situation in the UK.'

Mitch had wondered about this, as he had been absent for the plans for this link.

'Just some contacts down in the south. I expected the point to be on the east coast, but then your bloody contacts came up with this godforsaken island. Must have added more than a day onto the plan. We'd already organized a boat off the coast of Flushing. I didn't want to leave everything to your tart.'

Mike's tone was deliberately offensive and Mitch felt his color rise.

'Look, Mike, you wanted this whole thing set up and it's been done, so just handle your part of it, okay?'

'I just want to get out of this poxy place.'

'I'll see you downstairs, then.'

Mitch left his disgruntled colleague and went to pack his own things. He carefully repacked his metal box and surrounded it well with his few belongings. He took a last check in the mirror and saw that whatever else he might be feeling, he looked normal, and went downstairs for the last time. Derek was holding the flimsy type of paper that told of a fax; furthermore it had the pale pink line on its edge to warn the roll was running out.

'Everything has gone through correctly, Mitch. So now we send the shipment off across the sea.'

Mike dragged his bag downstairs, and Diane presented him with a large bowl of yogurt and a spoon.

'Normally, one would drink a toast with champagne, but this will do much more good.'

'I don't like this stuff much, you know.'

Ryan accepted the bowl and sat down.

'You'll thank me later.'

Diane watched him eat his way through the yogurt. Once he was finished, the party made its way down to the launch, which was rumbling, quietly, at its mooring. Derek helped Mike aboard and in Spanish asked that Pedro stow the Mephistos securely away.

'The captain has all the charts necessary to make a landfall where you need, Mike. There is a refueling trawler about halfway. You can call from there, or a little closer, if you prefer. Accommodation is not too luxurious, I'm afraid. The boat is built for speed. There are provisions aboard, and a small bar.'

Ryan settled himself in the bow with his bag in front of him, as the others watched the departure. Derek tried a smiling '*Bon voyage*,' but the Irishman stared stonily ahead. Just as the last rope was sent curling over the stern, he looked at Diane Stacey and said, 'Thanks for the yogurt, I think it helped a lot.' Then with a roar of the engines, the sleek bow began to move out into the Atlantic, and the captain pushed the throttle to fast forward.

Mitch watched the boat tear across the sea and over the horizon. Ryan never looked back, and Mitch watched the hunched figure disappear from view with a great sense of relief that he had gone. The last few days spent with him had been a tremendous strain. Mike's overall unpleasantness seemed to be far worse than when they were both back in Ireland seated around the war table. Taking that type of brooding suspicion out of its natural environment had intensified it. Mitch could only describe it as totally inappropriate. But then wasn't the whole sick business? The fanaticism, the deadly commitment and the terrible vengeance were all totally inappropriate. It was perhaps twenty minutes before Mitch turned and made his way up the steps in the blinding sunlight.

He had not realized how long he had stayed, pondering on the jetty. Also during his progress towards the house he had been deep in thought. When he arrived at the top, there seemed to be no sign of Derek, Diane or the sheik. The house appeared deserted, but, as he passed through the hall, he heard an engine start and a crunch of gravel. He hurried to the front door and, throwing it open, he saw the Seat turning out of the drive. He just caught sight of Diane and Derek in the back, with the sheik sitting alongside Rafael in his customary driving position. Rafael was not wearing his peaked hat and seemed to be talking animatedly as the dust covered their final exit from the premises.

'And so, my Colonel, we have tricked them all.'

Mitch wheeled around and saw Margitte standing at the foot of the stairs.

'Your face is a picture. I wish you could see it. So are you just going to stand there, or do I get a proper greeting? I've worked hard, you know.'

Mitch shut the door and Margitte was in his arms, the familiar perfume filling his nostrils, her body crushed against him, as he held her tightly.

'So, how long have you been here?'

He took her hand and led her into the salon, making a point to look out of the window to ensure that the launch had not returned.

'It's okay, Mitch, it won't come back. Pedro is completely trustworthy. He'll take your charming friend all the way to England, with his worthless cargo. Mission accomplished, I think.'

Margitte was dressed in her customary yellow, in a sundress that showed off her tan and her slim shoulders. She sat on the long sofa and smiled across at Mitch. He felt a huge relief at her presence and the fact the danger was over.

'So, tell me, Margitte, how long have you been here?'

'I arrived with Uncle Walter, about four hours after you.'

'Who the hell's Uncle Walter?'

'He's not really my uncle, but everybody calls him that. He was the sheik. Not a bad impersonation for a Dutchman, was it? They had one hell of a shock when Ryan barged in and caught them speaking Dutch this morning. My sister nearly had a fit.'

Mitch suddenly got it.

'Diane. Your sister? Right. I felt that she was familiar, but it never dawned on me.'

'Yes, my little sister, and her actor boyfriend. He's South African. I don't like him much, but for a fat fee, he played along.'

Mitch smiled with the full realization it was over. He sat back and drank Margitte in.

'And so, Mata Hari, who was genuine in the whole plot? Don't tell me they were all relations?'

'Everybody was false, except the two Arabs you met up in Holland. They were real representatives of the great one across in Libya. I am told they were particularly impressed with Colonel Ryan's hangover and by your attempt to buy their favors with Monopoly money. It will be a very long time before your friends in the IRA will ever be able to obtain help from that direction. I am sure the word has gone round to all their colleagues, from Damascus to Riyadh and even to the ayatollahs. All will think the Irish are even crazier than their reputation. Monopoly money, indeed.'

Mitch laughed out loud.

'You switched the cases, I know. I could tell, but you don't mean you actually gave them Monopoly money. That's priceless.'

'Of course, the top layer of notes was genuine, but underneath that it was the funny stuff. I would have loved to have seen their faces when they got back to their hotel.'

Mitch leaned back and almost felt a sadness come over him, but his inquisitiveness took over, and he asked, 'Who were all the people, Margitte? Pieter, Hans, who were they?'

'They were characters from my checkered past. People I could call upon. They all owed me in some way. Both houses were rented by the week. We have until tomorrow to vacate this one. It's normally rented out to Spanish film stars, I think.

'The biggest problem was getting hold of the explosives. We only had two that would go bang. The other supposed Mephistos were mock-ups start to finish full of putty. Your friend nearly wrecked the whole thing with his silly little request to try one out here. That took a lot of organizing, I can tell you.'

'What do you mean?'

'We didn't have any explosive here. We had to get some sent down in the night from Holland. Major difficulties. But it all worked out. I'm afraid that little effort cost another ten thousand pounds, though. You really must choose your friends more carefully.'

'Mike was not in the best of shape, remember. And I guess that was all your doing.'

Margitte smiled, went over to a carved cabinet and opened the doors. It contained a large quantity of beverages.

'Doesn't seem to be any Irish here. Will Scotch do?'

Mitch stood up and joined her. There didn't seem to be any ice either, so they poured two stiff measures neat and downed them in one. They topped up the glasses and went back to the sofa.

Mitch took another sip and asked, 'Tell me about Mike's various sicknesses, then.'

'It was pretty simple, provided you know a friendly chemist. The idea, of course, was to keep him below par, and keep his mind off what was happening. The first packet contained a powder just to ensure a really world-class hangover. Obviously it worked very well. I assume that he had been drinking anyway? It needed some alcohol in the system to work properly.'

'Oh yes, he'd been drinking all right. It's a way of life for the Irish, especially when they're abroad.'

'Well, the other stuff was a potion that gave him a form of gastroenteritis. When he stumbled on the three talking earlier, Diane gave him some more of the same, to keep him incapacitated.'

'But what was the medicine she gave him? Or was it medicine?'

'Oh, yes. We had achieved what we wanted, and there was no need to make poor Pedro suffer all the way across with a fully occupied toilet. The yogurt was Diane's idea. It really works.'

Mitch put his arm around the brown shoulders.

'I guess we have to leave for Vaduz soon. Just to make sure the money's really there.'

Margitte giggled in a throaty way.

'It's really there, I assure you. And we do have the place for, oh, another day. And we're the only ones here.'

Under those circumstances, Mitch suddenly thought of a use for a fat overstuffed sofa with a view out over a glistening sea.

Chapter Twenty-Four

Cape Town, 1787

Paddy had no idea if he would like South Africa or not. As things turned out, he had no chance of finding out during the long month that HMS *Falcon* was tied up in the lea of Cape Town.

The voyage from Rio had been arduous. The fleet had its largest death toll so far, and even on the *Falcon*, which was run as well if not better than most, there had been the sad sight of four rough-hewn coffins slipping over the side. On those occasions, the ship hove to and the crew stood silently along the deck with heads bared and bowed.

Shortly after leaving the South American mainland, the small wallowing ships ran into the doldrums. Day after scorching day, the sails hung limply from the yardarms and the still water passed sluggishly around them. Below decks, the heat was unbearable and the smell from the rotting bilges caused even the strongest to plead for air and relief.

Chipper had made a good recovery. Much of this was due to Paddy's successful bargaining with the authorities, to allow him to spend time helping him on deck with his animal charges. Few problems occurred on this leg of the journey, and Paddy's skills had not been called upon very often. However, he was known to be conscientious, and his simple requests were listened to.

The original goat that had suffered from a broken leg was testimony to his healing powers, and had become, along with Percival and Marmy, an important mascot on board. One of the junior officers had made a passing remark to the cook about a good goat stew in the hearing of another man, and was told off in no uncertain manner by Captain Jenks himself.

Tales came to the four friends by way of the fleet's rumor machine about the exploits of Chief Sande. He was constantly in the news because of his harsh methods. Comparatively unknown before the voyage, he was now developing quite a reputation with his extreme cruelty dispensed nearly every day. He had soon become too much for most of his sailing colleagues, and he had been transferred to three different ships since leaving Southampton.

He was now on the *Cynthia*, one of the fleet's smaller vessels that was transporting women prisoners to Australia. Perhaps due to his fondness for make-up and his attraction to men, he had been behaving himself among this group. Sande appeared to have an appetite for women, and these were mostly women from the streets who had developed some canny ways to deal with all types. They flattered him, which he loved, and seemed to find his presence acceptable.

In his turn, Sande strutted about the deck and played his role as a master seaman, which in truth he was. The captain of the *Cynthia* even sought the chief's views on aspects of his ship and the discipline of the working crew. Most of the crew were leading a life of total licentiousness with any of the women who wanted a small favor.

Such behavior was also taking place on the two other women's ships, much to the envy and disturbance of the other males afloat. The shouts and murmurs at night floated across the hot dark waters to men's ears, who in every other aspect, had been emasculated and made impotent with enforced celibacy. The proximity and the openness of so much sex was often too much for both captors and captives. On board the women's ships, the marines and most of the crew, with the exception of the senior officers, were easy targets for the predatory nature of such females.

But in spite of the promiscuous nature of this atmosphere, some loving relationships were formed. Few, however, could withstand the grim existence shared on board the cramped and dirty hulks, where a slip of cloth was a favor to be fought and bargained over.

In the sweating torpid air of the doldrums, the prisoners' clothes rotted and began to fall apart. They had little else to clothe themselves, and when the fleet eventually crawled into harbor, Captain Phillip, as head of the expedition, decided to do something about it.

After dining splendidly with his brother officers, he arranged for numerous sacks to be shipped aboard every vessel, for the express purpose of providing additional clothing. The prisoners were at first unimpressed but eventually accepted that the alternative was far worse, particularly if the weather ever turned cold again.

Ackers, although still stocky, had become leaner and more alert. He had an almost telepathic relationship with Marmy and could find the cat any time he needed him. He just seemed to know where Marmy would be hiding in the many nooks and crannies the *Falcon* provided. Every night the cat would disappear about sundown, but he would be back alongside Ackers' head as the sun came up again. Chipper had lost a little of his original feistiness since his illness, but his eyes were bright and he seemed to miss nothing of what was going on aboard. He used his spare time when he was down below, to carve his figures out of anything he could scrounge. These small statuettes were mostly of a religious nature and were highly sought after by the crew, who were the only ones who could afford them. Chipper felt it was funny he had this side to him, as he confessed to not having a religious bone in his body.

Prof seemed to drift further and further apart from the other three. He grew even leaner, which appeared difficult, as he had started out thin at the beginning of the voyage. A fierce light glowed in his eyes, however, and he would sit listening to the talk on board, twirling the long gray hair of his beard between his fingers. He had taught Paddy the rudiments of writing and, although they both knew that Paddy would never make a true copperplate scribe, he could form letters well enough for anyone to understand them.

The biggest problem Paddy had when it came to writing was he could not hear the words in his mind, and this made him keep sentences very short. But as Prof said, 'You have to look at it positively, Paddy. Before you joined our merry band, you were an illiterate, now you're a scholar.'

The food improved dramatically once they were in port. Security tightened up once again, however, especially after one man shinnied down the anchor chain and swam ashore. This caused most of the guards to become very jumpy and they reverted to allowing only two men on deck at a time.

As the day for departure came nearer, Paddy managed to persuade his friend, Varcoe, to enclose one of Chipper's short letters with a note he was sending back to his sister in Cornwall. He labeled it Cape Town, but he didn't know whether his family would even realize where this was. The sending of this small note again caused Paddy's feelings to well up inside him with the acceptance that he was unlikely ever to return to a life of normality. Something had been growing in him like a cancer for several weeks, and he was no longer the calm quiet farmer who had taken his crop of potatoes to market and fallen by the wayside. Seeing the few scratched words scrawled across the flimsy paper only heightened the change in him and made him unhappy, resentful, and determined that such wrongs should be righted.

More animals were loaded on board. The *Falcon* began to sink lower in the water as the supplies to sustain the fleet, as well as the new colony, were packed in tightly. Some of the seamen watched this with concern as the First Fleet prepared to set out for its final leg. The plan was known by all now, and even though few had experienced the roaring forties, tales were told of the roughness of the sea route the fleet was to embark upon. Overfull ships would not sail well in such conditions. And they had a two-month, six-and-a-half-thousand-mile journey to go, right across the Indian ocean.

Captain Phillip had chosen this path for his fleet against much advice from his so-called betters. Many of these learned officers had counseled a run down the west coast of Africa, taking a chance on the availability of supplies from whatever was catchable, huntable and bargainable, from whatever chiefs might be there. Captain Phillip would have none of it and insisted on the more conservative and longer route. This would add as much as six weeks to the journey, but would guarantee access to traders with some reputation for a degree of honesty, and with consuls and ambassadors who could help out when things turned bad. In Phillip's mind, Africa, apart from its most southern tip, had fully earned its nickname as the Dark Continent. Therefore he had elected to take advantage of the prevailing winds and currents and cross the Atlantic twice before arriving at this port that would afford the fleet their last sight of English colonization.

This final leg of the journey now took advantage of the continuous winds rushing around the southern ocean, uninterrupted by any landmass. To the north of Antarctica, the seas developed huge green waves in constant motion, and the movement of the small ships became unbearably uncomfortable, as they pitched and yawed from one crest to another.

The sails and spars creaked in the massive airflow, and the dark green water rushed past as they headed towards their goal, six thousand miles away. With such a different movement, the crew began to suffer from seasickness again, and most of the prisoners lay on their bunks braced against whatever they could find to keep them in place.

Paddy found the best method of dealing with his animals was to rope them together as closely as he could. This way the group, as a whole, swayed and slid around the constantly washed decks, rather than individual animals facing certain death in being swept overboard. Nonetheless, the menagerie squealed, mooed, barked and brayed with the discomfort of it all. Day after day, week after week, they sailed on. Officers became frantic at the possibility of losing men, or worse still, losing their escort vessels in the high seas. Signals became mixed with the inability of the semaphore men to see over the waves, and like a mother duck with her ducklings, Captain Phillip instructed his other captains to stay close in line.

With the wind fully close behind the sails, the only way that the ships' masters could regulate their speed was to lower and raise canvas. Before, where they had sailed with the wind abeam, the sails could be directed more and the rate of speed either increased or decreased. Raising and lowering canvas required men aloft to work the ropes. In such pitching seas, all the crew looked upon this job with fear, and some seven men in all fell into the roiling ocean beneath. One fell to his death on the *Falcon*'s deck thirty feet below, his neck snapping like a twig.

There was no attempt to rescue the men who fell into the water. They were left to drown in the endless wastes as the ships plowed onward. The maneuver required to bring the ship about, and then to tack its way back to where the man was last seen, would have taken longer than any of the crew could have stayed afloat. This was a comparatively short time, as most sailors of the time refused to learn to swim. They believed such a skill would only prolong the agony of drowning. Their cries were soon covered by the screeching wind and they passed from sight in a few seconds as their mates stared helplessly after them.

Christmas came and went on a relatively calm day. The journey's progress was not interrupted, but some of the crew sang a few carols on deck, and the captains of each ship authorized an extra helping of food for the midday meal. At least it allowed a little ease from the stultifying boredom of the endless mountains of sea.

After a few more days, however, the lookouts in the leading vessel sighted land, and the word was passed by signal throughout the fleet. Men stretched themselves to their full height, straining to see the first glimpse of this new land, with its frightening tales of monsters and strange beasts. As the ships fell under the lee of the new continent and its calming influence on the ocean, an air of anticipation affected both prisoners and seamen. The usual discipline returned, however, with resulting increases in security of the convicts.

This first sighting of land found the four friends in good health. They were thin and all had the same weathered hard look in their eyes, but they had survived the voyage with no more to deal with than Chipper's stomach trouble and some internal infection that Ackers had shaken off.

Prof remained withdrawn, but no more than he had been for the last three months, and his appetite had returned, as well as his tendency to tell stories at night.

Paddy had kept in touch with Lieutenant Blackman, and also Varcoe, who would pass on snippets of gossip about the fleet. Varcoe also remained the main conduit for news about Chief Sande. Since his transfer to the *Cynthia*, the rumors were he had adapted some of his harsh behavior to the less violent ways of the women, and it seemed he was certainly not averse to changing his sexual orientation as well.

'Just a bloody satyr,' Varcoe said, as he and Paddy crouched under the scrap of canvas over the animal pen. 'I've met blokes like him before. Even have to keep your eyes on the animals when he's around.'

Paddy found the idea amusing, but Varcoe continued with his views.

'I had a brother-in-law once, until he got drunk and fell off the fishing boat. Just off Mevagissey it was. Well, he was like this fellow, Sande, excepting in his case it was strictly women only. He would get a sight of a pretty woman and the red mist would come down. If the woman was available, he would try to monopolize her until he could get her alone. Then he'd start pawing her and making suggestive remarks. All the way, until he'd got her in the hay. Amazing how many liked it and came back for more. Fred, his name was. Funny though, he sort of regretted his appetite and his success with it. He never seemed to get a lot of fun out of it. Bit like being ravenous all the time, I suppose.'

The fleet made its way along the southern tip of the new land. Often they would lose sight of the low red banks that ran down to the sea, as they moved out more to where the wind picked up. Some scrub trees were clinging onto the land for support, and one day Paddy thought that he saw some people grouped on the shore but he couldn't be certain.

The rhythm of the ship's day changed dramatically, however, one day in the middle of January. The ships had been moving slowly north, with the officers constantly sweeping the coastline with their telescopes, when the signal was made to turn into a large flat bay and drop anchor.

The convicts, including Paddy, were sent below, with

the hatches barred, as the crew made ready to set foot on land for the first time since the tip of Africa some eight weeks previously. The anchor chains rattled and boats were lowered. The officers in full uniform stood smartly at attention as the crews rowed them in small jolly boats towards the land.

Through their grubby porthole, Chipper and Paddy stared at the progress of this first party of Englishmen to set foot on this soil since Captain Cook, eighteen years earlier. The formality of the blue uniforms with their gold braidings were in direct contrast to the roughness of the land.

A group of natives stood off to the side of the landing. They were completely naked and waved some crude spears over their heads. They remained where they were, however, as the party of officers stood in the hot afternoon breeze formally claiming ownership for His Majesty King George III.

During the rest of the daylight, most of the officers and the senior NCOs made their way over to the site that had been chosen. Their faces showed no pleasure on the return trips, and the rumors that came down the hatchway at feeding time did nothing to lift the spirits of those incarcerated below. It seemed a cheerless, empty land.

Over the course of the next five days, the convicts were allowed on deck under the watchful eyes of marines with their muskets loaded. They witnessed many attempts by the crews to establish a base camp ashore. However, the reports that filtered back showed the land was too marshlike, the bay too shallow at low tide, and the water too brackish.

The glowing reports brought back home by Captain Cook had either been about some other place, or the good captain had consumed more than his fair ration of port at the time. If this was the true Botany Bay, it would not serve the purpose of either jail or British colony center. An air of depression settled over the whole fleet.

Varcoe sent a message to Paddy and his friends that they should be prepared for another move soon. A scouting vessel had come back with news that better facilities existed further to the north. And so it came as no surprise to all that, on a bright, breezy mid-morning, the anchor was wound back onto its creaking capstan, and the flotilla set sail once more.

The journey took no more than a couple of days, and even before the prisoners were, for the last time, ordered below, they could see they were entering a natural harbor of giant proportions. High hills looked down on a flat seascape and trees grew in great profusion all around. Grass covered the low hills that witnessed the entrance of the small ships which had made their perilous way across the world's great oceans.

Although the shambling convicts grumbled as they were locked below, they all experienced a feeling they were now in a new place. This one seemed to have some permanence, unlike the Botany Bay area that had given everyone cause for concern about their survival. Along with this feeling of permanence, came one of uplift that perhaps this place might not continue the sadness of their previous lives. It was an infectious feeling that ran around the dark holds, and through the confines of the cramped areas that had been their home for nearly nine months.

Paddy sat quietly on his bunk, thinking of the uncertain future that lay ahead for him. He had become very fond of his companions and he realized they had effectively taken the place of his true family. Thoughts of Katherine and his children rarely entered his mind, and he rather guiltily accepted that the welfare of Chipper, Prof and Ackers now meant more to him than his previous family.

Since the return to port in Rio de Janeiro, Paddy had understood the way of the world more clearly than he had ever done before. His life in Ireland might have been considered blissful compared to the one he now endured. Such bliss, however, was rooted in ignorance, and he had come to the full realization that, although he could no longer relax in the accepted ways of the past, he welcomed being able to play a role in what he was convinced would be a revolution.

The injustices that were all around him only magnified what had always been there before in Ireland. The rich had everything and seemed to contribute nothing, whereas the poor did everything and owned nothing. As the *Falcon* had made its way across the southern ocean, Paddy had clung to his animal charges and put his mind to the problems that beset his world. Inevitably, at every turn, he saw only one general cause of his society's misery – just one agitator of peace and wielder of punishments. No matter where he turned his face, his conclusion was obvious. The evil in the world could only come from one source: the English.

At odds with this revelation was the fact, however, that all his friends, indeed the only people with whom he had any relationship at all, were themselves English. This caused him some confusion and much soul-searching.

As he returned to his bunk each night, the colleagues around him found him more than normally withdrawn. The severe movement of the ship did not allow much communication, however, and he could lie on his bed turning his thoughts over and over in his mind.

Slowly, the tortuous threads of a theory began to evolve into one. He realized it at almost the same time the fleet turned into the harbor. It all rested on the power of the aristocracy. And the center of that power was twofold: money and education.

The English controlled all the money in Ireland. They doled it out to their friends for work and favors, but it rarely found its way into the pockets of the Irish themselves, with the exception of those rare individuals, the educated Irish. Slowly, over the years, these individuals had learned how to be as English as the English. They talked the same, dressed the same, and were at ease in the company of the English. Paddy didn't actually know any of these people, but he had had them pointed out to him on the occasions when they were in his vicinity.

This process of realization had been a slow one for Paddy, but with every layer unfolding, he began to burn with a deep and furious resentment at the injustice of it all. So deep and personal was his resentment that he could not even bring himself to talk to Prof about it. Normally, he would talk openly about every kind of subject with the philosophic convict meditating down below, but on this particular issue, Paddy allowed his thoughts to ferment and brew in solitude. As the landing was made fast in this new land, Paddy watched the way men behaved and saw that authority, with no fear of limits imposed by those more compassionate, was a brutal and inhuman system. Furthermore, when practiced by the English, it seemed to be positively barbaric.

The land on which they eventually settled proved acceptable for the purpose of confining convicts, erecting a settlement for trade, and operating a port to support the expansion of the Empire. Trees were systematically felled, shaped and built into a stockade to keep in the visitors and keep out the natives. These primitive people had long since given up their fruitless wailing, and now hung around the encampment helplessly watching each stage of the encroachment on their territory.

The convicts were divided up into gangs and work parties, and given their duties by the marines and officers who had been their jailers on the voyage. The weather was hot at the outset, but within the first three months, the days became progressively shorter and cooler, with the approach of the antipodal winter.

Paddy managed to remain with his friends for this period, although he was detailed to use his talents to work in the animal hospital that was an offshoot of the main compound. Chipper and Ackers were involved in the construction of the government headquarters, while Prof assisted in the clerical function of the main stores.

This meant that, although they were separated mostly during the day, the four could live in the same tented area, and it was here they shared their meals and the gossip about their day's activities. Such gossip included regular updates about their nemesis, Chief Gunner Sande.

At first, he had been assigned to watching over the ships at harbor. Then he was transferred to a detail formed to explore the outer limits of the immediate area. Finally, within six months and almost exactly at the same time that Ackers first mentioned his escape plan, Sande was put in charge of tracking down and disciplining runaways.

Chapter Twenty-Five

Canary Islands, 1993

The strain of the last week had obviously taken its toll on Mitch. He woke up on the couch with a blanket tucked around his naked body. Twisting his head to scan the opulent room, he caught sight of an antique ormolu clock on the marble mantelpiece. It was nine o'clock. He lay back on the velvet and satin cushion and relived the previous evening.

Margitte and he had spent the whole afternoon enjoying their re-encounter. This had resulted in numerous raids on the cocktail cabinet, accompanied by many trips to the kitchen and its well-stocked refrigerators. His present condition confirmed his recollection that he had eaten, drunk and made love well, and in great profusion.

Swinging his bare legs over the couch, he blinked at the morning sunlight reflecting off the blue Atlantic. There was hardly a shimmer on the stillness of the deep. He stood up and paced over to the window. At the same time, Margitte came through the door with a large cup of steaming coffee in her hand. Mitch initially felt embarrassed, because he had dropped the blanket on the bed. He considered dropping into a crouch and making a grab for the cover, but he realized that would be even more undignified.

'A fine sight to greet a maiden in the morning, Colonel,' Margitte said, putting the coffee down, and putting her arms around him.

'I woke up alone, which is not what I expected.'

Mitch tried to sound disapproving but failed dismally in the attempt.

'I have to tell you that when you finally had done with me, you fell asleep leaving me nowhere to lie down. So you have spent the entire night alone. You should be more generous with your space.'

'Comes from living alone for too many years, I imagine.'

They sat down and looked at the sparkling water, while Mitch sipped his coffee.

'We should get out of here in the next hour. Do you need much time?'

'No. I just need a shower and I'll be ready to go.'

Margitte was wearing a pale blue tracksuit, with her customary yellow draped around her throat in the form of a silk scarf. White tennis shoes completed the outfit, which gave the impression of a well-to-do tourist enjoying the Spanish islands. She smiled at Mitch and looked modestly down at her slim hands.

'I took the liberty of booking us two first-class seats aboard the Iberia jet leaving for Zurich. I hope you don't mind, but I assumed you would want to disburse the funds as soon as possible.'

Mitch wrapped the blanket round himself and walked to the door.

'Why should I mind? You'll need to pay off all your actors and relations. First class will be a nice change, too. My last flights have been far from relaxing.'

Margitte was surprised at how quickly Mitch had changed. He had stopped shaving two days ago and his auburn and gray beard seemed more marked once he had changed into a fresh shirt. He looked like an IRA member trying to grow a disguise, and she told him so.

'Also that damned beard of yours nearly tore a hole in my chin. You'll have to go easy with me.'

Mitch grinned and rubbed his rough face.

They slammed the front door and put their bags into the trunk of the small Seat that she had been keeping locked up at the rear of the house. She gestured to two identical aluminum briefcases in the back.

'I bought another to match the one you generously gave to the Arabs. I think it makes you look dignified.'

Mitch was glad to remember it and its partner that they had bought together so many months ago in St Mawes.

She drove well and fast to the airport. Neither of them found it necessary to speak much and instead concentrated on the hot and scorched scenery. Both hailed from wet, grayer climates and felt a little strange in such desertlike surroundings.

Once again, Mitch felt the tension in his stomach as he handed his bag to the ground attendant. But no bells or sirens sounded as it disappeared through the plastic curtain.

As the 737 lifted off and turned northwards toward Europe, Margitte audibly breathed a sigh of relief and took Mitch's hand.

'It's been quite a strain setting things up and then watching it all unfold over the past few weeks. I think we've been pretty lucky, particularly in finding each other, don't you?'

Mitch didn't react immediately, and was grateful for the diversion of a small dark flight attendant requesting their order for drinks.

'Did I make too obvious a statement?'

Margitte looked out of the window.

'How do you mean?'

'I didn't mean to compromise you by making an assumption.'

'Margitte, no. You know how I feel. Don't you?'

There was a large fat man in the seat in front of Margitte's and he now let the back down to its fullest capacity. She moved her head closer to Mitch's.

'I think I do but maybe it's too early, yet. We need to spend some time together, don't you think?'

The drinks arrived and Mitch took a long pull at a cold Scotch and water.

'We have to put that time together into our plans, I know, but first, I have to get away and completely disappear. Remember where I've come from.'

'I guess that's bound to happen. But can't we do that together?'

'Margitte, listen to me.' He spoke softly, directly into her ear. 'What I've done, with your help, is tantamount to treason. Once the truth comes out, which will be in about another ten to fifteen hours by my estimation, it will effectively sign my death warrant. Frankly, I'm pretty scared about it.

'Now, if we travel together, we are going to be more vulnerable, as we'll be twice the target. It won't take them long to figure out you must be in on it. Mike Ryan was already suspicious, and the others were sniffing around too.

'I have a plan, and it will work out well for us, but we have to be ultra cautious. The "Army" prosecutes deserters to the fullest extent that it can. Frankly, there has never been a case where a deserter has stolen such a large amount, and at the same time made them a laughing stock. The effort to find me will be massive. So I have to completely disappear.'

Margitte stared at the back of the man's head that was nearly in her lap. Her hands gripped the glass balanced on the pull-down table.

'How long will we have to be apart?'

Her voice was low and betrayed no sign that she was dreading the answer.

'It could be three or four months. I know, I'm sorry, but I have to set some false trails and use up their resources.

Maybe even leave a false body so they can think I'm dead. I don't know exactly yet. But once it's over, I will send for you and we will escape to a new life. I can't even tell you where that is. But it's far away and it will be safe.'

The cabin crew decided everyone in the front end should have more of the same, and by the time they were into their second round of drinks, Margitte seemed to settle back in her chair.

'You okay about all this?'

Mitch knew he had been saying things she did not want to hear.

'Sorry, but I had hoped we could get away together. But I do see you have to be alone. One can travel quicker than two, and you know their ways. You're right. They will be pretty angry, and you'd better bury yourself from their hide-and-seek.'

Mitch was reminded once again that he had found a remarkable woman. His experience was limited, but he had learned enough to know that women did not respond well to desertion for even the best reasons. He so wanted to tell her of the crazy scheme he had in his mind, of following his ancient relative's footsteps to Australia, but some inner door was slammed shut against revealing this plan.

They held hands until lunch was served, and then again afterward, until Mitch fell into a fitful doze, frequented by dreams of bombs, boats, running and money. The jumble of images intermixed with the drone of the engines, propelling them through the thin high-altitude air.

Zurich airport was full of the mix of humanity that seemed to constantly populate such places. Again, the passage of Mitch's bag was uneventful. Hertz produced a clean, if underpowered, Ford, and after some confusion trying to find the right exit, they began the two-hour drive to the principality of Liechtenstein. They entered the town that served as capital, as well as country, as the last glow of daylight passed over the western mountains. After parking on the cobbled street and taking their bags from the Ford, they walked the short distance to the hotel that Margitte had booked.

'It's conveniently across from the bank over there.'

She pointed at a gray building, with imposing marble and glass, staring blankly towards them. The hotel processed their arrival with customary Swiss efficiency, and after rejecting assistance with their light luggage, they took the creaking elevator and found their room. Too tired to take advantage of the intimacy of their shared bath, they dressed rapidly, all the time peeking at the bank across the street.

'Makes you feel funny, doesn't it, Mitch, knowing the money is just over there, waiting for you to get it.'

Mitch had to agree it did feel rather comforting, although he would feel happier once it was moved from its present traceable account. They consumed a rich dinner quietly in the small wood-paneled dining room. The local red wine was acidic, so neither Mitch nor Margitte drank more than a mouthful of it. The conversation hummed at a discreet level as the other occupants each attended to their well-groomed companions.

There was an atmosphere of richness throughout the entire establishment. Margitte ventured the opinion that everyone was there for the same reason, namely, money. Also, to have financial dealings in this place, one was automatically in the higher bracket, with a need to keep transactions away from prying eyes. The end result was that people kept a low profile and slipped in and out of the principality without drawing attention to themselves.

'You seem to know quite a bit about the place,' Mitch commented.

'Some of my earlier duties involved coming here and moving money around for my lords and masters. Terrorism needs a safe place to keep its funds. And these people are the best.'

'I know that. The "Army" always keeps its funds moving around for safety. We tend to use American banks, and, strangely, British banks as well.'

'Well, tomorrow you'll get a chance to meet one of the original Swiss gnomes. He'll be the custodian of the account and will remain our obedient servant until we desert him, or unless we run out of money, of course.'

'I assume once we change the account number, we will be secure from any inquiries. The bank will be the first place they will look, I'm sure.'

'There's no chance of any problem there, Mitch. These banks are used to all types of inquiries. Governments even try to play strong-arm tactics to get at people's accounts. But it's no use.'

Mitch caught the smell of an expensive cigar wafting over, and his nose inadvertently twitched at the pungent fumes. He dragged his senses back with the consolation he seemed to be over the worst of the withdrawal symptoms of nicotine addiction. Margitte was watching him closely and sensed his reaction to the odor.

'Don't weaken, Mitch. You're doing awfully well on the non-smoking front.'

'I didn't think you'd noticed. It's been quite a strain, but I feel with everything else changing in my life, I might as well go for the big one.'

'Well, it's worth the effort; you look better already. Tired, but not so drawn. I don't know how to describe it, but you have more of a bloom on your cheeks. Not so sallow.'

They each took a coffee into the plush bar, which served as a lounge, and watched the other people in the hotel drinking, smoking and nibbling their way through the evening.

The following morning, many of the same guests were digging into breakfast rolls, boiled eggs and cold meats, as if they had been starved for weeks instead of merely being away from the dining room for a few hours. It was noticeable that most of the men were dressed in dark suits and kept looking at their watches, no doubt aware their appointments were of great importance.

Mitch and Margitte both dressed as formally as possible, considering their lack of outfits. They each carried a briefcase. Margitte's contained the balance of the first payment to be deposited. Mitch's held their remaining working funds, which they would divide later. The presence of so much money with them made them feel nervous as they crossed the busy street. Once inside, they asked for Margitte's contact, Herr *Doktor* Wolfgang Berman. They were directed to a waiting area of thin expensive French furniture, but no sooner had they sat down than a slim mature woman came to escort them into the manager's outer office.

Herr Berman was a tall well-built man in his early fifties. He had the kind of gloss about him that only came from years of expensive grooming and tailoring. He smiled affably at them both and shook Mitch's hand, while managing to pause only briefly to assess Mitch's informal jacket, open-necked shirt and slacks.

The high ceiling lights glinted off his rimless spectacles as he turned and directed them both across the deep-piled blue carpet into the inner sanctum of his office. Gesturing for them to sit down in the modern black-leather chairs, which blended strangely well with the mahogany paneled walls, he waited patiently to hear the nature of their request.

Previously, they had decided on their split. Already one portion had been used to repay Margitte's expenses. Mitch was to take an equal amount for his trip. The balance of the first payment, together with the second payment, would be put into a joint account for their new start, whenever that might be. Margitte, who, apart from a polite nod, had largely been left out of the formal greetings by the Herr *Doktor*, now explained their joint wishes, and handed over her briefcase with the remaining funds inside.

Wolfgang Berman's desk, which, like the rest of his furnishings, combined leather, chrome and mahogany, had no evidence of work on it. It held an expensive blotter and two empty trays, as if the intrusion of activity would somehow ruin the ambiance of his personal space. After asking for the account number and identification code attached to it, he produced a black and chrome pen and wrote the digits down on a small note pad that he kept tucked inside his jacket pocket. Obviously, he must have touched some device on his side of the desk, for, as soon as he had finished his task, the door opened and a young man in a very expensive suit came in and soundlessly took the briefcase and note away.

Mitch found this silent, almost oppressive, atmosphere, somewhat amusing, but no doubt the regular clients of the Sovereign Bank of Liechtenstein expected this sort of treatment from the guardians of their fortunes. Wolfgang Berman seemed to have developed a smile as a part of his permanent demeanor, but Mitch had no difficulty in seeing it would disappear rather rapidly if one were to spoil the atmosphere, by lacking funds, or even, God forbid, by asking for a loan.

'We want the new account to have a new number and no linkage to what has gone on before.'

Mitch tried to air his instructions in as civilized a way as he knew how, but it still came out sounding coarse to his ears.

The spectacles flashed as Herr *Doktor* turned away from Margitte and looked squarely at Mitch.

'You have no need for concern on that matter, Mr O'Doule. It is standard procedure for the Sovereign to take great care over its numbering system.'

Some pleasantries were exchanged during the wait. Mitch was very aware that inside this silent kingdom, Herr Berman's rule was absolute. They had no idea what was happening outside the soundproofed door, how long the wait would be, or even if there might be a problem.

Eventually, the banker rose from his tall chair and said, 'If you would both like to come with me, we will go along to the cashier's department and make sure your money is safely deposited.'

As they stood up to leave the room, Mitch wondered if Herr Berman was perhaps receiving his instructions via some form of telepathy, but as the banker's chair was vacated, he noticed that the gloss of its leather reflected several small lights that were sunk into the desk below sight level. He felt rather pleased to have cracked some of the veneer of mystique.

They followed the imposing Swiss along the corridor and entered another inner sanctum, that of the cashier. The office was smaller than Berman's but was fitted out in a similar theme. A small man with black horn-rimmed glasses sat across a neat table with a pile of US currency in front of him. The way these people behaved caused Mitch some amusement. It was all as if they were playing some sort of game – like Monopoly. The recollection of that started a smile to begin, with the picture of some very unhappy, confused Arab terrorists.

'If you will just sign your names here, we can make the transaction final. As you will see, with yesterday's transfer and this morning's deposit, and after our commission has been deducted, there remains seven hundred and forty-five thousand dollars in the account.'

He handed Margitte back her case and continued, 'As

this has been opened jointly, it will require both your authorizations to make a withdrawal in the future.'

Herr Berman's voice melted into the surroundings as he passed across his black and chrome pen.

'I am assuming that statements of account will be collected here, and all contacts between us will be at your instigation?'

Margitte smiled at the banker, and said their instructions seemed to be fully understood. Mitch opened his aluminum case and placed the account details inside with their remaining liquid funds. He closed the lid with a carefully suppressed click. God I am getting as affected as these finance types, he thought. Still he had enough to start his journey, Margitte had sufficient to settle her bills, and there was nearly three quarters of a million left in this marble mausoleum.

Herr Berman escorted them to the door and after a last dry hand-clasp and a flash of his rimless spectacles, they were out on the street once more. Dodging an accelerating Peugeot saloon car as it weaved its way across town, they arrived panting at the hotel. There was an annoyingly long wait for the elevator to take them to their room. The moment they entered, a depression seemed to settle on them like the gray clouds that would swoop in over Mitch's Northern Ireland. It was almost physical in its effect and assumed a third presence in the small neat room. Mitch began to put things into his suitcase. Margitte leaned against the closed door and watched him.

'I'm not going to cause a scene, you know. You don't have to look guilty.'

'It's no easier for me, I can assure you, Margitte.'

Mitch did not believe she was as relaxed as she pretended. The previous night had passed in a passion that left them both exhausted. The impending parting had acted like an aphrodisiac and had entered into their souls with such force that they both wanted to keep the intimacy selfishly to themselves.

Mitch's tin box was still allowing him to transport his small weapon through the checked luggage, and he slipped open the lid under cover of the suitcase lid and felt for the shape inside. He had no wish to alert Margitte to his readiness for danger. He was relieved to see she did not appear to notice. He closed the box again and continued with his packing.

'Am I going to be able to keep in touch with you at the number you gave me?'

Mitch tried to keep his voice steady, so as not to betray the anxiety he was feeling inside. This woman had continued to grow more and more important to him, and he knew he was afraid he would not recover if she ever left him. Still, nothing had really been decided between them. It continued to be all very loose.

'I'll have any calls transferred, if I move from that address. I'm going to see if I can't spend a little more time with my relatives. Being with some of them has been good for me over the last few weeks. I had grown away when I was with the movement. I don't know how vengeful your friend Ryan is likely to be, but I guess I should keep a pretty low profile.'

'I don't think there's any way they could find you. They never saw you or even had a description of you, so all their focus is going to be on finding me. And I'll leave a couple of false trails for them. I don't think they will have any idea where I'm heading.'

'That's not surprising, because I don't have any idea either. No, you don't have to say anything. I understand. It's just going to be a bit difficult until I hear from you again.'

Mitch completed his packing and closed the case. Then he put both aluminum briefcases on the bed and divided the money into equal bundles. He handed Margitte hers and then took out a small piece of paper and looked at his notes. He had booked himself on an Iberian flight to Madrid, with a layover of several hours before catching a Varig flight to Rio de Janeiro.

Margitte was booked to Amsterdam on KLM. They would both leave Zurich within forty-five minutes of each other. They would have ample time to drive back out of Liechtenstein and drop the car off.

As if in accompaniment to their depression, a light drizzle began as they vacated the hotel and swung the car to the west. Looking across at Margitte, in her long raincoat with the yellow scarf at her throat, Mitch found himself wondering how he would feel once her presence had worn off. Again, he realized how little experience he had had with women on a truly personal level. All those years spent in plotting and planning violence had insulated him from the normal life of those citizens among whom he lived daily. It had not been a conscious decision to avoid becoming emotionally involved. It was as if the level of commitment to the cause had removed from him whatever it was that lived in others around him.

Margitte turned the radio on to a Continental program, playing a selection of Abba hits from the Seventies. They sounded out of place with Mitch's thoughts. He concentrated on the road snaking its way through the mountain scenery, and turned his mind to the future. He definitely felt a sense of relief that he was finally free. Unfortunately, this was coupled with a feeling of uncertainty, for he knew his escape was still to be completed. For once, he was to be the stalked and not the stalker.

As the kilometers lengthened away from Vaduz, both sank deeper into their own respective thoughts. They stopped at a small café for coffee and a sandwich. The hustle and bustle of the place did something to take their minds off the imminent parting but as they inevitably drew closer to the airport, they were both feeling very sorry for themselves.

As Mitch was to leave first, Margitte waited in the background as he presented himself to the check-in desk. He had not disclosed his final destination, preferring to keep Brazil to himself for the meantime. He reasoned that there was no need for Margitte to have to hold his itinerary in her mind as he made his way around the world. He totally trusted her, but he knew that just one slip could create a lead. Anyone she had used to help her could pick up information that might lead his pursuers to them both. The IRA were not the best organized people in the world, but with a huge cache of their funds stolen, and with them being made to look fools into the bargain, the search would unquestionably be furious.

All paths would be explored. The trail would be sifted and the 'soldiers' would be called off everything in order to find and punish the traitor. It was possibly happening now. That boat from the Canaries is very fast, Mitch thought. A shudder ran through him as he turned from the check-in desk, clutching his boarding card to Barracas airport in Madrid.

Margitte, holding his arm, felt his shiver and turned to him.

'Are you okay, Mitch?'

'Just a fit of the heebie-jeebies, I'm afraid. I felt the chase was on and it will be serious. Are you sure you can keep hidden, Margitte? I'm worried. They're evil bastards, and they'll be as mad as a wasps' nest.'

'But they'll be on my ground. Don't worry. They don't know me, Mitch, do they?'

'I've turned the whole thing over and over in my mind. Should I take you with me or should I go alone? The thing is that I know their ways. They'll know I had inside help, and they will come after two of us. I'll look different and I can move faster. Probably, on my own, I'll be sharper. You're one hell of a woman, Margitte, and one hell of a find for me at my time of life. When I'm with you I'm not really conscious of things around me. I'm consumed with you. That's the truth, and I'm scared I'll be caught off my guard. I have to weather the first flush on my own.'

'Living like a terrorist again?'

'Yes, but this time on the other side of the fence. Alone, and with only a rough plan to work from. If you were with me, all I would want to do is check into the nearest hotel room and not come out for several months. That's what they'll be expecting – me going to ground with you. Being static increases the risk of capture tenfold. Moving all over the place makes pursuit and detection far more difficult, and remember, I know where they are strong and where they are weak.'

Margitte leaned against him as their fellow travelers washed around them like a rising tide.

'It's okay Mitch. You go now. I hate partings. We've said all we can. You know how I feel, and we must wait until it's safe. If it ever will be safe.'

'It will, Margitte. Just take care, and keep a watchful eye out for anyone who seems to be taking too much interest in your movements.'

They clung to each other and then he was away through the security arch, with a sideways glance towards her. But she was gone into the rush of people. His escape had begun.

Chapter Twenty-Six

Sydney, 1789

Paddy woke up to the distinct sounds of rain and the barking of dogs. It had been building up to a rainstorm for several hours, and now the sound of a downpour on the thin metal-reinforced roof put a stop to Paddy's fitful dreams. As always, they had been full of anxiety and fear; he never regretted waking up.

The dogs' noise was probably caused by some disturbance. They were a motley crew and always acted up whenever they were approached by someone they did not immediately recognize. Paddy's first conscious thought was to look over at Ackers' bunk, and he was relieved to see the ginger beard sticking out over the edge of the sacking that covered his friend.

Since Ackers had first voiced his thoughts on trying to 'run for it', Paddy, Chipper and Prof had all feared that the unruly countryman would be foolish enough to try it. In the eighteen months they had all been incarcerated in the jail of His Majesty's new land of Australia, there had been twenty attempts for freedom. All of them had failed. Three men had died of thirst, five had been shot trying to evade capture, and the remaining twelve had been summarily dragged back to camp to be flogged in front of the entire colony.

Since Chief Sande had been in charge of escaped prisoners, tales of brutality and perversion had cut down the number of attempts. Nonetheless, Ackers yearned for life away from the confines of the colony, and the three friends worried at the possibility of him falling under the control of Sande.

As the camp began its slow growth from its primitive beginnings at Botany Bay a year and a half earlier, Paddy, Chipper and Prof had all seen changes in their lives. Paddy assisted in the animal hospital for a year then virtually took over after the old veterinary surgeon, Doc Winslow, contracted some strange illness and died. Because of his prisoner status, however, Paddy was not allowed to remain as the colony's vet; that role had to go to a 'gentleman', and so one was found. 'Doctor' Jameson was appointed to this position, and spent his mornings sleeping off the results of his afternoons and evenings. He was a plump affected blimp of a man, with a burning eye and caustic wit, which was usually directed at the more unfortunate, such as the Irish, with whom he came into contact. His jibes at Paddy were received in brooding silence and only added to the list of sins by the English upper class that Paddy was keeping in his head.

Jameson came and went and paid no heed at all to what was going on in his domain of sick animals. To him, it was a badge of rank he had to endure in order to collect the measly stipend and pension he needed, since he had gambled and drunk away the small fortune bequeathed to him by his maternal aunt in England. Deeply in debt and unable to curb his appetites, he had sensibly taken his remaining family's advice and acquired a berth to a new life in the new land of Australia.

On arrival, he dedicated this new life purely to alcohol, as the little gambling available did not suit his sophisticated tastes. The failed medical degree he had tried to forget now came in handy as the need for an animal doctor surfaced. His interview took place within the governor's stockade, and Paddy did not even know about it until the new vet took over the cramped office at the end of the animal compound. The first conversation did not endear Jameson to Paddy.

'What's your job here then, my man? Are you the mick with the animal touch?'

'I look after the sick animals. I have done since we were on the First Fleet out here.'

'Well, as long as I'm in charge, you'd better look sharp and not let any of the damned animals die more often than they did on that old fool Winslow's watch. D'ye hear me?'

Without waiting for a reply, the new chief staggered off to attend to his luncheon. Paddy shook his head and returned to a particularly bad-tempered pig that had cut its leg on some wire fencing.

'Another example of England's finest,' he said into the pig's ear. As if in agreement, the pig stopped its squealing long enough for Paddy to bathe the wound.

As the weeks bore on, Paddy accepted Jameson's comings and goings with stoicism. He was exactly the type of person Paddy had come to despise. All the time on the boat and in his New World here, Paddy had thought of his circumstances, and his anger and resentment burned towards those who had captured him and sentenced him to such a cruel fate.

In passing, Paddy accepted a measure of blame in that he had forsaken his pledge to keep away from the bottle, gotten drunk and allowed himself to be captured. Since then, apart from the red wine he and Varcoe had shared in Rio, he had made good on his promise never to drink again. But all the craziness that once would only enter his head when he drank was again close to the surface. Now, it was centered on revenge for those who had taken his life away.

'It may take a lifetime, but the English will pay,' he swore on the heads of his long forgotten family.

As Paddy was working at his life in the repair of sick animals, so Chipper Johnson was also exercising his talents in the pursuits of carpentry. The small cockney still had a spry way with him, and he could still revert to his old cheeky self. However, since his illness on the voyage, he had calmed down considerably. He now spent his time in helping to beautify the buildings the colony erected.

The first of these was the governor's headquarters, then the stockade for the prisoners. After those walls had gone up, the prison blocks were hastily built, followed by officer quarters. In the months that followed, various immigrants arrived on the battered ships that plied their creaking way across the endless seas. Far and away, the largest number of these immigrants were incarcerated, but sprinkled in among them, were some intrepid adventurers anxious to try their hand in a new country.

Chipper's carving skills and general craftsmanship were well received by many of these new frontiersmen, and he was hired out to help finish the few dwellings that were dotting the landscape. He seemed content outside the confines of the jail to which he returned each evening. He had fallen under the spell of a Bible teacher, who had strengthened his lost faith, giving him new hope for his future. The outside life and the food that was supplied by the new householders had fattened him up and given him a ruddy complexion. Not so for Prof.

With Prof's ready knowledge and clerical skills, it did not take the authorities long to recognize his usefulness in the stores and other places where ignorance meant disaster. In a few weeks, he had become one of the staples in the keeping of books and counting of supplies – so necessary for the new colony. He was shut away from most of the penal colony's activity, and he was grateful for the silence and relative security his position afforded. The colony had swollen, and because of its remoteness, had been self-sufficient from the start. This was not to say the first year was not without great hardship on the part of those who were captives, and also those in charge. The four friends had weathered these times relatively unscathed and, although it was the merest glimmer, there was a dim light of hope at the end of the tunnel. Five years was easier to endure than seven were, although poor Prof had to endure much longer.

None of the four talked about a future life, but they all secretly thought of the time when they would be able to leave this empty deserted land and return to their lives once more. Paddy had quickly given up the utopian dream of a new land with a new life. Australia soon proved the old regime had a firm grip on the way things were and would remain. In the silence of the antipodean night, they all would dream of a rebirth far away from the brutality of Australia and its burgeoning convict population.

Ackers lacked any skill with which to elevate himself above common laboring work. At the bottom of the class system, he was often the butt of the most severe punishments. He had been picked on from the start, because of his country accent, his solid squat build, and his general clumsiness. Often he would return to his cell exhausted and beaten, and only his little cat, Marmy, seemed to be able to calm him. Although he spent the day roaming around and hunting the many small rodents present, Marmy always made it back to their mutual bunk before Ackers arrived. It was a small hint of normal domesticity in an otherwise institutionalized life.

Sleeping together, thirty to a cell, most of the men made noises and cries as they turned in their uncomfortable bunks, but Ackers above all, was the noisiest. Perhaps it was the general unhappiness of his life that caused his nightmares. But this was yet another excuse for his fellow prisoners to complain about him, and there was little his friends could do to help.

After a particularly hot spell in November, Ackers seemed to become even more depressed and withdrawn. Both Prof and Chipper had done their best to get him transferred to their work areas to get him away from his tormentors. Neither had been successful, and this had resulted in their friend making his own plans.

The compound they all inhabited was quite loosely guarded. Outside the settlement, nothing existed for men from the civilization of Georgian England. True, giants and monsters had never surfaced, although rumors still circulated about the great outback. Mostly, men could stray small distances but there was no nourishment, and everyone knew the severest punishments awaited those who stayed out beyond the end of the day's roll-call.

As the days lengthened and the heat increased, Ackers took to standing each evening looking out through the stockade fence towards the setting sun. Marmy would often join him and crawl inside the ragged shirt with his face peeking out. Ackers would hum quietly to himself, and his eyes would take on a faraway look as the land became bathed in the reddish glow of sunset. Both Paddy and Prof, worried at the slow introversion that had overtaken their friend, would walk out to Ackers and try to get him to talk. Ackers would hardly acknowledge their presence and would continue with his staring off into the distance.

'I'm really worried about him, Prof,' Paddy said one evening, as they had tried unsuccessfully to get Ackers to talk to them. 'He's never been this quiet before.'

'I know how you feel, Paddy,' Prof replied, walking slowly away from the silent man at the fence. 'He's never been the greatest conversationalist, but he was always pretty lively.'

'This place can drive tough people crazy. I'm worried he could do something really daft. I don't know how to get through to him in this mood. Not even Chipper can get a smile out of him these days.'

'Don't worry, Paddy, it'll all work out, I'm sure.'

Prof's words proved to be completely wrong. Three nights later, Ackers was missing from the nightly count, and no one had any idea where he was. A desultory search was made of the immediate area in the hope he might have fallen asleep or possibly been persuaded to indulge in some aboriginal drinking spree. The latter was known to happen from time to time for those with the insatiable desire to consume alcohol, even if it was only the native's brew of fermented leaf juice and saliva. After two days, there was no avoiding the fact he had 'done a runner'. The forces were amassed to carry out a local search – twenty miles around the camp. Marines and soldiers as well as prison guards mounted up and began their hunt for the missing prisoner.

An atmosphere hung over the entire settlement. The convicts to a man (the women were incarcerated elsewhere) prayed for his success. No one believed Ackers would get away, but they all willed him on, even those who had found delight in ragging him and were in many ways responsible for his flight. Small bets were laid on his chances of staying free for a week, a month, a year or for ever.

Chipper was almost immediately called in from his work outside the compound, and Paddy and Prof noticed they were being watched more carefully than usual. The four friends' relationship was known throughout the colony, and the authorities became very suspicious that the others would somehow attempt to join their foolish companion.

When a full day's search proved empty, the various groups involved became more and more stone-faced and angry that they had been challenged in this way. Inevitably, the word reached everyone that the hunt had been turned over to Chief Sande and his band of assorted natives.

Sande lived five miles from the Sydney settlement and was rarely seen. He had formed a group of failed settlers and aborigines into a small farm, as well as running a supply store. Neither ventures were particularly successful, except Sande had managed to secure a good supply of tobacco and London gin, both of which were much sought after.

His aboriginal band, numbering about twenty, did not understand the concept of working for wages. They were highly delighted with any personal adornments that the chief threw their way, and so, effectively they worked for nothing. Sande became their headman and they treated him with all the reverence of such a rank. The other dozen in his 'tribe' had been snatched by him from certain starvation, and instead of having to accept charity, they were able to get along on a small share of the profits from the import business while at the same time feeling superior to the natives. Sande's sadism and sexuality also played a part in the hold he exerted over the deviant group. On the occasions any of them came into town, people shrank from them, and hoped they would leave as soon as possible.

The governor sent a rider out to Sande's ranch with a letter urging him to make full haste and find the missing felon, contain him and bring him back to camp for full punishment. Paddy felt a shiver run through him when he heard the news. An awful feeling of imminent terror came over him, and he took to his bunk to contemplate the few alternatives open to his missing colleague.

If Ackers was fortunate, he would be found close to home, with some vestige of an excuse. The worst situation would be that he would be found weak and helpless by the band searching for him. Perhaps he might even have the luck to have fallen off a cliff and died. Paddy flinched in the realization that death was proving to be the best solution. He was sad to think their lives had been so reduced that this could be possible.

As he stared at the rusting roof, running the events of his recent life over in his mind, the feeling of hatred again ran through him as he thought of the rule of one man over another with the accompanying unfairness and hatred that built up. Under different circumstances, the entire population could be settled here with the focus on building a new land with fairness for all. A new opportunity to create a life, with equal shares and laws to protect everyone equally, was being squandered.

This place had become a more hostile copy of the society they had left, with one set of rules for those in charge and another set for those in captivity. This would have been more understandable if most of those incarcerated had committed any real crimes that deserved such brutality. God knew that murder, rape and violence should be punished, but most of these poor souls had been banished from their homes and country for little more than stealing food for their family, or perhaps a handful of thin rags to cover their shivering emaciated bodies. The price for this was a minimum of seven years. Most of them would never make it home again. Their lives were basically over.

Paddy had at first tried to put such thoughts out of his mind. He remembered that, years ago, his quiet demeanor and lack of temper had been the envy of his family and the pride of his wife. Unlike his uncles or his other family and friends, Paddy had not been one to fly into a rage at simple provocation. But since he had opened his eyes that first day aboard HMS *Distinction*, his mind had been altered. Slowly at first, like the beginnings of a small bonfire, the heat of anger smoldered within him. But unlike wood and peat, injustice and the plight of his fellow prisoners fueled his fire.

Now here was his friend on the run, dirty, distressed and the object of ridicule by nearly everyone, and the best that he could hope for him was death. And still the English upper class affected holier-than-thou ways. Taking their sherry on the verandah as the sun set on the second day of the search, they pretended they were back in their respectable English homes and lording it over the lower orders. The unjustness of it all made him grind his teeth with fury.

A movement beside him caused him to jump. It was Marmy coming alongside him in his bunk. Paddy had thought the little cat had run off with Ackers in his escape bid. But here was the animal purring alongside his original owner. What could have been Ackers' idea in leaving him? Paddy felt it only had one meaning. His friend did not expect to survive the outback in its wildness, and had left Marmy here to be looked after by his friends.

No doubt Marmy had been frantically looking for his master and had now returned to look around the camp. Having found Paddy, though, Marmy curled up and was soon fast asleep. The Irishman envied the cat the ability to slip into unconsciousness with such apparent ease, whereas he himself struggled through several hours of sleeplessness each night enduring fears for his absent colleague.

In the morning, Paddy awoke with more than his normally bad feelings. His head swam with such an air of foreboding he at first thought he was still dreaming. The ginger cat had gone, but there was a small cluster of white and auburn hair alongside the edge of the bunk. As Paddy's eyes focused, he reached out and felt the soft fur with his callused fingers.

He nodded to Prof, who was also awake, and went out to dunk his head in the wooden trough that served as the hut's main ablutions. There was not a sign of Marmy, so he sat on the bench and waited for the water and biscuit that was the regular breakfast for prisoners. The sun had already burst out of the east, and the compound was starting to attend to its various duties. Paddy watched it all with a baleful look.

It was some time before Paddy noticed a group of guards pointing towards the western horizon. A dust cloud swirled around the approach of a party of some dozen or so men. He did not need to look long before his fears were confirmed. It was the hunting party returning. The sad spectacle of Ackers dragged along by chains soon became apparent. Sande, the only one on a horse, led the broken man who stumbled and would have fallen but for the cruel kicks and pushes by the others in the band.

The stockade was opened, and two lines were formed inside the gate by the marines and soldiers who shared the compound and jailer duties.

Paddy stood up slowly, and walked to the front of the men who had gathered to watch Ackers' sad return. He glared at the few who chattered about the bets they had placed the previous days.

As the party came to the gate, Paddy could see that Ackers was hardly alive. His tongue hung out of his mouth, swollen and raw. His eyes were almost closed with bruises and gashes over both brows. One arm hung down at a terrible angle and had obviously been broken, as had most of his fingers. Paddy moved towards his helpless friend but felt a tight grip on his arm. It was Prof, with Chipper close by.

'Don't go in front of the line, Paddy,' Prof said between clenched teeth, 'it's just what they're waiting for.'

Chipper moved alongside Paddy on the other side.

'It's no good, mate. There's nothing any of us can do for the poor bastard. At least now he's back in camp, he'll be under the governor's eye, and away from that swine.'

A flash of orange tore out of the waiting line.

'Marmy!' Paddy cried and moved forward. Both his friends held him tightly, as the cat streaked across the dusty ground towards his master. Sande had just dismounted and was handing the reins to one of the aborigines, when he too saw the small animal tearing up to them. He pulled a blade the size of a carving knife out of his belt. As the cat reached six feet away from the sagging Ackers, Sande stepped in front of him and leaning down, skewered the little animal through the belly and hoisted it high in the air. A guttural groan escaped from Ackers' dry throat as the cat screamed its death in mid-air. Paddy also cried out, but was turned round by Chipper and held tightly by Prof.

Sande tossed the cat's body to one of his band and said, 'Give the skin back to me after you've stewed the rest. It'll make a nice baccy pouch. Me other one's getting a bit worn.' Then, after kneeing Ackers in the groin, he pulled the now weeping hulk over to the governor, who had hastily donned some clothing for this early reveille. Sande performed a navy-style salute and shouted, 'One prisoner reporting for duty, Sir.'

The governor stared at the crippled wreck whimpering before him. 'This man is in a terrible state, Chief Gunner Sande. What have you done with him?'

'Attempting to evade escape, Sir. Put up quite a fight.'

Paddy twisted in the grip of both his friends. Ackers was never a man to fight foolishly. Everyone knew that. It was one of the problems that had caused his baiting. He would not fight back unless absolutely necessary. Sande was a known sadist, and here was evidence he should never be trusted with anyone in a weakened position.

Paddy felt, rather than heard, Prof's words in his ear.

'Steady, Paddy, we're in danger here. Just keep your eyes down and, above all, keep still.'

Paddy nodded his understanding.

The governor was plainly upset by the condition of Ackers. He was known by all to be a rigid man, with an obsession for rules, but he was not cruel. He stared with unconcealed disgust at the scene before him: the upright, bald-headed gunner, with his cruel sneer, surrounded by his group of deviant followers, all looking pleased with themselves and the prospect of spending their reward indulging in further extremes.

'He fess'd up, Sir.'

Sande made his statement more to the whole assembly than just the authority in front of him.

'There was four of 'em in it.'

Ackers jerked himself upright and received a vicious blow in the kidneys from one of Sande's helpers. Sande himself turned round and hit Ackers full in the face, causing the helpless man to sag down on his chains, unconscious once more.

'That's enough of that, Sande.'

The governor motioned for a group of jailers to carry the returned convict away.

'What were you saying?'

'He confessed to there bein' four of 'em in the plot. One got out and the others would follow in a day or two.'

'Do you know the others, Sande?'

A silence hung in the heavy morning air.

Paddy stood between Chipper and Prof, realizing that they were completely trapped. Once again, Sande was his nemesis, his accuser, his fate.

With no hesitation, Sande raised his hand and pointed at the three standing just twenty foot away.

'That's them, Sir, always hung around together, they 'ave. Always been the same. Born trouble, all the way across on the boats. You'd best be done with 'em, Sir.'

'I'll make the rules here, Sande, if you don't mind.'

Sande walked back with a sly look over at the three men he had accused. His motley crew of helpers stood around him as they awaited the governor's words. Paddy felt anger rising up in his face. Prof and Chipper stood silently awaiting what would happen next. The governor sent four guards over to the three and had them pulled roughly in front of him.

He turned quietly to the men next to him and talked with them for a few minutes. Turning, he eventually said, 'Do you deny what you have heard said here?'

Prof as the natural spokesman for the three said, 'He was our friend, Sir, but we knew nothing about it, nor did we plan to escape. Ackers must have been delirious, Sir. He looks very bad.'

The governor stood silently for a long time, obviously thinking what the best solution might be. After several minutes, he said, 'The returned prisoner is guilty of escape. Bring him out to be flogged – fifty lashes. As for you others, I know you're all friends, and I can't believe you knew nothing about this sorry attempt. However, there is no real evidence against you apart from what amounts to hearsay; therefore I shall be lenient. Nonetheless, I consider you to be a risk to the security of this colony, so I shall send you away from here for the rest of your sentence. You shall be incarcerated on Norfolk Island. Stand by to witness sentence.'

At first Paddy did not quite understand what had been said. But he did hear Prof mumble, 'My God' softly behind him.

The trestle for flogging was dragged into the center of the compound, and several marines stood by as Ackers was pulled over to the wooden frame. He was strapped tightly to the edges and a piece of leather belt shoved between his teeth. A young drummer boy began the roll, as a sergeant of the marines pulled back his arm that held the wicked lead-tipped cat-o-nine tails. As the flail bit into Ackers' back, he let out a scream of such piercing horror that every man in the assembled group turned his face away. All except Sande, who leered at the sight of blood and fear, reveling in the moment.

Ackers did not last beyond twenty lashes. After his harsh

treatment from Sande, he was too weak to take such punishment. The cold water sluiced on him, to revive him between each stroke, finally failed to do its job, and the doctor pronounced him dead. He was cut down and his life and his presence was gone from his ashen friends, as they were taken away to solitary confinement before shipment to Norfolk Island. Sande did not see the look that Paddy directed at him as he was led away.

Chapter Twenty-Seven

Zurich, 1993

Mitch O'Doule felt totally mixed up. As the well-manicured Swiss countryside fell away underneath the rapidly rising 747, he had two strong emotions vying for attention inside him. For the first time in his adult life, he was away from the 'Army'. And he was not just away, he was actually on the run, a traitor. He had turned his back this time on all he had stood for over the last twenty-five years. The word would be out now. Ryan would know that he'd been taken, and the forces would be massing against him.

At the same time he was experiencing an overwhelming feeling of loss, having said goodbye to the only woman to have shared his excitement and his dreams for decades. Margitte had taken up a space in his life that he had always thought was non-existent. But having done so, she had now to be apart from him.

He leaned back in the seat and tried to focus on his next moves. First there was a four-hour layover in Madrid, then he would fly on to Rio de Janeiro. He would have to do something about his dark brown hair and also decide finally on either mustache, or, God forbid, a full beard. His present scruffy non-shaved look made him feel just scruffy. Maybe some glasses would help. It was extremely unlikely there would be any watchers in South America. All the eyes of his former colleagues would be on Spain or France, particularly the south of both those countries. Also, he was not on any active Interpol list as far as he knew. Of course, that had never been any real concern to him.

He would take advantage of his stop in Madrid to look around the city. Perhaps he would visit a few bars and wave some money about. Carefully, of course, he did not want to be too stupid, but it might set off a false trail or two. Afterward, he would spend a couple of weeks in Brazil, keeping a low profile, then he would go to South Africa, just like Great-great-great-granddad Paddy had done, all those years ago. Then eventually, it would all come together in Australia. That was where the future for Mitch lay. And once he had found the right place, he would send for Margitte, and they would live happily ever after. He smiled at the simplicity of it, also at his naiveté.

The aluminum briefcase at his feet gave him a wonderful feeling of comfort. Up until now he had never really had to worry too much about money. He drew whatever he needed from Army funds. His needs were small and his life only called for food, drink, clothes and that lonely converted farm flat. He paid for the flat, but everything else came as a result of sympathizers to the great cause. Pubs ran slates that were never cleared; shops did the same for food and clothes.

When he thought about it, it was quite a novelty to go shopping for anything. As a result he had no built-in gauge for how long money would last. This had the effect of making him feel very vulnerable and in need of Margitte whom he knew had no similar dysfunction.

The pilot dropped the huge vessel onto the tarmac of Barracas airport, Madrid, with a bouncing jolt. Mitch had dozed off until that moment. But pulling himself together, he took his briefcase and joined the slow meandering conga of his fellow passengers to leave the plane. Having checked his bag through to its final destination, he did not have to worry about another check of his luggage. There would be that in Rio, he imagined, but he put the thought out of his mind for now.

Outside the airport building there was a long line of passengers for a short line of taxis. He was struck by the difference in the people here, compared to the stoical Swiss whom he had left behind. Everyone in the queue talked loudly and waved their arms about while speaking. Passing cars seemed incapable of proceeding without honking their horns, and there was an energy that was all encompassing.

The taxi he entered was full of strong tobacco smoke that made Mitch's nostrils twitch with desire. It had been a long time since he had enjoyed such an aroma up close. The driver could speak no English at all, but seemed to understand the word 'Downtown', which Mitch repeated several times through the thick haze that enveloped them both.

The un-airconditioned car was hot and stuffy, and the driver continued to smoke as they made their way through the heavy traffic. Watching everyone hooting and waving their hands out of the windows, Mitch reflected that, although Spain was only a few hundred miles from Switzerland, it might have been a different world. After a bit, Mitch began to find all the hustle and bustle rather amusing. He decided he needed a drink. Leaning forward, he said 'Drink' to the driver, but it did not seem to register. It was only when he accompanied it with the gesture recognizable throughout the world that the driver understood.

'Tourista bar?' the driver asked.

Mitch thought that through for a moment, and felt he would rather go somewhere less exposed.

'No,' he replied and the driver smiled. It's funny, thought Mitch, how everyone hates tourist places, and yet they're always so busy.

The driver turned off the wide boulevard they were on, and jostled his way through some narrow streets made even more narrow by cars parked on both sides. The local citizens, Mitch could see, had made parking into almost an art form. Cars were even parked up on the corners of sidewalks, making it impossible for the people to walk through. No doubt there would be hefty fines for this, but so far it had not stopped the offenders.

Eventually, with total disregard for any other motorists, the taxi was aimed at a small spot next to a bar with tables outside, and the driver parked. Mitch pulled some dollars out of his pocket and handed about twenty's worth to the driver. To his surprise, the driver promptly got out of the car shaking his head. Smiling, he led the confused Irishman inside, and stood beside him at the bar.

There were a great number of men at the curved counter, and the white-shirted barmen behind seemed to be having a job to catch up with the constant demand. The taxi driver was obviously well known, however. One of the barmen shook his hand vigorously, as they rattled away in Spanish, Mitch looking on impotently. He caught the word '*amigo*', several times and realized the driver was explaining that he was a friend with 'dollares'. '*Americano*' Mitch also recognized, and he had to tell the driver that no, he was, in fact, Irish.

This seemed to please the man immensely, for no reason that Mitch could detect, but it called for a couple of drinks to come their way. Beer for Mitch and red wine for the driver, who had now introduced himself as Paco. All very nice, thought Mitch, as he downed his mug and gestured for another one. The cabby went to a small table in a corner of the crowded bar and returned with a plate of prawns. He offered them to Mitch and promptly pulled the head off one and began to eat the inside. Mitch ate his more conservatively, to the driver's amusement.

The taxi driver, it seemed, had accompanied Mitch here to assist with the money change, and also because the man obviously liked to drink. He was on his third glass before someone came over to him, and pointing at his cab outside, asked to be taken on to another place. The driver rubbed a stubby finger and thumb in front of Mitch's face, and Mitch realized he should now pay his fare. He wondered how much all this extra service was going to cost him.

The driver took two twenty-dollar bills from Mitch and handed them to the barman. He handed several Spanish notes back to Mitch as he pocketed some and left the others on the bar. With much '*Amigo, amigo*', he left Mitch and went outside with his new fare. The barman smiled amicably. I hope the rest of my trip is as friendly as this place, Mitch thought. It also occurred to him that staying here would save a lot of stupid travel time. He shook the thought off. It was too close to home by a long way.

After several beers, Mitch wandered around for a bit. Having eaten several of the prawns, he was not hungry, and anyway he didn't know what he would have ordered if he had gone into a restaurant. It made him realize that living in a new country was not going to be easy if he didn't speak the language.

No doubt the ancient relative was right in his choice of a new land, Mitch thought, knowing full well the irony of Paddy's life. His Irish ancestors had suffered as badly in the founding of Australia as any of the English prisoners of the time.

The traffic at this late afternoon time was heavy. The sound of horns never let up for a minute. Mitch looked into one or two shops, and admired the elegant way Spanish clothes were displayed. One particular mannequin showed off a brilliant yellow dress, which immediately made him think of Margitte with such a piercing twist it made him wince. On impulse, with an overwhelming need to call her, he turned into a smart hotel.

After asking at the main desk where the pay phones were, he was directed to a small window off to the side of the main area. Inside a cramped room sat three harassed phone operators. They were working old-fashioned equipment, while dealing with a number of guests who were sitting on chairs outside, waiting for their calls to come through. Mitch tried to make the operators understand him, but it took a tall distinguished gentleman to help him. After vigorously denying he was English – something that he was going to have to curb, he realized – he accepted the help, and sat alongside the gentleman to await his turn in one of the booths.

Mitch's new companion wore a mustache with points sticking up on both sides of his smiling mouth. He was about sixty years of age and he wore a gray suit that reeked of money in its cut and choice of material. Mitch smiled inwardly at the thought that, at present, he could certainly afford one like it, but his spoils were not enough to allow him to continue to think that way for ever.

The callers in the booths were men, he noticed. All the *telephonistas* were women. It seemed to Mitch that the latter stages of the feminist movement had not reached this hot and dusty city. He also realized he had absolutely no idea where Margitte stood on such issues. There was still so much to learn about her. He did not have long to ponder this, as his turn came up to use number four booth. The familiar ring came across the line and Margitte soon spoke.

'How long have you been home?' Mitch asked.

'About half an hour. Whereabouts are you?'

'A few miles to the south of you. Don't worry about it.'

'Are you okay?'

'Sure.'

Now he had her on the line he could not find what he wanted to say. He felt like a tongue-tied teenager, with too many thoughts and not enough words. She broke the pause.

'I've been thinking about you, you know.'

'Me, too. It was harder than I thought.'

'I know how you feel. As though there's a hole in one. Something important missing out of one's middle.'

'Same for me. It's not a very nice sensation. It's kind of a first for me,' he confessed. 'I suppose I should have had more experience at getting lovesick when I was a kid.'

'Well, you were too busy setting the world to rights, I guess.'

It was funny how just talking to her made the distance disappear. Margitte talked about her flight, and Mitch talked about his, then looking at his watch, he realized he only had a couple of hours before his flight out. He immediately began to freeze up, and then worried that he might upset her. But she seemed as balanced as ever.

'I know, you've got to go. It was great that you called.'

'I'll call again as soon as I can.'

He hung up and paid his fee at the *telephonista*'s window, deciding to have a final drink before leaving. The hotel bar was quiet and dark. He remembered he had considered laying a false trail in the city, although he had little hope of being able to do that effectively in such a short space of time.

Sitting at the end of the mahogany bar sat the distinguished gentleman from the telephone area. He looked very sad as he stared into his glass of wine. Mitch ordered a beer and went over to him. The man looked up and his face lost some of its sadness.

'Ah, the gentleman from Ireland. I hope your call was better than mine.'

'Fine, thank you. You have a problem?'

'I'm afraid it was a final call to my mistress. My wife insisted. She said it had been going on for too long, and our friends were beginning to find it, how would you say, unamusing.'

'I see.'

Actually Mitch didn't see at all, but the old gentleman was obviously very upset.

'You know, when we have a real trouble like that back home…' Mitch couldn't quite conceive of such a circumstance as this back home, but he pressed on, 'we would not touch that sort of drink. It would call for the real stuff.'

He waved at the barman who was silently polishing glasses, at the end of the bar.

'A double Bushmills, please.'

The barman obviously had some knowledge of his language, because he reached under the bar and withdrew a bottle of the Irish whiskey, and began to pour it out in front of Mitch. Mitch insisted on the glass being filled to its brim, and pushed it over to the sad-faced man.

'Try that and tell me if it doesn't make you feel better.'

The Spaniard spluttered a bit as he took the first swallow, but after the second, some color came into his face.

'You're right, you know. It does make one feel better. But this is a sad day for me. It is going to take me weeks to find a replacement for Pilar. She was so beautiful.'

Weeks, thought Mitch. It had taken him all his life to find Margitte.

He could see, however, that this was leading down the wrong path, so he indicated for the man to take another sip. Eventually, he got the whole story. His companion was called Joaquin (pronounced Wakeen, it seemed to Mitch). He had made a fortune in the slot machine business, and had four children. He was sixty-four, and since his early marriage, had always had a mistress – to keep him young, he said. However, no matter how deviously he tried, his wife always found out about them. Eventually, she would put her foot down and the girlfriend would have to go. The funny thing was this always happened about the time Joaquin began to think about a change himself. Nonetheless, he was a man of honor, and the inevitable tear-filled parting would always upset him.

'*Señor*, ah, what is your name?'

Mitch told him.

'Well, *Señor* Mitchell, we will have one final salute to Pilar.'

He motioned to the barman and in rapid Spanish ordered two single measures. They both toasted the end of such a fine affair.

'And now a final act, if you please, Mitchell. It is just my little tradition – normally carried out alone. But if you don't mind, we shall share this moment. You have given me strength to carry on.'

Mitch was rather apprehensive at what might next occur, but watched as, ceremoniously, Joaquin took out his wallet and removed a small passport-sized photo. He kissed it tenderly and then, after balling it up in his fist, placed it in an ashtray and set light to it with a gold lighter. They both watched the paper crumple as the flames engulfed it.

'*Señor*, it is done. Now I must look to the future. You have given me hope. The Bushmills will be my new drink if I ever find myself in a similar circumstance.'

Mitch somehow felt this was pretty much a certain bet.

'Please accept my card, and if I can ever be of assistance, do not hesitate to call on me. I am truly indebted to you.'

Mitch pocketed the finely engraved card and told Joaquin that as it happened, he was also in trouble, but he was going to solve his difficulties by running away to a different land. However, if he found himself back there, he would be certain to call. He was subjected to a light embrace from his new-found friend as he vacated the stool.

Out of the hotel, he walked towards a large square, to

search for a taxi rank. Thinking about his journey ahead, Mitch wondered at the strange course of events that had made him follow his early relative's footsteps. Paddy had presumably not come here, but he had been in the Canaries, and Mitch was now to follow the route to Rio, South Africa and then, finally, Australia. He remembered he had chosen the final destination after seeing those old yellowed pages from so long ago. The Canaries were definitely not part of his original agenda, and yet Paddy had been there. It was all such a strange coincidence. Once Mitch had found safety and settled in a remote part of the continent, he would try to make the effort to find out what had happened to Paddy O'Doule.

Right now, however, he needed a cab and an airplane out of here, and to leave the heat and danger of Europe far behind. As he climbed into a black taxi and slid over the hot plastic seat, he realized how much better he felt since talking with Margitte. He wondered how long the medicine would last him.

The taxi sped towards the airport and Mitch was glad this driver did not smoke or try to engage him in conversation. The windows were open and the dusty heat blew in and clothed Mitch in its warmth. He dozed in the back until the car reached the terminal.

In spite of some arcane air traffic delay that was announced over an ear-shattering sound system, Varig airlines eventually invited their passengers to board. Mitch entered the 747 and sank into the foreignness of its background music, dusky flight attendants and smell.

How many cultures since leaving that dark little flat? Mitch asked himself. English (he really was going to have to stop wincing at the mention of the place), Dutch, Canaries, Swiss (he was sure that Liechtenstein was not a separate culture), Spanish, and now Brazilian, or at any rate soon to be.

Not bad for the son of a shipyard worker, he thought, smiling to himself. My old dad would be proud of me. Or would he, I wonder?

Fifteen hours later, Mitch found himself in the over-crowded, noisy tourist capital of Brazil. He passed through customs and immigration, with no interest being shown on the part of the authorities. He knew Brasilia to be the real capital, but Rio was the place everybody always thought of as being the capital. It was somewhat like New York versus Washington. And like New York, this city's people ranged from the poorest of the poor to the richest of the rich. He was sure that the distinguished Joaquin, whom he had left sitting in front of his Bushmills at the Madrid hotel bar, would fit right in here. There were certainly enough glamorous women around to fill his recent void.

Mitch selected a plain-looking hotel from the board at the airport, and a taxi unceremoniously dumped him outside it. His room was neat and tidy but, apart from the rooms and a reception area, the hotel didn't offer much else. It seemed, in order to eat, Mitch would be spending his time and money outside. Opposite, there was an expensive-looking travel agent and a couple of bistro-type restaurants, so it was just a question of figuring out how best to find what he liked.

When he had deposited his bags in the room, he was drawn to the telephone, but he rejected the idea of calling Margitte again so soon. He needed to establish himself here before getting another fix from the comfort of her voice. He was rather pleased with his self-control, but he was also very excited at the prospect of being in such an exotic place.

Although he was tired, he felt he had to explore this energetic place, and so, for several hours, he walked around looking at all the different sights in this other world. He went into one cafe and ordered a cake from a display in the window. The coffee he chose to accompany it was thick and dark. That was the way Margitte liked it, he remembered. On his way back, he passed a barber's shop. On impulse, he went inside, and after a short wait, was offered a chair by an old stooping man. Mitch had no idea how to make himself look different, and the barber did not speak any English. So, to start with, Mitch pointed at the red of the leather on which he was sitting and then at his hair.

He was unaware he was in a city where, with its unlimited choice of lifestyles, men were often in the habit of changing their hair color. So he was somewhat surprised, when the barber produced a large color chart from which he could choose. Feeling rather embarrassed for some reason, Mitch pointed out what he felt to be a muted auburn to alter his thick brown hair. The old man went to work, whistling silently through his teeth.

The whole operation lasted an hour and a half. Mitch did not really like the result. He didn't mind the color so much, but the haircut that went with it made him look foppish. Mitch had never taken a lot of trouble with his appearance, and the image that now stared back at him from the barber's mirror was far too well cared for. He hated it. But the idea was to look different, wasn't it? Mitch paid and left, running his hand through his reddish locks.

Mitch continued enjoying Rio for five days. He took several tours, including one up to the famous Sugar Loaf Mountain with its huge statue of Christ. Each day he began with the thought that he would make this the day to call Margitte, but he forced himself to get through some hours of eating, walking, sightseeing and then lunch. After that, he would take a siesta, by which time he felt it was already too late to call, as it would be evening, and she would probably be asleep or out catching up with the family members, as she had said.

On the Monday morning, however, Mitch woke up early, and decided that he could go no longer without hearing the soft Dutch accent. He placed a call through the antiquated hotel system and lay back on the bed waiting. He was amazed at how excited he was at the prospect of speaking to her. The shrill ring, when the call came through, startled him, and he nearly dropped the handset as he picked it up. He knew immediately that something was wrong. Her voice sounded dead as he spoke her name.

'What's the matter? You sound bad.'

'Of course, she sounds bad, you bastard, how would you expect her to sound?'

The voice was Ryan's. Mitch felt a cold draft of fear run through him.

'What have you done to her?' was all he could force out of his dry mouth. Crouching on the edge of the bed, he began to shake over the top half of his body, and he gripped the receiver so tightly his fingers began to hurt.

'You didn't think we would forget about your lady love, did you?'

Mitch remained silent. All the color had drained from his face and he felt turned to stone.

'It took me a bit of tracking down, but Taffy felt all along she was the key to your turning, and for sport we had that fellow of Fergy's do some checking up.'

'You leave her alone,' Mitch growled helplessly into the phone.

'Or what?' was the mocking reply.

Mitch could see the sneer on Ryan's face as he pictured Margitte terrified in the background.

'So here's the plan, you bastard. I want the money. All of it. If you give me the money, you may get to see the girl. I'll have to think about that.'

Mitch could not get his mind into gear. He was completely helpless, but in an instant, something came to him in a flash. He slammed the phone back on its base, nearly breaking it. Once he did it, he regretted it immediately. He had cut the lifeline that was between him and Margitte. But the base instinct that had made him do it was a better reasoner than his conscious thoughts. It had gained him the initiative. Ryan was powerless right now. He had no idea where Mitch was, and Margitte could not tell him, God help her. As his brain slowly began to function again, Mitch – once again in his violent lifetime – thanked his instincts. Nonetheless, he was terribly afraid. Margitte was in the most appalling danger, alone, helpless, and with God knows how many of his former colleagues in control of her. He started shaking once again.

His eyes automatically searched for his cigarettes, and it was several seconds before he realized what he was doing. He got up from the edge of the bed and went into the bathroom and, throwing off his clothes, stood under a cold shower for several minutes before turning the temperature up. Even after cleaning his teeth, he felt physically sick and forced himself outside into the bright morning sunshine to try to get rid of his nausea. He walked to the cafe where each morning he had been taking a coffee to get himself started. As he sat at the table, his mind began to work more logically. How had they found her so quickly? This was the most pressing question. But then, solving that puzzle would not help him out of his present predicament. It was irrelevant. What he had to do now was somehow gain the ascendancy. Slowly he began to think of the facts, forcing his mind to function in a more rational way.

After several swallows of strong coffee, it dawned on him that, maybe, the key to it all would be the money. If the money was as important as he thought it would be to Ryan, he could get Margitte out of Ryan's clutches. That was the foundation of any plan he could cook up. The more he thought it all through, he realized how crucial the two signatures would be that were required to withdraw the money from the Sovereign Bank of Liechtenstein.

There would be no getting round the stern Swiss banking rules unless there was a certified death certificate. No, he didn't think that, even in one of his more violent rages, Ryan would try to pull that one off.

The coffee was helping to calm his nerves sufficiently to allow him to begin practicing the way he wanted the next conversation to go. He ran over his statement to Ryan, as he sat staring out at the normality of society going on all around him. Checking his watch, he worked out it had been a full forty-five minutes since he had cut the connection with the sneering Irishman, effectively taking the power away from his tormentor.

The call came through into his room very quickly after he had ordered it. Margitte answered at the first ring, but the phone changed hands immediately Mitch said 'Hello.'

'Don't you try that trick again, you bastard.'

Ryan spat into the phone,

'I'll do any damned thing I want, Ryan. So you better get used to the idea. That is, if you ever hope to see any of your money again.'

There was complete silence at the other end of the phone. Mitch could hear the blood coursing through his head, as his pulse beat like a hammer. He shouted into the mouthpiece, 'Put the lady on.'

'I make the deals here, O'Doule,' came the angry reply.

'There is no deal if you don't put her on.'

Mitch knew he had reached a moment of truth. He had to stare this situation down, otherwise everything he had planned and hoped for would be lost. Ryan began to bluster. Mitch said nothing. Eventually, Margitte came on the line.

'How many are there?' Mitch asked the question quickly, expecting that Ryan would be jamming his head to the receiver. She answered, 'One.'

By the sounds, Mitch knew that his suspicion was right;

the level of Margitte's voice had dropped a decibel or two. Ryan would be right alongside the earpiece now, but Mitch at least knew that so far he was only up against one adversary.

'Are you okay?'

'I'm okay.'

'I'll get you out of this as soon as possible. I think I know a way to get him the money.'

'Well, you better, my boyo. And there'll be no more little chats with your girlfriend from now on.'

Ryan's voice came harshly across the transatlantic link.

'I'll speak to her whenever I want, if you want your money. And there's a good reason, too. Are you listening?'

'Go ahead, I'm waiting for it.'

'Well, as she probably told you, we have to have two of us to get the money. There's one more reason, too. If she's in any way harmed, not only will I leave you to stew in your own juice, but I'll come after you. And you know it. So think about how you're going to look without the money, before you try anything rash. It's up to you.'

There was a pause of several seconds. Mitch could hear Ryan's breathing across the wires.

'So what's the plan? Assuming I agree.'

'I'll call you in two days.'

Mitch slammed the phone down for the second time. 'I think I've got you, my fine friend.' He went over to the closet and took out the tin box that had been so useful in concealing its contents through the world's airports. 'Just one more journey to go.' Mitch breathed to the contents. He took out the pistol and checked the action. He slipped the magazine into the handle and cocked the weapon, looking along the barrel. For the first time in his memory, the cold steel in his hand felt repellent to him. The old feeling of excitement, with its accompanying security, was not there. Shrugging, he pulled out the magazine and replaced the box in his luggage.

He walked quickly across the street to the travel agents and booked a direct flight to Zurich for that afternoon. Also, hating his new hairstyle, he returned once more to the barber's shop and indicated that he wanted all his hair off, down to a stubble. The long-suffering barber swept the gown over Mitch's chest and set to work, accepting the changing way men were these days. They're as bad as any woman, he thought.

Chapter Twenty-Eight

Sydney, 1789

Paddy, Chipper and Prof were held in solitary confinement for the next four weeks. Apart from a change of the slop bucket, and a plate of rough maggoty bread and a mug of water once a day, to prove the existence of other humans, they were to all intents and purposes alone in their dark world. Unbeknown to the other two, Prof had in his own soft, insistent way managed to find out information on their future. Since he was totally non-threatening, with a quiet modulated voice, people naturally trusted him, and the four jailers, responsible for their containment, responded to his various small questions. This meant when the time came for them to be led out into the sunlight, he knew the fate that awaited them. And the news was not good.

Shackled together, they were able to share the first words with each other since that fateful day four weeks earlier. Chipper looked gaunt and Prof was stooped and limping. They were shadows of the men that had walked up the gangplank of the *Falcon* nearly three years before. Chipper cracked a joke about nothing much changing around here, but his two friends could not bring themselves to even smile.

A small clipper was at berth alongside the quay. About fifty chained men were lined up with twenty assorted guards to shepherd them onto the ship. Many of the guards were familiar, and Chipper mumbled under his breath,

'Looks like we've got a few choice ones to look after us.'

A pint-sized officer in a lieutenant commander's uniform bustled about, shouting to his crew. He seemed to be typical of his class. There was also a stern bosun with a clump of rope swinging at his fist. He officiously passed on the orders down the line of responsibility. To Paddy, it was so terribly predictable, and he hated it all. He hated the uniforms, the shouts, the whistles and the overt show of power that these ships carried with them. It was a concentrated microcosm of the English social system, and there was no way out.

As they lined up on benches below deck, Prof was able to tell them what he had found out. Their destination was Norfolk Island, one thousand miles to the east of what was now being called Sydney. It was a stark rocky outpost with nothing on it but pine trees, grass and seabirds. The cocky officer on deck was to be its new governor, and they were all to have the privilege of colonizing this outpost for the king.

'It's the ultimate prison for the ultimate prisoner,' Prof smiled through his straggly beard. 'Even the guards are all terrified of the place. They say there's no shelter, nothing will grow, and it's the harshest place on earth.'

'It can't be any worse than when we arrived here,' Chipper spoke up. 'It can't be. Can it?'

They lapsed into silence and listened to the noises above, as ropes were untied and the crew made ready to head the ship off on its feared voyage. Paddy looked at all the men's faces. There was a mixture of every sad and anxious type of emotion on them. It was difficult to accept these were what the authorities considered to be the hardest of the hard; that these were the men who could not be contained because of their inherent danger to the colony. All Paddy saw was a group of dejected souls on their way to yet more cruelty and hardship at the hands of the English establishment.

Conditions on this ship were even more sparse than when they had made the long journey to Australia. The prisoners were allowed up on deck for much of the time, but they were always heavily chained. There was little to do, and even Paddy and Prof's interminable conversations were not what they used to be. Paddy had become less interested in Prof's knowledge, and he suspected that deep down, in spite of his pronouncements, Prof accepted the status quo of the system that had made such misery of all their lives.

Chipper found a few pieces of scrap wood and bone, and, with the Madonna's help, had made some carvings. He would joke with many of the men, but in keeping with the general atmosphere of apprehension, he tended to keep close to those he knew. As he hunched over each piece, he could be heard whispering the prayers he had learned from the Bible teacher. He had spent several weeks helping this fallen priest erect a farmhouse. In payment for his efforts, the man had immersed Chipper in his faith, and somehow kindled a flame that all of them, including Chipper, had thought was dead long before.

Paddy, though, had been losing his spiritual belief with every moment he spent brooding on his new view of the world. He remembered his difficult conversations with the atheistic Prof early on in the voyage. Had he voiced his new feelings now with all their strength, he knew he would shock the older man. But recognizing Chipper's resurrection, he also realized it helped to comfort the little cockney in his hard life. He could not despise him for it.

The voyage was prolonged by their inability to find a landing in the heavy swell. A huge storm had pounded against the granite coast of Norfolk Island, causing tremendous seas. It was several days before it subsided enough to allow the crew to put a boat ashore. When eventually they did manage to land the convicts and guards, the remoteness of the island affected all of them with a deep depression. It was a ghastly place, desolate and wet, with no shelter from the storms that beat down on the place In keeping with the harshness of the place, the authorities immediately instituted a fierce regimen of work in order to quickly turn this into a suitable possession of the Empire. Within months, the weight of work and the paucity of rations broke most of the convicts, and the guards took out their own misery on the few prisoners who exhibited any sign of spirit.

In years to come, Paddy would look back on the two years that he spent on Norfolk Island as being the final period of his great enlightenment. He tried to keep out of trouble, and he tried to maintain his loyalty to those things which he held dear, but it was an impossible battle. Each day they toiled to keep their small hold on this deserted, cheerless place. With no chance of any escape for body or soul, their lives were a constant misery.

The discipline exerted on the convicts was far harsher than anything they had experienced before. Beatings were a regular experience. In spite of keeping his normal quiet demeanor, Paddy had been given one hundred lashes over his time there. Chipper had received fifty and even Prof had endured thirty. The first time it occurred to any man, whether for a small or serious lapse of discipline, it was an agonizing shock to the mind to receive so unjust a punishment. But the horror of the leather-bound lead weights slashing across the bare back of a man took all thoughts away; the pain consumed his every fiber.

The effect of the beatings on the three friends was to drive them deeper into their inner characters. Chipper became more religious and prayed more devoutly for salvation. Prof became more withdrawn, and Paddy became more obsessed with his volcanic rage. The beatings made his hatred grow, and if he found himself forgetting his inner pain, the beatings allowed him to resurrect it.

Every day was a constant battle to avoid misery. On one occasion, a guard took exception to his stumbling on a rocky path they were taking to reach an outcrop of pines growing nearby. He lashed out with his billy club and the blow cut Paddy's mouth on the edge. It was a bad cut and, when they returned to their huts that evening, Paddy refused all help. Instead he rubbed salt into the wound saying the feel of the scar would help him remember. Many nights would find him sitting in solitude, fingering this physical mark against him.

In other men, such anger would erupt in pointless acts of violence against the tormentors, but, in Paddy, the hatred was driven inwards, and he welcomed it, fed on it and encouraged it to grow like an all-consuming cancer. It sustained him through the months of animal-like existence. And yet, to the world he was just a big silent mick, wandering around and keeping to himself. No one ever saw him cause trouble, and it was even thought he might be a bit slow. The image suited him perfectly.

Unfortunately, the life was turning others into shells of men who were facing extinction. Prof's spare frame had never been particularly strong, and the lack of sustenance on the island caused him to become sick and weak. The authorities refused to acknowledge any illness for fear of allowing slackers, so if one could walk, one went to work. Prof went to work. Because of his reputation and general demeanor, he was given lighter duties than normal, but still the effort needed was sufficient to drag his health down. He began coughing up blood every morning; then it was during the day; finally, he would cough all night. Everybody knew he could not last long, no matter what care his friends could provide at the end of each back-breaking day.

As Prof suffered from his illness, Chipper, too, began to lose his health. He had never healed properly from his flogging, and now, at night, he would shiver and moan as infection set in. Many men suffered similar problems, but such discomfort was shrugged off by the authorities as being of no importance. However, if allowed to go untreated, infection could lead to gangrene and ultimately to death. Chipper lacked the resilience in his small broken frame to fight off the inevitable.

Paddy had to watch helplessly, as the slow decline of the last two real friends he had on earth set in. It was like seeing small flames flickering lower and lower, as they turned into lifeless embers. At first he tried begging or stealing extra food, hoping to build them up and give them some extra strength to fight for life. But Prof could not eat more than a few crumbs, and Chipper just drank the brackish water with a few mouthfuls of rotten biscuits.

Over two months, Chipper had actually deteriorated more than Prof. The sores on his back had now spread to other parts of his body, and the leaves and water Paddy used to dress them only seemed to make things worse. There was no comfort or cure for illness. Those who died would soon be replaced from the ready supply on the mainland.

During their imprisonment in this dreadful place, men were driven to terrible deeds. Their sentences meant the convicts had all hope of a future taken from them. Most had been sent here because they were thought to be the worst of the convicts – perennial offenders – and on arrival, all differences between them vanished. Here, all became the same; they sank to the very end of the chain of degraded life, at the very furthest point of society and any hope of justice. These were men devoid of any hope and any dream; they had become subhuman wrecks, the forgotten trash of the world.

Within months of their arrival, a few desperate souls had tried to escape on makeshift rafts and boats, but the treacherous coast and high cliffs made these attempts all but impossible. Soon the authorities found it easy to check all the possible places from which any attempt could be made. There were so few that soon no effort was made. This was an impregnable place and it built an impressive record for containment.

With interminable sentences and no possibility of escape, soon the hopelessness of the convicts' lives encouraged them to seek the only possible way out. Discussed in hushed whispers, it became known as 'The Final Escape'. Thus, many of them chose the only solution left to them – suicide. After two years, the authorities began to realize that, in their own perverse way, the convicts were getting away.

Initially, it started with small rumors that began to circulate in the stone huts at night, when it was dark and still. But then a pattern began to emerge. At first it did not seem possible that men could be driven to such horror. But eventually, as the incidents began to mount, even the doubting had to accept the most desperate had found a way out of their living nightmare.

Many of the convicts were Irish and, consequently, Catholics. They mostly kept apart from the English, who were Protestant, but both groups shared a belief and fear of mortal sin. Suicide was mortal sin, and therefore all recoiled from it. But the rumors told of a way to die without paying the price of everlasting hell and damnation. Except for suicide, even the most foul criminal could be forgiven if he confessed his sins at the last. They all believed this, and as a result, many of them went to their deaths on the scaffold, muttering their confessions. Often the last words to croak from a beaten man's throat, as he passed out from the pain of the cruel lash, were supplications to his Savior to forgive him for his sins.

In order to make the final escape, three men, either by drawing lots, or by agreement, would play the roles of killer, or corpse, or witness. Those most desperate at the thought of further time in this accursed place could elect to die at the hand of another and then be free of mortal sin. This other man in turn would be set free by punishment at the end of a rope. The third would be witness to the crime. Even in such a place with no hope for anyone – jailed or jailer – the King's law must be carried out, and this meant a full judicial hearing in Sydney.

One rain-lashed night, with a howling wind beating against the rough sides of the hut, Prof spoke softly to his two friends. In between blood-flecked coughs and gasps for air, he told them of a plan.

'You know I'm dying,' he began. He waved away the protests and stammered on. 'I won't last much longer, and my dying is of no consequence to me. I welcome it. But it could be of use to you. You can use it to get out of here. It can mean life for one, or even the two of you. Have you heard the rumors of the final escape?'

Paddy and Chipper looked at each other in the gloom. The idea was so macabre when it first had been voiced among prisoners in the secret of the night, no one could believe it.

'Come on, boys, you've heard it – don't make this hard. Remember how we heard how fights kept breaking out? How one poor devil would be killed, and one or two of the others would snitch on the killer? Then what? Come on, you know how it works. The murderer gets sent back to Sydney to be hanged, and the witness gets to spend the rest of his sentence on the mainland.'

Chipper groaned in pain and hung his face in his hands. Paddy stared ahead at the two of them. He knew what Prof was suggesting, and he knew what would be involved. His stomach churned at the dreadful sacrifice they would be making. He turned away in silence and tried to shut out the awful images. He burned inwardly that the English could drive them to even think of this.

For a week, no mention was made of the subject by any of the three. Then the weather turned very bad and forced them to huddle in their huts, cowering from the driving rains. Some work was done on the few patches of ground that begrudgingly yielded up a sparse crop, but the overseers worried at the danger of too much erosion to risk work, so the encampment was allowed an empty day off to spend in their huts. They lay on their bunks as the rain dripped through the thin roof in puddles around them.

'So, Paddy, my old friend. Have you thought any more about my plan for you?'

Paddy drew a little closer.

'I can't think about it, Prof. You and Chipper are all I have in the world. The thought of losing either of you is too much for me to handle. God, that we have been driven to this.'

'But, Paddy, you know I'm not going to last beyond a few weeks. Everybody has helped me, but I can tell, I'm not much longer for this troubled world. It's not anyone's fault. I've lived longer than any of my relatives back home, and this place is worse than any hell could be.'

Chipper was lying on his bed, his teeth chattering as he fought his recurrent fever, the soft words of a prayer hanging in the wet air above him.

'Paddy, look at him. He's suffering terribly. He'll live in torment for what? A few months at most. We have to help him.'

The big Irishman looked at the little cockney and could see that he was almost in a state of delirium. His old happy state was now long since passed. Chipper would never play jokes or make them laugh again, unless some miracle occurred. He lay semi-conscious, an arm thrown across his eyes, to shut out the gray light in the room.

Paddy stared around the hut. The other fifteen or so occupants were all in a bad way. Either they were ill, like Chipper and Prof, or they were just broken husks of men. Their lives, either as a result of outright cruelty or plain exposure to this harsh place, had drained everything from them. Each day was as wretched as the one before, or, in many cases, even increased in hardship and pain.

Paddy knew that few of his fellow convicts on this, the furthest outpost of the penal colony, had any reason to want to continue living. They lacked the fire inside them to force them onto any goal. No one to whom he had ever spoken here ever talked about the future, apart from vague musings that one day they would go home and perhaps be reunited with their families. But the longer they spent here, the less these musings carried any hope or conviction.

Such ambition had now completely left Paddy's mind as the fires of injustice smoldered deep within him. Replacing these memories and hopes that had been sacrificed in the furnace of his consciousness was one driving goal – vengeance – against society, in general, and Sande, in particular. His last thought at night and his first thought on waking was he had to survive in order to be avenged. Now as he looked on the terrible physical condition of his two friends and remembered the cruel fate of Ackers, he allowed himself to once again dwell on his mission. He would punish all whom he could to pay back what had been taken from him.

Once he had passed this final test of incarceration, he would somehow track down Sande. He would destroy him and his vicious cruelty with the same efficiency he would one of the many rats that shared their current shelter. Once he had performed that execution, he would turn his attention to the English, for it was they who had created the misery surrounding them all, and brought it to this present level of horror. Any society that could punish men and women to this degree must not be allowed to survive. He could not bring down an entire empire, he knew, but he could inflict serious damage to it. The English would pay for destroying his two friends, suffering here in front of him, as well as Ackers, left back in Sydney, rotting in an unmarked grave.

Dragging himself back to the present, he whispered, 'What do I have to do, Prof?'

He knew Prof's mind after so many hours in deep discussion with him across all these many miles and years. But, lacking the courage to implement a plan such as he knew could be in Prof's mind, he needed the older man to speak the details. From the moment that Prof had brought up the final escape, Paddy understood what must take place. Just the realization made him feel responsible. It was this which was upsetting him. In some way it was as if merely thinking the thoughts made him the co-architect of the plan. Logically, he knew this was not the case but, emotionally, he had felt in torment for a week.

'Paddy, you have to do nothing. Just tell the guards it was me. That's all. You're fit and strong. You're going to survive, I know. Since we came here, you've changed. I think I know what's happened to you, although you've not talked to me. Vengeance is wonderful nourishment. I've seen it consume many men over the years, but I've also seen it drive men on.'

He broke off in a violent spasm of coughing. It took him several minutes to regain himself.

'There is no hope here for Chipper and me. We've paid too high a price to the world that's forgotten us. You know all the years that you were on your farm in Ireland, living innocently, Chipper and I, well, we were swimming against the tide. That takes a lot out of a man, being different, being non-conformist. We've talked about it together. We're not as strong as you are, because you've had the armor of innocence around you. Since we both got sick, we've known that we wouldn't survive this new trial. It's meant a great deal, in our darkest moments, that you would get out of here and live. In the last week we've watched you and known what must happen. There is no choice left for us.'

He laid a bony, almost translucent, hand on Paddy's arm, as the big man slumped beside him. With a strength and a resolve in his gaunt face, Prof rose and staggered over to Chipper, who was lying motionless on his bunk. He knelt beside the smaller man and stroked his hot brow.

'Chipper, how's it going, my old friend?'

Chipper did not reply, but opened his eyes and looked at his colleague, with a glazed smile.

'I'm needing to do a little job, Chip, could you let me have a loan of the Madonna?'

Chipper looked down at his belt and Prof put his hand on the buckle and pulled the thin stiletto out.

'Thanks, Chip. I'll put it back in a minute. Can I get you anything?'

Chipper mouthed the word 'Water,' and Prof motioned Paddy to fetch a mugful from the pail nearby. Prof took the mug and put his thin arm around Chipper and tilted his head to pour a few drops of moisture in. The heat from the small cockney was fierce as his fever raged within him. Wiping the sweating face, Prof let him sink back, the eyes closed into unconsciousness again. Paddy stared at the scene before him, knowing there was no role for him to play in this private Eucharist. Prof stared pointedly at Paddy, and then bent over the small sick man again. He began to stroke the fevered man's shoulders and then his chest.

The breath rasped in and out of the open mouth, as Prof felt gently around Chipper's chest. Placing his left hand to the side of the breastbone, he placed the tip of Chipper's thin knife between his splayed fingers. With one stroke, he plunged it deep into the prone man's heart. There was no reaction from Chipper. He died immediately, his weak heart pierced by Prof's incision. Prof left the blade in the wound and fell back sobbing onto his bunk.

'Fetch them, Paddy. Now. I killed him. You are the witness. Call the guard, for God's sake, Paddy.'

Chapter Twenty-Nine

Rio De Janeiro, 1993

Mitch O'Doule had developed a ringing in the ears. Once the ticket for Zurich was in his hands, he had to face an entire day in the city, waiting. The time went very slowly. He walked around the city with unseeing eyes, his mind fixed on what he had to achieve. Margitte floated in and out of his conscious mind, a jagged memory surrounded by fears and horrors as to what might befall her.

Over and over, he recalculated what his options might be. He had to get the money, he knew that. Once the transaction was made, Ryan would undoubtedly try to kill him. He was a simple man with more than a generous portion of pride. Mitch had destroyed his reputation, and Ryan would never forgive that. Also, he would wreak vengeance on anyone associated in the plot with Mitch. Somehow, he had to get Margitte out of the scene, before he and Ryan had their inevitable confrontation. As he made his final turns around the city, Mitch could only think of one thing: escape from Ryan's clutches.

His fingers would sweep involuntarily up to the hair that used to hang down over his eyes. Since his visit to the long-suffering barber, he now only had a reddish stubble. The bristle felt strange on his hands. It reminded him of the changes that had occurred to him since Ireland. He had changed inside, he knew, and now there was a constant reminder of this on the outside. With his short mustache and now this lack of hair, he looked a tougher man. Only Mitch knew that inside he was not the killer he once was.

As he put his things together in his room, he considered he had to face a more uncertain future than at any time since he had made the decision to escape from his former life. He also recognized there was every risk there might be no future. He had to find a way. Checking his gun once more, he wrapped it carefully and fitted it snugly in its tin box. He knew with every aircraft he boarded he was taking a chance. He felt he had used up more than his fair share of luck. He mouthed some hopes for one last try, as he pulled the zipper across the bag and went down to the lobby.

Almost as if Rio mourned his passing, a black oppressive cloud settled over the city as the taxi maneuvered through the streets to take him back to Europe and certain danger.

The ringing in his ears had stopped once he had begun to formulate a simple plan. Now he was back into his old life, living on his wits. At least if there were any watchers from the 'Army', or even the police of the various countries that wanted him, they would all be fooled by his changed appearance. For all his notoriety, Mitch had never sought disguise, outside of loose clothing and hats. His face was well known on posters in a number of post offices, but not this face. There was some comfort in knowing he looked so different.

The aircraft was full, and the flight, with its load of excited passengers and their many bags, lurched into the heavy, black sky. Mitch had managed to pick a seat near the door close to the galley. From here he could not see the film, and he spent the time ignoring his craving for nicotine and planning for the very worst consequences.

After a gentle landing at Zurich, he felt exhausted. He knew he was in no fit state to put up a tough fight. It would come down to firearms, he knew. But could he catch the dangerous Ryan off guard? He would be facing a deadly foe.

Once again, he passed through customs and immigration without any difficulties. This type of living was really pushing his luck. It only needed one nosy bag searcher to start rooting around and the game would be up. A look through the records would easily turn up who he was, and then he would not have to worry about Ryan any more. Except that he could be reached in jail, and at some time in the prison's night, there would be an unwelcome visit from someone with a sharp object.

The ride through the mountains took longer than the last time, and it certainly was not as pleasurable. His mind concentrated on the road and how to arrange his meeting. He would make two room reservations for a start. Midweek should not present a problem for visitors, he hoped.

On arrival at Vaduz, he checked immediately into his former hotel. There seemed to be few other guests. He dumped his belongings in the closet and took a long hot shower. Once he had dressed, he walked out and along the main street. He found exactly what he needed within a short block. It was a small hotel, which he found out had a total of ten rooms. He was able to reserve the largest, overlooking the street.

Still not quite sure what his next move should be, he called the number in Amsterdam. Margitte answered the phone immediately, and as before, it was snatched out of her hand.

'Where the hell are you, you bastard?'

Ryan's temper had not improved since the last time. He was obviously very angry at the fact his brilliant discovery of where Margitte was, as well as her importance to Mitch, had still not put him in control of the situation.

'I'm where the money is, Ryan, and if you want it you'll do exactly as I say.'

Under completely different circumstances, Mitch felt he could possibly enjoy the whole business of keeping Ryan at bay. He was a very nasty individual, and he deserved to be baited. However, Mitch knew he was playing a dangerous game. He had to be very careful. One slip and it could push Ryan over the edge.

'Now listen to me. Tomorrow you will check into the Gasthaus Jansen. It's on the main street of Vaduz. The woman knows how to get there. There'll be a reservation in your name. Arrive at lunch time and if you behave yourself and the woman is unharmed, you will have the money before the banks close that day.'

'If you try any tricks, she'll get it, O'Doule.'

'Sure, sure, I know all the threats, Ryan. Just be at the hotel on time. I'll be waiting.'

Once again, he hung up. Now he was faced with plotting his next move. He picked up the telephone again and asked for the number to the Sovereign Bank. Its ringing tone was as discreet as its general atmosphere. Mitch really didn't like it. He asked for Doctor Berman, and after a short wait, a woman answered. It took a few moments more for the good doctor to pick up his phone.

'Herr O'Doule, what can I do for you?'

'I'm afraid we are going to close our account with you, Herr Berman. We have had to make some changes in our plans.'

'I'm sorry to hear that, Herr O'Doule. You understand we will have to claim our full commission, in spite of the short time you have been with us. Most unfortunate.'

'Unfortunate, as you say, Herr Berman, but unavoidable.'

Mitch O'Doule went on to suggest they might be able to visit the bank the next day in the afternoon to complete the transaction. After hanging up, he lay down, thinking over his difficulties. He had less than twenty-four hours to go.

That evening, he revisited the Gasthaus Jansen, and let himself into the room he had booked earlier in the day. It was a big room, and he looked at every corner of it. It was here, he knew, that his journey of the last few months could end. How he reacted to the danger ahead would determine whether that journey might continue as planned, or whether he would see his last sight on earth here. He shuddered at the thoughts in his head.

Slipping the Luger out of his trouser band, he felt along the beam of oak that supported the large bay window, protruding over the street. He thought there might be some way that he could lodge the gun there, so that he might grab it when Ryan's attention was taken up with something else. The roll of tape he had bought earlier would help, but the surface of the beam was altogether too smooth. Ryan was a suspicious man. He could not take a chance.

He racked his brains and, in the silence of the darkening room, tried to think what Ryan would do. Although the room was large, there was not much in it. Two upright chairs, an overstuffed armchair, a small table, and two single beds. A door led to a cramped bathroom, with its customary bidet, bath, toilet and washbasin. He sat on one of the beds and sank into deep thought. He played the scenario through in his mind over and over. His long experience with his foe gave him several clues to how Ryan would want to handle things. There would be no assault until the money was safely in his hands, that was certain. Then, Ryan would make his move.

Finally, Mitch decided on his plan of action. It was risky, but then he had no choice. After ten minutes of careful work and after pacing round for a minute or two, he let himself out of the room and went downstairs to the reception desk.

'Tomorrow, there will be two guests checking into room number five. A Mr Ryan is arriving from abroad with a companion. Please see them up. I'd like to pay in advance.'

This seemed to please the clerk on duty.

Mitch slept badly. In the morning, he called the airport and rang around the various carriers, checking incoming flights from Amsterdam. He wanted to be able to see Ryan and Margitte arrive. He guessed it would be somewhere between ten and two o'clock. He was sure they would not be stopping to have lunch. There would only be a few minutes once they arrived, however, and he had to maintain the initiative and keep the pressure on Ryan. Speed would help.

At one thirty five, from a small table at a street-side café, Mitch saw a bright red Ford Mondeo pull up outside the *Gasthaus*. Margitte was at the wheel, with an unshaven Ryan leaning towards her in the passenger seat. It was easy to see both of them were in a very tense state, although Margitte looked the more relaxed of the two. She was in jeans and a brown woolen sweater. She carried her briefcase with her. Ryan clutched a dark raincoat to himself, and with one hand on her arm and another holding a duffel bag, he hustled her into the hotel. Mitch paid for his coffee and went directly back to his room.

'Mr Mike Ryan, please.'

There was a pause.

'Ryan.'

The name was spat into the mouthpiece. This was a man wound up to the fullest extent.

'Okay, now, Ryan, here's how it's going to be played. You come with us to the bank and wait while we get the money.'

'Fuck you, O'Doule. She's not leaving this room. Do you hear? You get your treacherous arse over here right now, and then we decide.'

In custom with his methods so far, Mitch put the phone down. It had been worth a chance, but Ryan was not going to go for plan A. He picked up his briefcase and went out of the room.

'Get your fucking arse in here, you bastard.'

Ryan had the muzzle of his silenced revolver in Mitch's ribs as soon as he swung the door open. He grabbed the case out of his hand and flung it on the bed.

'Right, up against the wall, legs spread. Just like in the Falls Road, you bastard.'

He patted Mitch down and, once satisfied that he was 'clean', he pushed him into one of the upright chairs.

'Where's the woman?' Mitch asked his captor.

'In there,' Ryan said, nodding towards the bathroom door.

'Get her out,' Mitch growled. 'You know my terms. Any damage and there's no money.'

Ryan placed the other upright chair next to Mitch and opened the bathroom door. Margitte came out. Ryan gestured with the gun, and she sat down next to Mitch.

'Are you okay?' he asked.

'I'm fine. A bit tired, but that's not surprising. Your friend doesn't believe in too much sleep.'

'Did he hurt you at all?'

Ryan waved the gun in front of them to silence them and, reaching round to the back of his belt, produced a set of handcuffs.

'Okay, that's enough out of the two of you. Give me your hands.'

'It's okay, Mitch. He's rather fond of his handcuffs.'

So saying, Ryan clicked their wrists together with the links of the cuffs passing through the front legs of Margitte's chair. It meant they had to lean forward. Mitch made a mental note that so far he had made one small mistake. He'd assumed it would be rope Ryan would use.

'I've a bloody good mind to finish the two of you off now. Treacherous bastards.'

'Look, Ryan, can we just get on with the transaction. We all know what you want – it's just the money. Now you need us both if you're ever going to collect it. So stop trying to act like an injured virgin, and let's make the trade.'

'That's okay by me. Let's get on with it.'

'Well, Ryan, this is all going to rely rather heavily on the bank manager across the street. If he's willing to play ball, then I guess you'll get your money brought over. If not, well, you'll have to trust us.'

'Just make the call, O'Doule.'

Ryan brought the phone over and placed it in front of Mitch. Mitch used his free hand and dialed.

'Herr Berman, about the closing of the account I was telling you about yesterday. We have a slight problem. Ms Ednas Ledenfeld is rather ill, I'm afraid, and can't make it over to you.'

'Oh dear, Mr O'Doule. I do hope that it's nothing serious.'

'Just a slight touch of food poisoning, I think. She'll be fine tomorrow. However, it's rather important that we complete our transaction as soon as possible. Could you possibly send someone over to us for the signing, and then have the money delivered?'

'I'd be delighted to come myself, Mr O'Doule. When would be convenient?'

'Could you make it right away? Ms Ednas could then get some rest. I'd really appreciate it. We're in the Gasthaus Jansen.'

He hung up the handset. Ryan snatched the phone away from him, and then paced around the room.

'All very friendly with our banker friends, aren't we? Well, this is where the account gets cleaned out in more ways than one.'

'Look, Ryan, let's get one thing straight right now. Margitte is only a link in the chain. She's nothing to you.

So here is the deal. She walks out of here, or there's no money.'

'You're in no position to make deals, O'Doule. You're the one tied up and I've got the gun. So keep quiet and let me think.'

'You may have the gun, Ryan, but without a good performance and our willing signatures, you'll have nothing. The banker will be here in a minute, so you better start letting Margitte and me get normal. The Swiss don't like abnormal situations, I think. So undo the cuffs.'

Ryan sat them together in front of the small table and, for an angry, preoccupied man, showed some creativity in undoing the cuffs and giving them a pack of playing cards.

Mitch forced himself to breathe regularly, and asked in a quiet voice. 'So how'd you find her, then, Ryan?'

'Had the phone listings checked. Taffy did it before I even left the country.' Ryan couldn't help but look pleased with himself. 'Also, I had one of our lads go around the hotels in Christchurch making inquiries. Turned up the address. Simple, really. Fergy's boy had the place down in less than two days.' He sneered at the two of them and lapsed into silence.

They had to wait no more than ten minutes before the phone rang to announce the Herr *Doktor*. Mitch invited him upstairs immediately. Ryan, who had insisted that both his captives remained sitting at the table, where he could keep an eye on them, answered a soft tap. Doctor Berman accepted Mitch's introduction of Ryan as a business contact traveling with them. Ryan slumped on the bed, directly in line with his prisoners. Berman produced a single sheet of paper and, being careful not to disturb the cards on the table, indicated where both should sign. On inquiring how Mitch would like the money, he nodded at the suggestion of dollars in large denominations.

Margitte asked him, 'Would you like a case for the

money to be sent over, Herr *Doktor*?'

'Yes, Miss Ednas, if you have one at hand. Thank you. I must say how sorry I am to hear of your illness, and I am also sorry we have not been able to be of more help to you both. Please call me if ever the Sovereign can be of service in the future. You, too, Herr Ryan. Please, my card.'

Ryan stuffed the card in his trouser pocket and handed over Margitte's briefcase, not taking his eyes off Mitch for a second. With a curt nod to them all, Herr Berman left with the promise that his assistant would be over with the money in ten minutes. He let himself out, as Ryan gave no indication he was going to leave his position across from Mitch and Margitte. As the door clicked shut, Ryan produced the gun from under the coverlet, where it had remained, pointing at them both, for the entire interview.

'That was very convincing. Keep it up.'

Ryan glared at Mitch who sat staring at the cards before him. He knew he would have a problem getting Margitte out of the room with the banker's assistant here, so he reasoned he had to make his move now.

Come on, me boyo, just give me a chance, Mitch thought to himself, as he watched his quarry.

Restlessly, Ryan stood up from the bed, placing himself three foot from the two of them. Mitch gripped the side of the table and hurled it at Ryan. At the same time he reached under his chair and pulled the Luger out from where he had loosely taped it the previous evening. His movement took Ryan completely off guard, and Mitch was on him before he had a chance to level his gun at the attacking man. Mitch grabbed the waving revolver and wrenched it out of Ryan's grip, hurling it to the floor.

But Ryan was not giving up his struggle just because he had lost his gun. He kneed Mitch in the groin and punched him in the face, splitting his lip. He seemed unconcerned that Mitch was the one now with the gun, and kept on punching and kicking. Mitch fell across the bed on top of Ryan and managed to point the muzzle of his Luger in Ryan's ear. But Ryan just kept on kicking and twisting. He seemed like a man possessed with some demonic spirit. He connected with Mitch's jaw sufficiently enough to make Mitch go groggy for an instant. Then, twisting around, he got a lock around Mitch's throat. Even though Mitch pointed the Luger at the frantic man's head alongside his, Ryan paid no attention.

The air was starting to go out of Mitch, as they rolled off the bed and staggered upright. He knew his gun was in his clenched hand, but somehow he couldn't force his finger to activate the trigger. He was struggling helplessly in Ryan's strong grip when Margitte stepped into the fray. She had retrieved the fallen revolver from the floor and stepped around to the back of Ryan. Raising her hand, she brought the butt of the gun down on Ryan's skull. He dropped to the floor like a stone. Mitch felt sick. He was choking, and he slumped back on the bed, his head hanging down.

'Why didn't you shoot him, Mitch?' Margitte asked, as she felt around in Ryan's jacket pocket, finding the handcuffs.

'I don't know,' was all Mitch could rasp out of his wounded windpipe. 'I just never thought about it. God, he could have killed me there, with his bare hands, if you hadn't stepped in. God, no wonder I'm out of the business. I'm supposed to be a bloody colonel, you know. Not some junior recruit on his first job.'

'And how many men have you killed in similar circumstances, my brave colonel?'

A trace of her humor was evident even at this time as she slipped the handcuffs on the unconscious Ryan.

'The truth is there would never have been similar circumstances. I would have done them in, as soon as they came at me.'

'So, how many has it been, Mitch?'

'I guess, around a couple dozen or so, over the years. Most of them were scum of one sort or another, but it's part of my former life, and I feel a bit ashamed about it.'

She smiled and said, 'That's a bit like confessing to the number of women you've had.'

'Something like that, I suppose. Look, we'd better get him out of sight. The banker will be here in a minute. Not a good idea to have an unconscious man in the room when we're counting out the money.'

Together, they dragged Ryan into the bathroom and locked his wrists together through the washbasin down-pipe. His breathing was steady, and apart from a huge lump on the back of his head, he seemed none the worse for wear.

'Jesus, if he was pissed off at me before, he'll be even more so now.'

Mitch closed the bathroom door shut, and pulled Margitte over to the nearest bed. He kissed her hungrily, and rubbed his face in her hair.

'My God, you scared me, Margitte. Falling into that man's clutches. I thought I would never see you again.'

He was surprised at the pricking sensation he felt in his eyes as he stared into her face.

'Are you really okay?'

'I'm fine, Mitch. Ryan was only after you. I could kick myself for going back to my flat. He kept me locked in my bathroom most of the time. He can get a taste of his own medicine for a change. He rang my bell as cool as you like, and burst in as soon as I opened the door. He slapped me a couple of times until he realized I didn't know where you were. But apart from that, he left me alone. Those handcuffs of his are pretty effective. He was terrified you wouldn't ring again. By the way, I hate your hair.'

Mitch grinned and ran his hand over the bristle.

'I was pretty scared to begin with, but I began to understand he was scared, too. He made me call the phone company to get the number transferred back, then I had to call the cousin I was staying with to tell her I was going to be home for a few days, to take care of some leaky plumbing. He watched me like a hawk while I made the call. He almost convinced me he understood Dutch. I didn't dare stray from the story.

'It took me a couple of days to figure it out, but then I realized he was on his own. At first, I expected a whole contingent of your ex-soldiers to come pouring through the door with pillage and rape on their minds, but it didn't happen.

'I never talked to him, but from the urgent pacings of the room and his mumblings when he thought I was asleep, I understood he wanted the money back so he could look his colleagues in the eyes again.'

Mitch watched this remarkable woman calmly telling him the circumstances of her ambushing. Her strength came through, and he realized that, if they were to truly escape, he would need that strength. He was secretly worried that his inability to pull the trigger as Ryan struggled with him was a manifestation of lack of resolve, or even weakness. He recoiled from the thought.

It was only a few minutes before the phone rang again. A young messenger, in a blue uniform with shiny brass buttons, came up and put Margitte's case on the table. It was affixed to his wrist with a heavy linked chain, which he undid with a flourish. He made no comment at the strewn playing cards all over the floor, although he tried to avoid walking on them. The money was neatly stacked inside the case, and both Mitch and Margitte signed their names once again. After the messenger left, Mitch took Margitte over to the armchair.

'I need to tell you something. It's about the money.

You're not going to like this, but I can't take it, Margitte. It's not right. I've damaged them badly, and I know we can escape where they'll never find us, but I can't keep the money. It's been on my mind, from the moment this blew up in our faces. Once the money has gone back, I'll feel better.'

'Mitch, do you have anything else?'

'I reckon, I've about enough to get us through a couple of years. After that, I guess I'll have to find a job.'

'Well, I've got some put by, so we've probably got enough for more than a couple of years. It seems a shame, though. It's all there in that case.'

She stood up and walked over to the table. Opening both cases, she transferred Mitch's money over to the freshly filled case. Then pausing, took out a bundle of notes, and transferred it to the other case.

'My expenses, Colonel, if you don't mind. I hate to travel broke, and wherever you intend to take us, I guess I'll need some new clothes. Where do you intend to take us, by the way?'

Mitch frowned quickly and strode to the bathroom door. He flung it open. Ryan was fully conscious and staring at him.

'Yes, do tell, Mitch, where are the two of you headed. Because wherever it is, I'll bloody well follow you.'

Taking the silenced revolver by the barrel, Mitch undid the handcuffs and led Ryan out to the room, recuffing him to the bed. Ryan glared at Margitte as he went past. She, in turn, shrank back from him, holding the briefcase against herself. Then, throwing the combination locks, she put it down nervously next to its twin, as Mitch restrained his ex-colleague. She was obviously very wary of the man, since she had immobilized him.

Mitch sat in the armchair, facing his enemy, the revolver loose in his hands.

'So, Ryan, you're trying to live with the fact you've been had. You poor bastard, I almost feel sorry for you.'

'I don't need your fucking sympathy, you're nothing but a bloody traitor.'

'Now, that's where you and I begin to differ. Come on, Ryan, it's over. The 'Army' has no future going along the path you've decided. It doesn't make sense. You're losing support on all sides. The young don't care any more. The Yanks don't give the money they used to, and the Arabs, well, even if they didn't think we were a bunch of crazy drunks, they're an unstable lot to get mixed up with. So, my ex-friend, I'm going to give you a break. In fact, I'm going to give you three breaks. You get to walk out of here, you keep the money, and one more thing...'

So saying, Mitch walked over to the telephone and picked it up.

'I want a number in Northern Ireland. Can you get it for me?' He spoke firmly into the mouthpiece.

He stood silently waiting. Ryan watched him, a confused look on his face. Margitte stood next to the two cases, on the far side of the room.

'Hello, this is O'Doule. Who's in the room? Put him on. Taffy, this is Mitch. Listen carefully. Ryan's with me. There's been a problem. It was all a fake. I wanted out, and I am out. Shut up and listen, Taffy. Ryan found me, but I turned the tables on him. I'm letting him go, and he's bringing the money back. There's some expenses missing from it, sorry about that. But it's mostly there. Don't bother to try and find me. You're going to need all the energy you've got to handle life in the future. Think about it, Taffy. The old ways are dead. I know it, and so do you, if you use your head. Try the negotiating table. Get someone respectable and sober, and talk your way to peace. Appeal to the Yanks. It's the only way. Good luck.' He hung up abruptly.

Ryan lay back, looking at Mitch.

'You're crazy, O'Doule, if you think we're going to pack up the struggle, just 'cause you suggest it. You might have gone soft, but the rest of us haven't.'

'Mike, think about it on the way back home. You don't have much choice, and if you hand everything over to the real maniacs, you'll be dead meat in time. The band is getting smaller. Pretty soon, there'll be hardly anyone left. Now, the lady and I are going to disappear. But first, as I promised, you get to walk out of here. No gun – sorry. But take the money and get back home where you belong.'

Mitch was very careful letting Ryan up off the bed. He tossed him the handcuffs' key, and kept the silenced revolver trained on him. Ryan rubbed his wrist and the back of his head. He grabbed the briefcase Margitte held out to him, then stared stonily at Mitch as he went to the door, but Mitch turned silently to look out of the window, down at the street.

Margitte joined him after the door was closed, and together, they watched Ryan in the street. He looked around furtively, then lay the briefcase on the roof of the car. He tried the locks and, when they proved impossible to open, he slammed his fist on the case and slung it onto the back seat. Climbing in, he tore away from the curb.

'We'll wait a few moments, before we leave, just in case he decides for some crazy reason to come back for us.'

'I wonder how long it'll take him to figure out your birthday combination, Mitch,' Margitte said and laughed. 'I guess he'll have to wait until he gets home, won't he?'

Margitte squeezed his hand.

'I hope we're going to have a moment or two before we travel.'

Mitch checked the street for any sign of the bright red Ford. But, evidently, Ryan had decided to return home and make the best of his good fortune.

As they walked along, Margitte leaned close to Mitch and said, 'Well, Colonel, is it safe for me now to know where I'm to be spending my life with you?'

'Almost,' he said, teasing her. 'But first of all, we're going to visit a friend of mine in Spain, to see if he's had any luck in replacing a much missed girlfriend. I need to send for some funds, and I must post a letter to my aunt. I promised to write to her. Just in case the mail is watched, it will look good coming from Madrid.'

'I have a small note to send as well. The same postmark will do for me to,' she said, smiling quietly. 'And do you think they might have some clothes that would suit me in... Madrid, was it?'

'Strangely enough, I know the very shop. They had a rather nice yellow thing in the window.'

'And shall I be able to buy a new purse there? I'm finding the briefcase to be just a tad unfeminine. Madrid, you said? And is that where we are to finish?'

'No, for that we're going to the ends of the earth.'

'Well, Colonel, before we get there, let's just take a moment or two in this fine hotel. I think I know what we both need to get the tension of battle out of our minds.'

Chapter Thirty

Norfolk Island, 1791

Chipper's body was removed in the most rudimentary way. After all, he was just another of the poor devils who had been sent to this accursed island. The jailers openly talked about a happy release, and how the lucky bugger had escaped with a simple stab wound. Prof was not treated as gently. Murder was still a serious crime, and all those in charge of the settlement knew that, without punishment, any of them could be next on a murderer's list.

Prof was very weak, and yet he was dragged out into the windswept compound, and made to stand for over an hour while the authorities decided the best plan of action. In calling for help, Paddy had identified himself as a witness to the crime of murder, and he was immediately put in solitary confinement, no doubt to ensure his memory of the events would not be diluted by contact with others.

Eventually, Prof was also sent to a cell to await the next boat able to transport him to a trial in Sydney. Through a friendly guard, he passed a message to his friend, saying he was well and strong and would see him on the ship. Paddy knew his own future was tied to his friend's will to live. If Prof were to die before the time of departure, Paddy would not be needed as a witness back on the mainland.

He kept reliving, over and over, how they had been driven to such an act of wretchedness. His two best friends, both at death's door, had been brought to this state by neglect and cruelty. Society at large was responsible, but the individual who could most be held accountable for their condition was Sande.

Paddy had not been able to get the horror of Chipper's death out of his mind. He kept seeing the knife going into the small defenseless chest. Paddy's soul screamed out for revenge.

In the confusion that had followed his calling for the guard, he had taken the knife. Then, quickly, he had pulled Chipper's belt from around his poor dead body. It had originally fit a much larger man, and there was enough room for him to put it round his own waist, slipping the thin blade once more behind the buckle. Fortunately, the guards were too wet, confused and weary to worry about a murder weapon. Nearly everyone of the convicts had some sort of crude weapon, from thin shards of glass stuck in crude wooden handles, to stilettos made of wood that had been hardened in fire.

The blood pouring out of the dead man's chest was quite sufficient for them to deduce he had been stabbed. It had happened scores of times. Prof put up no resistance, and there was a willing witness; it was all neat and tidy, and nobody really cared.

Chipper had been buried the next day, with a short service given under a windy but clearing sky. The acting chaplain spoke briefly of the weight of the tribulations of life being lifted by a forgiving Lord. There was a poor attempt at a hymn, and then the canvas-wrapped corpse of one of the friendliest, brightest and most agreeable of God's creatures was laid to rest. Inside his damp cell, Paddy pictured the proceedings in his mind's eye, and a river of tears ran soundlessly over his scarred and haggard face.

From the silence of this empty place, Paddy wrote a last letter to his family in Ireland. Their image and the life they had all shared was now a dim and distant memory, and even the act of penning the few short words did not bring them any closer to him.

During the next three days, Prof's condition was the subject of most of the jailers' talk in the cell block. He was hanging on and seemed to have recovered some of his health. But Paddy could hear the racking coughs and the awful struggling for breath. He knew Prof was fighting for enough time to get them both away from the island. His resistance to the hardships of their life was almost at an end, and if he won through, then it was just a question of whether he would give up his life at sea or at the end of a rope on the mainland. Paddy prayed for the hangman to be cheated.

Eventually, a packet-boat was ready to sail. Paddy and Prof emerged from the cells and were chained together for the short walk to the dock. No talking was permitted, and it crossed Paddy's mind that, if he really was the only witness to the crime committed by his partner, being chained to him was probably a very stupid idea. But then the way the rules were written by the Establishment, it came as no surprise to Paddy. It might even have been funny, if it were not so awfully tragic.

Once on board, the two men were separated. Paddy was confined to a cramped area below decks, and Prof was kept in a small iron-barred cell across the gangway from him. Mostly, they were left alone, except when Paddy was allowed up on deck for exercise. No such privilege was permitted for the accused. His health was of no importance.

The ship was returning to Sydney to rotate a number of guards, and also to pick up much needed supplies. Since it was forced to fight against the prevailing westerly winds, the voyage was predicted to take about three weeks. Paddy took his daily walks around the deck, and was allowed to spend an increasing amount of time up there.

When they were together, Prof spoke softly to Paddy

across the small gangway that separated them. He told of his sadness at what he had had to do to Chipper, but he knew that it was the only solution.

'A few more days of pain, and then a suffocating death, drawn out, probably alone, while the rest of us were away, digging holes in the rocks. I don't mourn that it happened, Paddy, just for why it had to be.'

His cough was now all-consuming. He kept a blood-soaked rag in front of his face as he heaved and struggled. After a week, it became impossible for him to talk, but he would watch Paddy with his rimed eyes, and would occasionally smile. It was as if he wanted Paddy to relish the fact he had cheated the system for all three of them.

Two weeks out of port, Paddy had spent the afternoon up on deck, watching the tipping of the boat's bow as it tacked its way across the empty sea. The crew had come to regard him as no danger, and with only the two prisoners to watch, discipline became relaxed for all on board. Many of the seamen were from Ireland, and Paddy had enjoyed swapping tales about the old country. One small deckhand, with a red beard and a giant silver earring, said that he knew Paddy's village.

As soon as he had told the seaman where he was from, Paddy regretted it. His life back there was something he had buried deep within him, and he did not want to unfold it. He had become a different person, and he could not get his mind to return to those far-off days with their innocence and simple pleasures. The seaman seemed to recognize Paddy's problem.

'I understand, Paddy. I lost everything when the landlord put the rent up. With no proper job, I couldn't pay, and we were thrown out on the street. My wife died of pneumonia and the baby starved to death.

'There was no work, so I was forced to leave the country and go to Liverpool. At first it was hard, living in the land of the bloody English, but there were many Irishmen like me there. Pretty soon, I found a job on a boat, and with nothing to keep me, I volunteered to come out here. I can't say as I regret it. But, Paddy, have a care. I've seen many a man get eaten up with hatred. It's as bad as a cancer.

'There were a few back in Liverpool that wanted to bring down the whole British Empire if they could. They had plans to use explosives, and guns. I spent some time with them, but somehow I couldn't keep the fire alight inside me.'

'Well, tell me, Red,' Paddy asked in a low voice. 'How would you meet such people?'

'It's not hard to find them, Paddy. Just walk into any pub where the Irish meet and say you hate the English rule. "Ireland for the Irish" is the slogan. You'll be amazed how many men will come up to you. But take care not to do it in a pub with too many English around – they get a mite upset.'

He went off, chuckling, and Paddy's eyes took on a faraway look again. So that was the way. Vengeance on Sande. Vengeance on the English. That would be his way. He would find those who had hate in their hearts, and join them. He would tear at the very fibers that held the British system together. It would consume all his energy and strength. It would probably take all his life, but he would pay them back for his losses. They would suffer.

Two days later, after walking the deck deep in thought, he went below and, as usual, looked at his sick friend. Prof was lying curled up like a baby. He was quite dead. His hand had fallen outside the cell and clutched the bloody rag that was drying in the salt air. Paddy pulled it from the thin fingers and put it in his pocket. At the same time, he felt the Madonna's handle nestling snugly in Chipper's belt against his hard stomach. The fires of hatred no longer flamed and exploded up inside him; they now smoldered with an even intensity at what he had to do.

On arrival in Sydney, Paddy's expected testimony was a short formality. The corpse had been interred on Norfolk Island, the killer had been buried at sea, and one more dead convict was nothing to become too upset about anyway. Nonetheless, rules and paperwork demanded a full accounting, and Paddy was made to stand before the governor, and told to tell his tale. It was a sad repetition of many such stories. Prof and Chipper had fallen out over the possession of some food. They took to fighting, and Prof had produced a knife – since gone missing – and plunged it into the other man. He had subsequently died himself a few days out of Sydney. He had been disposed of in the customary way.

The governor nodded sagely at the evidence, then looked down at the sheet of paper in front of him. He then turned, unsmilingly, to Paddy. 'It seems to me, O'Doule, we have a simple choice ahead of us for you. A return to Norfolk Island, or regular work here. What duties were you assigned on the island?'

'Hard labor, Sir.'

He thought to himself that the governor must be in a more than usually stupid mood; for convicts there was only hard labor in the place. But he stood passively, with his eyes downcast. It was a stance all the old lags knew kept their lords and masters happy.

'Well, O'Doule, I remember you were about the best animal doctor we had here. Would you be prepared to continue those responsibilities again?'

Paddy said he was good with animals, and he would be pleased to continue where he had left off. But where was Doctor Jameson? He was told the good doctor was dead from a liver disorder. It came as no surprise to Paddy.

So, the big Irishman, whose intelligence was usually questioned in most matters outside the healing of sick animals, re-entered mainland convict life. He lived at one end of the primitive hospital that served both people and animals. He made no friends, and after his daily duties, he spent most of his time watching the sky and humming softly to himself. At these times, he would be seen rubbing his fingers along the edge of a bad scar at the side of his mouth. It pulled his mouth into a downward scowl. But everybody said that he was a quiet simple fellow who would never harm a soul.

He always seemed to be very interested in how escaped convicts were caught, and more particularly, who had been responsible for the captures. Such inquiries would inevitably lead to an ex-naval bosun, named Sande, and his band of half-castes and degenerates, who lived far away out in the bush. A keen observer would have noticed a light in Paddy's eyes at the mention of the name. But, as was usual in the non-suspicious, such signs would pass without registering.

Nor did anyone notice Paddy's reaction one day when he learned that his nemesis had obtained a booking on a passage to England. Rumors told of how Sande had a fancy for the area around Brighton in Sussex. He had boasted of these plans many times in the rough taverns that catered to the growing population of immigrants and ex-convicts. At the time, Paddy had another six months to serve of his sentence, and although he enjoyed great latitude with the authorities, he reasoned that for him to attempt to reach Sande, he would be running a huge risk, and if caught, he would not be able to perform his great mission. He had already spent six years waiting; a little longer would not hurt him.

He therefore continued to be a model prisoner and looked forward to the eventual day when he would be able to begin his life's work in earnest. It was strange, he often thought, that no one could tell that, underneath his deliberately calm surface, there was a violent fire of hatred and loathing waiting to explode. He had never seen a volcano, but he understood what the phenomenon was. He readily identified with it.

Eventually, his sentence was finished, and as a free man he spent two years as a private animal doctor, earning the money necessary to pay for his shipment back home.

His small shabby practice at the edge of the burgeoning colony attracted the needs of the sheep and cattle farmers who had settled in the area. He showed no interest in turning it into the gold mine it could have become. He handled all the animals himself, with the help of a young mute Irish boy who had been convicted of picking pockets in the area of the law courts in London. It was a crime that was simple to catch, and even easier to judge, in view of its proximity to so many custodians of the law.

When the time came, Paddy paid with cash for his passage home. He estimated he had sufficient money left over to live for about six months, once he arrived back in England.

He spent the voyage walking the decks, eating well, and speaking only when he was spoken to. He shared none of his experiences, and only showed true friendship to the two Irish deckhands, who regularly swabbed the tar-filled planks, open to the elements. He even lost interest in them when they confessed to being happy with their lives and not minding the English. After that, he would just smile at them and wave, moving to a less crowded part of the deck to brood.

It was a gray day with a biting wind coming out of the west, when the ship eventually arrived back at Tilbury docks at the east end of London. As he made his way down the crowded gangplank, and through the thick throng of people waiting for mail and news from the colony, he spotted a small inn that seemed to cater to travelers.

He took a room for three nights, and after enjoying the rare privilege of a hot bath and haircut, he set out to re-equip himself with new clothes and boots. On his way around, he asked about the locations of Liverpool and Brighton. He was sorry to find they were diametrically opposed in their locations. Committing the locations to his mind, he pondered his best course of action. Brighton first, or Liverpool? The more specific goal or the more general? As he rubbed the rough scar and stroked the freshly trimmed beard, he weighed the options open to him.

Eventually, he came to his decision. He would make contact with some allies before he went after Sande. He now had a purposefulness in his step, as he went to collect his new clothes. Once they were fitted in the tailor's shop, he admired his new look. He hoped he appeared to be a simple farm type with good boots and a woolen suit that would last for many years to come.

He booked a seat on the next coach to the north-west of the country, paying in advance for stays at all the inns before he reached his destination in Liverpool. The journey lasted a week, as there was very bad weather and the coach became stuck on several occasions. Paddy smiled at what the other passengers considered an inconvenience. If they thought such a journey was intolerable, they should know what it was like to sail to the end of the earth, and then to that dreadful island that stamped out the life in a good man's soul.

On one night outside the city of Manchester, he had a nightmare. It woke the other passengers, sleeping in hammocks behind the rough drapes inside a dark communal room that they all shared. It was the same as all the other nightmares. He was standing with Sande out in the hot sun. He had been released from a trestle where he was being flogged. Sande had offered him a way out. He had to kill three bad men. Paddy was given a thin knife and led to a room where Ackers, Prof and Chipper lay, bound to their bunks. Sande pointed at the unconscious forms and Paddy walked forwards with the knife. Firstly he plunged the blade into Ackers, who died without a sound. Then he stabbed Prof, who also died without any noise. But when he put the knife close to Chipper, the little man woke up and screamed at him, 'He's the one, Paddy. Kill him. Do it for your old mates.'

It was at this point Paddy woke up, sweating and terrified. A couple of the other passengers had come to his assistance, but the Irishman waved them away and apologized for the trouble he had caused them. It was several hours before he could once again contemplate closing his eyes. It had been some time since he had had that particular dream.

Liverpool was as busy and crowded as London. There was a noticeable absence of the gentry, however. Most of the people seemed much poorer than in the capital, and Paddy heard many folk speaking either Gaelic or with a strong Irish accent. He felt he had come home. It took him no time at all to find an Irish lodging house with a good-sized bar. Each night, the place was full of hard-drinking men and women, singing Irish songs and telling Irish stories. There was even an Irish harpist, who would start early, and finish an hour or so later, when the noise level became too great to hear the gentle strumming.

For four nights Paddy stood at the end of the bar sipping a lemonade and enjoying the hubbub that enveloped him. He would nod at people and smile, but he would never start a conversation. On the fifth evening, a stocky man stood next to him. Like Paddy he appeared to like lemonade. He smiled at Paddy and indicated their two glasses.

'The best drop of the lemon this side of the old country.'

Paddy agreed that yes, it was good, although it had been

many years since he had been on the right side of the water.

'You're new, I've not seen you around these parts before. Where are you from?'

'Some call it the ends of the earth. But it's beyond that.'

'I know where you mean, my friend. I've lost some people to that place. My name's McBride, but you can call me Bridie. All my friends do.'

They sipped their drinks and watched the people milling around the bar, fighting and squabbling, drinking and arguing.

'Do you not like a drink then? What was your name?'

'My friends call me Paddy.'

'Well, here it'll have to be something different than that. There's a Paddy every three foot.'

'It's Paddy O'Doule'

'Well, then, we'll call you Paddy O. That should avoid any confusion. So, do you not like a drink then, Paddy O?'

'It was the undoing of me, I'm afraid. The drink let me be caught by the press gang, then I fell into the wrong hands, and ended up a convict.'

'I know the story, Paddy O. It's been the tale of many a poor man from across the sea, and it will be, I imagine, until it's "Ireland for the Irish".'

The words registered with Paddy immediately. The seaman on the boat had told him. He turned away from the crowd and spoke softly to Bridie.

'I'm thinking you might need someone like me to make such a thing possible.'

That's all it took for Paddy O'Doule to begin a life of murder and mayhem. Working quietly inside a small cell of fanatics, and then becoming its leader, he was responsible for the untimely demise of many small-time officials of the government. Mostly they were judges or policemen, jailers or crooked lawyers; all of them, however, were known for their prejudice against the people of Ireland.

He lived a dark and simple life, always walking in the shadows and turning away from those who looked at him. He forged no strong relationships with either sex, nor did anyone ever visit him in his single room over the top of a ship's chandler's store. But the rigors of his harsh life in the penal colonies, and the fact that he showed no concern for his health and condition began to have an impact on him.

A year after he had joined the band, and after plotting, tracking and carrying out his work to strike at the English oppressors, Paddy took a leave of absence. He would, he told them all, be away for about two months. He had calculated a month to find his quarry and lay his plans for his revenge. He had a little money left from Australia and planned to use it for the stagecoach to the South. The return trip would be taken rough, staying where he could. Sleeping in fields presented no problem to a man who had spent time in the penal colonies of Australia and Norfolk Island. No one asked him where he was going, and he said nothing of his plans, only that he would be back as soon as possible.

He was missed by the group. Although they all knew they were making little difference in the struggle for independence, they had the satisfaction that they were, at least, doing something. Paddy's dedication to the cause had a way of keeping the group's spirits up, particularly when they failed, which was more often than any of them liked, or admitted to.

The journey down to the gentle rolling countryside of Sussex took nearly two weeks. Paddy spent the time in watching the passing of the countryside, and as usual, he kept himself to himself. The dreams had stopped coming, but he worried that with his mission on his mind at every moment, he would once again draw attention to himself. He could not afford to be caught. His work was too important.

The last link was a bone-jarring coach ride to Lewes, the county seat of Sussex, and it was here Paddy began his search for the ex-bosun, Sande. Unfortunately, he had to perform this task without help, as too many questions would cause suspicion. As he walked around the old town, situated some twenty miles away from the Brighton area, he could be heard humming quietly to himself and be seen occasionally, rubbing the disfiguring scar at the edge of his mouth. Those passing by who noticed him assumed he was a smallholding farmer here for supplies. Anyone with a greater sense of perception would have seen that his well-made boots lacked the deep stains of mud from any farmyard.

He walked the distance to the outskirts of Brighton. The weather was mild, and the rain that often gathered on the peaks of the gentle Sussex Downs stayed away, so the countryside was bathed in a sunny glow. Farms spread out all around, and the workers would often wave to him as he strolled along the rutted highway. Nowhere did he see the round bald pate of his quarry.

He began to realize that, without the ability to ask, he was severely hampered. No doubt, Sande was disliked by most of those who knew him. However, Paddy could hardly stop at every turn to make inquiries and then expect to get clear away, leaving the human wreckage he hoped to create.

It was a Monday when Paddy had his great good fortune. He had been in Brighton for two days, walking around and just looking without any clear plan on how to proceed. Early in the evening, he came upon a market being put up for trading the next day. He reasoned that it was likely, if Sande was truly a farmer now, he would put in an appearance at a market most weeks. He inquired at a nearby hostel if the market opposite was the biggest in the area. He was informed that no, the biggest was on Thursday, near the northern edge of the town, but this local one was pretty good.

He spent a quiet night in the hostel, and decided to take a chance the following day. After an early breakfast, he went out to the market, which was already bustling with activity. He walked around, listening to the unfamiliar burr of the country accent. The stalls displayed a variety of produce, all basking in the morning sun. The people pushed each other, good-naturedly, and joked, as they carried out their trade. Paddy passed unnoticed among them with his ears cocked. Eventually, he heard the sound he was listening for. The sound of a voice from his homeland. It was from deep in the South of Ireland, but there was no mistaking it. It belonged to an old fat woman, who was laughing at a joke her customer was telling her. She sat in front of a big table, which bowed under the weight of many boxes of bright red tomatoes. As soon as her customer walked off with his bag filled with her wares, Paddy approached her.

Laying on his brogue, he picked up a large tomato and said, 'To be sure, you've a fine crop here, Ma'am. Better than you'd grow across the water, I'd say.'

'Poor miserable things they'd be, Sir, unless they was under a bit of glass, to be sure. And how long have you been away from the old place?'

'Too long, Mother, I can tell you. But this is a nice spot to be, I'm sure, apart from the English.'

He winked and smiled at her.

'I'll have a couple of pounds of your best, and maybe you could help me find a fellow. An old shipmate of mine. Bald he was, owes me some money. Name of Sande. Ever heard of him?'

Paddy watched her carefully, and as she started putting the fruit into a bag, she looked sideways at him. It was just a pause, but, immediately, Paddy was on his guard.

'Not the nicest chap, Mother. But I want the money he

owes me. To tell the truth, I don't much fancy seeing him again. He was a bad type at sea.'

She handed over the bag of tomatoes, and looked up at him from her clear eyes. The jollity all gone out of her.

'He's got a farm out on the Worthing road. You best take care, Mister; he's a bad lot. He drinks all day and lets that poor missus of his do all the work. Her and her poor kids.'

Sande married? Paddy had a hard time understanding that.

'I didn't think he was the marrying kind. You surprise me.'

'I only saw the man a couple of times. He's a real queer fish, if you ask me. Came here from Austraylee, they say. Had some money, but lost it all within a year of arriving. Then he met up with this poor woman – foreign she was – Europe, someplace. Anyway, she had a small place, but had lost her husband to the scurvy. Two little kids she had, and Sande moved right in and married her. She thought he would help her. Poor fool, she. He just drinks and lies around, that is when he's not beatin' the hell out of all three of them. Have a care, sir. He's a bad one. As for getting any money out of him, I'd be surprised. But the best of luck to you.'

'And to you, too, Mother.'

He handed over a coin and leaned close to her. Kissing her softly on the cheek, he mumbled the words, 'It may be best not to remember me, Mother.'

'To be sure, sir, I have too many good folks to serve to remember any one of 'em. You'll find the road to Worthing off to the west. Be careful.'

Paddy disappeared into the crowd, relieved he did not have to wait until Thursday. His idea of bumping into Sande at a market would never have worked. If the old lady was right, his wife did all the work. He had been lucky.

He found Sande before sunset the next day. His farm

gave him away. It was a mess, and the house, set back half a mile from the road, looked as if it might fall down any day. A few pigs were in a muddy pen, and some thin cattle grazed over the barren slopes among the chalk and flint rocks that protruded through the earth. Paddy followed a path, carefully keeping a beech hedge between him and the house, until he was only one hundred yards away. Then he sat in the hedgerow and watched for a sight of his enemy.

He heard Sande before he saw him. He was roaring like a bull from the back of the house. Two thin children came racing around the front, a boy and a girl of about ten or eleven years of age. Sande followed, shouting and waving his fist. He had put on an enormous amount of weight. He must be well over three hundred pounds, Paddy thought, as he watched the huge bald-headed man give a poor chase to his charges. A ringing started up inside Paddy's head. It took a lot of effort not to jump up out of the hedge and run towards the hated foe.

Sande gave up the chase, and the youngsters ran off into the distance where they forgot their pursuer and began a game of throwing stones into a pond. Sande sank down on a wooden block, used for chopping wood, and mopped his brow. His massive chest heaved up and down, as he sat there staring around at nothing in particular. He reached round into his back pocket and produced a black pipe. From his other pocket, he pulled out a purse of tobacco. It was well worn, but there was no mistaking the remnants of ginger fur that clung to its surface. The pressure inside Paddy's head built to an alarming state. Seeing this loathsome man sitting so close, with the last remains of the constant companion of the poor fated Ackers, took all reason from Paddy, as he crouched hidden by the copper leaves of the hedge.

Paddy struggled with his hate, and watched as Sande replaced the pouch and sat smoking. From the house,

Paddy could hear the preparation of an evening meal. Sande heard it, too, and stood up stretching. Scratching his huge belly, he walked off to the barn that stood alone at the side of the house. He came out a minute later with a handful of eggs.

Paddy continued to watch as the man returned to the house and slammed the door. Slowly he began to relax, as he felt the moment of his retribution nearing. He even felt a smile playing at the corner of his mouth. He was grateful he still had some of the old woman's tomatoes to munch on, together with a bunch of celery that he had gathered on his walk to Sande's farm.

As darkness descended, Paddy watched for a return of his enemy. Once dinner was over, the household retired for the night. By nine, all the lamps were out and silence took over. Paddy made his move for shelter in the barn to make his plans. Nothing stirred as he squeezed into the dark, foul-smelling interior.

As he became accustomed to the dark, he was reminded of his journey through the neat countryside of Cornwall, all those years previously. This was a situation of a very different condition, however. The barn was filthy. A few chicken coops were crowded along one side, and there was a half-roof some ten feet up, with a rickety ladder to it. Apart from the chickens, there was nothing else there except piles of trash and broken farm implements.

Paddy tried the ladder and was surprised to find it stronger than it looked. He climbed to the floor above and found it empty apart from several coils of rope and an old pulley. He sat with the rope running idly through his hands, humming softly under his breath and staring at the pulley. About ten o'clock, he left his position and went to work. It only took an hour, and, afterwards, he sat dozing until the various animals in the yard began to greet the dawn.

It had been more than seven years since Paddy had felt tears running down his face. That had been when he had sat alone in his cell, listening to Chipper's sad funeral. He had witnessed the sea burial of his last friend, Prof, without the same wrenching loss. He knew Prof had brought about his own escape from Norfolk Island, and intellectually had used his illness to free his two best friends from their prison. As he had watched the last remains slip over the side, Paddy knew his dead friend would have appreciated the elegance of the solution. Somehow, Prof's quiet death did not seem so heart-wrenchingly awful. It had carried a dignity that had been lacking in the others.

During the night, Paddy had sat staring into the darkness, and he had begun to feel that same pricking in his eyes, once more. The fact that Sande had actually taken the small dead body of Marmy and done what he had with it made Paddy feel sick. If ever there was evidence of evil in the world, and more specifically in the ways of man, then for Paddy, sitting in the darkness, this seemed the last act.

Even beyond what had happened to Prof, Chipper, Ackers and himself, Marmy's fate was unparalleled. In some way, the men could be said to have had some control over their lives. But this was a small, simple, loyal, little animal that only gave comfort to lonely men who spent their lives in torment. For Marmy to have been the victim of such bestiality was beyond any wickedness that Paddy could conjure up.

A shout followed by a bang caused Paddy to come to with a start. His right arm had gone numb, and he clenched and unclenched his fist to get it working. Through the slatted wood he could see Sande standing at the door of the house. Paddy was certain if eggs were a favorite of the huge man he would eventually come back for more. He hoped they would feature on Sande's breakfast menu. The chickens below him obviously reasoned the same, as they, too, began to stir and cluck in their cramped hutches.

Paddy crawled nearer the edge of his lofty hideout, and tightly gripped the end of the rope he had been working with earlier. As suspected, Sande made his way over to the barn, spitting a brown stream of tobacco juice through his yellow teeth. Paddy could hear the blood pumping through his head as he concentrated his every atom of energy on his plan.

Sande kicked open the door and, mumbling to himself, shambled over towards the chickens. His rancid odor wafted up to Paddy, ten foot above him. Sande stopped for a moment to let his eyes focus on the barn's filthy interior. With a grunt, he moved three more paces which placed him immediately under Paddy. Something must have alarmed him because he stopped momentarily, and his head was beginning to look up when Paddy threw himself over the side of his perch. Holding the slack end of the rope, he dropped like a stone on top of the bald head.

Sande was a massive man, but all the years of hard labor and fighting for his very existence had produced a strength in Paddy that culminated in solid muscle, bone and sinew. Both men, with a combined weight of five hundred and fifty pounds, fell to the dusty floor. But it was Paddy who made the next move. The night before, he had fashioned the end of the rope into a noose. This he pulled over the bald head and, grabbing both of Sande's ears, he wrenched him to his feet. Sande shook himself like an injured bull, and made a grab for his assailant. Paddy had moved swiftly to the side, and easily evaded the huge hands. Pulling on the other end of the rope, which now ran through the pulley, he twisted it fast round a wooden joist above his own head. The tension lifted Sande till his feet were barely touching the floor. Once secured, Paddy moved back to confront his captive.

Sande was transfixed. He swung his arms and even tried

to kick out at his assailant. But he was partially suspended and helpless. To make sure, Paddy gave the rope another knot. Then he checked the noose to make sure that his earlier work was sufficient.

'As good as His Royal Majesty's navy would require, eh, Chief?'

Sande could not talk. The noose held his mouth clamped shut and also choked off nearly all the air going into his throat.

'You remember me?'

Sande rolled his eyes in a way that confused Paddy.

'Well, Chief, do you or don't you?'

To allow his captive a jog of the memory, he slammed his hand against the rope. A choking sound came out of the closed mouth.

'Well, I guess you do remember. It would be such a shame if you were to have forgotten me. And particularly if you had forgotten my friends.'

Sande rolled his eyes again. Now Paddy understood the expression. It was all that Sande could manage as a shrug. He put his hand out to the rope again, and Sande stopped the gesture, staring first at the hand and then Paddy.

'There were the four of us, if you remember. Initially, Chipper and me fell under your control, then your lies. You are an evil presence on this earth, Sande.'

Suspended as he was, the guilty man could do nothing but witness his impending fate. Paddy's dedicated words and demeanor had a chilling effect.

'Now, let me show you why you are going to die, my fat, perverted friend.'

Paddy pulled a caked piece of rag out of his pocket.

'This is from the choking lungs of a man who hurt no one. He died after his illness on Norfolk Island. He never should have been there, but you sent him.'

Pulling the Madonna out of its hidden sheath, Paddy

passed it slowly in front of the bulging eyes. Sande made a gurgling sound and seemed to leap backwards, although he was incapable of movement.

'Now, this little knife came from another dead man. You'll probably remember Chipper. He was a friendly little soul, wasn't he, Chief? Unfortunately, you chose to pick on him and make his life a disgusting misery. Then he, too, was sent to that dreadful island to be flogged and turned into something no better than an animal. But we all cheated you. It was the quiet Prof that made all this possible. Nonetheless, Chipper suffered badly. Once by your filthy hands.' And here Paddy punched his closed fist into the heaving chest. 'And then you lied, so he was sent away from his land.

'And now we come to the last.' Reaching around the straining body, Paddy found the tobacco pouch. 'This was a small friend of mine. It brought comfort to me and also to another of your victims, the simple gentle Ackers. You remember him, don't you, Chief? You remember how he was tormented and tried to run away. His torment only began in earnest after you caught him and he was flogged to death. Well, this little cat was his, and for what you did in that single act alone, against a defenseless animal, you deserve no mercy.'

Paddy put the point of the Madonna onto Sande's chest, and then watched the terrified eyes in front of him. The beam above groaned under the weight of the man. Paddy allowed the moment to linger as his eyes bore into his victim. The beam groaned once more and then a rain of dirt and dust showered to the floor. Paddy looked up and, as his eyes filled with the debris of years of neglect, he saw the beam crack and the rope securing Sande fall snaking to the floor. As Paddy rubbed his eyes clear, Sande leapt on him, knocking the Madonna to the ground. The two men thrashed around on the straw-laden floor trying to gain the advantage.

Paddy could feel Sande's thick fingers grasping at his neck, and he pulled his head down to reduce the area, while at the same time blinking his eyes furiously. Sande fought like a tiger. He used his bulk to pin Paddy to the floor and beat on him with his hamlike fists. Recovering from his temporary blindness, Paddy twisted underneath and did his best to protect his face. Eventually, with a huge effort, he toppled Sande off him and, as he escaped across the floor, he desperately looked for the fallen knife. To his horror, he saw it glinting right next to Sande as he staggered to his feet. Sande saw it, too, and in one movement, he grabbed it and threw himself at Paddy.

Paddy felt the thin blade enter his side, but, by lunging, Sande had left himself exposed and Paddy smashed his fist into Sande's sweating face. Then, falling on Sande's panting frame, he brought his knee into his unprotected groin, and was rewarded by Sande buckling towards him. As in the previous fight they had had all those years ago in the New Forest, Paddy once again brought both his hands hard and fast crashing together over Sande's ears. As before, the huge man reeled backwards and threw his own hands up to offset the pain of his exploding eardrums. In so doing, he dropped the Madonna. Paddy leaped forward, grabbed the knife and swung it upwards into the sagging belly. He drove it in as far as his fist could reach, and Sande, with a roar like a bull, fell like a toppled oak tree.

Paddy stood over the twitching frame and saw the light gradually snuff out of his tormentor's eyes. It was over. There was a moment of inner stillness for the panting Irishman before he looked down at his own wound. It was bleeding profusely but, strangely, it didn't hurt. Picking up the blood-stained rag he had waived at Sande, he pressed it to his side. Then he put the other things in his pocket, slipped out of the barn and walked quickly away.

He took the road north, and stopped only once for refreshment at an inn. After a lemonade and a meat pie, he continued on his way, putting as much distance between him and his act of revenge as possible. With the use of an occasional trap, it only took him two weeks to cover the distance back to Liverpool. The pain in his side increased and often the wound would leak over his shirt.

One night, with twenty miles to go, he stopped on a lonely hillside. In a field, he dug a small hole with his bare hands. Standing quietly under a moonless sky, he dropped into the hole the Madonna, a blood-stained rag, and, finally, with a strong pricking sensation in his eyes, a strange-looking ginger pouch. Then, in spite of the pain in his side, he began humming softly to himself, while covering the hole and slowly pressing the earth back with his foot. After a moment more he turned, and with his hand pressed against his side, he journeyed onto continue his chosen fight.

Paddy knew, within a few miles of reaching his destination that his wound was serious. The searing pains that had been coming regularly were now almost continuous. He made it to Bridie's door and almost collapsed outside. His friend struggled upstairs with him and called for a woman, who knew some nursing, to come and look at the wound. As Paddy lapsed into unconsciousness for the second time that night, she took Bridie to one side and told him that his friend was badly infected and it would take a miracle for him to survive.

The woman and Bridie took turns caring for the deteriorating man, but the miracle they both prayed for did not occur. Paddy's infection spread and he had no strength to resist it. It was almost as if he had given up his will to live. He endured the terrible pains that racked him with a resignation that seemed at odds with his previous fight to survive.

One quiet night into the second week of his illness, he called out for Bridie. In a voice that was hardly audible, he told his friend about his mission to go after Sande. It seemed to give him no pleasure to recall the end of the man who had haunted him and his friends halfway across the world. Afterwards, Bridie gave him some soup and was about to send for the woman to come and re-apply some dressings, when Paddy called for him to come back.

'Bridie, there's another tale I want to tell you.'

'Paddy, it's enough. You need to rest. Tell me in the morning.'

'No, I need to tell you. I don't have too long, I know.'

Bridie sat down on the bed next to his friend.

'I've got a son, Bridie. I saw him a few weeks before I met you. I never told anyone before.'

Bridie learned that the only other time Paddy had left the Liverpool area had been shortly after his arrival and nearly a year before his dreadful mission with Sande. He had taken the boat across to his homeland. His intent was to find his family and try to put his previous life behind him.

Belfast had changed since his last experience there some thirteen years before. He landed at the docks close to where he had been forced aboard the *Distinction*. He walked quickly past The Rover, which looked no different, although he saw that there were some new buildings close by.

There was a trap leaving for Ballyhean in an hour and he hung around waiting for it, feeling confused and lost. It was the strangest thing but he didn't feel a part of this gentle urban scene, and his customary suspicions had no place here. The discomfort stayed with him on the bumpy journey.

Ballyhean had a similar distanced feel to it. It was late when he arrived and he stayed at the new post house that had been erected to deal with the service of regular traps to and from the city.

In the morning, with a continuing unease, he walked the two miles to his old home. He was not sure how he would react on seeing the distanced people who had been the center and focus of his early life.

The corner that he rounded to give him the first sighting of his home had become overgrown with thorns and did not allow him the view he expected. He had to walk out into the middle of the lane before he realized there was nothing to see. The house had completely disappeared.

He hurried on now, convinced his mind was playing him tricks, but there was no mistake. The land was ploughed over with a fresh growth of crop coming through. He leaned against a tree and let his eyes run over what had meant so much to his family for so many generations.

He was shocked to feel a change come over him. It was a feeling of relief. He recognized it and began to feel guilty at such a thing. However, there was no denying that he had been scared of what he might find and also have to deal with.

He turned round and returned to the village center. On the way he stopped at the entrance to a farm that had once belonged to a family called Hollister. The woman who was tending some plants was unrecognizable to Paddy. She looked up at the sound of the gate swinging open.

'I'm sorry to trouble you, Ma'am, but could you tell me anything about the O'Doule farms back down the road. I used to know the family.'

For some reason, Paddy had no desire to declare who he was, and waited for the woman to answer his question.

'My parents knew them, I think,' she replied, with a furrowed brow. 'They all died when I was young.'

'I see.'

Paddy kept his face blank as she continued to think.

'I'm sorry, Sir, I was forgetting. One of them survived. The young O'Doule, it was. He went away.'

'What went wrong? Here, I mean. It's all changed.'

'It was the cholera swept through. Took nearly everyone. My parents and brother. Nearly everyone,' she repeated.

There was a silence as if the memory was too painful for her. Then she picked up her rake and began to sweep.

'Do you know where I could find the young O'Doule?' Paddy asked quietly.

'Postman in the village could help, maybe.'

He thanked her and went on his way. It took him two more days before he met up with his youngest son. The trail took him back to Belfast and a small house in the inner city. A succession of postmen and lawyers had pointed the way for Paddy to find the address. As the trail became closer, it was obvious from the replies to his questions that David O'Doule was not any favorite with the officials from various agencies.

Paddy banged on the door of a shabby house and waited in the gloom of a late Saturday afternoon. A thin woman in a loose smock answered and pointed to an inner room just inside the door. Paddy was not sure what he expected on meeting his son, but the tired, stooping young man who stood up to meet him was not it.

'David O'Doule?' Paddy asked.

There was a nod and a wary look.

'I'm your father.'

The wary look became one of confusion, and it was nearly an hour later before the two men finally accepted who they each were.

Paddy stayed in the house for four days. He had breakfast, lunch and dinner in the same room that they both slept in. The meals were served by the thin woman who was called Nell.

Each evening, Paddy would leave the shared room, as men would come in and fill the confines with strong talk and even stronger tobacco smoke. At these times, Paddy would grow impatient with the endless arguments and walk the streets. On the third evening, he sat in Nell's kitchen drinking tea. He liked her, perhaps because she made no secret of her affection for David.

It was obvious to Paddy that Nell was pregnant, although the signs foretold that the event was still quite a long way off. She was attentive to Paddy and fussed over him as the meeting in the front room continued late into the night. Finally, she sat down across the rough table and looked into Paddy's eyes.

'You know about the baby, don't you?'

'I've been around long enough to know the signs, lass.'

'I told David about it only a few days before you came.'

'I'm sure he's happy with the news.'

Nell looked at her broken fingernails and said, 'I think so. Sometimes it's hard to tell with him.'

'How long have you known him?' Paddy asked quietly.

'About six months, Mr O'Doule. It seems a lot longer. I love him very much, you know.'

Paddy got up from his chair and poured some more water from the kettle into his cup.

'What do your parents think, Nell?'

'They're dead, I'm afraid. Killed by the same plague that killed your family, I shouldn't wonder, although it was a year later. These things hang around, though, don't they?'

Paddy could see that underneath the grime and weight of her life, Nell was a pretty woman. He promised himself to speak to David to make sure he did the right thing by the girl.

'Still, Mr O'Doule, they left me this house. At least that

makes me desirable, doesn't it?'

'You're being unfair to yourself. You're a pretty lass, you know.'

Nell brushed aside his words and continued with a look of concentration on her face.

'It's not been easy for David, you know. He told me all about what happened. The plague came about a year after you went away. It had taken them almost that time to find out that you'd been snatched by the sailors. Then the cholera came to the village and struck so fast that it wiped out nearly everyone in a few weeks.'

'Ireland has had those things before, I know. But not in my lifetime. We'd all thought that it had finished… please go on, Nell.'

'The family worried that, being the youngest, he might not survive. So they sent him off to his aunt in Belfast 'til it was past.'

'That'd be old Aunt Maud, I expect.'

'Well, as you can see, David came through. He'd had no contact with his family for a year, and then his aunt broke the news they'd all died.'

Paddy twisted in his chair as he formed a question.

'Did they all die together, Nell?'

'It was the little girl first, I think, then his mother and his brothers.'

'Dear God, poor Katherine.'

Paddy ran his thumb over the scar on his face.

'David came back to the farm when he was twelve. He found the English landlord had ordered it torn down and planted to seed. There were no markers for the buried, only crops to feed a man who had never shown his face there.'

Paddy stood up and stared out of the window, holding in the anger at the resurfacing of the images that had remained hidden for so many years. Nell continued with her quiet story.

'David came here to Belfast about a year ago. Now he's fallen in with this group who're dedicated to changing Ireland. But I think he's getting tired of all the talk.'

'I'm not surprised. I couldn't take more than an hour on that first night.'

'Well, now he wants more than talking, I'm afraid. He wants more action.'

Paddy took no pleasure in the knowledge that he and his son were engaged in a similar fight. Paddy believed his hatred and revenge were justified by the cruel events of his life, but, although David had been made homeless by the same system, it was a terrible way for a young man to start his adulthood.

'I think he needs you, Nell. Just to look out for him. Maybe a family will help him to settle down. He's still so young.'

But as the evening wore on Paddy came to understand that the great hardships his son had faced had eaten into him. He too had suffered at the hands of a cruel system, and lost his mother, and sister to one of the great famines that swept the small country, already weakened by illness and starvation. He watched the flickering candle, as he and Nell listened to the departing men leave the house. As he stood up to leave the kitchen, he bent down to kiss her. He felt the moisture of tears on her face.

'He kept the letters that arrived, you know,' she said, her back to him. 'They're on the shelf there.'

Paddy looked to where she indicated, and he could see the small pile of letters in a binder of string. He felt the paper on them, but had no need to look inside at the words over which he had labored under Prof's tutelage.

'His aunt managed to collect them for him. He's carried them around all this time, but he never talks about them. I've never looked at them. I can't read.'

'Don't fret yourself, lass. They're from long away and a long time back.'

The front door banged and David came into the kitchen.

'So you two are having a chat, are you?

Paddy went back to the table and sat down.

'Nell's a wonderful woman, David. You're a lucky man.'

'I know.'

David still had a hard time calling Paddy 'Dad' or 'Father'.

Paddy continued, 'You should forget this revolution stuff for a bit, you know. There are more important things for a young man to concentrate on.'

David took the third seat at the table and looked into his father's eyes.

'Look, I may be young, but I've seen a lot. I can't forget the way the English have treated us. Someone has to fight them.'

'David, this hatred will destroy you,' Paddy said. He lowered his voice and continued, 'I've been consumed by hatred for years. It eats away and steals your entire life. Don't make the same mistake as me. Live your life. Raise a family, enjoy the good things there are and don't mess with politics.'

'Well, you'll be glad to know I'm out of politics. I'm going out on my own. I know there's others that feel the way I do. Why don't you stay here and help me in my fight.'

'No, David,' Paddy shouted, 'I'll not help you go down the same path I've taken. I have only one thing left to do and my life will be complete. You have a family to think about. Give it up, David.'

Paddy's plea could not move his son, who stood up, his stool falling backwards and startling them all.

'No, I have the same right as you. I'm damned if I'll just lie down and take it.'

Paddy's voice rose again as he tried to correct his son's view that he had far from lain down, but David was out the door with it crashing behind him. Nell put her hand on Paddy's arm.

'Let him go, Mr O'Doule. He'll settle down. He's going to do what he wants, you can't stop him. I'll do what I can to make him a good wife.'

'I know you will, lass.'

Bridie leaned closer to hear Paddy's words. Hardened though he was by years of struggle, he was moved by the story of the two men meeting. He thought for a moment, then asked, 'Paddy O, would you like me to keep an eye on the boy for you?'

But Paddy had died with the telling of the tale of his family's dynasty across the Irish Sea, a dynasty that would take two hundred years to run its course.

Epilogue

The radio buzzed impatiently on the dresser. It was one of those mercilessly hot days that beat down on the Australian outback. The voice crackled before either of them could get to the set.

'Hey, Mitch, are you there? Pick up, will you? It's Rodge.'

'What's up, Rodge? You're awful damned impatient for such a hot day. Over.'

'I need to find out if you want to come over on Saturday night. Bit of a party. The missus keeps on asking me and I keep forgetting. Over.'

'Well, they do say the memory's the second thing to go, Rodge. Hang on, let me ask the wife.'

'Margitte, are you on for a party on Saturday night, over at Roger and Elsie's?'

'It's fine by me, Mitch. But we'll have to stay the night. I'm not driving back all that way. Unless you decide not to drink this time.'

'Forget it. It's Saturday night, isn't it? It's an Aussie's privilege. Rodge, we're on, but Margitte says we got to stay over, if that's okay. Over.'

'That'll be fine, Mitch. We'll look forward to it. Bring a bottle. Over and out.'

Margitte had already gone out to the long verandah, overlooking their ranch. The main heat had gone out of the sun, and she sat down on the double swing seat. Mitch put a Mozart string quartet on the P player and poured them both a glass of Foster's. After turning up the sound, he joined his wife in their customary evening drink outside.

'Can't say I'm overjoyed at the prospect of another piss-up at Roger's. I think I'm getting too old for it.'

'Come on, Mitch, it's only ten years since we got married. We're almost newly-weds. Don't go old on me now. Incidentally what did Joaquin say in his letter. You didn't show it to me.'

'I'm sorry, I'll fetch it. It's the usual stuff. He's got a new mistress. He's passionately in love.'

They looked at each other and said the word 'Again' to each other out loud. Then they giggled.

'Yes, Mitch, it'll be ten years in three months. Do you ever think back?'

'Sure, I sometimes think maybe Ryan is going to come over that rise out there.'

'Yes, I know. But it's too long a time now. I doubt he or any of his friends are actually looking for a Mr and Mrs Sande, located in the middle of Australia, do you?'

'Not now, although I did worry for the first couple of years. But old Joaquin helped us a lot in having all those postcards we wrote sent from all over Spain. He's a clever old bugger.'

'It comes from keeping all those mistresses of his hidden from the *Señora*, I would think.'

'We have to thank him for our name as well, too. He really took to that story about your relative from England. When was that now?'

Margitte took a sip from her drink and thought back to the tale.

'The old people always said it was about two hundred years ago. Poor woman, widowed twice. And the second husband murdered. Apparently it was no real loss. He was a cruel seafarer. Stabbed in his own barn, no less. Afterwards she couldn't face England alone with her children anymore.

So she just sold up and went back home to Holland. Then that curious idea of hers, turning her name around from Sande to Ednas.'

'Well, it allowed you to keep your name – sort of, anyway. It always seemed to fit us, too.'

He looked across at her and smiled, as he took her hand and held it against the soft yellow of her dress fluttering in the gentle breeze.

'It all worked out very well in the end. I would have loved to have seen Ryan's face as he showed Taffy he'd only recovered, what was it? Five thousand? I'll never really be sure if you switched those cases on purpose or not.'

Looking surreptitiously around, she nestled close into his neck and said, 'You know, my colonel, I can't remember now. It was a different world.'

*

Copy of descrambled communication received at GCHQ, Andover. Postmark, Madrid, Spain. Dated, March 15, 1994

> I HOPE YOU ARE SATISFIED WITH THE RESULTS OF OUR PLAN. I CONSIDER MY DEBTS PAID IN FULL. GOODBYE, MAGGY.

978-0-595-41721-6
0-595-41721-3

Printed in the United Kingdom
by Lightning Source UK Ltd.
125586UK00001B/5/A

9 780595 417216